deadly AFFAIR

USA TODAY BEST SELLING AUTHORS

K.A KNIGHT
IVY FOX

Deadly Affair (Deadly Love Book One).

This is a work of fiction. Any resemblance to places, events or real people are entirely coincidental.

Copyright © 2022 K.A. Knight & Ivy Fox, all rights reserved.

No part of this book may be reproduced in any form or by any electronic or mechanical means, including information storage and retrieval systems, without written permission from the author, except for the use of brief quotations in a book review.

Written by K.A. Knight & Ivy Fox
Edited By Jess from Elemental Editing and Proofreading
Formatted by The Nutty Formatter
Cover by Opulent Swag and Designs.
Photographer Wander Aguiar.
Model Aaron G.

He came into my life as my savior.
All blood-soaked hands and deep blue eyes.
But then he became so much more... he became my stalker.
And now? Now he wants to put a ring on my finger and call me his wife.
How could I possibly refuse when he's offering me my one chance at redemption?
Some loves are worth sacrificing everything for.
Even when they turn deadly.

deadly AFFAIR

USA TODAY BEST SELLING AUTHORS

K.A KNIGHT
IVY FOX

For Claudia.

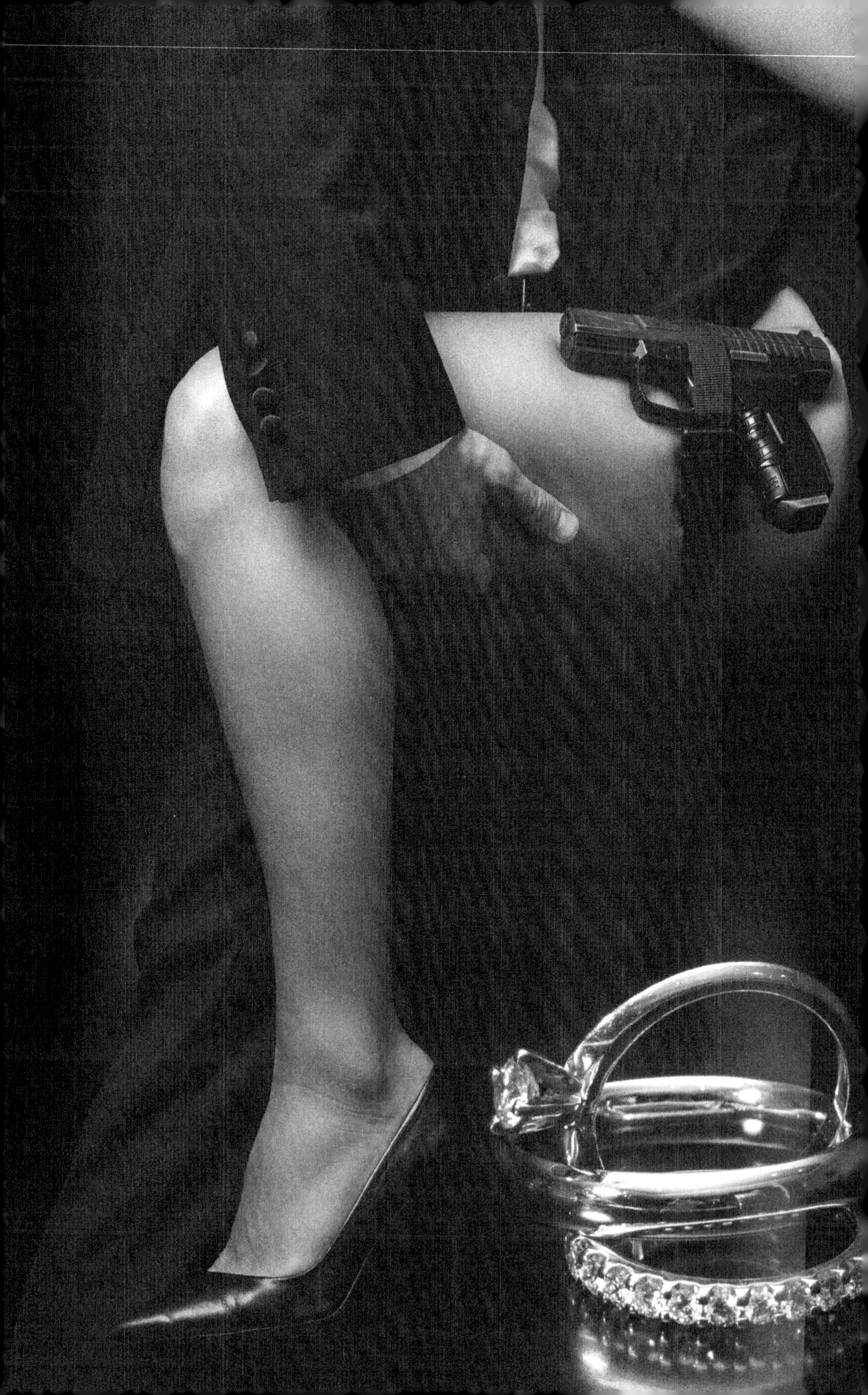

Prologue
LAYLA

"Mom, you have to slow down! You're going to get us killed!" I shout at the top of my lungs, my heart jumping up my throat from how fast she's driving.

She either doesn't hear me over the piece of crap car we're in as she speeds lightning fast or she chooses not to acknowledge me. It also doesn't help that my baby sister, Zoey, and kid brother, Gage, are whimpering in fear in the backseat. Even above the roar of the engine, their fear-filled sounds reach my ears. I throw a quick glance at them to check if they are okay and find their faces pale and sweaty, suggesting they are about to hurl at any second.

"Mom, please! Zoey and Gage look like they are about to throw up," I yell, holding onto my seatbelt like it's the only thing keeping me from flying out of the car, which is a possibility given the reckless way she weaves across the road, her eyes continually going to the rearview mirror.

"Layla, look in the glove box. There should be an empty plastic bag in there somewhere," she snaps, ignoring everything else I have said up until now.

Nevertheless, I do as she says, and I find the bag easily enough amongst all the clutter filling the tiny space. Holding it tight, I kick the glove box shut and suck in a deep breath, calming my nerves. My brother and sister need me right now. They are counting on me. So before I turn around, I put on my best comforting smile for my siblings.

"Zoey, Gage, if you feel sick, just use this, okay?" I tell them kindly, keeping my voice soft even as I hit my mom's seat from the force of her turning a corner.

Zoey remains rigid in her seat, as if she's too scared to move. Her eyes, which are silently begging me for help, hurt my heart. Gage, however, snatches the bag out of my hand and wraps his arms protectively around it.

"No one is yakking their chunks in this bag. This was a birthday present." He pouts, narrowing his eyes.

It's from the time Mom was able to take Gage to watch his very first basketball game in the city. One of her drinking buddies gave her two tickets—I shudder to think what she had to do to get them —and she surprised Gage with them as a birthday present. She wasn't able to buy him anything there, but she did manage to purchase the plastic bag Gage is currently protecting so fiercely in his little hands. It's unfathomable to me how that was only last month.

Our little family was happy.

Or at least our family's version of happy.

And now . . . we're in the chase of our lives.

Okay, maybe happy is a bit of an overstatement. We were content with what we had. Life hasn't always been easy in my household, but we made do.

Until yesterday, that is.

I can't help but remember why we're in this situation to begin with, the real reason our lives have been a constant battle of survival. The only thing that ever puts a genuine damper in our humble lives is Gage and Zoey's dad, Roy. His temper knows no bounds, and his fury is only matched by the hatred that fills his eyes.

Last night, he gave Gage the brand-new shiner he's now sporting. Every time I catch a glimpse of it, I get angry all over again. It didn't surprise me when Roy went berserk on my kid brother for messing with his things. What truly shocked me was my mother's reaction to all of it. Seeing her baby boy all bloody and bruised must have somehow coaxed out the last remaining sliver of maternal instinct in her. All it took was one look at Gage and my mother decided to leave Roy's sorry ass for good the very next day. It's astounding, really, since she has been just fine with him using her as his personal punching bag for years. But for him to lay a finger on Gage . . . Well, I guess it was too much for even my mother to handle.

Of course, she never once batted an eye when the creep would put his hands on me, but that's a different story.

My gaze flickers over to the woman in question, the very one who should have loved me and protected me but could never summon the will to do it. My mother's love was never in the cards for me. She always resented the fact that she was tied to a baby when she was just a kid herself. One of her high school hookups was too cheap to buy or wear a condom, and unsurprisingly, nine months later, I popped out, an occurrence that my mother seems to blame me for to this day. Sad thing is, she's all I've got in the parental department. I have no idea who my father is since she was too drunk when they were making me to even get his name.

Romantic, right?

After a slew of deadbeat boyfriends and dating more losers than I have fingers and toes to count on, Mom finally met and married Roy, and by the way they tell it, it was love at first sight. He had a dilapidated house big enough for the five of us, and she took the beatings like a trooper.

Win-win for everyone, huh?

Every time he hit her, she would always come up with an excuse that it was somehow her fault and that she deserved to be disciplined. She sang a very different tune, however, when people on the street asked her how she had gotten a big swollen lip and that gash in her cheek.

"Oh, this little thing? It's nothing. I'm just so damn clumsy when I get a few beers in me. You know how it goes," she lied, her first priority protecting the man who was abusing her.

I was only a child when it started, but even then, I knew what was happening in my home was wrong. I tried to protect her, to get her to fight, but all it got me was a slap across the cheek for my troubles. She funneled all the anger she should have shown her piece of crap husband and channeled it into me.

Instead of protecting me, she chose him.

Well, that's Alice for you. She always knew how to pick the worst in the litter. I hadn't met a guy in her life who didn't either smack her around or treat her like a piece of garbage. Mom always did take falling in love with the bad boy to a whole new extreme.

Hence why we're currently driving at one hundred and fifty miles an hour, trying to put as much distance between us and this last dirtbag. Everything was going swimmingly too. I was overjoyed she was finally leaving him and that I wouldn't have to creep around the house, scared of every shadow. We waited until Roy departed for work at the factory, and then we packed up our stuff and left.

It was just bad timing that as we were about to turn left on a crossroad, we caught sight of his pickup truck directly in front of us. It was even worse luck when he stared into my mom's eyes from a few feet away. He slid a finger from left to right across his neck in the universal gesture that if he caught her, she was as good as dead.

The silent threat was enough to spook my mom into panicked hysteria, so just like in the movies, this is the part where we cut to the chase scene. Mom has been driving like a crazy person for the past half hour, trying to lose his tail. I don't even think she knows where she's at. She's just taking the first roads she finds in an attempt to escape the man she said she loved so much.

"Layla," Zoey mumbles in the backseat, drawing my gaze to her and away from the road.

"Yeah, sweetie?"

"I think I'm going to be sick," she whimpers, her big green eyes filled with unshed tears.

"That's totally okay, baby girl. Gage, give Zoey the bag," I implore, glancing out the back window to check the road.

"No," he says, holding the stupid thing close to his chest.

I want to yell, but instead I take a deep breath to calm my temper. He's just a kid, after all, and he doesn't know any better.

"Yes, Gage. Give it," I order sternly.

"I said no. It's mine!" he yells.

"Will you three quit your yapping? I'm trying to concentrate here!" Mom screams.

Gage gnaws on his lower lip, like he's about to cry, before he reluctantly hands the plastic bag to our sister.

"Gage, honey, I promise that when we get to where we're going, I'll get you a new bag," I coo, trying to stop his tears from falling.

He's suffered enough in his young life, so if all he wants is a plastic bag, I'll get it for him.

"You promise?" he whispers, sniffling. He wipes the snot coming out of his nose on his forearm, his expression so sad it hurts me inside..

I hand him the package of tissues I always carry on me, wearing the most comforting smile I can muster considering the predicament we are in. Neither Gage nor Zoey have any clue as to what's going on, and I'd rather keep it that way. I don't want to scare them if I don't have to.

"I promise, sweet boy."

He sniffles into the tissue then casts me a soft smile, but it quickly disappears when Zoey starts retching into the plastic bag.

"Ew, gross, Zoey." He gags.

"I can't help it," she snaps, her own tears streaking down her cheeks.

"It's okay, sweetheart. Gage was just teasing. Weren't you, buddy?" I cut him a look, trying to urge him to help.

"But it stinks," he complains.

"Gage," I say slowly, "tell Zoey you didn't mean to make her feel bad because of something that's out of her control. It's not her fault she's sick."

"No, it's Momma's," Gage interjects, throwing a dark glare at the woman driving.

Although I try not to think about it, Gage has a lot of Roy in him. Sometimes when Mom gives him treats or does something nice for him, he acts like she just hung the moon only for him. Other times, like right now, I swear his stare alone would kill her on the spot. Zoey is more docile, and when I say docile, I mean she does everything in her power to be invisible in our home. If no one sees you, then you can't get beat on. She already has that mentality of an adult even though she's only seven and still just a child, and it hurts my heart that my baby sister has learned such a cruel lesson so early in her tender life.

"Layla! Do you see him? Do you see the truck?" Mom calls out, bringing my attention to her.

I squint. I think I can see a little spot of blue in the distance.

"I think he's maybe a mile or two behind us."

"You think or you know?"

"I think. How am I supposed to know? It's not like I have binoculars. I see someone on the same road behind us, but the car is just too far away to see if it's Roy's or not."

At the mention of his father, Gage perks up.

"Dad? Why are we running away from Dad? I thought we were just going to visit Aunt Lucy?"

"And we are, baby. We just need to make a little detour first," Mom lies through her teeth.

Gage's forehead wrinkles, he's not buying what our mother is selling. "I don't want to go to Aunt Lucy's anymore. I want to go home."

"See what your big mouth did?" Mom scolds, swerving so carelessly that the seatbelt cuts through my shoulder. I swallow the pain and turn to ease Gage's reluctance.

"But don't you want me to get you that bag I promised? I can't do that if we turn around and go home."

I see the wheels spinning in his tiny brain, but my optimism takes a nosedive when he starts shaking his head.

"I don't want it anymore. I want to go home. I need to apologize to Dad for messing with his things. I shouldn't have gone to the garage in the first place. I know that now. So let's all just go home so I can tell him I'm sorry!" he yells, shifting closer to Zoey just so he can kick Mom's seat in his tantrum.

"No one is going home!" Mom yells from the driver's seat. "Now shut your trap, Gage. It's all your fault we have to leave anyway. Why you had to mess with his guns is beyond me. How stupid are you? I swear I have idiots for kids. Not a winning one in the bunch."

I close my eyes and count to five so I don't lose it on her. I'm used to her being mean to me, but when she loses her temper with the little ones, my protectiveness comes out like a tidal wave.

"Will you just shut up?" I yell. "Can't you see you're making things worse for them? They aren't at fault here. You are, Alice."

She scoffs. "I've had it up to here with you and your mouth too. The minute we get to Lucy's, I want you out. You're sixteen. You can take care of yourself. I don't want you living under my roof anymore. You're a burden."

I know she's bluffing.

She's been threatening to kick me out since I was twelve and she found Roy copping a feel of my ass.

Yeah, sure, Mom. I'm the one at fault for your lousy life choices.

In the end, though, she never follows through, and that's because I'm the one who takes care of Zoey and Gage while she parties. I'm about to say as much when I see a stray dog run across the road.

"Watch out!" I scream.

Alice swerves to avoid hitting the animal, but her grip slips on the wheel and she loses control of the car. We veer off the road and ram into a tree. Shards of glass shower over me, leaving little cuts all over my face, chest, and shoulders. My neck hurts like nothing I've ever felt before, and my ears ring from the violent crash.

"Gage. Zoey," I mumble, trying to clear the fog in my head. "Gage. Zoey. Answer me. Are you guys okay?"

"My head hurts," Zoey says after an excruciating amount of time as I manage to stiffly turn to check on them.

There is an ugly gash on her forehead and blood streaking down her precious face. I unlatch my seatbelt and crawl my way to the backseat to make sure they are okay. Gage rubs his neck, the shock making him speechless for once. I grab another tissue and try to clean Zoey's wound to see how deep it is.

"You're going to need some stitches, kiddo."

"Will that hurt?" she whispers, crying silently.

"No. They put on this miracle cream first, so you won't feel a thing when they stitch you back up. You'll be good as new."

"Ah shit, shit! Look what you've done!" my mother shouts, turning her head toward us.

I'm about to tell her she has no one to blame but herself for her shitty driving when her face turns as pale as a ghost.

"Oh fuck! Fuck, fuck, fuck."

I turn around to see what she's staring at, only to be crippled with fear at what I find. Roy's blue pickup truck slowly pulls to a stop a few feet away from us. He shuts the engine off and waits.

"Okay, Alice, think, think," my mother repeats to herself. "Okay. We haven't done anything wrong. We were just going to visit my sister. Nothing wrong with that. I'll just say I didn't see him earlier and what a good thing it is that he did and followed us since we've just had a terrible car accident and need him to take us back home. Yeah, that's it."

As my mother gives herself a pep talk, my stomach twists into knots as to why Roy hasn't stepped out of his truck yet. Mom pushes her breasts up and smooths her blonde hair away from her face so that her big green eyes are on display.

Say what you will about Alice, but she's beautiful. She's a little run-down, but she's still gorgeous in her own right. When she unbuckles and opens the door, a sick feeling assaults me. On instinct, I reach out and grab her wrist.

"M-Mom," I stutter, earning a surprised look since I haven't called her that in years. "Be careful. Something doesn't feel right."

"Don't be silly. I'll get us out of this mess. You should be worried about yourself. I'm serious. I no longer want you in my house. I'm going to tell Roy that I was taking you to stay with my sister. He'll believe me. Men are stupid when it suits them." She smiles triumphantly, unlatching my grip from her wrist.

She doesn't give me a chance to say anything else as she gets out of the car and sways her hips while sauntering over towards Roy's truck. With bated breath, I watch her stroll up to him and stop at his side door window, relaxing her arms on the door's frame as she tells him her version of events.

"Zoey, Gage, I want you to sit down on the floor," I order without looking away from Mom and the pickup truck.

"What? Why? Gage retorts.

"Just do it," I demand, unbuckling their seatbelts so they can crawl to the floorboards.

Zoey does as she's told, looking awfully pale all of a sudden. It's most likely due to blood loss. My gaze flickers back to the road, catching sight of my mother's head falling back with laughter.

"I don't want to," Gage argues, pulling my attention back to him. "Zoey's stinky throw up bag is in my way."

Jesus H. Christ.

I'm about to grab the vomit bag when a loud, thunderous sound sends panic down my spine. It all happens so fast. One second my mom is all smiles, and the next she's falling to the ground with a bullet in her head.

"Oh my God. Gage, hide! Now!" I yell, hurriedly crawling to the driver's seat to get us out of here.

Although Mom never had any cash for me to take driving lessons, she's had me driving around town on school runs, grocery trips, and anything else I could do since I was tall enough to reach the pedals and see over the dashboard. My entire body trembles as I try to start the car, hoping the crash didn't fuck up the engine. Unfortunately, all I get are hiccups as the motor struggles.

"What was that sound? Why are you trying to start the car? Where did Mom go?" Gage questions rapidly.

With the crash, he must have suffered the same brain fog I did, and now he's finally functioning. When Gage turns in his seat, he sees Roy getting out of his truck.

"Layla, it's Dad. He came to help us," he says excitedly, not smart enough to know there's no way Roy is here to rescue us.

With our mom's corpse concealed by high bushes, he doesn't see that she's dead, and to my horror, he shoves his door open and runs to his father.

"Gage! No!" I scream, but it's too late.

The sound of Roy's shotgun being reloaded is loud enough that it can be heard over my terror. I sit frozen in place, my heart in a vise as I shake profusely. Helplessly, I watch my little brother run to his father with open arms, only for the bastard to unload another shot right in the very center of his tiny chest.

"No!" I scream, my tears falling down my face until I taste the salt on my lips.

He killed him.

That son of a bitch killed him.

And he's going to kill Zoey and me next.

Oh my God.

No. No. I can't let that happen.

"Zoey? Zoey!" She lifts her head, the blood matting her golden locks to her temple. "Zoey, I need you to be my brave girl, okay? I need you to slide out of Gage's door and hide in the field. Can you do that for me?" I beg, trying to hold it together when in reality all I want is to fall apart and lie on the floor in the fetal position until this nightmare is over.

The only thing that prevents me from doing just that is knowing that Zoey needs me.

I have to save my sister.

She shakes her head, her tears cascading down her pretty face.

"I know you're scared, Zoey. I am too. But I need you to do this, okay? I need you to be brave and run as fast as you can down that field and onto the pig farm. There will be people there who can help you with your cut, but you have to promise not to make a sound. If you hear anyone behind you, I want you to hide. Can you do that for me, Zoey? Can you be my big girl and do this brave thing for me?"

With tears still streaking down her cheeks, she nods and makes her way to the other side of the car. The field is large enough that Roy won't be able to find her, but I still can't take that chance. I need to stall him long enough to make sure she has a good head start. I need to give her a fighting chance since I wasn't able to give that to Gage.

"What about you? Aren't you coming?" she asks, looking back at me.

That one look will haunt me until the day I die, which might be soon.

"I'll be right behind you. I just need to do something first. Now go," I lie, each word tasting like lead on my tongue.

"I love you, Layla," she sobs.

"I love you too, Zoey. So much. Now run. Run."

With those painful words hanging in the dense air between us, my little sister slips from the car and runs as fast as her little feet will carry her. I sink back in my seat and send a little prayer to any god that will hear me.

"Please keep my sister safe."

I don't ask for more than that. It would be foolish of me to think I will get out of this alive. But if I can do this one thing and keep Roy busy long enough to give her some time, then by God, I can't think of a better reason to sacrifice my life.

I take in a long breath of air, and on wobbly knees, I get out of the car. Roy stands only a few feet away from his son's corpse. My tears continue to fall as I stare at his small motionless form, his body mangled by the shot.

"There she is. Just the girl I was looking for," he cheers.

"You're a monster," I sneer, my legs shaking.

I'm desperate to check on Zoey's progress, but I don't dare move my gaze from Roy since I can't give her hiding spot away.

"Aww, is that any way to talk to me? As I see it, I'd be nice to me right about now. I have your life in my hands, after all," he taunts, holding the gun with one hand and reaching for his crotch with the other.

"Why? Why do this, Roy?"

"Why?" he shouts, his eyes bulging from his skull. "Your bitch of a mother was going to run off and leave me. With my kids, no less."

What he's saying is absurd.

"So you killed her?"

"She needed to learn her place. It's her own damn fault for getting fresh with me and lying to my face, telling me she was just dropping you off at her sister's. Nah. She was leaving. I saw the truth in her eyes, even when she was blatantly lying to me," he shouts, the force of his anger almost bowling me over.

He really is fucking deranged.

"And what about Gage? Did he deserve to die too?" I demand, trying to hold his attention and give my sister a chance to live another day, even if I'll never see her again.

"If he was my son, he would have put his foot down and told his momma what's what."

"He's eight!"

"Old enough to know better," he retorts, spitting on the cement.

He's unhinged, a sadistic madman on a power trip.

"Is this the part where you kill me too?" I ask, strangely calm and detached about the idea of these being my last moments on earth.

"I'm considering it, but there is so much I want to do to you," he responds, running his eyes down my body as his tongue drags along his chapped lips.

Bile instantly rises in my throat.

"These past years, I've been dying to pop that cherry of yours. I told myself to be a little patient and give you another year or so, but now I'm thinking why wait when your body looks like it's prime for the taking."

Suddenly the thought of dying doesn't seem so bad. I prefer death over having his filthy hands on me.

"That pretty mouth of yours has been begging for my cock for ages now. How about you be a good girl and come closer? Who knows, maybe if you show me that you can take your bitch of a mother's place, I'll let you live. You won't get a better deal from me."

"I'd rather rot."

"Oh, I like the sound of that too. The idea of fucking all your holes when you're no longer breathing is getting me hard, Layla. I think I'm going to try my hand at both options and compare what I like most—you moaning like a bitch in heat under me or the dead silence of your obedience."

What did my mother ever see in this asshole?

The thought is just a blip in my mind as something vital catches my attention. In the distance, I see a black car racing toward us. I have a split second to decide what to do. I choose to fight.

"Help!" I wave my arms in the air so the driver of the car can see what's going on. I hardly think whoever is in the car can stop a madman with a shotgun, but maybe it's enough to scare Roy back into his truck and make him drive away. Roy turns in the direction of the car, cursing under his breath when he sees we have company.

"Guess our time is up, Layla. I really am disappointed that we didn't get to have fun, but that's life," he comments before racking his gun.

Oh my God.

He's not going to run.

He's going to kill me.

For the second time today, I stand frozen in place, unable to move a muscle as fear cements me to my spot. When I stare down the barrel of the gun, I know all is lost. This is the end of me. What a wasted life. I had so few moments of joy for this to be the end of such a miserable existence.

I guess if I'm to meet my maker, at least I'll go out with the same bravery my little sister showed earlier. I square my shoulders and look Roy in the eye with all the resolve I still have in me.

"I hope you rot in hell, Roy. I hope they catch you for what you've done and that the rest of your days are spent in a cage. Only iron bars and a tiny cell are a good enough home for you. Let's see who is going to use your mouth and ass then, you sick fuck!" I shout, unwilling to beg or cry for mercy.

"You fucking bitch!" he yells, aiming the shotgun at my head.

The next ten seconds feel like they happen in slow motion, and although my eyelids scream to be closed, I force myself to keep them open, not missing a single second of it. The black car—now just a few yards from us—slides to the side, stopping only when it's directly across the middle of the road. I watch in complete astonishment as the driver rolls down his window and extends his arm with a gun in his grip. Another loud roar of gunfire pierces my eardrums, deafening me. I continue to gawk as the bullet slices through the air until it finds its target. Roy's head explodes as I watch. He starts falling to the ground, but not before his trigger finger jolts and makes his last shot. I wait for the bullet to find me, and when it does, the sensation is so violent, I drop to the ground.

As I'm falling, I focus on the blue eyes of the man who is stepping from the car with his gun still in his grasp. They are the color of midnight, mesmerizing me with their beauty.

He meets my gaze, and then I do the most idiotic thing.

I smile.

It's not a bad way to die if the last thing I see are such beautiful eyes.

As I'm about to thank this kind stranger for giving the last seconds of my life the beauty it has always been deprived of, my head hits the hard cement.

Instead of the sapphire blue I wish to hold onto, all that's left is cold, dark blackness.

CHAPTER 1

Layla

N ightmares.

I've had plenty of nightmares in my short life, but none of them were as vivid as the hazy images that assault me now.

I'm running toward something.

No . . .

Not something.

Someone.

There is an urgency in my rapid footsteps.

It demands I pick up the pace.

Run faster.

Harder.

It might mean life or death if I don't.

Instead of running away from the danger like a sane person would, I run toward it.

Fearlessly.

Relentlessly.

But the road is filled with so much blood and chaos, and no matter how fast I go, I can never seem to outrun its cruel madness.

And then, suddenly, I stop.

I freeze.

My legs are unwilling to move an inch closer to the horror now lying before me.

The blood of the innocent stains the cold concrete, turning the ugly gray to pools of red crimson.

My blood.

My heart.

Those are the things I now see splattered on the ground.

Something inside me snaps like a frail twig demolished by a harsh wind, and that's when I truly run.

Not out of desperation, but rage.

So much rage.

An angry wrath consumes me from within and refuses to let go.

The adrenaline that swims through my veins as I furiously trudge on, however, can't compare to the inexplicable feelings of loss and misery that clash within my soul.

Just as I start to give in to my grief and anger, the flash of sapphire eyes reminds me to resist the lure of my emotions.

It only happens for a split second, but those blue jewels are followed by a shout, reminding me of a word that I forgot even existed—*hope*.

Just as the foolish thought washes over me, a bullet pierces through air, and the sound of it hitting bone is so deafening, it springs me awake from my slumber, forcing me to face what is now an uncertain reality.

My breathing comes out in bursts as I try to wipe cold sweat off my brow with my forearm, but just as I try to wipe my forehead clean, crushing pain paralyzes me for a moment and my breathing becomes even more erratic. I count to ten, inhaling through my nose and exhaling through my mouth, pushing the debilitating pain away. Once the ache is somewhat manageable, and my breathing slows, I try to open my eyes. Unfortunately, my lids refuse to cooperate since the harsh light above me is so bright it's almost blinding.

Where the hell am I?

What happened?

These questions bombard me all at once as I force myself to open my eyes, pain be damned.

My lids carefully flutter open, slowly at first, just until my eyes can grow accustomed to the white light overhead. The smell of antiseptic fills my nostrils with bitter undertones of some artificial fragrance from cleaning materials. It's a distinct smell that can only be found in a hospital or clinic.

Hospital, why am I in a hospital?

My panic quickly subsides when I find my baby sister snuggled up beside me in the small bed, holding my free hand so fiercely in her sleep it's as if she's afraid I'll vanish. A tender smile begins to curve my lips, but it's wiped away when I hear nurses and doctors talking right outside the small room, confirming my initial suspicion of where we are.

I'm in a hospital.

Why are we in a hospital?

But just as the question comes to the forefront of my mind, the ache in my shoulder answers it for me.

I was shot.

I was shot by my stepfather, but I wasn't the only one.

Gage.

Oh God! Gage!

It's all coming back to me in a flurry of terror-filled flashes.

All of it.

As hard as I try to expunge the image of my baby brother being struck down, erasing the beautiful light within him, all I can see is his lifeless body. It's as if I'm back on that abandoned road, living the last seconds of his life all over again, helpless to stop it.

My silent tears stir Zoey awake.

I quickly wipe my tears on the pillow before she's fully awake.

"Layla! You're okay!" Zoey squeals in excitement the instant we lock eyes.

"Of course I am, kiddo. I'm like a cat. I've got nine lives, didn't you know?" I tease, rubbing the tip of my nose against hers, praying she doesn't see the crippling misery in my eyes.

As my kid sister hugs me, I try to hide that every part of me hurts—my head, my shoulder, and every limb on my body, but it's my heart that bears the brunt of the pain.

Memories of Gage's last seconds continue to replay in my mind, and it takes extraordinary effort to keep the small smile on my face for Zoey when my soul cries in utter misery. I widen the pathetic smile even more when guilt starts to creep into me as I realize that not one tear I'm holding back is for my mother.

Roy killed her too, and like one would discard an unwanted piece of trash, he left her body to rot in a field.

Although a part of me must have loved her once, I can't seem to find any lingering shard of that love—not when I'm mourning the loss of my brother, a life she failed to protect.

Like she failed to protect all of us.

"How did we get here?" I ask, hoping that Zoey's tale on how she was able to get me to the hospital will take my mind off Gage.

I immediately regret the question when Zoey kneels on the mattress and starts talking gibberish about an angel that came to save us. I play along, because no matter how improbable her description of the event is, it's still better than the one I have.

Unlike Zoey, I didn't see an angel.

All I saw was the devil himself in my stepfather.

"He was huge, Layla! I mean, he was as tall as the sky and as big as a house, and he picked you up like you didn't weigh a thing. You should have seen it," she continues animatedly.

"I'm sorry I missed it." I grin, my cheeks hurting with the effort, like plastic stretched too thin, about to crack and break. Brittle, that's what I feel like.

When the twinkle in her eyes starts to dim, I know she's thinking about how if her so-called angel would have gotten to us ten minutes sooner, then maybe we wouldn't have lost Gage to that monster.

"Zoey—" I start, but she just shakes her head, not wanting to hear whatever consoling words I have to offer her. Good thing, too, since I'm not sure any words I have could make up for the horrific ordeal we just suffered.

How could I ever justify the loss of a brother and mother to someone so young? I'm still trying to wrap my head around what happened to us and how our little fucked-up family just got cut in half.

"He wasn't a good man," she mutters under her breath, unwilling to make eye contact with me. "I knew it all along. Gage never saw it, but I did."

My shoulders slump at her words, the hate in them so palpable I can almost taste its arsenic.

"It doesn't matter now. He can't hurt Gage anymore. Or Mom. And he'll never hurt us again. Never," she seethes through gritted teeth, making me wrap my arms around her tiny frame, even if it hurts like hell to do it.

"It's okay, Zoey. We're okay," I lie, since I'm not sure that we will ever be okay after this.

She lifts her head from my embrace, her eyes filled with unshed tears.

"What's going to happen to us now, Layla?"

I open my mouth to lie to her again, but the way she squints at me, silently demanding the truth, has me sealing my lips tight for a second. I let out an exhale before kissing her temple.

"I'm not sure. The only thing I am sure about is that whatever happens next, we'll face it together. You and me, Zoey. Always."

That brings a genuine smile to her lips.

"Us and our guardian angel."

"Sure. Him too." I giggle.

I refuse to take that idea away from her.

If believing in angels who come to our rescue brings her a small smidge of solace, then the least I can do is let her have that. Lord knows we don't have much else aside from each other.

The soft knock on my door and featherlight feet walking into the room have me releasing my sister in favor of trying my best to sit up to greet the strangers who walk into my room.

"Good. You're up." A soft-spoken woman in a white coat smiles at us. She proceeds to walk to one side of the bed as another woman, a nurse, checks my vitals.

"You must be my doctor," I state evenly, holding onto Zoey's hand while my eyes trail from the doctor to the nurse who is hurriedly scribbling on a chart.

"I am. My name is Dr. Levi, and you, young lady, gave us quite a scare. I was starting to think you didn't want to wake up. Our own living, breathing Sleeping Beauty."

My forehead wrinkles at the absurd comment.

"If I'm here with a bullet wound to my shoulder, then you know my life is no fairy tale." When the smile on her face immediately drops to the floor, I kick myself for being so blunt. "I'm sorry. I didn't mean to be rude. I know you were only trying to be nice and help me. Thank you."

Dr. Levi tries to grin at my lukewarm apology, but her smile doesn't hold the same happiness it did when she walked into the room to see me. I guess I should be grateful for it since it's more in tune with my current circumstances.

"There's no need to thank me. It's my job to make sure you get out of here on your own two feet, after all."

"And when will that be?" I ask, tightening my hold on Zoey's hand.

Dr. Levi glances over at the nurse, who in turn gives her a curt nod, before she gives me an answer.

"If all goes well, in two days' time you'll get the all-clear from me. We just want to make sure there aren't any complications from the surgery we had to perform on you yesterday. We were able to remove the bullet from your shoulder with ease, but we still want to make sure it wasn't in your bloodstream long enough to cause any lasting damage. There will be some physical therapy in your future since cartilage and muscle were damaged, but luckily no bone or any vital arteries were hit. All in all, you are one lucky young lady."

I let her words hang in the air, making no attempt to tell her just how ridiculous that statement is.

I've never been lucky a day in my life, and if such luck was to come my way, then it's a day too late and a dollar short.

Dr. Levi clears her throat, looking like she would prefer for the floor to swallow her whole than stay a minute longer in this room with two orphans who, just by the blank expressions on their faces, are making her feel inadequate with her bedside manner.

"Doctor?" the nurse calls, taking mercy on her. "The woman from Child Protective Services is still waiting outside. Should I tell her that she can come in now?"

"Child Protective Services?" I blurt anxiously as Zoey hugs my side, racked with the same fear those words provoked in me. "Why is child services here? Didn't anyone call my aunt? Why isn't she here? Why are they?"

Dr. Levi turns two shades paler as the nurse quickly leaves to fetch whoever is waiting outside for Zoey and me.

"Dr. Levi," I continue, "did anyone call my next of kin and tell them what happened? Did anyone call Aunt Lucy?"

"I really couldn't say either way, but I'm sure everything will be perfectly fine," she replies with a fabricated, upbeat optimistic tone.

"Right," I snap, no longer caring that my venom-filled voice makes the young doctor squirm where she stands. "Because all fairy tales begin with a visit from child services."

CHAPTER 2

Alaric

"Argh!"

"Oh, quiet down. It's just a fucking flesh wound, you pussy," I bark at the man tied down to my workstation.

The fucker continues to moan in pain, twisting and turning like a live worm on a hook. I'm not worried he'll get away. The leather binds around his wrists and ankles keep him from going anywhere, but if he keeps fidgeting like this, sooner or later, I'll end up killing him just because I feel like it. If I do that shit instead of cutting him nice and slow like the contract ordered me to, I'll have to refund half the money that was paid to me upfront just because of my impatient follow-through.

Needing something to get my head back in the game, I pick up my remote control and increase the volume of the sweet sounds of Wagner blasting through my sound system, succeeding in muffling this jackass's whimpers and useless pleas for mercy. My fingers trail over my shiny instruments of pain, yet none of my preferred toys call out to me like they should, making me choose the last one by default.

I crack my neck, hoping it will ease the tension in my shoulders, but to no avail.

"Fuck," I mumble, pissed off. "Get it together already, Alaric."

No matter how much I castigate myself for it, my head hasn't been screwed on straight since that fucking day I saved those two young girls from certain death. Everything reminds me of them lately, especially how I just left them to fend for themselves back at the hospital without a second thought.

Jesus fucking Christ.

Having a heart is bad for fucking business, my pops once told me.

He gave plenty of advice like that back in the day. Some I took to heart, while others I just chalked off to him being bitter and jaded with the life he led.

I mean, being a contract killer will do that to a man.

We get numb to it all.

The screams.

The begging.

The blood.

After a while, none of it affects us much.

So why the fuck am I letting two little girls get the best of me?

"Fuck!" I yell, knocking all my toys to the floor with one quick slide of my hand.

The bruised and beaten naked guy lying on the hardwood table freezes, wary of what I'll do next.

"Oh, now you decide to keep still, huh, fucker?" I shout, aggravated that not even work can take my attention away from all these feelings inside me.

Feelings.

Isn't that just a kick in the head?

I caught fucking feelings just because a little girl stood up to me while the last remaining member of her family was slowly dying in my arms.

"You know what? Maybe you're not the only pussy here. I think I might have grown one too," I choke out sarcastically then laugh at my own poor attempt at a joke.

His beady eyes widen as I pick up his file from a nearby table and come closer to where his head lies so he can get a good look inside it.

"Says here you're a bad man . . . Paul," I start, pointing to his name on the file. "The kind of guy who gets drunk on a Sunday afternoon and then puts himself behind the wheel of a car. See this right here?" I point to where his sins are written down in black and white. "It says here that you killed a woman, a pregnant woman, and the little boy she was pushing in a stroller, probably taking him for a nice walk to the park."

Like the coward he is, he closes his eyes when he's faced with the truth. I grab hold of his jaw and fiercely make him look me in the eye, forcing him to see it, hear it, and live with it the way everyone else will have to.

"It must take a real piece of shit to run two people over like that and just keep on driving. Didn't even call for help, did you? Did it even occur to you to call nine-one-one before they bled out and died? You were probably too worried that if you did, the cops would trace the call back to your pathetic ass."

My nostrils flare in disdain when he doesn't even try to deny it.

"I wish I could say it was just dumb luck that the woman and kid you killed were none other than the wife and only child to the district attorney. Worse luck still is that for all his holier than thou talk about putting the scum of the earth behind bars for their crimes, he's not so keen on trusting the justice system when it's his own blood on the line. That, shit head, means you got me instead of Lady Justice."

His sudden calm reaction to everything I'm saying hits a nerve, and when he starts mumbling something, something that sounds awfully like a prayer asking for absolution, I lose my shit.

"Are you fucking praying?" I shout in his face, my spit hitting him in the eye. "You think God is going to come for you and save you from this? Open the pearly white gates of heaven for your ass to walk right through just because you decide you're sorry now? Newsflash, motherfucker! There is no fucking God. If there was, he wouldn't let a piece of shit like you kill two innocent people and just go about your business like nothing happened."

The thought of Layla and Zoey immediately comes to mind as I shout those words.

But they aren't the only image I focus on.

It's the small, defenseless boy whose mangled body must have needed to be scraped from the concrete with a shovel that ends up increasing my fury.

I stare at the camera that has been filming this scene for the past hour and offer a shrug.

"Consider this a freebie," I say to the camera, and then I slice the fucker open from navel to jaw.

I drop the scalpel in my hand and wipe the blood spatter off my face before I turn off the camera.

Sloppy handiwork.

I hate it when I'm sloppy.

I prefer a level head when I'm working.

I'm clean and calculating, and this was anything but.

It seems that's how this shit is going to continue to go on if I don't get some intel on how those two girls are doing. I can't concentrate on anything else if I don't.

Goddamn it.

My pops was right.

Having a heart is a bitch.

And worse, it's bad for fucking business.

* * *

Two hours later, I'm strolling through the same hospital where I left an inconsolable Zoey and her big sister, Layla, not two weeks ago. The only difference is that this time, I'm not just dropping them off and making a quick getaway. This time I'll need some answers first before I leave. Stupid, I know. I shouldn't get involved, especially since I committed a murder and it will be handled by the police, but I have to know they are okay.

"We've been trying to reach you, but you didn't leave a phone number or a name," the male nurse sitting behind the counter explains after I ask about the girls' whereabouts. "The police wanted to speak with you too."

That's the precise reason why I didn't leave my name and number, idiot, I think to myself. "That can wait. Right now, I just want to see how the girls are doing," I reply curtly.

"They left. Child services took them."

"Already?" I cock a brow. "The girl was shot, for fuck's sake. What kind of butcher shop are you guys running here? Patching them up with a Band-Aid and kicking them to the curb is not how you deal with gunshot wounds," I growl, my blood starting to boil out of nowhere.

Before I have time to analyze why the fuck I'm acting this way, the male nurse is scribbling on a piece of paper.

"Here. This is the address they were taken to. That's all I have," he says before handing me the yellow Post-it note, his fingers trembling in fear.

What a fucking pussy.

If all I had to do was talk a little loudly to scare him, then he would pee his pants if he knew that I was scrubbing guts and blood off my beard a few hours ago.

I snap the Post-it out of his hand and turn my back to him, walking outside to my car and hoping the address he gave me isn't some wild goose chase he's sending me on.

I chuckle.

Nah.

The fucker knows better than to make me pay him a visit a second time in the same day.

I get into my car and add the address to my GPS, grateful to see that it's only a twenty-minute drive from here. The only thing I'm not so happy about is that the address leads me to a house that looks like it's on its last leg in a bad part of town. I see two kids open the iron gate and pass by me with skateboards in their hands.

"Hey," I call out, fishing a twenty-dollar bill from my pocket. "What is this place?"

The skittish kid just walks past me, while the one who isn't afraid to talk to strangers for a buck stays rooted to his spot, opening his palm. I reluctantly give him his money before I get an answer.

"What does it look like? It's a foster home, old timer."

My forehead wrinkles since this pissant should show more respect to the guy who just paid him for barely any info.

I swipe the bill out of his hand faster than he can blink.

"Yeah, I get that it's a foster home by how run-down it is. What I want to know is if there are two girls inside. One must be like . . . I don't know . . . seven or eight and her sister has a banged-up shoulder. Any of that familiar to you?"

He crosses his arms, not one bit frazzled by the scowl on my face.

"All depends," he retorts.

"On what?" I snap. Usually I'm better at this, but my patience is wearing thin where my two girls are concerned.

"If you're going to pay me or not."

I almost roll my eyes at the little dipshit. "Here," I bark, handing him his money.

"Nah, man. I'm going to need a little bit more than that to get your intel."

"How old are you?" I arch a brow.

"Fifteen."

"Want to make it to sixteen? I suggest you talk. Now."

The nonchalance in his expression is wiped clean when I give him the look.

In our business, we all have it.

It's the same one that says don't fuck with me or else.

Else usually means a quick slash to the throat. This kid hasn't lived long enough to earn my wrath, but if he keeps playing with me, then I'll have no choice but to rough him up a bit.

Just a bit.

"Gray!" his cowardly friend shouts, looking like he's about to throw up. "Just tell him already."

"Better listen to your friend." I smile menacingly.

"I don't have friends, asshole," he spits back.

"Not with that attitude." I smirk, liking the kid just a little bit more, but not enough that I won't bitch slap him if he doesn't get it together and give me what I want.

The pissant stares me in the eye like he's a man and shit. If he wasn't such a pain in my ass, I'd actually find him amusing.

Since I'm not one for patience and slapping him about would only take more time than what I have right now, I relent and grab another twenty from my pocket.

"Make it good," I tell him, giving him his money.

He counts the two bills like they are hundreds, and this time he stashes them away before I have a chance to steal them out of his hands again.

"You're looking for Zoey. Zoey and Layla, right?"

My chest tightens at the mention of their names.

"They are not here anymore. They got out just in the nick of time."

My brows furrow at the ominous comment, but right now the only thing I can focus on is where they went.

"Where did they go?"

He runs his tongue over his teeth, making my hands ball into fists.

I don't even wait for the little dipshit to blackmail me again for more money. Instead, I just grab the rest I have in my pocket.

The little prick even has the nerve to smirk at me.

"Give me two secs, old timer, and I'll tell you."

Before I have time to ask what he means by that, he drops his board against the chain-link fence and races back to the foster home. I stand outside for what feels like an eternity as I hear more than one voice coming from inside the shabby house.

Is this really the best we can do?

Leave traumatized kids in a place where they are bound to get even more scarred?

Fuck this decaying society.

No wonder there are men like me walking about.

I start to tap my shoe on the sidewalk, counting down the minutes for Gray, or whatever his name is, to come back outside. I'm about to lose my patience and go in to find the prick when he finally emerges from the rat infested house he calls home.

"Here," he says, handing me a piece of paper.

"Great. Another fucking Post-it."

"Huh?"

"Nothing, kid. You did good," I praise him, eyeing the new address written on it, this time with a name.

"I thought they only had that aunt of theirs who came to pick them up. You don't look like family to me," he remarks suspiciously.

"That's because I ain't, kid. Stop asking so many stupid questions when you already know the answer to them," I advise with a leveled tone.

His face suddenly looks almost subdued, which raises my hackles since this kid has been nothing but a jackass since I met him.

"Are you going to look out for them? For Zoey?" he asks with genuine concern in his voice.

"That's the plan, kid."

"Good," he retorts, looking somewhat grateful, or at least as grateful as a kid like him can be. I eye him for a moment, noticing his black eye, his worn clothes, and his too skinny frame, all covered up by a big mouth.

Safe to say, kids like him have never been grateful for anything that has happened in their lives.

"They are good, you know? You don't see much good in this place." He tilts his head back to gesture to the place he just came from.

"Yeah, well, let that be a lesson to you, kid. There isn't much good anywhere these days."

Gray nods, almost as if he understands exactly what I mean by that.

"I'm glad they have you then. They need someone big and mean to scare the wolves away," he adds before picking up his board and walking toward his friend who is now standing on the opposite side of the road.

"Hey," I bark out before he gets too far. "When I see them, do you want me to give them a message from you or something?"

I don't know who is more surprised that shit came out of my mouth, but here we are.

Gray stares at me for a split second before placing his foot on his skateboard.

"Tell Zoey I'm sorry and for her to forget this place ever happened. I sure the fuck will." And just like that, he glides down the street on his board and flies away like he never existed.

I take one more look at the house behind me and can't help wondering what the kid meant by that. Suddenly, the urge to see if both girls are okay with my own eyes multiplies tenfold. For the second time today, I get behind the wheel of my car and race to an unknown address, this one closer to the outskirts of the city where normal, wholesome families reside. Knowing that the girls are living in such a place is the only thing keeping me from driving like a madman.

Thirty minutes later, I park my car just three houses down from theirs. The lawn looks like it's been looked after, so at least someone inside gives a crap about what their neighbors think. That's good. People who believe they have eyes on them at all times are less likely to do something that will get them in trouble. I crack my knuckles, my leg bouncing up and down. I hate that I don't have a clear view of the inside. The curtains are too thick to see anyone moving, and I'm too far away to hear anyone talking from inside too.

But I have to see them.

I'm not sure what I'll say, or do for that matter. I haven't exactly concocted a plan up to this point, which is very unlike me, but then again, I haven't exactly been myself since they came into the picture.

"Fuck it," I mutter, my hand already on the door handle, ready to get out of this car and bang their door down if I have to.

Just as I'm stepping out, I hear a familiar bratty voice giggle behind me.

"Slow down and watch where you're going, Zoey. I need those eggs whole when we get home."

Zoey giggles at her sister, raising the two plastic bags in her hands that most likely contain the eggs Layla is talking about.

"If they fall, then we'll have scrambled eggs tomorrow for breakfast. No big deal."

Layla laughs at her little sister, rubbing the top of her head with her free hand since her other arm is still in a sling.

"You know, for a little thing, you sure have a mouth on you, sweet girl," Layla says with no malice to her tone, only undying love.

"Don't I know it." I chuckle under my breath, my gaze glued to both girls.

Zoey gives Layla such a sweet smile, it physically hurts me that I made the decision to stay away for as long as I did.

That shit is going to change now.

From here on out, I'll never take my eyes off either one of them again.

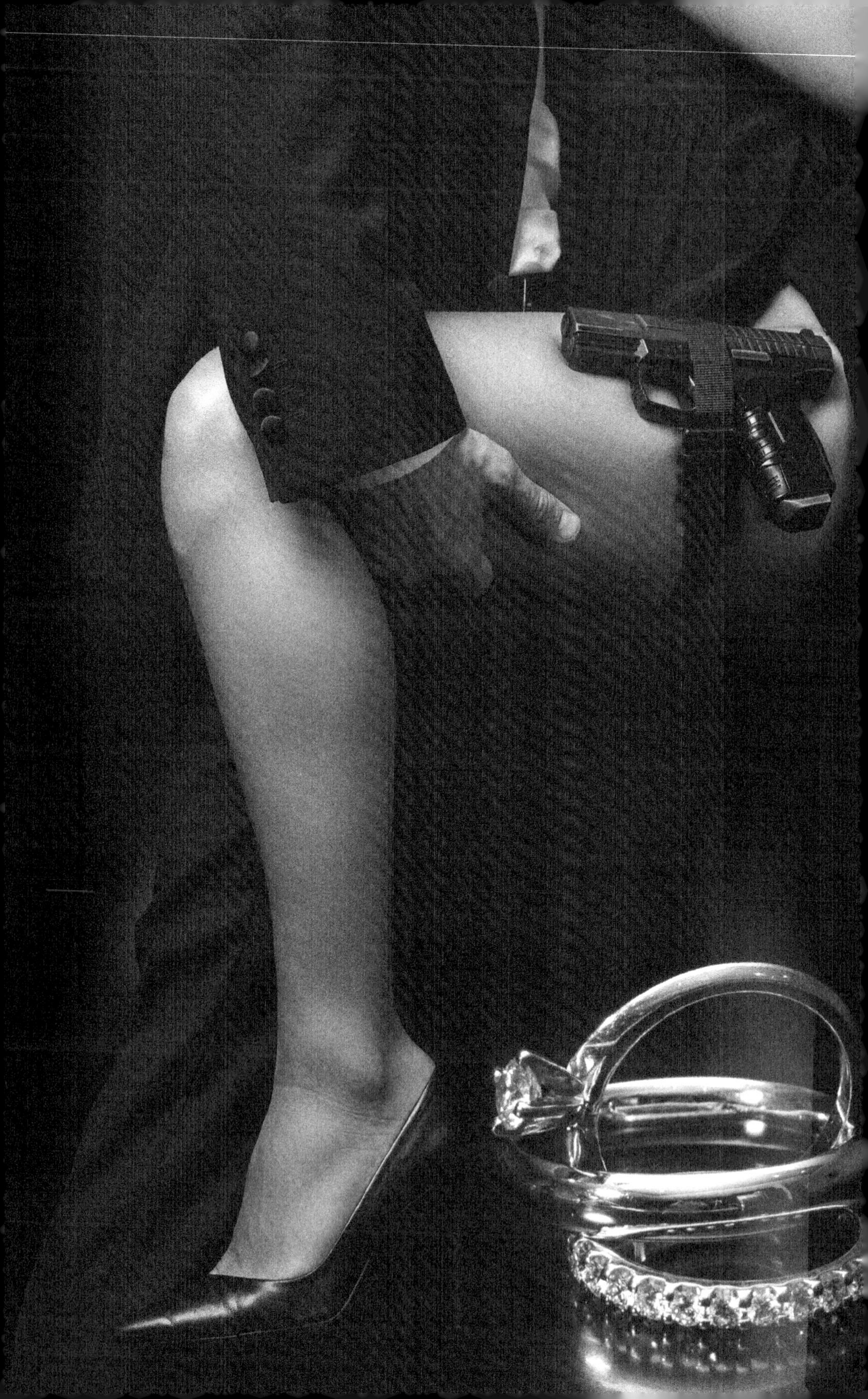

CHAPTER 3
Layla

Eighteen months later

It could be worse.

This path life has given Zoey and me could definitely be a million times worse. We could still be back in foster care.

It took dozens of calls to Aunt Lucy, begging her to take us in, to prevent that from happening. She only changed her tune after I promised that I would quit school and do whatever I needed to do to carry our weight.

That got her attention just like I knew it would.

Aunt Lucy might have a little more money than my mom did, but when it comes down to it, they are both made of the same fabric. If it's free, they want it.

To them, life couldn't get any better than having an inhouse maid who will do their dirty work for them so they can kick back, drink cheap box wine, and chain smoke menthol cigarettes while they watch bad reality television all day. I really don't care if I spend my days cleaning after a drunkard like Lucy, her handsy slob of a husband, or her two obnoxious sons.

All I care about is Zoey.

Knowing that she's safe and healthy is the only thing that really concerns me.

Mind you, my aunt does have days where she makes life less than bearable. Anytime my mother's name is even mentioned, I either get a snide comment or an evil side-eye. So far, she hasn't hit me, but I can tell she's dying to lay her hands on me. In my aunt's eyes, I'm the reason Roy killed her sister. She believes I must have done something to piss him off for him to retaliate the way he did.

She doesn't blame the deranged monster who almost killed his entire family by the side of a road.

No.

You can't curse a dead man for his wrongdoings, but apparently you can take it out on the girl who still bears the scar of his bullet on her body.

According to my aunt, I'm the one at fault, especially since it seemed dear old Alice told her sister Lucy of her plans to kick me out of the house the minute we got here.

It was stupid of me to think my mother was only talking trash for the sake of hurting me that day in the car. I honestly believed we were leaving Roy as a family so we could start over after the way he hurt Gage. Apparently, Alice had plans to start her new life with my brother and sister without me. I think I would have been okay with that decision if she would have stepped up to the challenge of being a good mother to my siblings, but with Alice, history had a tendency of repeating itself. Sooner or later, some other lowlife would have come along, and she would have forgotten Gage and Zoey in a heartbeat. Without me there to look over them, I couldn't imagine how that would have gone.

But that is neither here nor there now. She's not here to cause more damage to our lives, and to my bitter agony, neither is my sweet little brother.

It's only Zoey and me against the world now.

If I have to cower and nod whenever Aunt Lucy yells at me just because she's in a mood, or if I have to swallow down my puke anytime my pervy uncle gets up from his seat just as I'm passing by so he can rub his junk against my ass, then so be it.

These are the thoughts that tumble through my head as I iron a stained T-shirt that should have been thrown in the trash years ago, but as Aunt Lucy always says, if it isn't broke, you keep it. Maybe that's why she stays in her loveless marriage.

"Are you almost done in there? Dinner won't fix itself, you know," my aunt hollers above the loud television show she's been watching all morning.

"Yes, ma'am," I reply on cue since no other answer will win me any brownie points with her.

I quickly iron the last two shirts and pack their clothes in their respective drawers before putting the iron and board away. I walk into the kitchen, bypassing Lucy on her recliner as she laughs at some joke a guy made on TV. I open up the refrigerator and sigh in frustration when I find little inside that will enable me to cook a meal for six people.

I hate this part.

I have to ask my aunt for money just to feed her own family. Somehow, she always manages to twist it in a way that makes it seem like the reason why her refrigerator and cupboards are always empty is due to having two extra mouths to feed.

Of course, I have lived here for close to two years now, so I know the real reason.

You see, Lucy is what you call a stay-at-home mom. At least, that's what she tells people. In reality, she got hit by a bus when she was in her twenties and has been living off disability and the money she got from her settlement case. Uncle Dave, on the other hand, earns his living from working at the post office. He's bragged more than once about how it's his government work that really keeps a roof above our heads. Whatever they both bring home, I know it is enough to pay for their four-bedroom house, but I also know for a fact that they could all be living much better if my uncle didn't gamble so much of their money away.

Not that Lucy says anything about it.

To her, it's my and Zoey's presence in her home that has them counting pennies.

Damn it. I hang my head for a moment, mentally preparing for the fight to come. I'm so tired of it.

I loosen my shoulders and put on a fake smile as I walk to the living room, mentally preparing myself for the words I know will come out of her mouth. As I get into the room, though, Lucy is on the phone, cackling away with someone. I stand rooted to my spot, waiting for her to get off the phone.

"God. Stop being such a creeper, Layla. I can feel you breathing on my neck."

Sometimes I fantasize that it's my hands around her neck instead of my breath, but every time I do, guilt immediately surfaces. She gave us a home, so I should be grateful, and I am. I just wish she would show us a little kindness too. Unfortunately, in this family, kindness is a luxury no one seems to be able to afford, which is something I should have learned from my mother. After all, her and Lucy are practically the same. I guess I could blame their upbringing, but at what point do people just decide to be assholes, make bad decisions, and keep blaming it on past events instead of being decent?

"Anyway, that was Dave on the phone. He's going to bring home some fried chicken for dinner. Guess you're in luck tonight," she mutters, throwing me a narrow-eyed glare as if my very presence pisses her off.

The smile that springs free on my face is immediate. Thank God.

If he's bringing dinner, then I don't have to ask her for money. At least not for another day.

"Hmm. You know what would go great with fried chicken?" she muses, staring at me. "Some mashed potatoes and collard greens."

Fuck my life.

"I . . . Uh . . . We don't have any of that."

She arches a brow, and I bite my inner cheek when I see a twinkle of triumph in her eyes.

"What does that mean exactly?" she drawls, and I know she's gearing up to fight me.

I swallow dryly while trying hard not to fidget under her scrutinizing gaze. "It just means I have to go to the grocery store around the corner. That's all."

"And am I stopping you? Go, girl, and stop wasting my time. I've got better things to do than stare at that ugly face of yours all day."

My broken, dirty nails dig into my palms while she admires her perfectly manicured ones. "I'll need money, Aunt Lucy. To go to the store, I mean," I tell her.

"Again? By God, you really are a leech, aren't you?" she spits in distaste, grabbing her cigarettes and lighter. "My dear sister, God rest her soul, always said you were one, and now I see she was right all along. Here," she barks out, retrieving her wallet from the side of her favorite recliner with one hand while doing a balancing act with her lit cigarette with the other. "Go and be quick about it. Dave should be home in a few hours, and you know he likes to eat his dinner the minute he steps foot inside this house. Don't make my man wait, you hear me? He's been dying for an excuse to kick you out, and if he finds one, I won't do a damn thing to stop him. You little bitches are bleeding me dry as it is."

I feel the metallic taste of blood pool on the tip of my tongue as I swallow down yet another one of her provocations. I won't give her the satisfaction of talking back. I know the minute I do, she won't stop at beating me down with her words. Her backhand or a belt will be her preferred method to get her message across.

I wait for her to hand me her credit card and walk out the instant I have it in my hand. When I close the front door behind me, I let out the air that was trapped in my lungs.

Trapped.

That's how I've been feeling lately.

Completely trapped in my circumstances.

I just have to hold on for six more months. As soon as I turn eighteen, I'll ask for custody of Zoey then find a job and a place for us in the city. Once I do that, then I'll cut ties with the last remnants of my mother's family. Aunt Lucy's charity comes with too many strings and a kick to my already low self-esteem. There's no way I will let Zoey live in this house long enough for her to feel like she's an unwanted burden.

Zoey is so much more than that.

Right now, she's my lifeline and the only thing that keeps me going.

As long as she's happy and well cared for at the end of the day, that's all that matters. With new resolve, I walk down the front yard, open the little white gate, and walk to the nearby store just a block away.

Although I hate asking my aunt for money, I do enjoy these

little trips to the store. It's usually the only time I can get out of the house. It's when I can just be Layla. Nothing else. Not their housemaid, the caretaker, or the survivor. Just me, a teenage girl, and for a few moments, I can be anyone with any type of life.

I could be an aspiring singer or dancer. I could be in the throes of new love. I could be happy.

No one gives me sad eyes because they know about my past.

In fact, no one knows much about me at all.

The only person I talk to aside from my family is the boy who works the counter at the store after school. His name is Nathan. He doesn't make my heart flutter or my knees weak, but he's nice to me. He always has a big smile for me when I come into the store, almost if I'm the highlight of his day.

It's nice. He's nice. Most importantly, though, I feel seen by him, and that's a feeling that has evaded me most of my life. The only time anyone has ever seen me is when they want something from me.

Ruthless Aunt Lucy.

Pervert Uncle Dave.

My selfish mother when it suited her.

Even Roy.

The only people who ever truly saw me and never demanded anything from me in return were Zoey and Gage.

It's amazing how they were the very ones I'd do anything for when all they wanted was to play with their big sister.

Adults have a way of making me feel worthless in their eyes.

Less than worthless.

Disposable.

Maybe it's because Nathan is around my age, or maybe it's because he's lived a charmed life, free of trauma, that I feel so at ease with him. No matter the reason, it's nice to at least have one friend.

"There she is. The most beautiful girl in town," he shouts out when I walk into the store.

I shake my head and keep it low since I don't like the attention his usual greeting always draws from the rest of the shoppers in here.

"Hey, don't be shy. Come over here and talk to me for a bit."

"After I get my groceries," I reply meekly, trying very hard not to make any eye contact with anyone.

Who knows? Maybe my aunt has spies here who will rush to tell her that I've found a friend.

I very much doubt Aunt Lucy would be thrilled to find out anyone likes me, much less a teenage boy.

Since I don't have much time today to chat with Nathan, I hurry to get all the vegetables and ingredients I'll need before I make my way to his counter.

"Guess what?" he says as he passes the produce over the scanner.

"What?" I reply with a smile.

"A friend of mine is throwing a party at his house. Want to come with me?"

I shake my head. "I can't. Sorry."

He frowns. "It doesn't have to be a date if you don't want it to be. We can go as friends if that's easier for you."

My forehead creases. "Why would that make it easier? We are friends."

"Oh, I know. Some girls just like to DTR before going out with a guy." He coughs awkwardly.

"DTR?" I ask, hating that I'm so naïve when it comes to normal teenage lingo.

"You know? Define the relationship or whatnot," he explains with a smile as I place the produce in a plastic bag.

"You have to tell your boss that these bags really aren't good for the environment. You can get paper bags or those recyclable totes," I reply instead of giving sway to that loaded comment.

"So you keep telling me." He chuckles before telling me how much I owe him.

I hand him the credit card while I pack the last remaining items in the bag.

"No smokes today?" he asks.

"My aunt didn't ask for any." I shrug.

"Good. That means I get to see your pretty face again today."

I smile because he's being sweet. "Maybe." I wave before grabbing the bags off the counter to leave.

"Raincheck on that party then. I'll keep inviting you, and one of these days, you'll say yes just to shut me up," he calls loudly.

"Okay. If you say so." I laugh and stroll out the door, feeling a little bit lighter than I did before I went in.

Just as I start walking back home, there's this nagging feeling that someone is watching me.

It happens from time to time.

I usually chalk it off to my own paranoia, a side effect from all the shit I've had to endure in my life, but then other days I actually have to look behind me just to make sure no one is following me.

It's the oddest sensation.

While this sixth sense should tell me to be cautious of my surroundings, it actually feels like I'm safe somehow. Like someone up there is looking down on me, making sure I don't take a false step or do anything that will bring danger to my doorstep.

It's only late at night, while I'm lying in bed with Zoey, that my mind travels to darker territory, wondering if, in fact, there is a real live person who is tracking my every move.

Later that night, I whisper, "Zoey?" wondering if she's already fallen asleep.

"Hmm?" She yawns.

"Have you seen anything weird lately? Experienced something that felt wrong to you?"

"You mean like Uncle Dave eating a whole bucket of chicken for himself and only giving us a wing to share? That kind of weird?"

"Are you hungry?" I ask, now worried that my baby sister isn't getting enough to eat.

"No. I stole two pieces when he wasn't looking." She giggles.

"You did? You little devil." I laugh under the cloak of night, pinching her back affectionately. She turns around to face me on our shared bed, the rays of moonlight streaking through the curtains making it possible to see her mischievous grin.

"Uncle Dave can stand to skip a meal or two." She shrugs.

"That may be true, but next time, come to me if you want more food. I can get it for you."

Her smile turns upside down. "Do you think if he caught me stealing that Aunt Lucy would send us back to the foster home?"

"No, of course not," I lie. "That would be silly of them to do so. Besides, they like having us here."

"If you say so," she mumbles, unconvinced.

"That's not important right now." I shrug, not wanting my little sister to be worried that my aunt can change her mind at any minute and send us back into the foster system. "I'm going to ask you something, Zoey, and although it might sound weird to you, I need you to answer me truthfully. Can you do that for me?"

She nods.

"When you go to school or play out on the street with the other kids, do you feel like someone is . . . I don't know . . . watching you?"

"Of course I do," she answers as if it's the most natural thing in the world.

"What? You do?" I blurt out, unable to hide my worry.

Zoey yawns again, turning to the other side and snuggling farther under the covers, as if her answer didn't just put me on high alert. "It's our guardian angel, Layla. He's always watching us. You don't have to be scared. It's okay."

My shoulders slump in both relief and defeat.

Zoey hasn't let go of this angel talk since the incident.

Maybe it's the only coping mechanism she has to deal with what happened to us, our family, and Gage, and although I don't want to encourage such delusions, I don't have the heart to take away the only comfort she seems to have found to deal with what transpired.

"Of course. How silly of me," I mutter before placing a kiss on the back of her head. "Goodnight, sweet girl."

I turn to the other side of the bed and close my eyes, hoping that sleep will take me under and away from thoughts of stalkers and murderers.

Like clockwork, however, just when sleep starts to seep in, making my eyelids heavy and my heart rate slow, sapphire blue eyes shine brightly at me, guiding me to dreams of a life that could never possibly be mine.

A life where both Zoey and I are happy and loved.

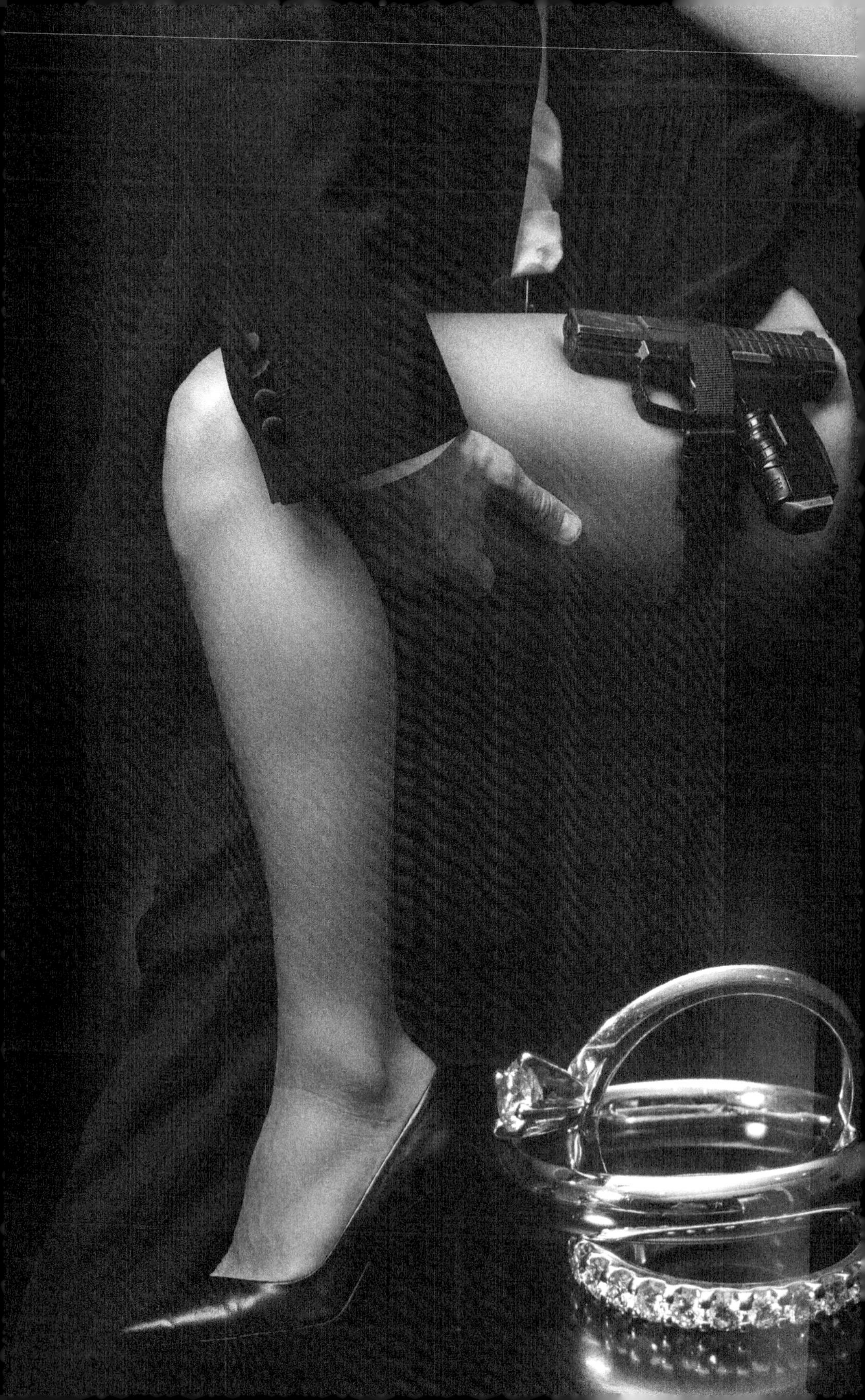

CHAPTER 4
Alaric

L ife really flies by when you have two full-time jobs to occupy your time.

One is a little messier than the other though, and surprisingly enough, I'm not talking about the job that forces me to burn my clothes because the blood and guts on them won't come out no matter how many times I put them in the wash.

Yeah.

Lately, keeping tabs on Zoey and Layla has become more of an obsession than anything else, and if that isn't messy, I don't know what is.

No, that's not entirely true.

Zoey's good. The girl is thriving in that wholesome neighborhood she's shacked up in. It's been a year since I found the little scarecrow of a girl on the side of an abandoned road and she gave me shit about where I was taking her sister. Every time I check on her, she's giving two boys, who I assume must be her cousins, hell at the park. She runs circles around them in the jungle gym, and all the other kids in the park seem to prefer her company over her cousins'. She even has a little more meat on her bones and has grown a few inches since the first time I met her.

Yeah, that girl is going to be a handful when she becomes a teenager, but right now, she's kicking ass and taking names.

The only time I get worried about her is when Layla shows up at the park after her cousins call her, telling her that Zoey just blew her chunks in some bushes again. The little one has spells of throwing up from time to time. I'm not sure if she eats too much junk food, and that's why she's always tossing her cookies, or if there is something else that's wrong with her.

Maybe it's her head.

Anytime Layla comes to pick her up after she's had those types of episodes, I see how she always brings a wet towel with her to clean her sister's face and then wrap it around her temples.

Aside from that happening occasionally, compared to Zoey, Layla is the one who looks like living in the suburbs isn't working out for her. She's also harder to pin down. While I make sure to always keep my distance from both girls, it's been harder to stay away from Layla, especially because the dark rings under her eyes tells me she's been working to the bone and getting very little sleep for her trouble.

Since she rarely leaves the house, it doesn't take a genius to figure out that her aunt has her working from sunup to sundown doing chores. For the past year, I've also watched Layla take little Zoey and their two snotty cousins to school before Layla rushes home right after, not attending high school like she should at her age.

I mean, how old is Layla now?

Seventeen, maybe?

Hmm.

This is where things begin to get messy for me.

Anytime I start on this path of figuring out how old Layla is, my gaze begins to wander down her body. At first, I tell myself it's only to see if she's healthy or if she's been eating right, but I know all those excuses are nothing but bullshit.

It's in the way my eyes linger a little too long on the blossoming mounds of her breasts, but my wandering gaze doesn't stop there. No. The fucker has the audacity to drop to her ass, a tight little ass fit to bounce a quarter off of. On the days she wears skirts, I almost weep for joy when the wind hears my secret thoughts and gives me a little view of the plain white cotton underwear she wears—underwear I could snap off with my teeth.

Thoughts like that can get a man like me in a world of trouble.

So I lie to myself.

I tell myself that I haven't gotten laid in ages, or felt a woman's touch for longer than I care to admit, and that's why Layla summons all these fantasies out of me. Fantasies about getting out of this car, putting my hand over her mouth, and finding a hidden spot where I could sink my cock inside her virgin pussy then ravish her for hours on end until she walks home with a fucking smile on her face instead of the solemn frown she always carries.

When I first started keeping tabs on the girls, it was for pure reasons. Well, as pure as a man like me can be. I needed to know they were safe, and it should have ended at that. I should have stopped coming around when I saw that they were living in a nice house, a place where the trauma they went through wouldn't happen twice, but for the life of me, I couldn't stay away. I'm not sure why though. Maybe it was the fact that I felt some sort of responsibility for them. I mean, I did save them once. It would be a shitty thing to do to just leave them to fend for themselves after I came into the picture.

Lately, though, I don't feel like that obligation or even that ounce of responsibility is what drives me to see them every day.

It's her.

Watching Layla blossom into womanhood has been a guilty pleasure I can't seem to quit. Just the thought of staying away for a day or two has my chest tightening and the air in my lungs burning me from within.

So I come here and sit in my car a few houses down from theirs just so I can get a glimpse of my girls—of *the* girl.

When the light from a small room in the back of the house turns off exactly at nine P.M like clockwork, I stay just for another half hour to watch over them as they go to sleep, wishing I was in their room to kiss them both goodnight.

Zoey on the forehead.

Layla on . . .

Fuck.

Best be on the forehead too.

It's another lie I tell myself that I pretend I follow, even if only in my mind.

I'm doing just that when an unexpected movement catches my eye. White curtains fly out of the small window, the autumn wind blowing them away when a shadow creeps out and jumps off the small ledge.

"The fuck?" I growl when I see Layla silently and carefully closing her bedroom window behind her and making a mad dash through the front gate without anyone inside being the wiser.

"The fuck are you doing, sweet one?" I ask out loud, even though she can't hear me.

I keep my eyes locked on her as she looks from left to right and crosses the street from her home. Like a sucker, I lower my broad frame so she can't see me when she passes my car, even though my tinted windows would make it impossible for her to do so.

When she's a few steps into whatever direction she's going, I break my number one rule of staying hidden at all times and hurriedly climb out of my car, slamming the door a little too loudly for comfort. Luckily, Layla is so focused on her nighttime getaway that she doesn't even register that I'm walking right behind her. Since this isn't my first rodeo in tailing someone, I keep to the shadows and maintain a healthy distance between me and my mark.

Confusion, frustration, and ultimately anger has me quickening my pace when she turns a corner, vanishing toward the faint sound of hip-hop music. Just as I turn onto the street she disappeared to, my shoulders slump at what I find.

It's a fucking house party on a Friday night thrown by a bunch of teenage kids, whose parents are probably out of town.

Layla doesn't do parties. With her aunt forcing her to drop out of high school so she could have a live-in housekeeper, Layla doesn't have time for friends, much less time to attend high school parties.

So why the hell is she going to one?

I watch, helpless to stop her, as she goes inside the house. A bunch of kids all stand in the front lawn with red solo cups in their hands, dancing and having fun.

With a good ten years on all of them, if not more, I can't just follow her inside without alarm bells going off. Sure, some of them already look drunk as shit, but the presence of any adult at this party will sober them up with a snap of one's fingers.

So I wait, leaning against a light post with my hands in my pockets. I wait until I catch a glimpse of her again. Unfortunately for me, Layla doesn't come out for a full twenty minutes, making each minute that passes that much more excruciating for me to bear.

"Fuck this!"

I've been here long enough to get the layout of the house and its surroundings. I can sneak through a neighbor's backyard and hop the fence into some bushes to see if I can get a better view from there and into the house.

Without a second to lose, that's exactly what I do.

It's through those damn bushes, squatting down like some damn stalker, that I finally lay eyes on my Layla sitting on the back porch steps, being chatted up by a pimple-faced loser.

She seems into him though.

Really into him.

Anytime the idiot opens his mouth to say something, Layla laughs a real laugh.

One I've only heard her give to Zoey.

Then the little dipshit covers her hand on the step between them with his.

To anyone else, that small touch would mean nothing.

To me though?

Well, the fact that I instantly grab my gun, prepared to shoot the dipshit's head off, should be an indication of how innocent I think that touch is.

Suddenly, the idea that someone else can do that, and that she's allowing a stranger to hold her hand, is too much for me to handle.

Instead of standing up and telling this kid who probably isn't old enough to vote yet to keep his hands off my girl or risk dying on the spot, I turn my back on both of them and go home.

Layla deserves a bit of happiness, and if that little twerp can give her that, then who the fuck am I to stand in her way?

I'm no one.

She doesn't even know who I am.

I doubt even little Zoey remembers me after the past two years they have had.

When I walk through the door of my brownstone, I take two steps at a time up to my room and lock my sorry ass inside. I strip off all my clothes and take a cold shower to cool my temper, but it does very little to ease the burning rage inside me.

Still a ball of nerves, I drop on top of my bed and cover my eyes with my forearm, needing to expunge the last image of Layla from my mind.

The way her cheeks turned pink at his smallest touch.

The way her breath hitched when he looked at her.

Fuck, I think I almost heard her heart pound in her chest with that small show of affection.

Kindness.

That's what my girl has been deprived of for so long.

A little show of kindness, and she lights up from inside.

"I could have been kind to you, baby. So fucking kind," I mutter as my hand falls to my crotch, rubbing the ache away. "And you're a good girl, aren't you, sweet Layla? You'd repay my kindness with a little of your own, wouldn't you?"

I groan when the image of Layla kneeling in front of me comes to the forefront of my mind. In my imagination, I wipe my thumb across her luscious bottom lip and open her mouth for me.

"Show me, sweetheart. Show me how sweet and kind you can be," I order.

Layla's mystical eyes go half-mast as her fingers run up and down my hard length. She doesn't even wait for me to order her to take my dick into her hands and just follows my silent command with true eagerness to feel my velvet skin.

"Shit, baby. Stop teasing. Open that mouth for me," I demand.

My eyes roll to the back of my head when I feel her wet tongue run circles around the tip of my cock. I grab the nape of her neck and slide my cock down her throat with gentle ease.

"*Just like that, baby. Take it all in.*"

Like the good girl she is, she swallows me whole, moaning my name while my dick slides in and out of her wet mouth.

Layla brings me to my knees, making me come so fast and swallowing every last drop of what I have to give her.

It's only when the image fades and reality hits that I realize what I just did.

I jerked off to the girl I swore to protect.

A girl who is barely legal in the eyes of the law.

My young, sweet Layla.

Fuck!

I need to stay away from her before I do something I might regret—like kidnap her and keep her all to myself.

Or worse.

Kill anyone who gets in my way.

CHAPTER 5

Layla

The day I've been waiting for has finally arrived.

It's my eighteenth birthday, which means as far as the world is concerned, I'm a legal adult.

I can finally book a meeting with our social worker—the same social worker who, almost two years ago, waited patiently outside my hospital room to take me and Zoey to that god-awful foster home.

It's hard for me to relive those days.

Not only was I still in mourning, but the drugs the hospital had given me to deal with my bullet wound would knock me out cold for the better part of those days and nights. Any time I was lucid enough to do something about our wretched circumstances, I was on the phone begging our aunt to take us in.

But that was then, and this is now.

I can no longer live under Aunt Lucy's roof and accept being her favorite punching bag just because the mood suits her. Lately, she's starting to pick on Zoey too. No longer satisfied with making my days miserable, she has set her sights on my baby sister, yelling to anyone who has ears that Zoey's constant migraines are starting to become a nuisance for her.

She doesn't even care enough to take Zoey to the hospital or see a doctor who might be able to shed light on my sister's ailments. All she cares about is that while I'm taking care of Zoey, I'm unable to keep up with the chores she expects me to do.

Enough.

I will no longer tolerate us being bullied like two rejects by a woman who couldn't care less about us—blood relation or not.

We'll do much better on our own.

That is, if the social worker in front of me allows me to get guardianship of my baby sister.

"This is a tall ask, Layla. Before we can go to family court and ask a judge for custody of Zoey, you'll need to have all your ducks in a row to be seen as fit to care for her," she hedges.

"I'll do whatever it takes, Ms. Barry. I have to. Just tell me what to do and I'll do it," I reply with urgency, fully committed to resolve the task.

Her golden-brown eyes soften before she lets out a deep exhale and starts giving me a checklist of dos and don'ts.

"You'll need to prove employment at a job that will enable you to take Zoey to and from school, which will be a hard thing to get for a girl with no high school diploma."

"I'm hard-working. I can find and keep a job," I reply quickly.

"There is also the question of housing. You need to find a place where Zoey has her own room, otherwise it will make it difficult for you to get custody."

"Understood." I nod, trying to remain optimistic that I can and will do all these things she's telling me to. "I'll make it happen."

"I know you say that now, but if you think getting custody is hard, then keeping it isn't any easier. You need to make sure Zoey is enrolled in school and that she doesn't skip. She must have good grades, and she can't get into trouble of any kind."

My smile never wavers from my lips with her warning.

She knows, as well as I do, that my baby sister has a knack for finding trouble. It's not like she goes out to find it; it just comes to her on its own accord. It doesn't help that I've never been able to stop Zoey from speaking her mind the minute a thought comes to her. Unlike me, she's a free spirit, and I've done my best to nurture that part of her.

It's bad enough that I'm damaged goods.

Zoey deserves to have a normal childhood and make foolish mistakes along the way.

I don't have that luxury.

I make a note of having a serious talk with my baby sister to tell her that when—not if—we're on our own, that she will have to do her very best to be on her best behavior. It's the only way I can guarantee she won't be forced to live with our aunt or be thrown back into foster care.

"How fast can we get this all done?" I ask, my heart twisting in my chest, eager for us to start fresh.

"I can try to set everything up for you to see a judge as early as the end of the month. That means you have exactly two weeks to get all this sorted. My reviews on you and Zoey for the past two years should also help. Although you dropped out of school at an early age, you've always shown great maturity, and I've seen how well you take care of your sister. Hopefully the judge will take my reports on you girls into consideration."

"Thank you, Ms. Berry. I appreciate that more than you know," I gush.

She nods with a tender smile. "Well, don't let me keep you. You have plenty of things on your plate that you need to accomplish in the shortest time I can get you. My advice is to find a job as fast as you can. It doesn't have to be glamorous. As long as it pays the bills and enables you to take care of your sister, that will be enough."

I get up from my seat and stretch out my hand.

She follows my lead, wearing that same gentle smile on her face.

"I really do wish you two the best of luck, Layla. Life has been unnecessarily cruel to you both, and I wish I could tell you that you are an exception to what I see coming into the office every day, but files like yours are more common than I'd like them to be. It would do my heart good knowing that at least you girls were heading on a different path—one filled with joy instead of tears."

Again, my heart feels like it's being squeezed into a pulp with her words, but they give me the necessary strength to walk out her door with my head held high.

Since her office is smack-dab in the city center, I take advantage of being here and start walking down the busy streets of New York, praying that I'll find a help wanted sign somewhere.

I'm not naïve enough to think I'll get some paid desk job at my age with my lack of experience, but I can cook and clean. I've had plenty of practice these last few years to prove it. I stare up at all the tall buildings, wondering if there is a family or a single mom or even a single dad who needs someone to give them a hand around the house.

I guess there is only one way to find out.

With rigid shoulders, I start to walk toward a lobby of a swanky building, only to be stopped by a doorman.

"Anything I can help you with, miss?" He eyes me up and

down, and I know by the raggedy chucks I have on, he can tell I don't belong here.

"Maybe." I paste on a smile, hoping it does the trick of easing his stiff upper lip.

Unfortunately, when his bushy brows come together at the bridge of his nose, I know a nice smile won't get me through this building's doors.

"I . . . Um . . . Do you know if anyone in this building needs a maid? Or a cook? Maybe a family who has small children and is looking for a nanny? Maybe? Anything like that?"

His eyes keep trailing up and down my body, and unlike the way Uncle Dave sometimes looks at me, or even my evil stepfather used to back in the day, this man's glare holds nothing remotely close to sexual interest. It's the look someone gives another when they think they are out of their depth.

It's pity mixed with a smidge of worry that someone might walk by and see me standing here talking to him, polluting that perfect IG lifestyle the people living inside this building wish to maintain.

"No one here matches what you're looking for," he replies with a strict tone.

"Oh." I kick the ground at my feet. "Well, thank you anyway," I reply on autopilot, turning my back on him so I can continue my search.

I only have a few more hours before I have to return to Charleston and back to Aunt Lucy. She was okay with me coming into the city today, thinking it preferable that I see my social worker at her office than have Ms. Berry make an unannounced social call at her place.

If there is one thing my aunt hates more than me, it's having to fake that she likes me for the sole benefit of getting child services off her ass. I know she gets paid for having Zoey and me living with her, but whatever the amount is, it must be pretty low since my aunt doesn't seem to think it's enough to justify nice treatment, even if only for an hour while Ms. Berry takes inventory of our care.

I'm just a few steps away from the building when the doorman behind me calls out for my attention.

"Miss? Miss?"

"Yes?" I ask, confused on why he's calling me since it was very apparent he didn't want me loitering in front of his building.

He takes a few steps toward me but stops when he's satisfied that there is still a safe distance between us—enough that people passing by might think he's only giving me directions or something. I guess I do look like I'm lost and in no way, shape, or form belong in this side of the city, much less this street.

"I'm sorry if I came off rude before," he says, a little contrite.

"I don't think you were being rude, just merely doing your job of keeping people like me away." His shoulders slump, and his severe expression morphs into that god-awful pitying look I despise. "No need to apologize. I understand. I'll be on my way," I add, turning my back to him again.

"Wait," he pleads, taking another step closer to me and coaxing me to face him. "How old are you? Nineteen? Twenty, maybe?"

"It's actually my eighteenth birthday today."

He lets out an aggrieved exhale. "Damn it. I knew you were just a child."

"Believe me, sir, I haven't been a child in years," I rebuke a bit too harshly.

He takes a long look at me, and to my confusion, smiles. "I have two daughters roughly around your age. I've made it my life's mission to make them comfortable enough that they don't have to have the spirit you do now."

"Good for them," I reply sarcastically then bite the inside of my cheek for being so mean. "I'm sorry. I didn't mean that. I'm glad your girls have a father who cares enough for them to give them a good life."

His smile is timid, but I see that my words hit a chord inside him. "You've been to hell and back, haven't you, kid?"

"I've been closer to it than most, I guess." I shrug.

"I figured as much. Well, if you can survive one hell, then going to another won't scare you."

My brows furrow at his ominous statement.

"You need a job, right? Maybe a place to stay?"

I nod expectantly.

"Then take the subway to Hell's Kitchen. I'm sure you'll find what you're looking for there."

Although the name he gave me should strike fear into my bones, it does the very opposite—it gives me hope.

"Thank you." I grin with sincere gratitude.

"Good luck to you. You're going to need it." He gives me a curt nod and goes back to his post.

Yeah.

Luck has never been on my side, but that's okay.

Hell's Kitchen seems like the exact place where girls like me end up anyway.

I might as well see if I can start fresh there and get a small slice of heaven in such a place.

It can't be worse than the hell I've lived through so far, that's for goddamn sure.

* * *

I got it!

I can't believe I got a job!

It's only a waitressing job at a run-down diner at minimum wage, but with tips and being able to eat at least one meal there on my shift, it will suffice.

It's the best birthday present I could have hoped for. I've been walking on cloud nine since the owner of the diner said I could start as early as the beginning of next week, but my joyful mood is fading away fast as the bus to Charleston gets closer and closer to Aunt Lucy's.

I squirm in my seat, thinking of how best to approach the subject with her, how I intend to get full guardianship of Zoey and that I will no longer be able to be her housekeeper for zero pay.

She's not going to like it.

In fact, I'm counting on her shitting a brick the minute I give her the news that I got a job.

I have to swallow my pride, though, no matter how many curses she slings my way, and beg her to let Zoey and me stay at her place until I'm able to save enough money for us to find a place in the city. I cringe at the thought of how that conversation is going to go down, but it's a necessary evil I'll have to endure and muster through.

With all the bravery I can conjure, I get out of the bus and walk the two blocks to the place I've called home for the past two years, and hopefully for the last time soon enough.

The minute I unlock the front door, I hear my aunt bitch at me for how long I took and that she expects dinner on the table in the next hour or else.

"I'll be right on that, Lucy, but do you mind if we talk first?" I ask, trying my best not to fidget or show an ounce of the panic I feel that she's going to make my life harder than she needs to.

"Talk? Talk? Girl, didn't you hear me? We're starving! While you were off gallivanting in the city doing God knows what, who do you think had to pick up your slack? Me! Now get your ass in the kitchen before I lose my patience with you."

Right.

Because she's had so much of that for me lately.

Unwilling to let her deter me, I walk closer to where she's standing and square my shoulders, my chin a little too high for her liking judging by the scowl she's giving me.

"I told you I needed to talk to Ms. Berry today. I wasn't gallivanting anywhere, as you put it."

"Oh, you were doing something alright. I called your so-called social worker two hours ago, and she told me you had left her office ages ago. So where were you, huh?"

"I got a job," I reply assertively.

"A job?" She laughs.

"Yes."

"And who would give a high school dropout a job?"

"It doesn't matter who gave it to me. All that matters is that I have one, and I start it next week."

"Is that so?" She crosses her arms over her chest. "And who is going to do your *real job* here at the house? Don't think you can stay here, eat my food, and raise my electricity and water bills for free. You have a job, fine. I expect a check every Friday for having to put up with you and your sister. *And* I expect all the chores here to be done too. I won't tolerate slackers."

Cold sweat starts beading down my spine when I realize she's serious.

She actually believes that I'll just hand over whatever money I make at the diner and still work in her home for free.

I swallow dryly and shake my head.

"Unfortunately, I can't do that, Lucy. I'll need to save up so Zoey and I can find a place to live together. I've already told Ms. Berry my plans, and we are working for me to get full custody of my sister. All I ask in return is that you give me a little time to save up, and then we'll officially be out of your hair for good."

My aunt's eyes widen for a second, her blue gaze turning lethal just like my mother's used to get when she was about to wreak havoc on us. The sting of a slap across my face takes the wind out of my sails, making me step back an inch to keep my balance.

"You ungrateful slut!" she curses, swinging the back of her palm against my cheek. "I have put my life on hold for the past two years to watch over you brats, and this is how you repay me?"

Another slap.

"Because of you, my beloved sister Alice is dead. Dead! You are a curse! Everything you touch turns to shit, you ungrateful bitch!"

Before she's able to swing her hand across my face for a fourth time, I hold onto her wrist, stopping it midair. I never would have before, but seeing how close we are to being free has made me brave. Stupid too.

"I'm not ungrateful, Lucy. You, on the other hand, have plenty to learn about being a decent human being. If my presence here has caused you such pain, then fine, I'll leave. I'll leave today. Just please keep Zoey for a bit until I have a suitable place to take her to. That's all I ask. Please."

Her nostrils flare in contempt, her blue eyes the color of a thunderstorm.

"Zoey! Zoey! Get your ass in here!" she yells, making my hackles rise.

The instant my sister walks into the living room, Lucy grabs her by the shoulders and gives her a hard shake. "You want her? Have her!" my aunt shouts. "I never want to see either one of you as long as I live. Get the fuck out of my house. You're both dead to me—as dead as the sister you killed!" She points a menacing finger at me.

My protective instinct takes hold of me as I slap my aunt's grip away from my kid sister. I lower to her ear and whisper to her, my gaze never leaving my aunt's unhinged stance.

"Go to our room and pack, baby girl. Get as many clothes as you can and anything of value to you. I'll be right behind you."

Zoey hesitantly walks away, but she doesn't move past the hall into the back room where we have our stuff, determined to stay exactly where she can see me.

"It's okay. You can go." I try to give her a comforting smile.

"I'm not leaving you alone with her," she retorts, giving my aunt her best scary scowl.

God bless my sister.

She's so small yet so fearless.

"We'll be gone in twenty minutes," I tell my aunt.

"Make it ten, bitch, before I call the cops and have you booked for trespassing."

My hand itches to lay one on her, but I know that her threat to call the cops isn't an empty intimidation tactic. She'll call them for sure, and having an arrest record won't look good in family court.

I do as she says and head toward Zoey, urging her to go to the room and pack up our meager belongings while inwardly freaking out about where we are going to sleep tonight since I still haven't found an apartment for us. I hurriedly stuff a backpack and a duffel bag with all the clean clothes I can find while Zoey goes God knows where.

"Zoey! We don't have time. You heard her. We need to leave," I call, ordering her back into the room.

"Just give me three minutes. I'll be quick."

Thinking that maybe she needs to use the bathroom or something, I take it into my hands to pack her backpack for her. I'm not sure how I'll be able to transfer her from the school she's going to now to one in the city, but I'll figure it out. That's tomorrow's problem. Tonight, I still have to figure out where we're going to sleep. That's the only thing I can focus on.

"Okay. I'm good to go," Zoey proclaims at the door of our room.

"Here. Take this," I tell her, handing my baby sister her bag.

She puts it on her back and doesn't once complain about how heavy it is.

"Let's blow this joint," she chirps cheerfully, like we're about to embark on an adventure that she's been dying for me to take her on for years.

I put on a brave face and stretch out my hand for her to hold.

She squeezes my fingers tightly in her tiny grip, as if knowing I need a little bit of her bravery to walk out the door, fully knowing we are about to plunge into uncharted waters.

My aunt is standing post at the door, which is flung wide open, tapping her flip-flops on the floor as if counting down the beats of each second that we are still in her domain.

Neither one of us says even as much as a goodbye as we pass the threshold of the front door, only to hear it slam the minute we're standing on the front lawn.

I hold onto my sister's hand as we walk toward the white picket fence, then in the direction of the bus stop. As we keep walking to this unknown future, all I can think about is where I'm supposed to take Zoey now. Maybe I can go back to the diner and ask if I can start work tomorrow instead of next week. And maybe, if I do a good job on my first day, the owner will take pity on me and pay me the week's wage upfront just so I have a little money to at least feed Zoey. Maybe there is a shelter in the city that we can go to for the time being. It's not ideal, but it's better than making Zoey sleep on the streets. My head starts to hurt with so many maybes rummaging around in it.

"Are you scared?" Zoey asks, pulling my mind away from my troubling thoughts.

"Not even a little." I smile encouragingly.

"Me neither." Zoey grins back, her smile splitting her face in two.

"Good, I'm glad."

Once we reach the bus stop, we grow silent for a moment, waiting impatiently for a bus that will take us to our new destination.

"Promise you won't get angry with me?" Zoey questions worriedly out of the blue.

"Why would I ever be angry at you?" I retort, confused.

"Just promise, okay?" She pouts.

"Fine. I promise."

Zoey chews on her bottom lip before she takes an envelope full of cash out of her backpack.

"Where did you get this?" I shriek a bit too loudly.

"Before you came home, Uncle Dave said he had a good day at the track, so when Aunt Lucy kicked us out, I sneaked into their room while he was taking his nap and took the big envelope he had been swinging in our faces for the better part of the afternoon. Are you mad?"

I count the hundred-dollar bills in the white envelope and see that there is over two thousand dollars inside it.

I should be mad.

I should be very mad.

I don't want my kid sister to steal from anyone.

But Zoey just provided a way to get an apartment sooner than I could have ever hoped for, as well as give us a safe place to sleep tonight.

Now how can I ever be mad at that?

CHAPTER 6
Alaric

I once read that to kick a habit, it takes around three months of going cold turkey to do it.

It took years of research to come out with that load of shit.

It's been well over three months since I've set my sights on Layla, and I'm still a fucking addict.

Somewhere along the line, she became my most seductive drug.

I can't seem to find it in me to quit her, and with every day that passes that I don't see those beautiful jade eyes of hers or hear her laugh, it feels like I'm going through the worst withdrawal known to mankind.

I still stay away, or at least I stay away from her.

Not wanting to give in to temptation and do something reckless, I've forced myself to alter my vigilant routine, staying away from places where I might get a glimpse of my girl.

Instead, I follow the little one like my very life depends on it.

If Zoey is okay, that means Layla is too. That girl would move mountains to make sure her kid sister is happy and healthy, which means if Zoey's cool, then all is right in Layla's world. I don't have to set eyes on her to know that.

Hence why I'm sitting in my car, watching a bunch of unruly kids run out of the school gates like they just spent a stint in the slammer. I turn down the music in my car when I see their two snot-nosed cousins walk through the gates with Zoey nowhere in sight.

Seeing that shit immediately makes me tense.

The same thing happened yesterday, and the day before that.

Zoey never skips school unless she's sick, but she's never been sick this long.

Fuck.

I try to breathe through my nose, since my jaw is locked in place, as I scan the school looking for anyone who would be stupid enough to give me some intel. My sinister smile comes to life when I see a young teacher's aide wave goodbye to the students like they are her entire world.

She'll definitely know what's up with Zoey, and since she looks like a woman who is eager to please, she'll give up any info she has to a total stranger as long as I can fabricate that I'm some concerned parent or family member.

I take one quick look in the car mirror and quickly nix that idea.

I don't look like a parent, and I sure as shit don't look like some estranged family member who just dropped into town to see Zoey of all people.

But I can sure as hell pass for a cop.

Considering the girls' background, a cop dropping by to check on them wouldn't raise any eyebrows.

With this plan in place, I get out of my car, and with laser-eyed focus, I walk straight to the overly green teacher's aide.

"Can I help you?" she asks the minute she sees me heading her way.

"All depends. I'm looking for Zoey. She's about this size and has blonde hair and green eyes. Has a big mouth on her for her age. Know who I'm talking about?"

"And you are?" She arches a brow defensively.

"Detective Wagner," I lie straight to her face. "Just wanted to see if she's doing okay, all things considered."

Her tense posture instantly relaxes before my very eyes as she tucks a loose strand of hair behind her ear. It takes everything in me not to scoff when she doesn't even ask to see my badge and takes my word as gospel.

"I really wish I could help you, detective, but unfortunately, all I know is that Zoey no longer attends this school. I'm unsure what the dynamics were behind her transfer either, I'm afraid. Sorry I can't be of more help, but maybe her aunt and uncle can be of more use to you."

"Yeah, you might be right about that. I think I might just give them a visit."

"I hope they can help. Zoey will be missed. She and her sister, Layla, were such sweet girls," she replies in earnest.

I can tell by the way she keeps playing with her hair that she'd like to continue this conversation somewhere more private. I guess playing around with kids all day has her biological clock ticking or some shit, or maybe she's just horny. I really couldn't care less.

My dick already has an owner.

Even if she's too fucking young and clueless to know it.

I give the woman what I hope resembles a fucking smile, or maybe I just gruffly mutter a thank you for her time, but soon enough, I'm back behind the wheel of my car, driving like a mad man to the girls' house.

Just as I'm parking at the curb of their house, I see the fat fuck they call an uncle get out of his car in the driveway with his postal worker uniform still on.

This time, I don't even concoct a plan or an elaborate ruse to approach him.

I want answers, and this fucker is going to give them to me.

"Hey, you!" I point a finger at him as I jump over his stupid ass white fence.

The asshole's eyes widen in fear as he gropes himself to find his house keys.

"Not so fast, you ugly fucker. I have questions for you."

"If this is about the money I owe Big Tony, I told the other guy that he'll have his money by the end of the week. I just need to get paid, that's all. I'm good for it. I promise."

"Do I really look like a guy who works for a fucking loan shark?" I bark, already gripping his nape.

"You look like someone who's here to break my kneecaps," he replies on a sob.

"Hmm. Not wrong there. But I'll tell you what. I won't hurt a hair on your head if you tell me where your nieces are."

He tries to lift his head, confusion plastered on his pathetic, ugly face. "You're here for those bitches?"

I snarl and hit him hard in the back of his head—so hard, in fact, that the fucker falls to his knees, hugging his ears like the inside of his head is ringing too loudly for him to take.

"Let's try this again, asshole, and this time, be careful how you talk about those girls in my presence."

His indignant glare just pisses me off more, so I give him a little kick in the stomach to get him talking.

"I don't know! I don't know!" he shrieks in pain after I landed my foot in his rib cage a second time.

"What do you mean you don't know? You're their fucking guardian, aren't you? They are not a pair of keys you just lose. They are two girls! Talk, fucker, because I'm losing my patience."

His eyes sweep around us, then he curses under his breath when he sees a neighbor across the street hurrying inside his house, making no attempt to help him in any way. I guess this sack of shit isn't beloved in his neighborhood if no one is going to give him a hand while he's getting the shit kicked out of him in his own front yard.

Why am I not surprised?

My fingers lodge into his short, greasy hair, pulling the asshole up by the strands just high enough for me to place my mouth next to his ear.

"I'm going to give you exactly ten seconds to start talking. If you don't tell me where the girls are, then you'll force me to take you inside this nice home of yours and have some real fun with you. Trust me. You don't want that."

When the foul smell of piss scents the air, I let the piece of shit fall to his hands and knees, disgusted as I watch him soil himself.

He raises his hands in clemency, his face red as tears streak down his cheeks.

"I don't know where they are. I swear. Those bitc—I mean the girls," he quickly amends, "stole some money from me and left. I swear that's the God's honest truth."

Hmm.

Stealing cash, even from a piece of shit like her uncle, doesn't sound like the good girl Layla is, but it does sound like something Zoey would do.

"Because of them, I'm in deep with Big Tony since half of that money was his. I should have called the cops on them," the stupid shit for brains adds.

I'm two seconds away from kicking some sense into him and making it clear that in no way, shape, or form will he call the cops on my girls when I take a step back to get my bearings.

I still need to get some information out of this human excrement on how I can track the girls down, and I can't get that if he's all banged up.

"What's the name of their social worker?"

"What?" he blurts, wiping his tears away.

I slap him across the face, my knuckles doing a fine job of splitting his lip.

"I said, you worthless piece of shit, what is the name of their social worker? Are you deaf as well as stupid?"

"I . . . Uh . . . I . . ."

"Talk, motherfucker!"

"It's Berry. Viola Berry!" he spits out in a panic.

"Now, was that so hard?" I snarl, storing the name away for later as I lean down to his level. "This is how this shit is going to go. You're going to forget the girls ever existed. I don't want you or anyone in your family to make any contact with them, and if I hear that you called the cops or tried to reach out to them in any way, then you'll get a visit from me, and it won't go as nicely as this one did. Believe me, you don't want to make me mad."

He nods pathetically, snot, blood, and tears now covering his beet-red face.

Not wanting to spend a second longer with this filth, I turn my back on the asshole and walk to my car. Good thing, too, since I have half a mind to end the fucker and wipe him off the face of the earth. I barely spent more than ten minutes with him, and I already know that living with that piece of trash must have been hell for my girls, especially my Layla. A guy like that probably looked at my girl and got a hard-on just watching her walk through his house.

I white knuckle my steering wheel, imagining all the ways he might have made my girl's life miserable.

I should have killed the fucker.

I would have, too, if I wasn't so desperate to find out where my girls are right now.

I turn on my car and speed dial the one man I know who can get me what I want and shed some light on where the girls could be at this precise second.

"Hale!" I shout the minute I hear him answer the phone.

"Alaric?" he retorts, his deep, rough voice indicating he's just woken up. "What time is it?"

Fuck my life.

It's way past three, and this fucker is still asleep.

Not surprising, since he likes to do most of his work at night, but I need him fucking alert.

Stat.

"It's time for you to wake the fuck up and get to work."

"You always did have the worst bedside manner. What do you want?" He yawns, making me crack my neck from side to side with his nonchalance.

"I need you to hack into child services and find out whatever you can about Viola Berry's case load. I need an address or contact about one of her files. Layla and Zoey Johnson. You got that?" I bark out, speeding back into the city.

"Yeah, yeah, yeah. When do you need it by?"

"Yesterday."

"A rush job, huh? That will cost you." I hear him smirk.

"Money isn't a problem. Just get me whatever you have. You have exactly one hour."

"Like I need that long," he scoffs, sounding offended. "I'll call you back in ten."

It's the first time my lips actually form a smile all day.

Hale Rhett might not like to get his hands dirty like I do, but he's the best in the game when it comes to hacking into places no one wants others to take a peek at. His forte is finding shit people want to keep hidden in the shadows, and he gets paid a pretty penny to bring those same secrets to light. In our line of work, there are plenty of people who prefer to pay a ransom to destroy a man rather than just killing him off. Sometimes I wonder if my way of doing things isn't a mercy.

I've seen what Hale can do with just a push of a button.

If there is anyone who is going to help me find Layla, it's going to be him.

I'm barely out of Charleston when my phone rings with his incoming call.

"That was way too easy," he says the minute he comes through the line.

"I don't care how easy it was, just give me an address."

The line goes quiet, raising my hackles.

"Hale!" I shout impatiently.

"Give me a minute. I've never seen you like this before. It almost seems like you care. I thought cold robots don't have hearts." He chuckles.

"I swear to God, Hale, if the next words out of your mouth aren't an address or a phone number or something, my next stop is your place where I'll fuck up that pretty face of yours just for wasting my time."

"Ah, there he is. Gratuitous violence has always been your defense mechanism." He continues to laugh. "I've already hijacked your GPS with the address you're looking for, asshole. I'll expect my twenty grand in my account by the end of the day. It was just too damn easy to ask for my usual fifty. You're welcome."

I don't even care that he hangs up on me, too eager to follow the GPS direction to my girl.

He's right though.

I'm not acting like myself, but that's not new.

Since Layla came into my life, the Alaric of before has been nothing but a distant memory.

I do care, and that shit, however frightening, can't be helped.

I'm in this now.

All in.

When the voice of my GPS tells me I'm heading toward Hell's Kitchen, my foot pushes down on the gas pedal, cursing under my breath. Out of all the places she could be in New York City, this is where she's been hiding.

It's a miracle I didn't get pulled over with the way I sped through the city just to get to what looks like a run-down diner where only the locals would be stupid enough to eat. Unfortunately, not knowing where Layla was has made me a little crazy, so I do the unthinkable—I get out of my car and waltz into the diner, grab a table at the corner, and wait.

If this is the address Hale got me, then Layla either works here now or is living with someone who does. For all our sakes, it better be the first scenario, since the thought of her living with anyone, a man most likely, will end up coaxing out an angrier version of the possessive beast inside me.

Then shit will really hit the fan.

Just as that thought starts to take hold of me, it instantly vanishes as if the sun finally parted the dark gray skies from my eyes, shedding light and warmth into my cold existence, all because I see her.

My Layla.

Holding two bowls of soup in her hands, she comes out from the kitchen in an ugly waitress uniform, with a twinkle in her green eyes and a bright smile on her lips.

Wouldn't you fucking know it, my heart stops.

Fuck.

It's worse than I thought.

So much worse.

Hale accused me of caring, but it's so much more than that.

I love her, and I was a fool to think I could ever let her go or let another day pass without seeing her, which only gives me one option.

I'll have to wait.

I'll wait until she's ready for me.

Until then, I'll keep watch until it's time to make my move.

And then . . .

All bets are off.

CHAPTER 7
Layla

Three years later

I can't help but look around at the tiny apartment I share with Zoey before I shut the old, rickety door with the broken lock behind me. Luckily the building's outer doors do lock, so there is very little risk that anyone coming into this building would steal anything from us—not like we have anything worth stealing anyway.

All you have to do is take one look at our tiny one-room apartment to see how true that is. There is barely any furniture except for a stove, a microwave, a bed for Zoey, and a shared dresser in the corner of the room. Oh, and how could I forget to mention the couch I found on the sidewalk one day? I made my baby sister help me drag it upstairs. That little find became my new bed. The old floral pattern is outdated and in desperate need of a good cleaning, but despite how many times I've tried to wash the upholstery myself, its funky smell continues to overpower the room. Its iffy odor is a piece of cake, though, compared to the springs that poke my back every time I turn over throughout the night.

But the little apartment is all ours, as is everything inside it, even down to the rat droppings.

One day I'll provide a better life for Zoey. My job as a waitress doesn't pay enough for much else, but at least we are alive and safe, and most importantly, we have each other.

I still wouldn't mind earning more money. I barely make ends meet as it is. Not that I would ever tell Zoey that. She doesn't need to worry, especially after everything she's been through. I promised myself I would protect and care for her, and that's what I did and intend to continue doing.

So even though I was still a kid myself when our world got flipped upside down, I shouldered the responsibility of being Zoey's only parental figure. She's my family. She's all I have left in this world, and I wouldn't trade that for anything.

All we need is each other.

Not that it doesn't hurt to know we're alone in the world. We still cry over our mom and our brother being dead.

Gage.

Even his name brings pain to my heart as I stomp down the three flights of worn stairs. His memory hurts so much that I'm oblivious to the music blasting from Mrs. Rodrigues's place and the laughter of the drug den on two. He was too young. He had his whole life ahead of him. I still have nightmares of his face before he opened the car door and ran with open arms and an open heart to the man who snuffed out his light.

Gage was too trusting . . . and now he's gone.

Zoey is all I have left, and raising a twelve-year-old girl is harder than it seems, especially when you are working constantly to provide for her. I make sure she never goes hungry, even when I do.

Sure, my lack of money means her clothes are often tattered, and I'm not stupid, I know she gets picked on in school. But God bless her, she never complains. No, she smiles. She never did that before, and it's the only thing keeping me going, knowing I'm doing right by her. I don't care that I'm giving up my life for hers. All I care about is giving her a better one.

The leaflet of the private school I've been trying to get her a scholarship to crinkles in my shoulder bag as I hop down the last step. *One day*, I promise myself, hiking it higher.

My worn leather jacket keeps the chill away as I step outside, ducking my head. I learned to survive fast here in Hell's Kitchen. The rules are easy enough to follow considering my upbringing. Don't make eye contact and do your best to be invisible. It's pretty simple to do when I've been practicing these same rules for most of my life. I follow them to a T. Besides, all I do is work, cook, and pass out over and over again until each day becomes a blurred repetition of the other. I bother no one, and no one bothers me. I like it that way. What I don't like is this horrendously uncomfortable uniform I have to wear to work every day. The stiff, skintight fabric itches every patch of skin it touches as I walk quickly toward the diner.

I can't be late again.

The three hours of sleep I got after staying up to help Zoey with her homework and cooking for her still wasn't enough.

Sighing, I watch the cracks on the pavement as I walk. It could be worse. But my back aches, reminding me that at just twenty-one, I'm already showing wear from the lack of sleep and nutrients. The pain gets worse every day. I know what's causing it, but the solution is for me to eat properly. I can't afford to, and my inability to eat three square meals a day shows. My bones stick from my skin, and my rib cage can easily be seen through my shirt, but all the money I earn goes to rent, utilities, and food. Medicine, too, when I can afford it.

Ever since *it* happened . . . well, since the incident, as we call it, Zoey gets migraines. They get so bad sometimes, she actually blacks out. She can't speak or eat or even move for hours, occasionally even longer than that. It got to such a scary point that I took her to the hospital and they prescribed her some medication to help manage the episodes, but it's expensive. It keeps her healthy and out of pain, though, so I scrape by and make sure I have it for her when I can.

Which isn't as often as I would like.

Through my reverie, I hear hoots and calls as I cross the road, the diner looming just ahead. The cheap, outdated, musty-looking establishment makes my nose crinkle. It's all I could get with no high school diploma and no prior experience. I'm lucky I have a job; I know that. Still, as I round the stinky alley, pass the overflowing trash bins, and hop over rats to the open back door, I wish my life were better.

But life only gets better if you make it so.

I suck it up, putting my bag and jacket in my locker, and tie on my apron. I smile and wave at the cooks in the kitchen and grab a pad and pen before heading to the front of the diner to wait tables for the next ten hours straight.

Three hours in, my stomach is clenching with hunger pangs, my feet hurt, and my head rings from the rude customers. My apron is sparse of tips, thanks to the cheapskates who come in here at this time of night.

I hear the bell above the door chime, and I jerk my head up. My heart starts to race when I see him walk in—my mystery man with the cerulean eyes. He has short black hair with a chiseled jaw darkened with stubble, a bumpy, broken-too-many-times nose, and sharp cheekbones that only add to the dangerously mysterious aura about him. He's incredibly handsome, which only makes him stand out more amongst such unflattering surroundings. Wearing an expensive leather jacket, luxurious black jeans, and a tight white T-shirt that shows off his impressive muscles, he's the polar opposite of the usual clientele, yet for as long as I can remember, he comes every day, rain or shine. He always sits in my section, but he never talks and hardly ever drinks the horrible coffee he orders. Instead, the mug usually sits lukewarm and untouched while he just . . . watches me.

As always, his gaze roves over the sticky booths and tables before landing on me. The shock of meeting those bright blue eyes locks me in place, holding me captive as my heart pounds and my palms turn sweaty.

"Hey, enough!" The rude voice snaps me back to reality, and I look down to see I'm spilling coffee all over a table.

Fuck.

"I'm so sorry!" I say, grabbing a towel and wiping up the mess as the patron grumbles. When I'm done and look back up, my mystery man is already seated, watching me. His jacket is off, sitting in the booth beside him, and his arm is spread across the backrest, showing the intricate, beautiful tattoos spanning his bicep. His thick arms and huge hands make my mouth water.

I wouldn't often call a man beautiful, but he's exactly that. There's something so unique about him, so utterly captivating, that I often dream of him—usually in a dirty way. I like to imagine those large, scarred hands touching my sensitive flesh. It's unladylike, I know, yet I can't help myself. He would probably stop coming in if he realized how much I perv on him all the time. He's clearly not from around these parts though, so why does he come here? He's not like the boys who try to chase me or the old farts coming from work to stare at my ass while drinking their beer, and he's definitely not like the homeless who pop in begging for a meal.

No, he's rich, scary, and downright sexy.

And right now, he's crooking his finger at me like I'm a naughty girl. So what do I do? I cross the black and white tile floor, hurrying to him like someone just lit a fire under my ass. Swallowing nervously, I smooth my hands down my uniform like the action will purge it of the dirty stains covering most of the fabric.

"Hi, what can I get you?" I squeak before I sweep my tongue over my lips, wetting them.

He watches the action intently, his eyes darkening with something forbidden. I almost gasp at the alluring sight, stumbling against the table just to keep myself from falling.

Brilliant.

Smooth, Layla. Real smooth.

"Coffee," is all he says before he turns and looks out the windows lining the front of the diner.

Now free from his penetrating gaze, I slump and quickly rush to the back of the diner to catch my breath.

"You should just screw him already," Will, one of the cooks, jokes.

I smile and duck my head instead of giving Will a reply. He's always giving me shit and teasing me, but he's a good man and often sneaks me food without ever saying anything to the owner about it.

In my dreams, I think to myself as I make his coffee how he likes it, wincing at the chipped old mug it's going in. I force myself to approach his table and hand it over. He takes it from me, like always, brushing his finger against mine. Electricity thrums through my body and shoots straight to my throbbing clit.

"Thank you," he murmurs, his voice dark and smoky, the mug looking dainty and tiny in his hands.

I nod and swiftly move away, getting back to work. As I take orders and bus tables, I sneakily look at him. He watches me the entire time, as if I'm his whole focus. I might find it unnerving if it wasn't for the comforting sensation I feel when I'm around him. With just one look, he makes me feel safe from everything. It's a strange and disturbing feeling for a girl like me.

His blue gaze calls to me, almost like I've seen them in another life, but I can't place it. I grab the coffee carafe and head over, refilling his mug even though he's only sipped it.

"So, been up to anything?" I ask, but instead of the witty banter I'm hoping to coax from him, all he does is look at me. I cock my hip out and smile, unable to help myself. "You know, conversations work a whole lot better when two people do it," I tease, leaning in and touching his arm to flirt, but he jerks it back as if he were burned by my touch.

My cheeks heat as he turns away, grabbing the spoon in a white-knuckle grip as he stirs his coffee, dismissing me. Humiliated, I scurry away with my tail tucked between my legs.

Idiot. Of course he doesn't want to flirt with you, never mind talk to you. Men like him are out of your league, Layla. You can look, but never touch. That little fiasco proves it.

Stupid, so stupid.

I spend the next hour or so purposely not looking at him, too embarrassed by my flirtation and his blatant dismissal. Yet I'm very aware of his presence, of his eyes moving over my body, and it puts me on edge.

He finally departs without a word, leaving me a hundred-dollar tip, as usual. I pocket it for Zoey's medicine, wishing I could thank him. His tips are the only thing that's helping my sister.

The rest of my shift is uneventful, and when it's done, I'm exhausted. I grab my coat and bag and wave goodbye, munching on the fries Will gave me. I drag my feet as I head home, knowing Zoey will be back at the apartment. Carol, who lives on the first floor, watches her while I work.

As I turn the corner, the bright LED lights of the strip club Tease catch my eye. I draw closer, not knowing why, seeing the crooked poster in the window asking for dancers like every day this week. Not for the first time, I debate whether or not I should apply for a job. I probably wouldn't get it, but I hear it is damn good money. Money I could use.

I really should strip. My customers, the dirty ones, tell me often enough I have a banging body, as they call it. I don't see it. All I see are bones. Still, the idea has merit. I could at least make more money for Zoey to see a professional about her head and then get her the proper care and medication she needs, instead of having to choose between her food or medicine.

I stare at the building, finding the courage to go inside, but when a certain pair of blue eyes flash in my head, I turn away and head home.

It's a stupid idea anyway. I have no experience and only an okay body and face. I would probably get booed off stage, I think bitterly as I drag myself up the steps to my apartment.

But when I open the door and see Zoey's smiling face as she waits for me to feed her, I know every sacrifice I've made so far is all worth it.

CHAPTER 8
Alaric

"**F**uck," I mutter under my breath when my butcher knife fails to slice through the bone in one clean break.

With gritted teeth, I manage to tug the knife out and add more elbow grease to my next swing. This time, my blade cuts through the cartilage with one loud thud.

"Now that's better." I smile, giving the dead congressman's chin a fake punch.

I turn the volume up on my earbuds, enjoying the sound of Tchaikovsky's *Swan Lake* melodies as I continue to work. I have a playlist for every type of job, but when it comes to dismemberment, I always find that classical music makes the grueling work more pleasurable. It gives the tedious task of slicing and dicing human flesh and osseous matter a certain type of elegance. Unless the client has personally requested that the target sees the end of the barrel of my gun, I have free rein on how I execute the kill. That also extends to how I dispose of their corpses too. I refuse to dump a body in the Hudson like some fucking amateur. I never leave any trace of my kill, unless it's what the client has previously requested, that is. Some of them like to leave a message and have the rotting corpse paraded on their turf as an intimidation tactic.

To each his own, I guess.

I personally don't like leaving loose ends and prefer to erase the evidence of my crime from the face of the earth. You'd be amazed how easy it is to dispose of a body. For instance, I have a few funeral homes that don't bat an eyelash at me handing them some quick cash just so I can use their furnace and cremate the evidence to ash. If you're short on time, then you can always shove your kill into a barrel full of lye solution. As long as it's heated up to three hundred degrees Fahrenheit, then the oily brown liquid will dissolve everything in just three hours. I'm also fond of having a few pig farmers on speed dial. Nothing gets through bone faster than a hungry hog.

Unfortunately, the congressman lying on the slab of my work table must have pissed off someone very important, since they were very clear on how to get rid of him. They wanted his head to be hand delivered on a silver platter and the rest of him cut into tiny pieces so they could feed him to his dogs.

And what the client wants, the client gets.

Especially when they are paying me a cool million for the job.

Yeah, I'm not cheap.

You want to pay less, then do it your fucking self.

I take pride in my work, which means I demand to be paid accordingly. Thankfully, my high fee hasn't injured my workload in any way. Not a week goes by when I don't get a call with a new job. Sometimes I get more than one call each day, which means I have to turn some jobs down. It's not ideal, but it's a necessity. When I was younger and hungrier, I'd take every job that was offered. Now that I have years of knowledge and experience under my belt, however, I know that to do a job well, I can't have my focus divided. My mind should be on the task at hand and not on my next kill, hence my one job at a time rule. Again, I don't get many complaints since most of my clients are willing to wait their turn.

Pulling myself out of my reverie, I take a deep inhale, swing my arms in the air with the music, and then continue to butcher this poor bastard into tiny pieces. Spurts of blood spray every which way, my goggles and black leather apron taking the brunt of it. Every so often, I take a break to rehydrate and wipe my sweaty brow. Another smile tugs at my lips when I finally finish the job in record time. All the stiff's limbs are wrapped in plastic and placed in an icebox, and the congressman's head is positioned at the very center, just as requested.

I leave the icebox behind in the basement so I can go upstairs, take a quick shower, and change clothes for the drop off. Once I'm all cleaned up and in my usual black attire, I grab my car keys, ready to finish the job.

Luckily for me, the abandoned warehouse I'm supposed to leave the congressman's remains in is in Queens, just a twenty-minute drive from my brownstone in Brooklyn. I scope the place out first, and once I'm sure no one is casing it, I get out of my car and leave the icebox inside, patting myself on the back for yet another job well done.

I slide back into my car and log onto the darknet, sending an encrypted message that the parcel is ready to be retrieved. Less than a minute after it's sent, the other half of my million dollars is deposited in my offshore account. Like a well-oiled machine, the whole process, from start to finish, ensures that my client never knows who he is actually working with.

Anonymity is another thing I greatly value, and I go to great lengths to preserve it. I've set my business up so that anyone who is willing to pay my price can find my services online on the darknet. Once they have made their submission, an automated call comes through my phone with only a password. I log into my account, use the generated code, and gain access to all the information I need about my next target and any special requests the client may have. If I accept the job, then my new employer has exactly one hour to cough up half my fee as a down payment. Should they fail to do so, the job is null and void, and the person is barred from making any new submissions to me.

I don't have time for fickle people.

They are either as committed to the task as I am or they can fuck right off.

A quick glance at my watch tells me I'm right on time for the real highlight of my day. Sure, I've been up all night working and should probably go home to get some much needed shut eye, but there's no way I could go a day without seeing her glorious face.

Layla.

My sweet and fearless Layla.

Lately, I've been feeling restless, like something is missing from my life. Maybe it's due to the fact that I have no friends or a social life to speak of. It's kind of difficult to create any lasting bonds when you can't even tell people what you do for a living. Passing strangers are easy enough to fool, but to actually open myself up in order to let someone get close to me, well, then the nondisclosure of my line of work ends up being an issue.

The only thing that lifts the weight off my chest of such self-imposed solitude and gives me some semblance of peace is when I go to the little corner diner Layla works at. The food there is shit, but if I had to, I'd gobble it all down with a fucking smile on my face. Fortunately, I can get away with only ordering the horrid slush they call coffee.

With the image of her jade-green eyes flashing in my mind, I put the car in reverse and hightail it out of Queens and over to Hell's Kitchen, needing to get my fix as my second reward of the day.

Although it really isn't a contest.

I'd take one of Layla's genuine smiles over a million dollars any day.

Once I've parked my car across the street, I wait a few minutes just so I can watch her through the glass windows of the diner. Even though the place is a total shithole, with even less savory clientele, Layla never fills a cup of coffee or delivers a plate of food to a table without a smile stitched onto her face. I'm sure she's extra pleasant to the clientele in the hopes they will shell out a buck or two as a tip. Of course, you only need to take one look at the hovel to know that no one who willingly goes in there has spare cash to dole out, even if it is to give it to the prettiest waitress they have ever laid eyes on.

Still, Layla does the best she can to go about her day with a cheerful grin plastered on her face, even though her eyes tell a different story. They speak of utter exhaustion, and like the kindred spirit I believe her to be, they scream of loneliness too.

Aside from the younger sister she dotes on, my Layla's only companions are the burdens and aches of the life she was forced into. Since she was sixteen, she's had to fend for herself and Zoey, making an effort to always have a roof over their heads and give her baby sister a home filled with love and happiness—even if they are lacking most of the usual basic material possessions. She lives and breathes for Zoey, and that sisterly bond is what drives her to wake up in the morning and face the dire challenges of the day ahead without complaint.

I should know.

I have spent the better part of the last five years watching her do it.

Unbeknownst to Layla, I've been a constant shadow and a permanent fixture in her life since that fateful day I found her on an empty road, seconds away from being killed. I was on a job and on my way to one of my favorite pig farms when, lo and behold, I encountered a hellish scene that has played center stage in my nightmares more times than I can count. Right before my very eyes, I witnessed a delicate flower stand up to a monster and face certain death with a courageous dignity none of my targets have ever been able to muster when I paid them a house call.

Sometimes I wake up late at night in a cold sweat, thinking what if I had chosen a different road on that day? What if instead of feeding the pigs the rotting corpse stashed in my trunk, I had used lye instead? Or a funeral home's oven?

What a sin it would have been for such a beautiful soul to die at the hands of such filth. The world would have been a miserable place without her light, of that I am certain.

I recall how my heart stopped when the fucker was still able to unload a shot, even after I killed him. In a mad dash, I left my car running in the middle of the road and ran to the young, innocent girl who faced the devil and lost. Air filled my lungs when I realized the shotgun wound was only to her shoulder, missing all of her vital organs, but the impact of the shot made her fall hard, her head bouncing off the concrete with a loud thud.

I had to think fast.

I couldn't exactly call nine-one-one, since the stiff stuffed in a black plastic bag in my trunk would raise questions, ones I had no intention of answering, but there was no way I was going to leave her behind to bleed out either.

So, without further thought, I picked her up in my arms with the intention to leave her in the closest hospital I could find. Before I left her in the doctor's care, I would also hand a note to the receptionist for the police, so they could make their way over here and see the bloodbath the prick I killed left.

I cringe every time I remember the young boy's mangled body lying in the middle of the road, and the woman's at the side of it, amongst the bushes, with her head blown off in such a way there was no telling what the woman looked like before.

It was only when I had her in my arms that the tiny little creature flew at me from God knows where and swung her tiny fists against my leg to grab my attention.

"You let her go! Layla, wake up! Wake up!" she shouted behind me as I made my way back to my car. After I made sure the girl in my arms was safely tucked in my backseat, I kneeled to the little warrior giving me shit.

"Listen here, kid. We don't have much time, so I'm going to need you to cool it for a bit. Can you do that?"

The little blonde spitfire wiped her tears, her lower lip quivering as she kept her gaze fixed on the girl inside my car.

"Is she your sister? Layla. That's what you called her, right?"

She nodded between sobs.

"What about you? You got a name?"

"Z-Zoey," she stammered, lifting her chin just enough to make eye contact with me. "Layla told me to run, but I couldn't leave her. I just couldn't. So I hid. I hid really well. But now you're going to take Layla away! Just like Daddy took Mommy and Gage away. I won't let you! I won't!"

She was a scared little rag doll of a thing, but she had heart.

"Okay, kid. Listen here, because the clock is ticking. No one is going to take your sister away. But she's hurt, really hurt, so I have to take her to the hospital so the doctors can fix her up, okay? So, as

I see it, you've got two choices. Stay here all on your own or get in the car and help me help your sister out. What will it be?"

Zoey's little nose crinkled for the briefest of seconds before she ran to the other side of the car and hurriedly buckled herself into the passenger seat.

"That's what I thought." I smirked, standing up and getting into the car with her.

I was about to put the pedal to the metal when Zoey placed her tiny hand on mine.

"Thank you, mister."

"No problem, kid."

"My name isn't kid, mister. It's Zoey," she corrected, shaking her head at me like I had a few screws loose for forgetting her name so quickly.

"Whatever you say, kid . . . I mean, Zoey."

After that serendipitous interaction, I made sure to keep tabs on the two girls at all times. Something inside me just had this need to protect them. The little one, because she showed bravery when most kids her age would have cowered when faced with the likes of me. And Layla, for having shown the same courage in her selfless pursuit to save her sister, since it was obvious she had failed to protect her mom and brother.

I had some hiccups keeping track of them when they lived in the foster home and then later at their aunt's house in Charleston. But the minute Layla turned eighteen and made the decision to move into the city—my city—I made it a point of knowing every move she made from there on. And when I learned she got a job as a waitress in this dump, there was no way I wouldn't use it to my advantage.

Over the years, my urge to protect her grew into an obsession, one I did very little to curb. Watching Layla grow up from a well-intentioned teenager to the fierce, kind woman she is today stirred something inside me that went beyond the basic need to keep her safe.

The need to possess her heart, body, and soul became a compulsion that has taken over every thought in my head. The only time I'm not thinking about having her under me is when I'm taking the light out of someone's eyes. After that, Layla is all I think of.

Shit.

My cock gets hard just from recalling how she blushed yesterday when she tried to innocently flirt with me.

And when she touched me . . .

Fuck . . .

When she touched me, it took monumental effort on my part not to pick her up, lay her on top of the table, hike that ugly skirt she wears as a uniform up, and fuck her right there where everyone could see. The insatiable need to devour her body and ravish it so completely that she would have no choice but to scream my name for all of New York to hear was so strong, I had to leave before I did something stupid.

Wiping my sweaty palms over my thighs, I lick my lips as I watch her sashay around the tables, her cute ass begging for my teeth to mark each cheek. She laughs at something the cook just whispered in her ear, and she's still smiling when she retrieves the plate full of food he puts on the counter, destined for her next client. Even though he's old enough to be her grandfather, I can't help the illogical jealousy that invades me, my hands balling into fists.

Layla is prone to smiling, but she hardly ever laughs.

Those moments are rare, so when she does it, it feels as if the sun just parted a cloudy sky for me, warming my insides with its transcendent, heated glow.

Layla places the plate on the table, shoving a stray lock of hair behind her ear. Disappointingly, her fiery red locks are in their usual bun today. Every time I'm near, I secretly beg her to let me untangle her hair from the top of her head just so I could feel the silk pass through my fingertips.

My cock swells in my pants to the point of pain. Unable to stop myself, I free my steel shaft from its confinement and wrap my hand around its base. Shame and embarrassment should snap me out of my lust-filled haze, but sense has no place in my mind when all I see is her. With the tinted windows of my car giving me the privacy I need, I jerk my cock with images of Layla playing in a seductive loop in my mind.

I stare at her full, lush lips and envision them parting for me, her tongue peeking out to tease the crown of my cock. I hiss when she takes me into her warm wet mouth, her jeweled eyes fixed on mine. My fingers weave into her hair as I push her down as far as she can take me, my cock hitting the back of her throat as tears begin to stream down the corners of her eyes.

I loosen my grip on her, afraid that I'm hurting her with my unbridled lust, but my temptress doesn't like that. Her hands cover mine, pushing me to continue my onslaught. She rubs her thighs together, her slick, wet pussy needing to be filled.

So small, so delicate, so . . . perfect.

I ask her if she wants to jump on my lap and ride me, and she nods as she sucks me down, making me delirious with want.

I ask her if she'll let me fuck her long and hard for days on end, and I get another nod, causing me to leak into her mouth.

And when I ask her if she's mine and I see her green eyes sparkle with utter love for me, I come undone. It's too much for me to take, and I come down her throat, loving how she never takes her eyes off me as she milks me dry, swallowing every last drop of cum.

When I feel my release on my hands, I see the mess I've made on my designer jeans, and cold reality sets in.

Fuck.

There's no way I can go in looking like this. I slam my fists on the steering wheel, hating myself for not having better restraint.

When it comes to Layla, however, my self-control has been slowly dwindling, and I'm not sure how long I can keep my urges at bay. Today was a perfect example of how unhinged I've become.

I throw a quick glance over at the diner, hating that I'll have to postpone my visit until tomorrow.

No.

Fuck that.

Tomorrow isn't good enough. I'll go home, take a quick shower, and come back. Why waste time on sleep when everything I could ever dream of is right here for the taking?

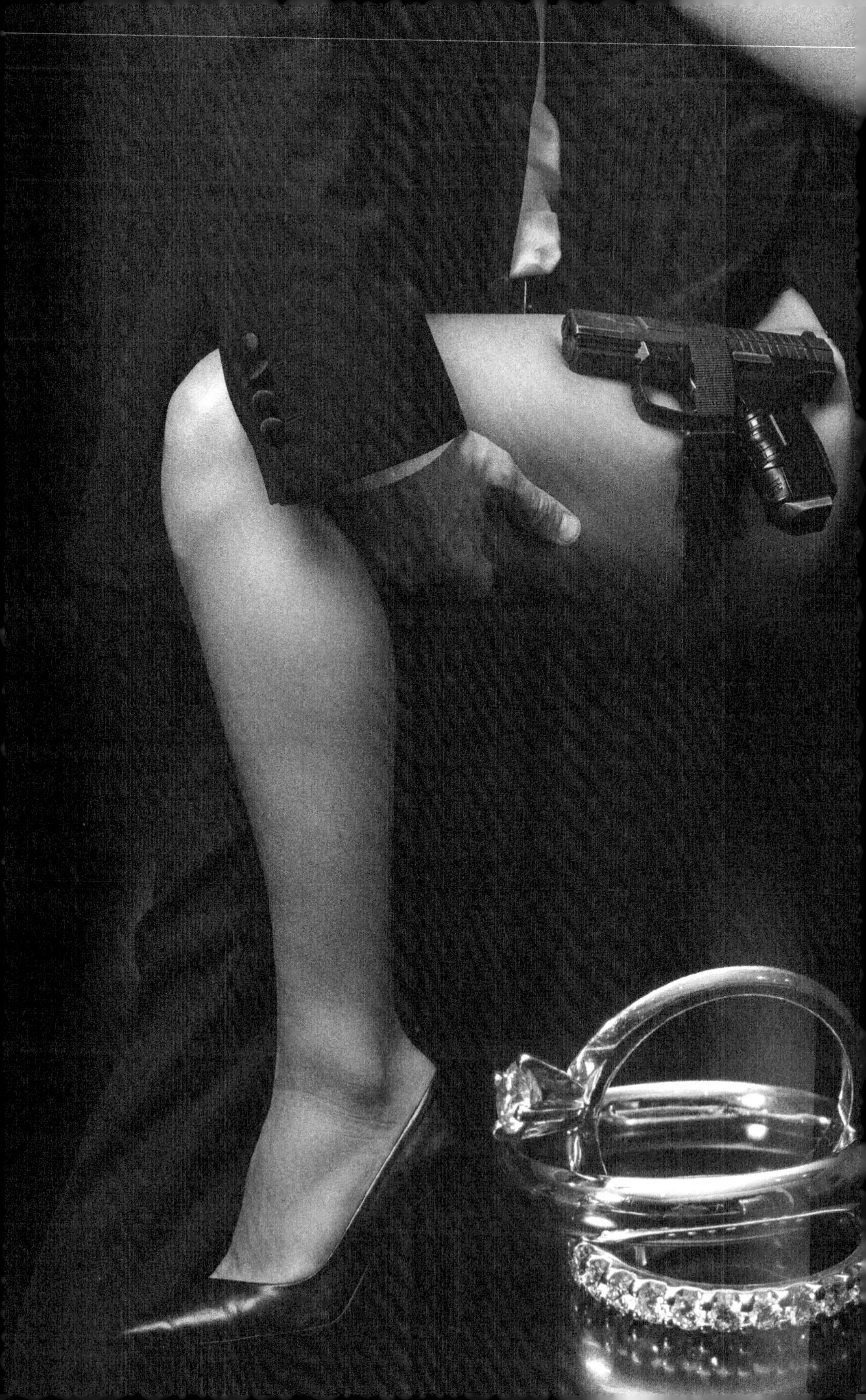

CHAPTER 9

Layla

Three nights . . . It's been three fucking hellish nights.

Three nights of holding Zoey's hair back, wiping her face, hands, and mouth while pressing cool compresses to her back as she heaves over the toilet, moaning in pain. I feel helpless and utterly inept. The medicine isn't helping. She can't eat, and she's barely drinking. My little sister is wasting away before my eyes, and all I can do is just sit here at her side spewing useless words of encouragement.

I promised to protect her, but I'm failing miserably.

I need to do something. Anything. She needs help, help I can't provide. So despite my stiff muscles and lack of money from having to call in sick, I pack us a bag, some water and snacks, and gently pull her from our apartment. She's barely able to take one full step, protesting that it hurts too much as her legs collapse beneath her. Before she falls to the floor, I pick her up and hold her in my arms, passing her a bag to keep across her chest in case she needs to puke. I ignore my shaking arms as I take each step down the apartment building ever so carefully. My legs are threatening to give out from lack of food, but I still push on for the precious load in my arms. She's weighing me down, but I wouldn't let go for anything in the world.

She's missed school, and I've missed work, but none of it matters as I look down at her pallid, gaunt face. Her lips are chapped and pale too. She looks so little, so young and scared. I move faster. I should have taken her to the clinic sooner, but I knew I wouldn't have the money for a consultation. Nonetheless, that's no excuse. I messed up, and because of my fuck up, she suffered for it. Never again. I'll do whatever it takes to get her better. She has suffered so much in her little life, and I refuse to be the cause of her misery.

Usually, I would walk or catch the bus, but not today. Zoey needs to get there quicker, so even though it pains me, I hail a taxi, already wincing at the fee he'll charge me. I give him the address of the free clinic, hoping they can help, but deep down inside, I know they will want to send us to a hospital to run tests and scans—scans that cost money I don't have.

It takes us twenty minutes to get there, twenty minutes of Zoey moaning and heaving. The taxi driver warns her not to get sick in his car, and I glare at him, my seething gaze making him thin his lips instead of uttering another word. When we reach the clinic, I toss my money at him and get out, carrying her up to the bulletproof glass door. I let myself in, groaning at how busy it is inside. I should have known. The old, mismatched chairs in the waiting room to the left are filled with junkies, homeless people, and just poor helpless souls hoping for assistance. They are all waiting patiently—some sleeping, some angry, some eating. The brick walls all have warnings that cameras are keeping a vigilant eye on us, and there's a security guard behind a glass shield next to the desk.

Hurrying over, my shoes sticking to the dirty floor, I beg the old, weathered receptionist to look up. I'm trying to be patient when all I want to do is scream at her to look at me. She continues to type on the chunky old computer, chewing gum as I narrow my eyes and curse her very existence.

"Excuse me—"

"Fill this form out and wait," she mumbles, slowly handing over a clipboard. I have to juggle Zoey in my arms to take it.

"Ah, thank you, how long will it be? My sister is really—"

"Take a seat and wait," she snaps, finally looking up, her eyes compressed into two tight slits. There's no compassion there whatsoever, so I swallow my retort and offer her a tight smile before I move to sit down. Luckily there's an open seat in the corner. It's an armchair, so it's big enough for me to sit in with Zoey next to me, even if it smells and is partially ruined. She curls up, finally going to sleep as I fill in her information and wait.

Tapping my feet, I look at the clock as the time ticks by slowly. Impatience claws at me. I spot a doped-up guy staring at me and quickly avert my eyes, not wanting to give him the wrong impression. Not wanting to get involved in anything.

An hour crawls by and hardly anyone is seen. I start to get antsy, and when Zoey begins throwing up two hours later, I get up and storm over. I'm done being nice.

"I need to see a doctor now!" I demand, slamming the clipboard on the desk.

"You will have to wait—"

"Can't you see she's sick? Very sick! She's just a kid! Help her!" I scream. Every eye is on me, but I don't care. The security guard stands, and I hear Zoey weakly calling out for me, but I'm not moving until I get help.

"Miss, I don't know what your damage is, but unless you're

blind, you can see that there are plenty of people here waiting their turn to see a doctor. You don't see them complaining, do you?"

I bite my cheek just to keep me from launching at her neck.

Fuck the glass.

Like I used to do as a kid when dealing with my mother's bitchiness, I count to five and then offer her a sinister smile.

"Listen, lady. My sister is sick. Very fucking sick. Now get me a doctor right this minute or live with the consequences."

"Are you threatening me?" she blurts in outrage, her ugly muddy eyes going wide in astonishment.

"You have to go home sometime." I shrug. "Don't test me, lady. My sister is all I've got. Believe me, I wouldn't waste a single night's sleep worrying about the beatdown I'd give you."

Her eyes trail over my thin body, a smirk tugging at her lips.

"Yeah, I'm skinny as shit, but don't let that fool you. I'm scrappy and I know how to throw a punch, so try me. I dare you!"

When she raises her hand to call security, I kick myself for being so hotheaded. If Zoey suffers yet again for my poor decisions, I will never forgive myself.

Luckily a doctor must have heard my rant, because he rushes out to see what all the noise is about. Wearing a pristine white coat, he rushes toward us. His belly protrudes over his pants, and his hair is graying, but he has warm, kind eyes.

"What's the problem here?" he asks softly.

I suck in a shaky breath and point at Zoey. "She's really sick, please help."

"Okay, let's get her into a treatment room."

I nod, thanking him as I rush over.

"Layla?" Zoey whispers, her face covered in a sheen of sweat as she wipes her mouth, peering up at me.

"It's okay, baby girl. We are going to get you the help you need," I promise as I brush her hair away from her forehead.

"But it will cost money. Just take me—"

"No, shush, don't you worry about that. Let this nice doctor check you over," I coo as I lift her into my arms and follow him as he leads me down a corridor to a treatment room. Pulling the door shut, I lay her on the bed and wait, looking around. All the drugs are locked away, as usual, but at least it's nice in here.

"Hi. Zoey, was it?" he asks as the doctor steps closer to her, the friendly smile on his face instantly calming me. "I'm Dr. Rhoads, and I'm going to help you, okay? Can you tell me what's wrong?"

She looks at me, silently asking me to answer for her since she is too frail to carry on a conversation, so I step up. "She's been throwing up for three days, her head hurts, she can't drink or eat, and she's weak. She's also fainting a lot."

"Okay, what's your name?" he asks.

"Layla," I reply, clearing my throat. "I'm her sister."

"You did good bringing her in. Let's take a look. Is there a history of anything I need to know about?"

"She has migraines," I begin, and then I instantly reel off the list of medications she's on while he nods, taking it all in. When his thick brow furrows in worry, I stiffen.

"What?" I question as he continues to examine her. When he's done, he steps back and sighs.

"I'm worried this could be something serious. She needs more than I can give her here—fluids to replace those she's lost, a banana bag for sure, and almost certainly a scan."

My world crumbles, but I nod and listen as he explains that he's going to call me a cab since I'll have to leave here and take Zoey to the emergency room. I thank him and carry her out, ignoring the unease pooling in my stomach.

"Layla, it's okay, take me home," she insists, picking up on my anxiety.

I smile down at her to try and reassure her, but I must not do a good job.

"It's going to be okay," I promise. "Just focus on getting better, okay?"

It doesn't take long to get to the emergency room, and the difference between it and the clinic is astounding. There are comfy blue chairs in a calm waiting room with vending machines and a polite, smiling receptionist. Everything is all clean and happy. Zoey is checked in and rushed inside on the doctor's orders, and I stay by her side as she undergoes blood tests, CT scans, x-rays, and everything in between.

The hours go by quickly, and before I know it, we are waiting inside the room with the paper curtain pulled for privacy. I hold her hand as she sleeps under the blankets in the bed, an IV in her other arm with fluids and nutrients to replace what she lost, as well as pain medication. Watching it being pumped into her tiny body that barely fills the bed, I let a few tears fall.

I suddenly find myself wishing someone else were here to support me, to help us—even if it was only to tell me I'm doing the right thing. Worry clouds my mind, but as the curtain is pulled back, I wipe away my tears and suck it up. My feelings can wait; this is more important.

"Hi, Layla, I'm Dr. Ramos. I'm the head neurosurgeon—"

"Neurosurgeon . . . So it's her brain?" I interrupt, standing as Zoey starts to wake.

He smiles softly and moves over to her side, checking her vitals. "How are you feeling, Zoey?"

"Better," she croaks and looks between us. "What's happening?"

"I have your results," he tells us both kindly, but the sadness in the tilt of his lips indicates it's not good news. My ears ring and my body shakes. I can't lose her, I can't.

"It seems you have a blood clot in your brain."

I almost throw up as he explains what it means for my little sister.

"It is fixable," he finishes. I missed most of what he said, but I fixate on those words as they make me slump. "With surgery."

"Surgery?" I gasp. "You're going to open her brain?"

He looks at me and nods. "If I don't, she could bleed into her brain and she would end up back here. Worse, she could end up on machines or even brain dead. It has to be done to save her life. Don't worry, we'll take very good care of her. I've put it in as an emergency, so I should get a date very soon."

"But I don't even have health insurance," I murmur in panic, making him freeze.

"Oh, erm, let's talk outside," he whispers under his breath to me, then he looks at my sister with that same warm smile on his face. "Don't worry, Zoey. We'll get you all fixed up. Just rest for now while I have a private word with your sister outside in the hall." He squeezes her arm and steps past the curtain. With a worried look at her, I follow him out, shutting the curtain before walking into the hall. Once I join him, he sighs.

"I understand your worry, but if Zoey doesn't have this surgery, the impact could be catastrophic," he explains as I wrap my arms around myself as my world falls apart. "Unless you can find healthcare or come up with the money for the surgery, I'm afraid all we can do is give her medication to ease her pain. It won't stop future attacks or the decline in her health though. She'll have good days and bad days until the bad days get so frequent, she will be hospitalized. I realize this is a lot to process, and I empathize. Is there anyone we can call? Parents? Anyone to help you through these trying times?"

"No, it's just us," I whisper, my voice hoarse. "I'm all she has."

And she is all I have too. I'd be lost without her.

"I'm so sorry," he murmurs, squeezing my shoulder. "Take a moment to decide if we can proceed. If not, we can discharge her with some medication, but you must promise to bring her back if she gets worse."

I nod, not really listening, still lost in the terror that's saturating me. My eyes go back to the curtain where she waits for me to make it all better. To save her.

Sucking in a calming breath, I walk into her room, pull the curtain in place, and sit again at her side, holding her hand more for my own support than hers. There are tears in her eyes.

"I'm sorry, Layla. I hate to be a nuisance. Maybe I should move back to Jersey with Aunt Lucy," she whispers, her lower lip trembling.

I squeeze her hand and force a smile. "Don't be silly, sweet girl. You could never be a nuisance. I'll find a way to fix this. I promise I'll make all of this better," I vow, kissing her hand. I never hide the truth from her or risk breaking this trust we have.

I need that money and fast before she gets too bad.

Money . . . I know where I can make it.

I close my eyes as she watches me. I know what I have to do.

If I want fast cash and lots of it, then I know exactly where men shower women with it every day. All they have to do is dance for it.

It might also chip away at their dignity, but who needs that when a beloved sister's life is on the line?

I sure don't.

CHAPTER 10

Layla

T*ease.*

    That's the name of the strip club I've passed on my way to work a number of times.

Now, it teases me into thinking that maybe I can earn enough to pay for my sister's surgery.

A blood clot.

That's what Dr. Ramos said.

My baby sister has a blood clot in her head, and lord knows how long it's been there untreated. I think of all the times she complained about her migraines, or when she would throw up at my aunt's place because the light coming through the curtains in our bedroom at night was just too bright for her to keep her dinner down, and it has me questioning my capacity to protect her. I should have known.

I should have demanded that my aunt take Zoey to the emergency room.

I should have yelled and pleaded and broke everything in my way so she would finally take Zoey's illness seriously. Lucy would have had the money for this surgery. She might have even been able to add Zoey to her husband's healthcare provider, if only I had insisted.

Back then, though, all my pleas went unheard, and I was just trying my very best to keep my aunt happy enough not to send us back to foster care.

I should have tried harder.

I failed Zoey then, but I won't fail her now.

If stripping is how I'll make her better, then so be it.

So I went in, plunged myself into this world.

My pride went out the window long before now, and if there are any remnants of it, then I pray it leaves me alone long enough for me to do what needs to be done.

"You'll need a stage name, honey. Have anything in mind?" Betty, a woman who looks like she's old enough to be my mother, asks as I fidget in my seat, waiting for her to pull out whatever outfit she thinks might fit me from the rack. We are in the back room, and before me is a row of polished mirrors with vanity tables. The walls are a bright red with posters of the girls plastered all over. Even back here, the music pumps through the walls, sending my heart into overdrive. At the back of the room, which Betty kindly pointed out, are rows of silver lockers I've stored my meager belongings in.

"Whatever works. I really don't care," I reply on autopilot as I watch some of the other girls paint their faces with their warpaint, while others slither into thongs and cheap costumes.

"Well, you better start pretending that you do. The best way to get those dollar bills is for the clientele to think you are loving every second of being on that stage," she offers softly, but there is steel in her voice.

"I thought we were being paid to dance, not act."

"Here at Tease, it's one and the same, girlie. Here. Take this," she says, handing me a cheerleading uniform.

I laugh just so I don't cry my eyes out.

"What? Don't like it?" she asks.

"No. It's fine. I just never stayed in high school long enough to wear one of these."

"Take it from me, being a cheerleader was overrated." She chuckles. "Prom queen too. I did all the normal things girls your age are supposed to, and it still landed me in this dump."

"I'm sorry," I tell her in earnest, staring at the little age lines around her eyes.

"Don't be. I made my choices, and I have to live with the consequences," she explains and then stares a little too long at me for comfort. "You can leave, you know? The DJ hasn't even told the horn bags outside that there is new blood in the show tonight. You can go. Just walk out the door and never turn back. It's not too late."

I get out of my chair and take the cheerleading outfit out of her hands. "I don't have a choice."

"We all have a choice, girlie. You just have to know which one is the right one."

Saving Zoey is the only choice I have.

It couldn't get righter than that.

"I have to do this. I need the money, and this is the only way I know to get it quickly without having to sell my organs on the black market," I say, albeit with a poor excuse of a joke to lighten the tense atmosphere.

Before I can stop her, she pulls at my arms and pushes my long sleeves up to my elbows.

"You're not a junkie, so it isn't for smack. Let me guess? Is your man a crackhead or does he have a gambling problem or something?"

"I don't have a boyfriend. Never have."

Her brows furrow at my confession. "A pretty thing like you? Soft spoken and polite and never had a man on her arm? Sorry, girlie, but that's hard for me to believe." She snorts.

"It's true. It's only ever been my baby sister and me. That's it."

"Ah," she murmurs, her eyes softening. "So you have a kid?"

I nod.

"Now I get it." She smiles sheepishly at me. "Got two of my own. They are both little heathens, but they are what gets me up in the morning so I can come to this dump and work. There isn't a thing I wouldn't do for my boys."

"I feel the same way about Zoey. That's why I need this job," I divulge seriously, needing her to understand I can do this. I have no other choice, and stripping isn't all bad. I've seen the fun they have and the sisterly bond between some of the girls.

Her expression turns motherly, which takes me aback since I've never seen such concern on a woman's face. Other than Ms. Berry, I haven't exactly had too many women who gave two shits about my sister or me, so I guess it's only natural that I feel a bit uncomfortable with the tender gaze she's showering me with now.

"Then let's get you ready." She smiles, showing me to an empty makeup mirror and chair. "Get dressed while I tell the DJ that you'll go on in a few. Ask one of the girls to help you with your makeup if you don't know how to put it on."

"Thank you."

She gives me a nod and starts walking out of the changing area. "Brandy," she shouts back at me just as she reaches the door.

"What?" I ask, confused.

"That's your name now, girlie. Sweet as sugar but has the strength to knock you down before you know what hit you. It's perfect for you."

"Brandy." I roll the name on the tip of my tongue. "I like it."

"The boys out there will too." She laughs. "Every last limp dick in there will be raining dollar bills when they see you. Best be ready for it."

I square my shoulders and look dead ahead at the mirror.

I have to be ready for it.

My sister's life depends on it.

Not wanting to look at myself in the mirror for too long, I start taking my clothes off to put on the cheerleading costume Betty gave me. When I'm done and I start fiddling around with the makeup on the table, two other women take pity on me and help me out. One of them fixes my hair into two braids, while the other gives me smoky eyes and red lips to finish up the look. They are just adding the finishing touches when Betty comes back into the room.

"You're up, Brandy," she announces, causing me to go into a mild panic.

"No. Don't even go there," Betty protests, apparently catching the sliver of dread in my eyes. "When you're out there, remember who you're doing this for. I won't lie to you. You'll probably cry your eyes out the minute you're off that stage, but when you get home and count your money and see all that you can do for the one person you love above all else, those tears will dry up pretty fast. You might get numb to it all, but as long as you keep your focus on what's important, none of it will matter. Do you understand?"

Her words of encouragement have me standing out of my seat and picking up the two pom-poms.

"I understand," I answer confidently.

"Good. Now give them hell, girlie."

I'll have to, because at the end of the day, I'd sell my soul to the devil if it meant saving Zoey.

She's all that matters.

CHAPTER 11
Alaric

Seven days.

It's been seven days since I last looked upon Layla's beautiful face.

She hasn't been to work all week, justifying her absence by calling in and saying her sister is sick. That's all the info I was able to pry from her friendly cook, Will, before he got protective of her, something that made my jealousy roar. My gut twists at the thought of little Zoey in discomfort, but it's not having my daily dose of Layla that really does a number on my head.

I'm going crazy with withdrawal.

One day without seeing Layla is one day too many.

Hence why I'm standing on her street, in the rain, waiting like a stalker.

I'm inundated with irrational concern, and I'm hardly able to breathe. I'll wait for however long it takes just to get a glimpse of her, just one quick look to assure myself she's okay. I restrain myself from storming inside and kicking down her door, but since I don't want to scare her, here I stand. A quick glance through her window or seeing her when she leaves will suffice. She'll have to leave her apartment to stock up on medicine and food eventually, so until then, I'll wait.

The drizzle of rain continues to fall on my face as I stare up at her broken-down building, watching the light in her apartment turn off. The heavy shower soaks me through until my clothes plaster to my body, and a deep chill starts to set in, but I've been in worse situations. I can remain still and silent under any conditions—the jungle, the arctic, anything my job entails. Usually it's only for a paycheck, but this is for something much more important—my girl. A speedy glance at my watch tells me it's a little past midnight, which means she's probably turning in.

Fuck.

Frustrated, I run my fingers through my dripping, jet-black hair, slicking it back before stepping into my car and making myself comfortable for the night. There's no way I'm going home. If Zoey is as sick as she says, Layla might have to leave in the middle of the night to take her to a doctor, and if that happens, I want to be here to help her in any way I can. The notion that she could have needed me this week and I wasn't here kills me as it is, so I settle down for the long haul, refusing to leave.

I still haven't come up with the ins and outs of what I'm going to say if that happens though.

Layla isn't stupid.

She won't believe I was passing by her street in the middle of the night and just happened to bump into her. She'd either assume that I'm stalking her ass—which I am—or conclude I have some kind of brain damage since no one with any intellect takes a stroll at night in this neighborhood unless they want to get mugged. Not to mention everything about me stands out. Even my Aston Martin sticks out like a sore thumb in this part of town, and when an expensive ride like mine pops up in this hood, it's usually because it's stolen.

But that doesn't matter.

Right now, the only thing that matters is knowing if she's okay. I need to know every detail of what the fuck is going on and not depend on hearsay from a work colleague either. I have to see it with my own eyes. *See her.*

I settle deeper into my seat, the heated leather interior doing very little to relax my tense muscles or dry me off. There's no way I'll grab a wink of sleep tonight. Good thing my phone hasn't rung in the past two days. I wouldn't be able to wrap my head around work at the minute when it's so consumed with worry over my girls.

Half an hour passes before I see movement. Her apartment building's outer door swings open. I jerk upright, ignoring my stiff body. A flash of red hair blows in the wind. It's the first thing that catches my eye, making my heart race as I squint through the dark to see her. Layla closes the door behind her, pulling up her hood while tugging at the belt of her trench coat to keep herself warm. She looks around before ducking her head and moving quickly down the road. I leap out of my car, silently locking it, and follow her on foot. Blending into the shadows in case she looks back, I keep my entire focus on her. My possessive nature screams for me to drag her into my arms and demand to know what she's playing at by going out at this time of night. The idea she could get hurt or worse fills me with dread. I've seen the very worst of human nature and know that someone so beautiful, so fucking innocent like her, is a sure target.

Breathe, I remind myself, and when my anger settles to a low burn, I think logically. She's probably going to an all-night pharmacy for Zoey while she sleeps. That makes sense, and I'll make sure she gets there safely.

I can work with that.

Bumping into her in a pharmacy isn't as far-fetched as crashing into her on the street. Still, for this to work, she can't see me trailing her. I make sure to give her a wide berth, my gaze never wavering from her slender form.

When she passes the only pharmacy in her neighborhood, my hackles rise. I've mapped out and checked every inch of her building and neighborhood, memorizing it for emergencies. She's not going to the pharmacy . . . so where is she going?

"What are you up to, Layla?" I mutter to myself as she shivers from the cold rain that hits her face, continuing her power walk through the dismal street.

She bows her head farther, walking dead straight and ignoring everyone else that passes by her. It's true what they say about New York. The city never sleeps, especially in the worst parts of the metropolis. Even at the most ungodly hour, you can't throw a rock without hitting some junkie, hooker, or homeless guy in need of a fucking break. And those are just the ones you don't have to worry about. The worst of the worst always comes out at night, and having Layla out here, so exposed, is making my back molars grind so hard that I'll probably end up breaking one.

When a big LED neon sign saying Tease comes into view, every muscle in my body tenses, and when I see her nod to the bouncer standing outside before she ducks into the strip club, my vision blurs with rage. I hurry to follow her inside, but the minute I step into this cesspool, I lose sight of her.

"Where the fuck did you go, Layla?" I growl, tightening my fists at my sides.

I ignore everyone else, desperate to catch another glimpse of her. I scour the place for a sign of her familiar red hair, but I come up empty-handed. The club is packed to the brim tonight with every specimen of pervert you can imagine. Maybe not all of them are bad, but they are not good either. There is a group of twenty men who look like they are part of a bachelor party, here to have a good time with the first girl who winks at them. Then there are those types of guys who had no better place to be on a Friday night, filling their plates with the all-you-can-eat buffet. You have your married men who called their wives and told them they had to work late tonight so they could sit alone in their booths, nursing their drinks and reminiscing about what it was like to have a hot young thing under them.

But those aren't the worst clientele strip clubs like this one hold. Not even close. It's the pigs that come here every night to get their cocks sucked by the talent on stage that are the scum of the earth. I know damn well that in a joint like this one, when a client asks for a private dance in the VIP room, what they really want is some pretty pussy to jam their cock into. To them, every girl that walks on stage has a price. If they are desperate enough to shake their tits and ass in front of them, then it's safe to assume that if one of these fuckers offered a few Benjamins for a ten-minute fuck, they wouldn't turn them down.

I hate places like this.

They reek of desperation and predatory intentions.

Fuck, Layla. Why the fuck are you here, baby?

Unable to track her down, I sit at the bar, making sure to grab the stool closest to the exit. I might not see her now, but if she came in here, then she'll have to pass me on her way out. When she does, she has a lot of explaining to do. My head is spinning with every possibility of why she left Zoey on her own when she's sick to come to Tease of all places.

Maybe it's not as bad as I think it is. Maybe she's moonlighting as a waitress here to make a few extra bucks. I know things have been tight for her and that she's barely keeping her head above water. That's another reason why I go see her at the diner each day. If I thought it wouldn't raise suspicion, I would leave more than just a hundred-dollar tip for her. I'd leave a fucking check with a whole lot of zeros on it. But Layla also has her pride, which means she would probably decline me handing her a wad of cash out of the blue.

Loud cheers break my concentration, and I instantly investigate what the ruckus is all about.

That's when I see her.

I ignore the DJ introducing her as Brandy, my eyes locked on her lithe, sure legs as she climbs onto the sticky stage. The woman who has been fucking with my head and heart for as long as I've known her is currently up there in nothing but a skimpy cheer-leading outfit with pom-poms in her hands. I'm so shocked that I'm incapable of moving. When the house DJ plays that old song by The Waitresses, "I Know What Boys Like," the irony isn't lost on me, since the pretty waitress that has consumed my every thought with all the things I'd like to do to her is about to throw one hell of a sucker punch to my gut.

The loud catcalls and cheers grate on my every nerve. She throws her cheerleading accessories to the ground and does a high kick, making these fuckers drool up a storm with her flexibility.

I can't take my eyes off her, studying her every move. It's sick, wrong. I should leave or take her with me, but I can't stop watching the graceful slope of her back as she spins or her perky round ass as she bends. But unlike the girl who smiles when she gives me coffee at the diner, here, Layla is all business. She doesn't crack one grin as she sashays over to the pole, wrapping her leg around it like it's her new best friend. My gaze travels down every curve of her body, and my chest tightens at the sight of her defined rib cage. I knew she was getting skinnier by the day, but never to this extent—not that any man here cares if she's too thin. To the patrons looking on, she has all the right curves in all the right places, starting from her double D tits under the small white crop top to her perky, pear-shaped ass in the skimpy skirt. My cock begins to swell as I imagine pushing her breasts together so I can slide my dick between them, jerking at it until hot spurts of my cum coat every inch of her chest.

I shift uncomfortably on my stool, watching Layla bend down and give her captive audience a perfect view of her thong-covered pussy underneath the little belt she calls a skirt. She continues to dance, ignoring all the shouts about how they want her wet pussy in their faces.

But she's not wet.

In fact, nothing about this gets her hot.

I've met enough strippers to know that some get off on the attention—but not Layla. Even if I didn't see the proof of her dry panties, I can tell by the blank expression in her eyes. This is just a means to an end. She looks almost dead inside, and that's what pushes my arousal away, replacing the feeling with anger.

Why is she doing this? To what end?

Why, Layla? Why?

I want to scream it at her, but instead of getting up and demanding answers, I remain on my stool. My furious, horny state prevents me from moving, and I'm too transfixed on what she's going to do next. Layla shimmies out of her skirt first, her plump ass making every man here salivate to get a bite.

Jesus fucking Christ.

The fantasies that assault me just from her ass alone has precum coating my now very hard, very visible throbbing dick. I lick my dry lips, palming my shaft just to ease some of the misery I'm in. To the tune of the beat, Layla continues to put on a show, dancing away like a fucking pro. When she feels the crowd getting antsy, she takes off her crop top, revealing her glorious braless tits, and the horde of horny men roar in delight. The only thing that slaps me awake is when I catch the slight tremor in her fingers as she tugs at the sides of her thong.

That's it!

I've had enough of this bullshit!

I'm hard and angry, and if I don't do something this very minute, I'm going to lose my shit.

Before she even thinks about showing these motherfuckers what's mine and only mine to enjoy, I push my way to the front of the club and jump on stage. When she sees me, her eyes widen in recognition, and a pretty shade of pink coats her cheeks. If I had it my way, the only color her body would blush into is the red imprint of my five fingers on her ass.

"You," she gasps.

"Yeah, me," I growl, picking her up by the waist and hoisting her over my shoulder.

A loud chorus of boos ensues when I pull her off the stage. I was half expecting her to protest with my caveman behavior and sling her fists against my back, demanding to be put down. However, that's not what happens. Instead, Layla's body slumps over mine in complete defeat.

I push through the crowd and into a side corridor, heading away from their grabby masses.

Once I have her backstage, I stride to the dressing room where the rest of tonight's strippers are getting ready for their set. It's only then, once I set her feet on the floor, that she shows an ounce of embarrassment for her nude state. Her arms instantly cover her breasts. As much as I would love nothing more than to have another peek, or better yet, suck on her pretty pink nipples until she comes in ecstasy, now is not the time to mess around.

"Grab your shit. We're leaving," I order, leaving no room for argument.

With her head bowed, she walks into the dressing room, stuffs her clothes into her bag, and opts to only put on her coat and shoes. It's cold as shit outside, and I'd feel better if she had more clothing on underneath her trench coat than just her panties, but I'm so fucking pissed that I don't even insist she should dress appropriately. Right now, all I want to do is get her out of here and burn the memory of tonight from my mind—it's either that or get the names of every guy who saw my woman naked and pay them a nasty visit. She shuffles toward me, and once she's close enough, I grab her hand and pull her the hell out of there.

I have to remind myself she's fragile, so I loosen my grip when all I want to do is drag her to my car, bend her over the hood, and smack her ass red for daring to do that.

The minute the cold air hits us outside, Layla starts to shiver beside me. Although I'm pissed as all hell, her discomfort unsettles me. I drop a warm arm around her shoulders and pin her to my side. She melts into my heat as we both walk back to her apartment building in total silence. I'm not sure why she hasn't pushed me away or why she's letting me lead her—to God knows where, for all she knows—without putting up a fight. If I were thinking rationally, then maybe I could make sense of it all, but as far as my logic is concerned, it all flew out the window the minute I saw her dancing on that godforsaken stage.

We get to her street in less time than it took her to go to work. The best thing for me to do is drop her at her doorstep, go home, cool down, and talk to her in the morning. Unfortunately for me, my torn heart won't settle in my chest until I get down to the reason why I found her working at Tease in the first place. So instead of leaving her and bidding her goodnight, I force her to cross the street to my car.

"Get in," I order, and again, the submissive way Layla obliges has me cringing. Taking a moment to suck in the cold air, I try to settle my possessiveness with a quick glance. She's sitting in my car, waiting for me like a good girl. Shaking my head, I round the front and open my own door, sliding into the driver's seat.

I slam the door behind me and turn to face her.

"What the fuck were you doing there, Layla?" I yell, unable to keep my temper in check. I'm still too angry that other men's eyes lingered on her porcelain skin. "Why the fuck did you feel the need to leave your sick sister all on her own in the middle of the night to go fucking stripping?"

Her big green eyes stare back at me, her jaw slack in shock as she's left speechless for a spell.

"How . . . How do you know my name? How do you know where I live? How do you know I have a sister?"

Good. Progress. At least her protective instincts are coming back to her. I hate this meek, silent version of my girl.

"Layla, I don't have time to answer a round of twenty questions. Your buddy, Will, told me when I asked him why you were a no-show at the diner this week. I got worried about you and wanted to drop by to see if there was anything I could do to help. Imagine my surprise when I see you perfectly content walking to your side gig at the strip club!"

"Stop yelling at me!" she retorts, the fighter I know her to be finally making an appearance. "You don't know me. You don't know anything about me or my life. How dare you sit here in your two-hundred-thousand-dollar car and pass judgment on the choices I have to make to care for my sister."

"Oh, I don't know you? Okay then. Tell me what possible good reason you could have to shake your ass in front of all those pervs. Tell me, Layla. I'm dying to know," I growl, our faces so close in anger it only amps up my need to kiss her.

"She's sick, okay? My sister is very fucking sick, so sick she needs surgery if she's going to make it. So excuse me if my need to keep my baby sister alive prevails over some dude coming in his pants while watching me dance. I couldn't give a rat's ass, and because of you, tomorrow I'll have to grovel to get my job back, seeing as being lifted off stage like a bag of potatoes is a big no-no and a sure way of getting me fired."

"Zoey's sick?" I whisper, the winds of fury completely knocked out of my sails.

Layla's fiery green gaze softens at the sound of her sister's name.

"Yes, very," she responds, her voice lowering an octave.

I should have known.

Every decision Layla ever made can be linked back to her sister's well-being.

I run my hand over my face, hating how I let my imagination get the better of me. Layla would have only resorted to stripping if she didn't see another alternative. Her back is against the wall, and here I am making her feel like shit for not having come up with a better solution to her problem.

"I'm sorry. I didn't know. I shouldn't have talked to you like that," I apologize, her eyes beginning to glisten with unshed tears.

"No, you shouldn't have. You have no clue what the past few

days have been like. You have no idea what it's like to feel so useless and helpless, watching the only person you love in the whole world deteriorate before your very eyes," she sobs, unable to keep her suffering at bay for another second. "She's all I have. She's my everything. And she's going to die because I can't save her." Her tears fall freely now, stabbing a ragged knife into my heart, each tear slicing a new, fresh lesion into it.

"Shh, baby. Everything will be alright," I coo, cupping her face as I dry her cheeks with my thumbs.

"No, it won't. Haven't you been paying attention? I'm about to lose my job at the diner because I can't leave Zoey alone throughout the day. I had to beg my neighbor to sleep at my place just so I could take a shift at the strip club in the hopes I could save enough money for her surgery, but now I'm out of that job too. My life is crumbling, and worst of all, I'm failing Zoey worse than my mother ever did because I'm going to be the reason she dies. Me! And there is nothing I can do about it!"

Her misery is a living, breathing thing hanging in the air between us, making me choke with emotion with every word that leaves her lips. In her mind, she's as good as lost, alone and adrift in her harsh existence.

But she's wrong.

She's not alone.

She never has been.

Because she has me.

Before I have time to talk myself out of the crazy plan I just concocted, the words are out of my mouth.

"I can help you. I can help Zoey and make sure she has her surgery and everything else that you two could possibly need," I tell her while continuing to dry her tears.

"I don't understand. You want to help us? How? More importantly, *why* would you want to do something like that? You don't even know us."

"I know enough. And I'll help you because I can. All I ask is for one thing in return."

"What?" She arches a suspicious brow.

"Marry me."

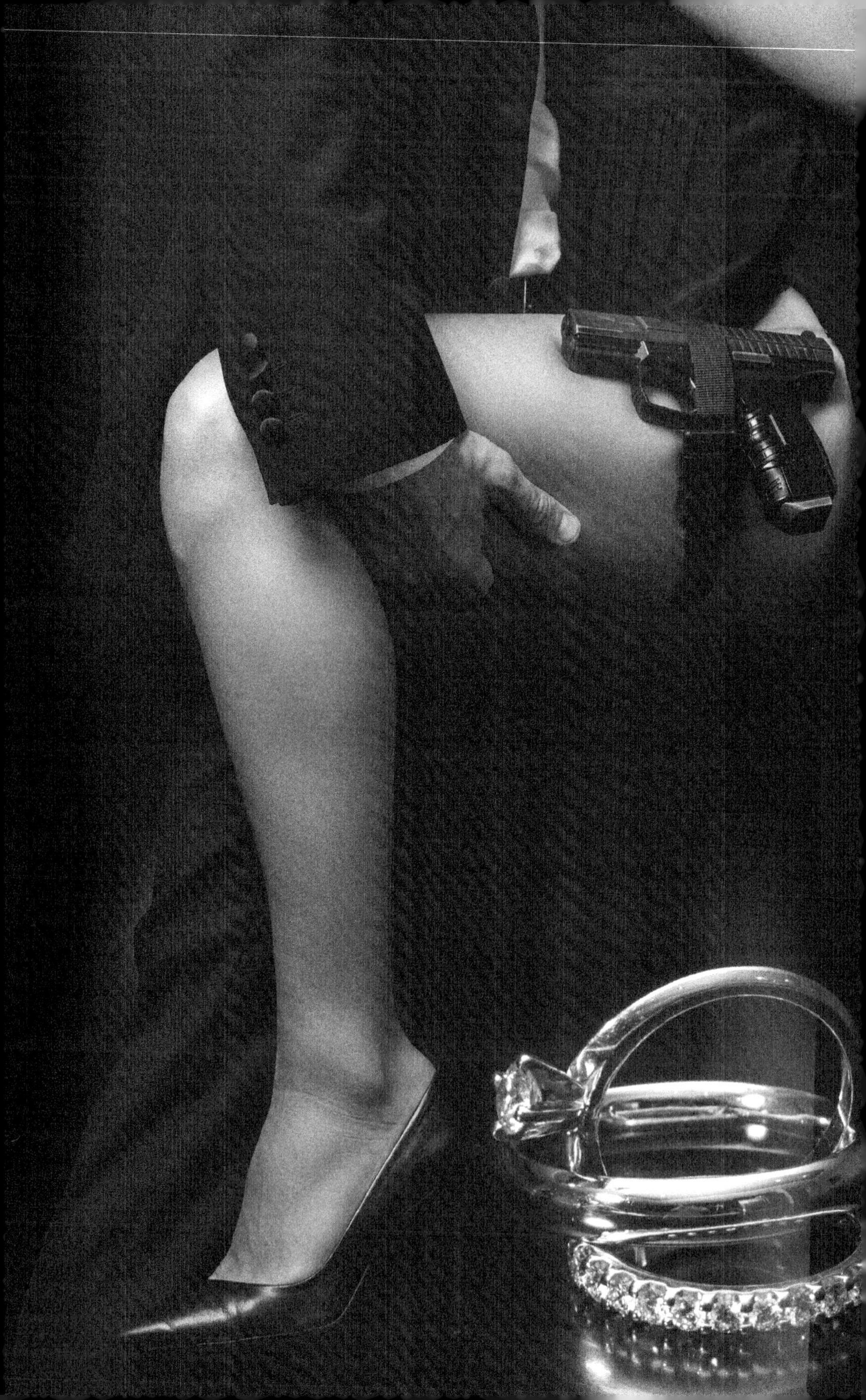

CHAPTER 12

Layla

Sitting in the dim lighting of his Aston Martin, I can't be sure if he's joking or not. I push him away as I wipe my face, drying the useless tears as best as I can. I feel the weight of his gaze on me the entire time. I don't know why I suddenly began crying. I haven't cried this whole week, needing to be strong for Zoey, but as soon as I was with this man, I found myself breaking apart, and I hate it. I hate that this stranger has that power over me. Maybe it's because I've finally reached my limit. Or maybe . . . it's because I feel safe with him sitting so close to me. I ignore the whole calling me baby thing, or how he knows my sister's name . . . for now. Especially since he just dropped a hot coal on my lap that I have to deal with first. I narrow my eyes on his face in utter disbelief.

"You can't be serious?" I ask obtusely.

Surely I heard him wrong. He barely knows me. I didn't think he even knew my name. But then why was he at Tease tonight in the first place? Was he looking for me? No. That's absurd. He doesn't seem like the type to follow a girl to a club like that, never mind rip her off stage, almost vibrating with jealousy. My skin heats at the memory of his possessiveness as he dragged me out of the strip club and into his car, demanding answers as if I owed him any.

The recollection has me shivering in my seat, and he mistakes my sudden chill for being cold, turning on the heat so I'm roasting.

"What did you say? Because I'm positive I must be hearing things."

"You heard me just fine, Layla."

I swear his lips tilt in a teasing smile before it quickly disappears. The whiplash from his shouts to the calm, sure way he's watching me leaves me blinking in astonishment. He leans forward into the light, allowing me to see his face clearer. Those bright blue eyes mesmerize me as always, but tonight they lack their usual icy stare. The heat filling their depths has my heart flipping in my chest, his gaze a silent plea.

"Marry me," he repeats in that smoky voice of his that has my insides quivering.

"You can't be serious." I laugh, turning away. "This is a joke, a cruel joke to play on a girl who's at her wit's end with all the shit she has in her life."

"I'm deadly serious," he promises, his voice hard, leaving no room for compromise. When I look back at him, I see his eyes are the same, his face set in concentration.

He really means it. He wants me to marry him.

"Why?" I blurt, beyond confused.

I thought he didn't even like me, and now he wants to marry me? It's absurd. There has to be some logical reason as to why. Is it because he feels sorry for me? Well, if that's the case, then I don't need his pity, but even as I'm about to decline his offer right here and now, Zoey's face comes to mind. She's the only thing that pulls me from my own depressing thoughts and back to the moment.

To the lack of space between us.

I can feel the heat radiating from his body, his big hands inches away as he leans closer, consuming my vision. He's lethal, that's for sure—not just to my racing heart, but to my future.

"I'm very serious. You need the money, and I have money. I will give you all that you need for Zoey's surgery and more, but these are my terms. You will marry me, live with me, and be my wife in all ways. That is, if you'll have me," he states, his hard tone softening at the end as he gives me the option.

I stare silently in shock. A half hour ago, I was shaking my ass on the pole. Even now I can smell my own sweat and the customers' desperation, and I can feel the glitter sticking to my skin. I feel disgusting, like a sore thumb in this car which is worth more than my apartment and savings combined—okay, so that wouldn't be hard, but still. Who is this man?

He waits for my answer patiently, watching the cogs turn in my head.

It comes down to this: could I really marry this man, this stranger, to save my sister's life? To stop my sister's pain? Isn't that just another way of selling myself? Only this time I'm selling myself to a blue-eyed, unknown man who claims to be my savior, coming to rescue me from my troubles and make it all better.

But no one is that perfect, that good. He must get something from it, but what? It can't just be me. I'm not much of a prize. With one look at him, I can see that a man like him could have any woman he wants. So why me? Why now?

My mind goes back to that one phrase—selling myself. Isn't that what I've been doing for the past few days? I've made three thousand dollars from allowing men to put their hands on me as their sneering, lustful eyes follow my every move. I've let them absorb every inch of my skin like they own me while I dance for their pleasure, wishing I were anywhere else but there. And now I'm here, being given everything I could ever want, but this time I won't flinch when he puts his hands on me. I'll want him to, since I've been fantasizing about him doing just that for longer than I care to admit. It still feels like a trap, though. I just need to decide if it's a snare I'm willing to walk into.

The truth is, I don't know this man. I don't even know his name. I know nothing more than how he likes to drink coffee and how he enjoys watching me with those bright eyes of his while I work, ensuring I go home with wet panties. For the first time in years, I dream of being under a man and letting him do very bad things to me. He makes me feel alive, vulnerable, and needy, and I hate that. I hate that he makes me feel weak with just a flicker of those cold eyes that only seem to warm for me, especially right now. I see his hands tighten into fists. Impatience or nerves?

"We don't know each other. Aside from you coming in for a cup of coffee at my workplace, you're still a stranger to me," I murmur, and he flinches, leaning back, but I surge ahead, knowing I'm walking the line. I could fall into madness by saying yes, but if I don't, what will I regret more? Not only would I save my sister, but I would get a chance to peel back the layers of the mysterious stranger I've been obsessing over. "I don't even know your name."

"Alaric," he growls. "My name is Alaric."

I nod, swallowing. "Alaric," I repeat, licking my lips. I swear I hear a groan as he shifts in the leather seat. "I-I don't know."

Can I really marry him? This stranger?

I always thought that if I married someone one day, it would be for love, and if I accept Alaric's offer, in a way, it will be. The love I hold for my sister is the driving force behind even considering such an offer. But can I actually do it, though, knowing nothing about this gorgeous man sitting beside me?

The truth is, I don't know.

"You need time to think. Let me take you home. I expect an answer tomorrow," he tells me. I nod, reaching for the handle, but he stops me, stretching his arm across my body to stop me from getting out of the car. The thick, corded muscle of his forearm slides across my breasts, making my nipples pebble to the point of pain, and my clit throbs in time with my heartbeat as I squeeze my thighs to ignore it.

"I promise to protect you, to give you everything you could ever have imagined if you say yes," he vows, those eyes melting me to the seat until I'm a puddle of mush.

When he slowly pulls his arm back, I breathe in a deep breath and stumble from the car, needing to escape his strong magnetism and the plea in his eyes for me to say yes.

He rushes around the car, taking my hand as he leads me to the door where he lets go. Alaric watches me as if he wishes he could follow me inside, and a small part of me wants that too. He doesn't speak, just observes me.

"Goodnight, Layla. I will see you tomorrow, and I want my answer then."

"Goodnight, Alaric," I murmur before I turn and rush into the building, only stopping when I'm safely in our apartment. My heart hammers in my chest as I press my back to the door as if he might chase me, bust it down, and demand I come away with him.

Is he my savior or my damner?

I guess only time will tell.

"Layla?" Zoey calls.

"Hey—" I clear my scratchy throat, pushing all thoughts of

Alaric and his offer out of my mind for now. "Hey, it's me. I'm home. Why are you up? Are you hungry, kid?"

"Yes, old cranky pants next door went home after putting me to bed. Complained about us not having any food in the house," she replies as I hear her little feet rushing from her bedroom. "Do we have any cereal?"

"We do," I murmur, moving to the cupboard. "Let me make you some. How are you feeling?"

I listen as she tells me about the dream she had before she woke up with her stomach growling. I nod and hum in the right places, but when she begins to eat, I stare at her, thinking back to his words. I will wish for nothing, which means Zoey won't either. She could go to a nice school, have the surgery, and live a good life.

But didn't my mother sell her soul to the devil with a silver tongue who promised to take care of her only to be led to her death?

Can I really put Zoey through the same kind of situation again, or will I learn from my mother's mistakes?

The night passes quickly, and I tuck Zoey into bed and stumble to my makeshift one on the couch. The memory of Alaric's rough, strong hands on my skin and his bright eyes begging me to say yes replay in my mind. I can't help myself as my hand drifts inside my shorts to my aching pussy. I've only felt this desire since he came into my life. Yet I refrained from touching myself, from begging for what I can't have. I was never into sex before since my teenage experiences were never something to write home about, but with him? Alaric? Even his name oozes sexuality. I lick my lips, just about to touch my sensitive wet flesh when a heaving noise comes from the bathroom, stopping me. Jerking my hand back like a teenager up to no good, I rush to the bathroom and find Zoey throwing up over the toilet with tears in her eyes.

I quickly wet a rag with some water and hold her hair back,

rubbing her for support as she throws up again and again. All the food she just ate, and then some, is purged from her stomach, and then she drops to the left, her body quaking.

"Zoey?" I yell, reaching for her as she flips and shakes, her limbs spasming as her eyes roll back in her head. "Oh God, baby, look at me. What's happening? What can I do?" I scream in panic.

I watch helplessly, but the trembling doesn't stop. I want to get help, but I can't leave her alone on the cold floor. I cry, I scream, begging for God to save her, and after what feels like a lifetime, it stops. I press my head to her chest and listen to her thundering heart. She's alive, and the realization makes me sag even as I move her into the recovery position, beseeching God for Zoey to wake up.

As I do, I know I'm begging the wrong person. God won't save us. He didn't help Gage or my mom when they needed him either. No, only I can save us, and I know how.

I have to do it. I have to marry him.

I can't watch my sister suffer and die from something I could have prevented just by accepting his proposal. His money could save her. If all he wants is me in return, then he can have every inch of me if it saves my baby sister. He'll be the one who is disappointed in the end, not me.

Yet somehow, that thought hurts.

I'm going to get married . . .

I'm going to be this stranger's wife.

* * *

"She's getting worse, Dr. Ramos," I say with tears in my eyes, watching the nurse insert IV fluids into her little veins with a concoction of meds that will ease the pain in her head and ensure she sleeps for a few hours.

"I told you as much, Layla. I'm growing concerned that she's deteriorating faster than expected. Unfortunately, the only thing I can do right now is keep her comfortable."

His words hold an edge to them, as if he wishes he could operate on my sister, consequences be damned, but I know he won't jeopardize his career for her.

I'm her last hope.

"If I had the money, how soon could you operate?" I question, wiping the useless tears off my cheeks.

"I can set it up for next week. Two if you need extra time to get your affairs in order," he replies hopefully.

I lower my gaze from the optimism I see in his eyes and look into the room where my sister is now comfortably sleeping.

"She'll be out for most of the day. If there are places you need to go, then you can trust we'll look after her," he adds, sensing my need to leave.

"I'll just be away for a few hours. There's someone . . . I mean, something I need to do."

"Take your time, Layla. In the meantime, should I book the surgery room for Zoey?"

My eyes never leave my sister. She frowns in her sleep, the pain in her head not even letting her dream. I finally turn my attention to Dr. Ramos, pure resolve etched on my face.

"Yes, please. Give me two weeks, doctor, and I'll get the money."

He lets out a small, relieved sigh and smiles at me.

"You are the best big sister Zoey could have ever hoped for. I have absolute faith you'll come through for her. I'll do the rest and make sure she's fit as a fiddle afterwards. I give you my word."

I give him a curt nod, trying my darndest to push all thoughts of my sweet baby sister's head being cut up with a drill and scalpel out of my mind.

"I'll return in a few hours. If she wakes up in the meantime, tell her I'll be back."

"I won't need to. She knows you'll never leave her," he replies.

Damn right.

Too many people in our lives have either left by their own two feet or because forces beyond their power made them—Gage being the one that still hurts the most.

I couldn't save him, but by God, that will not happen to Zoey.

Somehow, I was given a lifeline.

It's not an ideal lifeline if I'm to accept a total stranger's wedding proposal, but it's a lifeline all the same.

While I may have had plenty of valid hesitations when Alaric proposed to me in his car last night, in the light of day, with Zoey lying on a hospital bed, I realize his proposition came when I needed it most. Now all I have to do is tell him so.

If he wants me, he can have me.

All I'll ask in return is that he writes a check big enough to cover all my sister's hospital bills. Whatever happens after that, well, I'll cross that bridge when I come to it.

Thinking he'll drop by the diner to see me, I rush out of the hospital and take the bus there. The minute I walk through the doors, my body slumps in sadness.

Alaric is nowhere in sight.

"Layla!" Will calls out when he sees me, gesturing for me to come behind the counter. "Where have you been? The boss man has been threatening to fire you if you keep not showing up for your shifts."

"Zoey's sick again, Will. I can't come to work when she's sick. I just can't."

"Damn it. I thought as much. Still, I don't think you'll have a job if you keep pulling all these no-shows."

"Yeah, I know," I mutter in defeat. "I'll just have to deal with it after I've made sure Zoey is getting better."

Will gives me a gentle smile and tells me to wait for a few seconds before heading toward the kitchen. When he returns, he has a brown paper bag filled with two containers of today's special.

"Don't get excited. It's nothing much, only lasagna, but I know it's Zoey's favorite."

"Thank you. You're a good friend." I grin, genuinely grateful for the food. "Speaking of friends, I was wondering if a friend of mine came by asking for me?" I inquire sheepishly.

"A friend?" He raises his eyebrows. "I thought I was the only one," he teases, but I can tell my question took a bit of the wind out of his sails. "No, Layla. Sorry, but no one's come here looking for you."

"Right. No worries," I retort, putting on a smile and feigning indifference. "I should head back. Thank you, Will, for everything."

"Why do I feel like you're saying goodbye?"

I shrug and offer him a solemn look before I lean in and give him a side hug. He tightens his hold for a split second and then releases me from his grip.

"I wish you all the luck in the world, Layla. If there is anyone who deserves a little of it, it's you."

"Thank you," I reply and wave goodbye to the one true friend I've made since I came into the city three years ago.

I'm going to need so much more than luck though.

I need a miracle.

For all intents and purposes, it seems like the only man who can give that to me is my soon-to-be husband.

Since Alaric was a no-show at the diner, I go home, praying

he'll come here for his answer like he said he would. I pace the old rug in my living room, leaving it even rattier than when I bought it. My eyes go to my phone every few minutes, wondering how long I'll have to stay here and wait.

My soon to be fiancé must be in the same rush as I am—thank God for small mercies—since he knocks on my door less than two hours later. I swing it open, my face expressionless as I stare at the man who wants me to be his wife, even though he doesn't know me from Adam.

He doesn't budge from the hall, waiting for my permission to enter my home.

If I had time to spare, I probably would have accommodated him, but time is a luxury I don't have.

"I'll do it. I'll be your wife," I say in greeting.

His sapphire eyes light up just a tad before they turn an icy shade of blue.

"Although I'm glad to hear you say that, I thought maybe you could invite me in, and we could talk a little and get to know each other."

"We'll have plenty of time to talk after we're married," I reply, my tone arctic.

"Hmm," he hums, and I watch his large hands ball into fists.

Damn it.

Is he violent?

Does he lose his temper on a whim?

I mean, I should know what the hell I'm getting myself into, shouldn't I?

That would be the logical step to take.

Zoey's face instantly comes to mind, and I recall how she's been withering away before me these past few days.

"I don't mean to be rude," I explain, my voice coming out more anxious than I want it to be, "but I don't have time for idle chitchat, much less time to entertain whatever kind of *talk* you might have in mind," I add, making it very clear that if he thought I was going to bang his brains out when I gave him my consent to marry him, he has another thing coming. "Like I told you last night, my sister is very sick, incredibly so. I need to focus all of my energy on her. I'm sorry if that offends you in any way or if it's a deal breaker for you, but it is what it is."

Alaric looks me dead in the eye, and I swear my heart does a backflip just from the way he's looking at me right now. It's the most unsettling feeling.

"You're right. Zoey is what's important. I wanted your answer today, and you've given it. We can deal with the rest afterwards," he offers softly.

My shoulders nearly shake with relief, and it takes everything inside me not to show how comforted I am that he's not demanding anything of me right now.

I, on the other hand, still have some demands to make before I can return to the hospital.

"I've spoken to my sister's doctor, and he says he can book her surgery in two weeks. Will that be a problem for you? Moneywise?"

The way his nostrils flare in offense tells me no.

"Good. I'll probably need your phone number then so I can tell you how much it will cost and where to transfer the funds to." I hand him my phone so he can add his digits to it, but I become somewhat confused when I don't see him call his phone with it so he can have mine.

"There's no need for that. I'll go to the hospital myself and get it sorted out today," he promises.

"If that's the case, then I'd appreciate a ride over. Zoey is there right now, and I'd really like to be at her bedside when she wakes up."

Alaric doesn't even flinch at my request for a ride, and he steps out of the way so I can pass him. I hurriedly put on my coat and grab my bag, locking my apartment door behind me once I have everything.

Alaric walks silently beside me as we head down the hall. His breathing alone causes the hair on my skin to stand on end, making my heart skip a silent beat.

I don't know this man.

I don't know a thing about him.

But one thing is clear.

My body responds to his like a moth to a flame.

I just hope that the path I'm on now won't burn me alive.

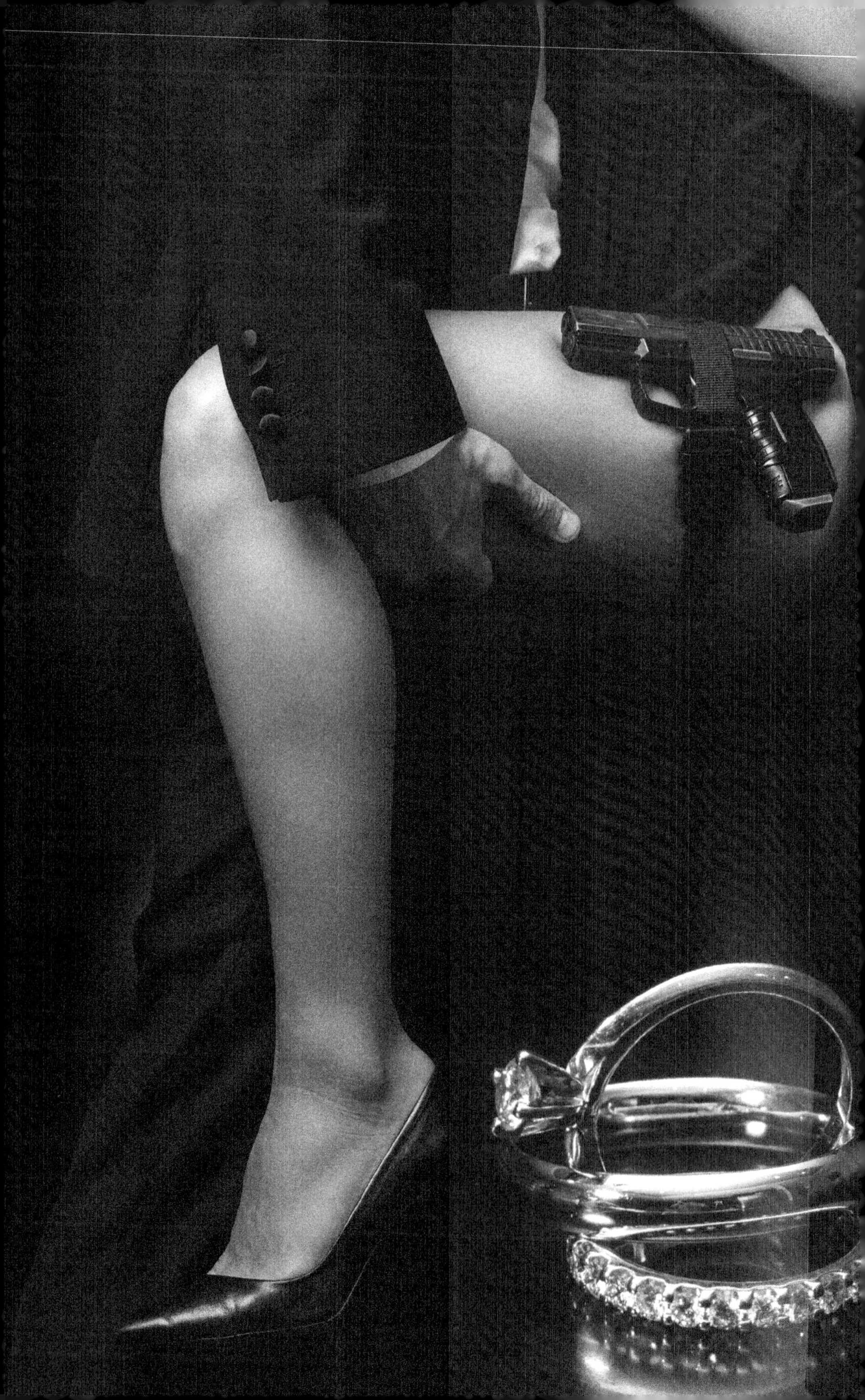

CHAPTER 13
Alaric

Ten days.

That's how long it took for Zoey's doctor to pencil her in for an emergency operation to remove her blood clot. To say I was pissed that it took that long to set up is an understatement.

The day Layla told me she would be mine, I couldn't drive to the hospital quickly enough to pay the hospital bill and dot all the i's and cross all the t's so Zoey could finally get the surgery she needed.

A part of me should have felt guilty that I manipulated Layla into agreeing to marry me before I wrote her a check. I mean, there was no way in hell I would have let little Zoey suffer another day after I learned that this surgery was the life and death kind. I would have paid whatever was necessary for her to get better, no question about it.

However . . .

Keeping that information away from Layla, although underhanded, was the choice I opted for to get what I've been craving for the past five years now.

Her.

I never said I was a nice man, and soon, Layla will know how true those words are.

As if she can read my thoughts across the room, her gaze bores into me, making me raise my eyes to meet hers. Like always, though, Layla breaks the connection, preferring to pace back and forth inside this hospital waiting room as she worries her lower lip. She doesn't look at me once after that, only lifts her head every so often to glance at the clock on the wall before flinching in despair at how long it's taking to get news about her sister.

I keep silent, knowing full well nothing I say will ease her concern. It's been four hours since Zoey was taken into surgery, and so far, no one has come out to give us any updates on how it's going.

"Something's wrong," she mumbles more to herself than to me. "It's taking too long. The doctor should have been back already."

I wish I could alleviate her apprehension, so I try even though I know it's futile. "I'm sure everything is fine. No news is good news."

She snaps her head in my direction, visibly upset at my response.

Fuck.

I should have kept my mouth shut.

"What I meant to say is that if anything went wrong, we would be the first to know. The doctor said the surgery would take four to five hours. We're right on time, Layla. Zoey will be fine," I promise, trying to reach for her, but she sidesteps my hand, glaring at me. If we weren't in such a serious situation, it might even be cute.

"You don't know that," she rebukes bitterly, unappeased by my poor attempt at optimism.

"You're right. I don't. But neither do you," I retort calmly, getting up from my seat.

I bridge the gap between us, but when I get closer, her body stiffens, and she hurriedly takes a step away from me. Rubbing the back of my head, I let out a frustrated exhale, but I don't try to cover that distance again or push her. This situation is tense as it is, and I know my presence only heightens her anxious state.

It's been close to two weeks since I came to her door, eager for her answer to my proposal, but when she accepted, there was no kiss to seal the deal or even excitement in her tone. In fact, Layla made sure that her tone was very businesslike throughout the whole exchange. To say I was disappointed, even when she said yes, would be an understatement. Layla made it very clear that her main concern was getting Zoey the operation as fast as possible and that our wedding would have to take a back seat until her sister was in the clear.

Albeit disillusioned by her stern reaction, I understood where she was coming from perfectly, and I told her I would deal with everything, even the preparations for our upcoming nuptials, so she could put all her focus and attention on her sister. I wasn't surprised that aside from asking me to write her a big fat check, Layla had made no attempt for any interaction between us. She didn't even ask for me to be here today, but there was no way I wouldn't come and support her while her beloved sister went under the knife. If Layla is to be my wife, then it's my duty to stand by her side during both good and bad times. And for Layla, today definitely constitutes being one of those undefined days. It can either be the happiest of her life or the worst. It all depends on what Dr. Ramos says when he walks through those doors.

Layla crosses her arms over her chest, staring at me while I try to think of something I can say that will ease her worry. I rack my brain for something, anything, but I come up with jack shit, since being sensitive on occasions like these isn't exactly my strong suit.

People die.

People die every day, every damn second. Shit, I, myself, have had a hand in making sure of it. What can I say to her that will give her some semblance of hope? What words could I utter that won't piss her off or make her cry?

I've got nothing.

My chest tightens to the point of pain with how fucking useless I am. I'm unable to ease her suffering. So instead of acting like someone I'm not, I choose a topic that might get her mind off her sister's surgery.

"I got us an admission meeting with St. Augustine's next week."

Layla blinks twice, gaping at me like I've just grown a second head.

Shit. Did I overstep? Am I fucking this up so royally even before it starts?

Goddamn it!

"It's the best private school in the district," I explain.

"I know it is," she snaps, still staring at me with confusion etched into her features.

"So you have heard of the school before? That's good. I thought that maybe when Zoey got better, she could start classes there. That is, if you want her to," I say hurriedly, not wanting her to think I'm taking over her life. I just want to look after them and make them happy.

Her shoulders slump as she rubs her forehead as if to ease an oncoming headache—from the stress or me, I'm not sure, and I'm not sure I even want to know.

"I've been trying to get Zoey a scholarship to St. Augustine for ages. They won't accept us, not when we don't have enough money to pay for the bare minimum like uniforms and school supplies," she replies, her voice tinged with sadness, and when her eyes flicker up to mine, I see self-hatred in her gaze. She thinks that's her fault. I wish I could wrap my arms around her and let her lean on me, but I know she needs to come to me on her own. Instead, I try to settle her reservations about the school.

"Zoey won't need a scholarship. I'll provide for her schooling," I offer slowly.

Her eyes snap up to mine, round and hopeful, but then it dashes away. Her expression drops and her lips tilt down, as if she's taming her own excitement at the prospect. I hate that. One day, she won't suppress her hope once she realizes she can have anything she wants in this world now that she's mine.

"You don't have to do that."

"Yes, I do. Once you marry me, Zoey will be my responsibility too." I shrug like it's easy.

And to me it is.

Zoey is her family, and Layla is mine now, so therefore we are all family, and I plan to take care of that family.

Layla opens her mouth to say something, but she's interrupted from doing so when Dr. Ramos walks into the waiting room. She rushes over to him, her pale face filled with fear. When the good doctor just smiles at her and says that Zoey's surgery was a success, Layla breaks down and starts to cry. Her relief is such that she turns to me and wraps her arms around my waist just to keep her knees from buckling. Her tears soak into my shirt as the doctor gives us a moment for Layla to collect herself. I hold her tightly as the weight of the bricks that settled on my heart suddenly vanishes with the news that little Zoey made it just fine.

I knew the tiny rag doll would. She's a fighter, just like her big sister.

Layla pulls away to face the doctor once more, her bright smile incandescent as she dries her tears. She's so beautiful, I can barely pull my eyes from her.

"When can I see her?" she asks hopefully.

"She's resting now, but I can take you to her. I'm sure Zoey would love it if you were the first person she wakes up to," Dr. Ramos offers kindly.

"Thank you, doctor," she says, starting to follow him in, but I don't let her get very far. I hold her wrist to stop her from taking another step.

"Doctor, when can we take Zoey home?" I inquire, ignoring the way Layla is trying to get out of my grasp. Like a hissing kitten, she digs her nails into my hand, making my lips kick up into a smile.

His confused stare bounces off Layla and onto me, unsure if he should give me that information.

"I'm Layla's fiancé," I deadpan so he can just come out and say what I need to know.

"We'll need to monitor Zoey for a few days, just to make sure there are no complications. I'd say she should get her discharge papers in three days, four tops."

With those words, I pull Layla to me once more, her chest gently pressing against mine. I lift her chin so she can look me in the eye and see that I mean business.

"Five days, Layla. In five days' time, I expect you to be at city hall waiting to be my wife. Is that clear?" I demand. I will give her this time with her sister, but then she's mine.

She swallows dryly, her green eyes fixed to mine. Fear and trepidation swim in her emerald gaze, but there is a hint of curious excitement too.

I can work with that.

I lean down and press a chaste kiss to her forehead before leaving her to do her sisterly duty by being at Zoey's bedside as she recovers.

* * *

The past five days leading up to our wedding have been utter and complete torture. I should know, since I'm an expert at inflicting pain, but never in my wildest dreams could I have imagined that watching the clock turn could be such a miserable affair. I did everything in my power to keep busy and not allow the insecure voices in my head room to grow.

During the day, I began the process of preparing the life Layla and Zoey deserve, while at night I took every job I could, entertaining myself one kill at a time.

One of the first things I did this past week was purchase us a townhouse in Tribeca and hire a professional decorator to make sure the four-story building felt like a home worthy of my girls. It was a feat getting the house ready in time, but when money isn't an issue, people tend to go the extra mile to get whatever you want done in record time. It would have been simpler to decorate an apartment, and I even considered buying us a penthouse apartment on the Upper East Side, but I nixed that idea fast. Such a home would draw too much attention to us, and the prospect of having nosy neighbors wanting to know our business isn't something a man like me really wants.

The minute I walked into our Tribeca home, I knew it was too perfect not to buy. Not only does it have ample space indoors, but it also has a large, secluded backyard any kid would be happy to play in. It's also situated close enough to St. Augustine's that Layla will be able to take and pick Zoey up every day from school if she so wishes. And knowing Layla, the knowledge that her sister is just a five-minute walk away will certainly please her protective nature.

I, however, like the townhouse for more practical reasons. It's a convenient twenty-minute drive to my brownstone in Brooklyn, which means I can keep my work life and personal life separate. I'm sure Layla wouldn't appreciate me coming home with brain matter on my shoes after a hard day's work, so having a place where I can work freely and clean up before coming home for dinner is vital for the success of our marriage.

Hmm.

That's another thing that's been keeping me up at night.

Layla has been so wrapped up with Zoey's condition, she hasn't thought to ask anything about me yet. The only question she did ask that very first night in my car was for my name—not even my full name at that. However, her lack of curiosity will dwindle once she's confident Zoey is back to her healthy self. Then, every question she can think of will start coming to her like a tidal wave, and I have to make sure I'm well prepared to have answers to all of them. Coming right out and telling her that she's about to marry a professional hit man isn't high on my to-do list.

I'll cross that bridge when I come to it.

Right now, I've got bigger concerns, like figuring out just exactly why the fuck my fiancée hasn't arrived yet. What could possibly be keeping her?

You know why, my forlorn heart whispers. It's a quarter to two, the time we're supposed to get hitched, and Layla is nowhere to be found.

Last night when I texted saying she needed to be here at city hall at two P.M sharp, I held my breath and watched the blue dots flicker on my phone then ultimately disappear. I didn't even get a thumbs-up emoji.

It unsettled me.

Now that Zoey is okay, there is nothing stopping Layla from not going through with our deal.

What should I do if she doesn't show up?

Do I scour the city until I find her then drag her kicking and screaming to the altar?

Or do I bow out and leave her the fuck alone once and for all?

These are the thoughts that plague me just minutes before my wedding. The obsessive animal in me that needs to possess every inch of Layla's body, heart, and soul yells that she will be my wife whether she wants to or not.

But the beating organ in my chest that loves her, that worships the very ground she walks on, slaps that caveman notion away. If Layla doesn't show up, then I will have to make my peace with it. All I want is her happiness, and if she doesn't believe she can have that with me, then I have to respect her choices.

"Argh," I grunt, running my hand over my face, hating where my head is at. "Pull your shit together, asshole."

Easier said than done.

I look at my watch and verify that it's now five past the hour.

"She'll come," I mumble as my heart deflates with each ticking second that passes by.

I keep my eyes peeled, waiting to catch a glimpse of her fiery red hair amongst the sea of people here. With each minute that passes, my hope of her coming starts to wither.

It was naïve and foolish of me to even think someone like Layla would want me.

How could she?

She doesn't even know me.

Fuck!

I shouldn't be doing this.

I shouldn't have given her this ultimatum. I should have just offered to help with Zoey's hospital bills and leave it at that. It was absurd of me to ask her to be my wife. What was I thinking? Aside from stalking her, what do I really know about the girl? I don't know her, just like she doesn't have the faintest clue about the man I am.

Stop lying to yourself. You know Layla.

She's the only real thing in your life.

The only peace you will ever know.

Fuck it.

If this is my only chance to have her, then by God, I will.

If Layla doesn't show up today, then not only will I bend her over my knee and fuck her senseless when I do find her, but I'll bring her right back here and put a goddamn ring on her finger, kicking and screaming if I have to.

Fuck her being happy without me.

I'm her happiness, just as she's mine.

Layla just doesn't know it yet.

With that thought in mind, the weight on my shoulders begins to lift, but any air I had in my lungs disappears when I see Layla running toward me in a simple white summer dress, her hair in total disarray. She stops right in front of me, her palm to her chest as she tries to catch her breath.

"I'm sorry I'm late. Traffic was horrible," she tells me, panting nervously. Her eyes dart away from mine for a moment.

The lump in my throat from seeing her here prevents me from uttering a word.

"Have they called us yet?" she asks worriedly, looking around.

I shake my head mutely, unable to even speak. She came . . .

and more than that, she's fucking stunning. She doesn't need a million-dollar wedding dress to look gorgeous. Every inch of her is perfect and made for me, down to the old, worn heels she teeters in.

Her brows wrinkle as she continues to stare at me.

"Is everything okay?" she questions softly, watching me nervously. Fear blooms in those emerald depths as she begins to fidget. Fuck, I put that there. I need to fix it and fast.

Everything is more than okay—it's perfect.

But instead of uttering those words, I limit myself to a nod.

"Good. I'm glad." She smiles hesitantly, straightening as some of her confidence returns.

I swallow down the lump of emotion in my throat and take her in, from the soles of her feet to the top of her head. She looks absolutely stunning in her cream heels and a simple spaghetti strap dress. It's perfect in its simplicity, although I'm kicking myself for not thinking of sending her something more expensive for her to use today just to show her how serious I am. But then again, I doubt any Vera Wang could possibly top her thrift store dress.

"Aren't you cold?" I mumble, nervous she's going to end up catching pneumonia wearing such a dress in the middle of winter.

"Not right now. When I realized the cab wasn't going to make it in time, I had to run two blocks over here. I must have taken off my coat somewhere in the middle," she answers, holding up her coat.

It's at this moment that I realize something else is missing too.

No. Not something.

Someone.

"Where's Zoey?" I rush out, panic filling my voice.

"I left her back at our place. She's still too frail to be walking about the city. I got my neighbor to watch over her for a few hours," she assures me and smiles. "She's okay, thanks to you. She doesn't like the pain meds and whatever else they have her on, says they make her drowsy, but she really liked the Xbox and new games you dropped off for her. Thank you." She reaches for my arm then, laying a hand on it. That one, innocent touch heads straight to my cock and hardens it in my tux.

"I thought she might need something to entertain her while she recovers," I reply gruffly. Luckily, I'm saved from saying anything else when a voice cuts through the air.

"Alaric Mathew Holmes and Layla Marie Johnson," the clerk calls.

"They are playing our song. Shall we go in?" she asks, tilting her head to the clerk.

I want to, God do I want to, but suddenly I'm frozen in place, my feet unable to follow through with my brain's orders.

"We don't have to do this if you don't want to," I hear myself say and immediately regret being such a fucking pussy.

Layla takes a beat and lets my words sink in.

"I'm serious. You don't have to do this," I repeat. I can't tie this beautiful creature to a monster like me, no matter how much I want to. It's selfish.

"I know I don't, but we made a deal. You saved my sister. That means something to me. You upheld your side of the bargain, so here I am to uphold mine. Now, are we doing this or not?" Her eyebrow arches high on her forehead.

Unable to help myself, I grab her hand and speed walk us into the chambers we were just summoned to before she has time to reconsider. I squeeze her hand as we step into the room and greet the city hall officiant ready to perform the service.

It's not how I envisioned Layla would ever get married one day. She deserves a big wedding, a fancy dress, and hundreds of guests to watch her walk down the aisle. But somehow, this little affair is more than perfect for us. Neither one of us has many family and friends, so a big wedding was never in the cards for us. I do wish I could have had the self-control to wait longer just so Zoey could be here. That's the only thing that feels off about doing it like this.

The officiant starts his speech, but he stops when I raise one finger to ask him for a minute.

"What's wrong now?" Layla questions, her hands perched on her hips. "You know, between the two of us, I thought I was the one who was supposed to have cold feet."

"Give me your phone," I order instead of fueling her sass.

"Now? We're about to get married and you want my phone now?" She huffs.

"Yes, Layla. I'm very aware of what's happening. Now give me your phone," I demand.

She glances hesitantly at the officiant before looking back to me, but in the end, she gives me what I asked for. Without a second to lose, I scroll through her contact list and find the number I'm looking for. It's not too hard to locate since she hardly has more than a handful of numbers in her phone. I open the FaceTime app and dial the number, and Zoey's face comes up within seconds.

"Wait . . . You're not Layla," she grumbles when she comes face-to-face with my mug.

"That's right. I'm not." I grin, unable to help it.

Layla shifts from one foot to the other, mauling her lower lip as I talk to her sister.

"Do you know who I am, kid?" I ask outright, wondering just how much Layla explained about our peculiar situation.

Like Layla, Zoey pauses for a second, taking in all my features before she says anything.

"You're him. The guy my sister is going to marry," she finally responds.

"That's right, I am." I beam, pleased that Layla told her at least that much.

"Huh. You don't look crazy to me," she retorts pensively.

"Is that what your sister said?" I laugh, noticing Layla's cheeks turning a pretty shade of pink.

"No, not really. I kind of thought you might be. I mean, no offense, mister, but you don't know us. Are you sure you want to marry into our family? We're not exactly very lucky," Zoey says solemnly. For such a young little thing, she's very smart.

But then again, she always was.

I can't help but feel a pang of sadness in my chest that she doesn't remember me, especially since the first encounter I had with her and Layla was so life-altering for me. I try to shake that melancholic feeling away, telling myself it's only natural Zoey has no clue who I am. She has probably done all that she could to put the memory of that horrific day in the past and move on.

And today, I'll ensure that Zoey's future will be a million times better than what her past doled out on her.

Both of theirs will be.

"We make our own luck, kid," I retort with a small grin. "I'm sorry you couldn't make it today, but I know your sister would want you to be here. Since you're still gathering your strength, I thought a video call would be a good alternative."

Zoey's eyes sparkle in delight, while Layla's soften. I ask one of the paid witnesses to hold up the phone so Zoey can watch the whole ceremony from the comfort of her home.

I grab Layla's hands in mine and tell the officiant to start.

"Thank you," she says softly before he begins.

I pull her hands to my lips and give her knuckles one soft kiss.

"There is nothing I won't do to make you happy. I promise."

Her nose crinkles at my words, and then her attention snaps to the officiant who's growing restless with the delay. She gives him a nod to proceed, and he continues.

"I call upon every person present to witness the union between Alaric Mathew Holmes and Layla Marie Johnson."

As he presses on, I stare into my beautiful girl's eyes and make a silent vow that one day, I will be deserving of her love. I'm not foolish to believe I have it yet, but hope blooms in my chest that she'll grow to love me someday.

The officiant clears his throat, breaking me out of my reverie.

"Do you have the rings?"

I nod, showing him the two simple gold bands and placing mine into Layla's hand.

"Then repeat after me," he adds, and I happily follow his lead word for word as I slip the wedding ring on my love's finger.

"I, Alaric Mathew Holmes, do take thee, Layla Marie Johnson, to be my lawful wedded wife. I give you this ring as a sign of our love, trust, and marriage."

Layla stares at the ring in a daze, and when the officiant calls for her to do the same, I wait with bated breath to see if she will follow through on her promise.

"I, Layla Marie Johnson, do take thee, Alaric Mathew Holmes, to be my lawful wedded husband. I give you this ring as a sign of our love, trust, and marriage."

It takes profound restraint not to grab her by the nape of her neck and kiss her.

"And now by the power vested in me by the city of New York, it is my honor and delight to declare you husband and wife. Go forth and live each day to the fullest. You may seal this declaration with a kiss."

I cup her face in my palms before pressing my lips to hers. I groan the instant I get my first taste of her lips—sweet like cotton candy and decadent like the most exquisite dessert. The little whimper she lets out when my tongue meets hers has my cock standing at attention. It takes everything in me to break away from her and not deepen the kiss.

But all good things come to those who wait, and Layla will be mine mind, body, and soul.

"I am so pleased to present the newlyweds, Mr. and Mrs. Alaric Holmes."

I stare into her half-mast, jade eyes, the shy smile on her lips melting me from the inside out. I have pictured this day a million different ways, but nothing could have topped the reality of finally calling her mine.

"Let's go home."

CHAPTER 14

Layla

It wasn't a traditional wedding, but it was perfect. I guess I never really saw myself getting married, never looked further than the next paycheck, but I couldn't imagine it any other way. I have the only person I care about sitting next to me as Alaric drives us through the city. He helped us pack our meager things from the apartment and let us into his Aston, all while Zoey smiled widely at him. She already loves him. Me? I'm not that easy. Fancy things are impressive, but I prefer the person behind the objects. I look at him now as he drives. There's a sure, cocky smile on his lips that sends a shiver through me as he meets my eyes in the rearview mirror. Possessiveness radiates from his every look.

I'm his now and he knows it.

"Where are we going?" I find myself asking.

"Home," is all he says. Zoey and I share a look but quiet down, enjoying the drive.

When we pull up outside of an impressive townhouse, I'm almost blown away. I'm too shocked to do much except stare, but

Alaric rushes around, helps Zoey and then me out of the car, and hurries us inside so we don't get cold. When the door shuts with a resounding thud behind us, I almost shiver.

This is it, the start of the rest of my life.

Zoey and I stand hesitantly in the foyer as he continues on, walking inside like he owns the place—which, I guess, he does.

It's impressive, really impressive, like something you would see in an interior design magazine. As if the huge exterior isn't incredible enough, the inside blows me away. It's all tasteful, modern designs with huge arched ceilings, a wooden staircase, old original flooring, and a chandelier. It's a mix between charm and sharp edges, just like Alaric himself. I instantly love it, almost feeling . . . at home.

Which is scary enough as it is.

I peer at the sliding barn doors hiding the rooms, but beyond the foyer is a hallway that I assume leads to a kitchen and the backyard, if there is one. He lets us take it all in before his smoky voice sounds close to me.

"Bedrooms are upstairs. Zoey, yours is on the second floor, and we're on the third. There are four baths, four bedrooms, a game room, a dining room, and a lounge. There's a pool on the roof and a garden out back—" He stops and turns to look at us, frowning. "What's wrong?"

"This is all for us?" Zoey inquires quietly at my side, holding my hand like we're strays—which we are.

I'm used to sleeping on a couch, and our apartment is the biggest space we've ever had, but it could fit in this foyer. It's both embarrassing and depressing, and it makes an ugly feeling rear its head for a moment. I want to defend our life and protect Zoey from feeling unworthy, but the look in his eyes stops me.

I see the sadness in his gaze before he masks it, strides over, and kneels before her, taking her hand as he shoots me a smile. "It's all for us. This is our home now; we are family." With that, he stands and kisses her forehead. "Tomorrow, you can pick out anything you want for your room."

"Really?" she squeals and throws herself at him for a hug, laughing as he pats her back.

"Of course. Let me make you both some food before we settle in." He winks at me, sending a shiver through me once more at the intention behind his words.

He turns and starts to walk away, calling, "Feel free to explore. What's mine is yours now."

"Wow," Zoey whispers. I can feel her excitement. She's also bouncing on the spot, ready to investigate.

"Go, but be careful," I tell her with a laugh, pushing her forward. With a grin, she starts to rush off, but then she slows down as she remembers my warning. After all, she's still recovering, and the bandage around her head is a perfect example of that.

"Thanks, Layla!"

I watch her go with a smile on my face and my hand pressed over my heart, still standing in my thrift store wedding dress. Unlike her, I feel out of place, so I don't explore. I peek into a dining room as I pass before following the path he took. I do notice it's all very . . . empty. There are no photos, no memories or personality. It looks like something out of a catalog, all clean modern lines. It screams money, but it feels . . . almost cold, until Zoey's loud laughter rings out. Even in her frail, weak state she's making the most of this fresh start and giving it her all. I have too as well for her. There could be worse lives . . .

We can make this work, I assure myself.

We have to.

* * *

Alaric cooked an impressive meal. He wasn't sure what we would like, so he made a whole buffet, with chicken, pizza, burgers, fries, cheese boards, fruit, and everything else you could imagine. He even gave Zoey some ice cream. After helping her with her meds, he shows me the way to her room so I can get her settled while he cleans up.

It's pretty, if a little empty like the rest. She has her own en suite bathroom, though, a double bed, and more space than our entire apartment back in Hell's Kitchen. The walls are a beautiful robin's egg blue with crown molding and high ceilings, the floor is a lovely, soft plush white carpet, and there's even a fireplace on the left wall framed by two huge windows looking over the back garden.

It's like a dream or a fairy tale.

But nothing is that good, right?

Shaking off my doubts, I help her get ready for bed, telling her a story and tucking her in. I know she's too old for that, but Zoey indulges me anyway. I wait until she's snoring happily, clutching a new stuffed bear she found, before I leave. When I reach the foyer again, I hesitate, unsure what to do. I got married today, he's my husband . . . but we are still strangers.

Hell, I didn't even know his last name until the ceremony. Will I be expected to sleep in his room? I'm guessing so. As my worries take over, he strides from the corridor and smiles at me. "Is she okay?"

"Better than okay, thank you. Her room is beautiful," I reply, remembering my manners.

"I hoped she would like it, but she can change anything. You both can. I want you to be happy here," he murmurs as he steps closer, his eyes darkening as he looks me over.

Lustful.

It's the only way to describe his gaze. I look down, unsure what to say to his generosity. The sparkling gold wedding band on my finger catches my attention, reminding me I'm now his.

"Come on, Layla," he whispers softly.

Alaric takes my hand and leads me up the grand staircase. I notice that each step is cushioned as nerves fill me. He doesn't speak, but the hungry looks he keeps throwing my way leave no question about his intentions.

He plans to consummate the marriage, to take his wife.

To fuck me.

Surprisingly, I'm not against the idea. My pussy clenches at the thought, and I get wet, embarrassingly so, until each step has my drenched panties rubbing against my sensitive pussy. I may not know everything about this man, but there's time. I tell myself it's only like a one-night stand or a fling. Even though it's a lie, the premise is the same. People fuck strangers all the time, so why can't I? This stranger just happens to be my husband.

When we finally get to the top, I'm trying to control my heavy breathing. He spares me a considering look, his lips parting as his eyes run down my body before he turns and practically drags me down to a set of double doors at the end of the hall. They are partially open, and I barely have a moment to notice the wood is decorated with orange designs and golden handles before I'm rushed inside.

A hand cradles the back of my head, and in the darkness of the room, Alaric towers above me. He commands my obedience as he steps closer, pressing his hard body to every inch of my soft frame. The slip dress doesn't give me much protection from him in his tux, and he looks dangerous and sexy as hell.

"Little Layla," he coos. "I've been dreaming of this moment for a very long time, imagining you in my bed with your nails in my back and your pussy wrapped around my cock."

I gasp at his words, almost recoiling at how forward he's being. Up until now, he's been tame, but it seems with the marriage completed, he's not holding back anymore. No one speaks like that, but he doesn't allow my retreat. He stares into my eyes as he surges ahead.

"I've spent a lot of time imagining fucking you and making you mine, and now you are. You're my wife . . . but I won't force you." He drops his hand and wanders away. I follow him like a moth to a flame, watching him wordlessly. My mouth feels dry, and my thighs clench together, hoping he doesn't notice my desire for him.

My husband.

The thought repeats in my head.

"I don't take what isn't mine." He looks over his shoulder at me. "So know this, I can sleep at your side tonight, and I won't touch you. But if you step into this room and look at me with those big fuck me eyes one more time, I'll throw you on our new bed and have you. I'll lick and taste every inch of that delicious body until you scream my name. I'll fuck you all night, Layla, until you can barely walk, until you know exactly whom you belong to. It's your choice." He disappears into another open doorway to the left, leaving me gaping after him.

He's . . . letting me choose?

The shy part of me demands I go sleep in Zoey's bed, but that's a child's fear. Because me, Layla, the adult who just married this rich, dangerous stranger really wants to take him up on his offer, on the promise in his dark voice. I want to see what lies behind that tux and find out if sex with him is as really as good as he stated.

I step after him hesitantly, holding the side of the dress with one hand, gripping the material for courage. Can I really do this? He's my husband, that's legal and true, but can I take him in every way he demands? Can I let him into my body when he's already barged into every other inch of my life?

But the pleasure he spoke of and the way he looked at me . . .

Hungrily.

It's seared into my mind, and I know before I even step foot into that bedroom what I'm going to do. I'm going to trust my husband one more time. Not to save us, but to damn me. To make me his.

Kicking off my shoes, I follow like a good girl.

He's standing next to a huge, king-sized bed draped in silks and pillows. His eyes are fixed on his task of slowly removing his cufflinks and rolling back the sleeves on his shirt, his jacket discarded on a sofa. I don't notice much other than that. As always, my whole focus is drawn to the man expertly removing his wedding clothes with a surety that has the mundane task seeming very sensual. Or maybe that's just my filthy thoughts. He doesn't look at me, but I know he's aware of my every move as I step farther into the room, sinking into the deep gray carpet beneath my feet.

It's now or never.

I swallow my nerves and gather my courage. "Alaric?" I call, my voice shaking only slightly.

He stops and turns his head, those dark eyes blasting through me until I actually jerk from their impact. My heart begins to race as nerves fill me, and I know if I don't do it now, I'll chicken out.

I grab the zipper on the side of the dress and slowly pull it down. My fingers shake as I stare into his eyes, and when it's undone, my panting is loud in the awfully silent room. I let it drop to the floor, the fabric flowing around my feet like a declaration. I'm wearing nothing but silky white underwear and a strapless bra as I stare at him.

He watches me back.

"I want the second option." I tilt my head back, lifting my chin.

He narrows his eyes and drops his hand from his arm as he prowls toward me like a predator hunting its prey. "You want what, little Layla? Say it."

Fuck. Licking my lips, I meet his eyes as he circles me and then stops before me. "I want you to fuck me."

His lips quirk up for a moment, and his eyes drop to my body. I almost want to shield myself from his gaze. Even at the club, I wasn't this shy, but suddenly, before this man I've just taken as my husband, I'm an embarrassed, quivering mess.

"Don't," he warns harshly. "Never be embarrassed in front of me."

Nodding, I watch as he reaches out and drags the tip of one finger over my collarbone and down the valley of my heaving breasts. "You're fucking perfect, too perfect to be real." His hand drops away, and he meets my eyes. "Are you sure this is what you want? I won't ask again, my love. If you commit to this, you are mine. I'll fuck every inch of you, push your limits, make you cry, and make you come, so that every time you look at me, you'll be nothing but a dripping mess begging for my cock. I won't take it easy on you—I can't—I want you too badly." As if to prove his point, he cups the huge bulge in his trousers, rubbing it as I watch, mesmerized. "If you want someone to love you gently, slowly, I'm not that man for you."

He's giving me an out, just like at city hall.

And yet again, I'm not taking it.

"I want you," I reply, my gaze still on his hand which is stroking faster now. "Are you going to keep talking, or are you going to keep these promises?"

"Layla, keep pushing me and your teasing little mouth will be filled with my cock so you can't speak again," he warns as he steps closer, pressing against me. This time he doesn't plan on stopping, and neither do I.

When I stepped into this room, I knew what I was doing. I've made my bed, and now I have to lie in it with him, my husband. Whatever else happens tonight, I'm finally going to give into this electric arousal that arcs between Alaric and me.

The heady, powerful feeling that grows inside me makes me smile as I realize he wants me as badly as I want him. Maybe he always has. As if he heard my thoughts, he tips up my chin with one finger and tilts his head down like he's going to kiss me. I inhale, waiting, but his lips simply move against mine as he speaks.

"Every shy look you gave me, every stolen smile and touch, no matter how innocent, drove me fucking wild. I tried to be good and stay away, but you're just too fucking tempting, Layla. I couldn't. I wanted you so badly, still do, and every fiber of my being tells me I'm yours, demanding I take you, fuck you, and prove those doubts in your eyes wrong. I saw the embarrassment and sadness whenever you thought I rejected you . . . but, love, I was protecting you. One more touch, and I would have bent you over those sticky diner tables and slammed into your tight little cunt in front of them all." He swallows my gasp, kissing me gently, the action contradictory to his dirty words. "You are my entire reason for living, my fucked-up dirty little secret I couldn't walk away from even though I knew I should. You are so innocent, Layla, so perfect, and me? I'm a scarred mess, yet it won't stop me, not now. You begged me to fuck you, and that's just what I'm going to do." His lips slam onto mine.

A promise.

I have to fumble to keep up as he tilts my head the way he wants, licking and nipping at the seam of my lips until I whimper, and then his tongue slips in my mouth. He tangles it with mine, sucking on it and dragging his along my teeth. He tastes and claims every inch like he promised. When he pulls back, I'm breathing heavily, my eyes are closed, and heat blooms in my stomach and pussy. Just from a kiss. But a kiss has never felt like I couldn't breathe without it, as if I might cry if he doesn't do it again.

My body sways into his even as he steps back, forcing my eyes open. "On the bed," he orders. I hesitate only for a moment, my mind clouded by desire, but it's too slow for him. He grabs my waist and tosses me. I squeal as I fly through the air, the impact forcing the breath from my lungs as I bounce before sprawling out across the bed in a very undignified manner.

He's on me in an instant, pinning me down with his huge body, his hands on either side of my head as he watches me. I wiggle beneath him, and his dark orbs narrow. "Keep doing that and I'll come across your incredible breasts before I even get to taste your cunt."

My eyes widen at his words. He can't mean that, can he? I mean, the only experience I have is limited, I'll admit, but the one guy I've been with didn't want to do that. He almost looked disgusted when I suggested he give me head like I had given him, and instead we had very unsatisfactory quick sex that left me dry and hurting. I know this won't be the same; my pussy is already slick with desire, and the hunger in his kisses only has that growing.

"You want to . . . taste me?" I finally ask.

"Every fucking inch of you," he vows. "Starting with these fuckable breasts spilling from this little bra. I can see your hard nipples." He groans and lowers his head. "And I need to have them."

"I—" I stumble over a response, but it doesn't matter. My words die in my throat as that hot mouth wraps around my nipple through my bra. The feel of his mouth, even through the material, has me crying out. Chuckling, he lifts his head and meets my gaze again.

"How sweetly you cry out. You're so fucking responsive. I can't wait to find out what else makes you scream."

My cheeks heat at his blatant dirty words, and his grin widens. "So fucking sweet. Tell me, Layla, are you a virgin?"

I stutter, closing my eyes before they meet his. "No." He doesn't seem angry as he tilts his head. "I didn't enjoy it that much. I've only been with one man, and yeah, it was bad," I blurt, embarrassed all over again.

"Then he didn't fuck you right, the moron. Having such a perfect creature like you beneath him and not making you come?" He shakes his head. "I'll rectify that. Did he taste you?"

"No," I whisper, knowing he will only keep asking.

"Fucking kid," he spits. "Little Layla, you will enjoy this. I promise you that. You'll enjoy it so much you'll crave it every second of every day. I'm going to eat that sweet little cunt until your cream drips down my chin, and only when you beg, fucking beg for me to fill you, I will. Even then, you will come over and over again, all across my cock, until that fucking idiot that took your virginity doesn't exist. Only I do and the pleasure I can give you. That, I promise you."

He leans down and kisses me again, and I whisper into his lips. My thighs clench together, but he doesn't like that. He forces himself between them, his material covered knee sliding up until it's pressed against my damp panties. The friction—oh God. I gasp and he swallows it, trailing his fingers up my arm and across my chest to my breasts. I can't help wiggling again, only now it's against his knee, and the hardness hits my clit, making me cry out.

Smirking against my lips, he deepens the kiss, tangling his tongue with mine as his expert, lithe fingers tug at my bra. He pulls it down, freeing my heaving breasts. Ripping my mouth away, I close my eyes, wanting to cover up, but he doesn't let me. He kisses down my cheek, stopping at my neck to lick and suck, before continuing across my chest to my breasts. I part my eyes slightly, looking at him through my lashes, and I see the hunger on his face as he takes them in.

"Fuck me, they are even better than I imagined." Alaric groans, reaching out reverently to stroke them.

When he circles my nipple, I bite my lip, trying to stifle a noise that wants to escape. His eyes dart up and narrow as he does it again, this time flicking my hard bud. The arc of pleasure goes straight to my pulsing clit, making me cry out as I grind into his knee. He likes my response and does it to the other side, eliciting a whimper from my lips. Alaric does it again, but this time, he plucks my nipple, twisting and playing to determine what makes me cry out and what makes me arch into his touch.

"Please!" I finally yell, and with his dark eyes on me, he pushes my breasts together, my hard nipples pointing at him as his mouth hovers above them.

"Please what?" he demands.

"I don't know," I whimper. "I need more."

Chuckling, he laps at my nipples, turning his head to lick both at once. The ache from his hard grip only seems to add to the pleasure that's rolling through me from his mouth. I close my eyes; it's too much. I can't look at his dark head and stormy eyes as he licks me like I'm his favorite dessert.

"Look at me," he demands, stopping. "Don't take your eyes off me for a moment."

They snap open automatically from the harsh command, and when mine meet his, he lowers his head again. This time he sucks my nipple into his hot mouth, the pressure and heat making me arch as my hips roll. I can't stay still, it's too much. My own desire makes me wild. I didn't know it could be like this. I can barely catch my breath, and he hasn't really touched me.

And yet I'm rubbing against his thigh unashamedly. I try to stop, I really do, but I need the pressure. I have to have it.

Popping my nipple from his mouth, he blows across it before giving the same treatment to the other. When they are both red and glistening with his saliva, he releases them, rips the bra off, and tosses it away as he continues down my body. He licks and kisses every inch, from my prominent ribs to my flat stomach. Alaric circles my belly button with his tongue before dipping inside, making me gasp his name.

"Good girl," he praises as he kisses just below it, and I stiffen.

He ignores it, stroking at sides until I relax, and then he continues on, kissing and licking along the edge of the tiny panties hiding my embarrassingly wet pussy from him.

But he's not a man to be denied, and he already said he owns every inch of me.

"I want to see every part of you," he murmurs against my skin, and he hooks his fingers under the side of my panties.

I throw my arm across my eyes. I can't bring myself to look as he slowly tugs them down. He stops to place open-mouthed kisses across my hips, and then I feel the glide of the fabric over my thighs before he moves them over my calves, stopping to kiss both. Lifting my arm slightly, I peek to see him watching me as he lifts one foot, kissing the sensitive underside, then tugs the panties off before tossing them to the floor with my other scattered clothes.

I'm totally naked under him, shaking, flushed, and so turned on I want to cry. But my embarrassment takes that edge away, and I slam my thighs closed.

His eyes narrow. "Layla," he warns. "You're mine, every delicious perfect inch. Now let me see you." When I don't move, he reaches up, grips my neck, and squeezes. "Now," he snarls, and when I obey him, parting my thighs a few inches, he strokes my sensitive neck and lets go. "Good girl. Wider, let me see my pussy."

Biting my lips, I let my thighs fall open. I squeeze my eyes closed, unable to look at him as cool air blows across my overheated wet pussy.

"Fuck, you are so goddamn wet, baby girl."

I try to close my thighs again, but his big hands are there, parting them farther, and when I look, he's staring at my pussy and licking his lips.

"Is that a good thing?" I ask.

"Good? Fucking phenomenal," he snarls. "You're so fucking perfect."

Reaching out, like the first time he touched my breasts, he drags one fingertip down my lips. I gasp, and he lifts it into the air, watching it glisten with my cream before he meets my gaze and sucks it into his mouth. His tongue wraps around the tip, tasting me. I still as he sucks it hard before popping it from his mouth.

"Holy fuck, baby girl, you taste so sweet. I can't wait to feel my tongue bathed in it."

He slides his entire palm down my core like he can't resist and sweeps his tongue along his hand, tasting more of me as he groans.

"Oh fuck," I cry out, my pussy clenching from his attention. "Alaric."

"I love the way you say my name," he murmurs as he touches me again. He parts my lips and stares at my pussy. "I want you to keep saying it while I taste this pretty pink cunt of yours."

Then, without warning, he drops to his belly between my thighs and throws them over his wide shoulders. My hands scramble on the bed, fisting the silk as his fingers part me again and his tongue drags down my folds, tasting every inch just like he said. The warmth and the feel of it makes me whimper his name as I give into the desire heating my veins.

"Alaric!" I cry out, hoping Zoey can't hear, but I couldn't stop myself even if I tried. He slides his tongue along me, again and again, circling my throbbing clit and then down to my clenching hole. He tastes every part of me, leaving nothing untouched.

"Greedy fucking girl, aren't you?" he growls between my thighs, the vibration making me whimper as my hips gyrate.

His big hands span my thighs, holding me in place for his eyes and mouth, leaving me open and vulnerable. My cheeks redden, knowing he can see how wet I am—embarrassingly so for him—but if anything, it only seems to please him more.

"Please," I beg. "I need to come."

"Soon," he promises, soothing my clit with his tongue then lashing it before sucking it into his mouth like he did my nipple.

The pleasure slams through me and I scream, threading my fingers through his hair and tugging on it. Suddenly he rips himself away, panting.

"Fuck, you're too goddamn sweet," he growls, watching my pussy as his fingers stroke down to my hole. He circles it, round and round. The touch drives me crazy until I'm about to yell at him, but he steals the words by slamming one finger inside me. Not slowly, no, he forces me to take it.

I fall back and lift my hips to take it deeper, and he quickly adds another, stretching me for him as his mouth attacks me again. He licks and sucks my clit in that circular manner that has me fucking myself on his fingers and mouth.

"Oh God, so good, don't stop!" I call out, rolling my hips, the pleasure nearly making me choke.

Sweat breaks out across my skin as I grind myself against his mouth. He adds another finger, the three digits stretching me so deliciously that when he crooks them along my walls, dragging against a spot inside of me I didn't know existed, my release explodes through me.

I can't even scream, locked in a cycle of pleasure that starts where his mouth is. I writhe beneath him, my pussy clamping around his fingers, and he still doesn't stop. He thrusts slowly, fighting my clenching channel as his tongue licks me through it and straight into another—something I didn't know was possible. When it's over, I slump into the bed, trying to push him away from my oversensitive pussy, but he doesn't relent. He presses a soft kiss against my clit and slowly pulls his fingers out. Meeting my eyes, he sucks and licks them clean before getting to his knees above me. His chin drips with my release, and when he leans down to kiss me, I lift my head to meet him.

I taste my sweetness on his tongue, my body slack and mind hazy with pleasure.

But he's just getting started.

He slides from the bed and watches me as he strips, exposing hard muscle after hard muscle, some covered in intricate artwork. The tattoos cause me to stare longer. There's a gun on his rib cage, pointing upwards, a cross on his right pec, wings on each shoulder, and his whole thigh is covered in a complex piece. I gulp, trying to look everywhere at once, from his impressive eight-pack leading to a delicious deep V pointing straight at—oh fuck—his cock.

It's massive. I can't stop staring, watching as it bobs. Precum beads at the tip, and the veins bulge. He's hardly got any hair there, as if he shaves, and I think that only makes it that much more impressive. There's no way that will fit inside me. I'm still staring when he climbs back up on the bed, settling between my thighs and stealing my view of his monstrous dick.

He grasps both of my wrists and pushes them to the bed above me. He holds them there with one hand as his lips descend on mine again. It makes all thoughts except for ones of him disappear once more as my arousal returns with a vengeance.

I wrap my left leg around his hip as I rock into him, trying to urge him on, but he ignores me. I didn't know it could feel like this. Didn't know I wanted this so much. I feel like I'll die if I don't get him inside me. My pussy glistens with his saliva and my own cream, aching to be filled, and my clit throbs in time with my hammering heart. My cheeks are red with embarrassment, even though he told me not to be, but I'm a little ashamed by how badly I want him, how fucking wet I was before he even touched me, and now? I'm actually dripping, begging to feel that massive length I glimpsed inside of me, and he's still taking his time, kissing me like he has all the time in the world.

I impatiently grind into him, feeling his hard length rub along my pussy. When it catches my clit, my breath hitches. He pulls back with a groan and presses his forehead to mine, my lips raw from his dominant, sure kisses.

"You are enough to test a man's control, my love," he murmurs against my skin.

"Who said I wanted your control?" I whisper. "I want the man who ripped me down from the stage because he couldn't stand it. I want the man who couldn't wait to tear off my wedding dress. I want my husband," I purr, knowing it will drive him wild.

I saw him earlier when I first said it, those blue eyes darkening, and I felt it in the way he threw me down. I don't know where the boldness comes from, but in my desire, my hunger for my new husband, I find myself uncaring. He likes my fight, likes my fire, and he'll get all of it.

All of me.

And I'll get all of him.

Preferably now. I want to know how good sex with him can be. I want him to show me over and over again what I've missed out on all these years with nothing but my imagination and fingers. I want to be painted in his need. I don't want the worry for Zoey, the ghosts of my past, and the terror that's always with me anymore. I want to be consumed by him until all that exists is pleasure.

"Layla," he groans, his body vibrating above me. That one simple word, my name, is a threat and a promise.

"Please," I whisper, lifting my head to chase his lips, kissing and nipping at the puffy flesh. I taste my own release there again, and I know it's wrong, but it's so addictive. "I need you. I need you inside me. It hurts."

That does the trick. He snarls, grips my hands, and slams them back to the pillow above me.

"We can't have that, can we, wife?" he growls as he kisses me once more. "Don't move your hands. If you do, I stop. Understand?"

I nod desperately, and he slowly uncurls his fingers from around my wrists. When I don't move, he sits back, looking down at my naked, vulnerable body spread out for him like a feast.

"You are so goddamn beautiful, and all mine," he mutters more to himself than to me, dragging his hands up my legs again. He parts my thighs as he lowers, and I wrap my legs around his waist as he reaches between us and grasps his cock.

"What about a condom?" I suddenly remember.

"I'm clean, I've been tested, and we'll get you birth control," he answers patiently, kissing me. "But I want to feel my wife raw around my cock."

I want that too, so I don't protest as I feel the tip of that huge cock press against my entrance. I stiffen though, but he leans down and kisses me until I relax, and then slowly, ever so slowly, he pushes into me. The stretch of my dripping channel has me groaning.

He's big, so fucking big.

He has to fight my body to get inside of me, and by the time he's buried to the hilt, we are both panting. He waits, just breathing, as he allows me to adjust.

"Okay?" he asks, cupping my cheek.

When I nod, he kisses me again and starts to move, pulling free of my body and pushing back in. He moves softly at first, almost lovingly, but when he speeds up? When he slams into my cunt with hard, quick thrusts? That's when I moan, feeling his length drag along those nerves, relishing the snap of his hips against mine as he reaches down and tilts my hips. He changes the angle until I'm crying out and he's sitting back, fucking me on his knees. My lower half is in the air, and his lips are twisted in a fierce snarl.

It's a beautiful fucking sight and has me reaching for him. I slide my hand down his rock-solid abs, feeling slightly raised scars beneath my fingers.

"I said don't move," he snaps angrily.

I whimper, I can't help it. He arches an eyebrow, waiting but not moving.

"I need to touch you," I rasp. "Please, Alaric, I want to touch every inch of you the way you did me."

His eyes close for a moment, and when they snap open, the shock makes me jerk as he leans down and blankets my body.

"Then touch me, wife, but know I won't be held responsible when you make me nothing but an animal rutting into you like a wild beast."

I clench around him, the thought making me swallow hard. He groans, snapping his hips forward to fill me again before he pulls out and thrusts back in as I drag my hands down his back to cup his supple ass. I feel it clench as he fucks me.

"You like that, don't you?" he growls above me, his huge cock spearing me. "Like the idea of me like that—fucking you until you can only scream for me, until no one can save you from the darkness inside me. The one that wants to swallow you whole and stain every inch of your perfect young skin with its mark and my cum and see every hole dripping with it for me."

I cry out at his words. The images of him doing just that fill my head until I'm clenching around him again like the greedy girl he called me earlier. Those dark, all-consuming eyes hold me prisoner beneath him, but I'm a willing one, and I dig my nails into his ass to urge him on.

"Yes, I would like it," I finally admit, arching my back to rub my aching, hard nipples along his wide, muscular chest.

Every inch of me is being consumed by this man, and there is nowhere left untasted, like he promised. My every nerve ending is alight with pleasure until I can scarcely breathe. I let my body take over; it knows what to do. I rise to meet his thrusts as I scratch down his back, cutting it as he pummels into me. He roars at the pain, and I feel blood under my nails, but I don't stop. I claw like an animal, writhing and rocking beneath him, chasing another release, and then it's there.

It slams through me, and my pussy clamps around his cock as I scream.

My channel milks him as he tries to fight it. He pulls out and pushes back in twice before it's finally too much and he gives in. Yelling, his hips stutter as he finds his own release. The warmth of it splashes inside me, making me groan as I collapse back onto the bed. I feel boneless, my body limp as he rolls his hips again and again as if shoving his release deeper inside of me. I whimper, unable to protest, too busy sucking in air as my body quivers beneath him.

Well and truly fucked.

"Good girl," he croons, his voice deep and rough. "You took my cock so well, my perfect little wife."

His words shouldn't make me float on air, but they do, and when his lips touch mine softly, I swear I melt into the bed. I don't even move when he pulls free of my aching core.

Rolling to his side, he leans on his elbow above me as I force my eyes open to meet his sparkling ones. He's never looked so relaxed, so happy and open.

I did that.

"Perfect in every single way," he whispers as he leans down and kisses me. When he pulls back, he strokes his hand down my body possessively. Reaching my throbbing, sensitive pussy, he trails his fingers along my folds, making me whimper lazily. He brings his hand toward my face, his fingers covered in our mixed cum, and then he coats my lips in the glistening fluid.

"Taste us, wife. Taste what we are like together," he demands, and my tongue darts out, tasting us as I moan. "We are perfect together. Now rest, I plan on waking you up in an hour or two with my head between your thighs."

I can't help but snuggle closer. We might have started as strangers, but after tonight, he knows my body better than I do. Everything else can come after.

I fall asleep right there in his arms with a smile on my lips, fully relaxed for the first time in forever.

Feeling safe and cared for.

With him.

My husband.

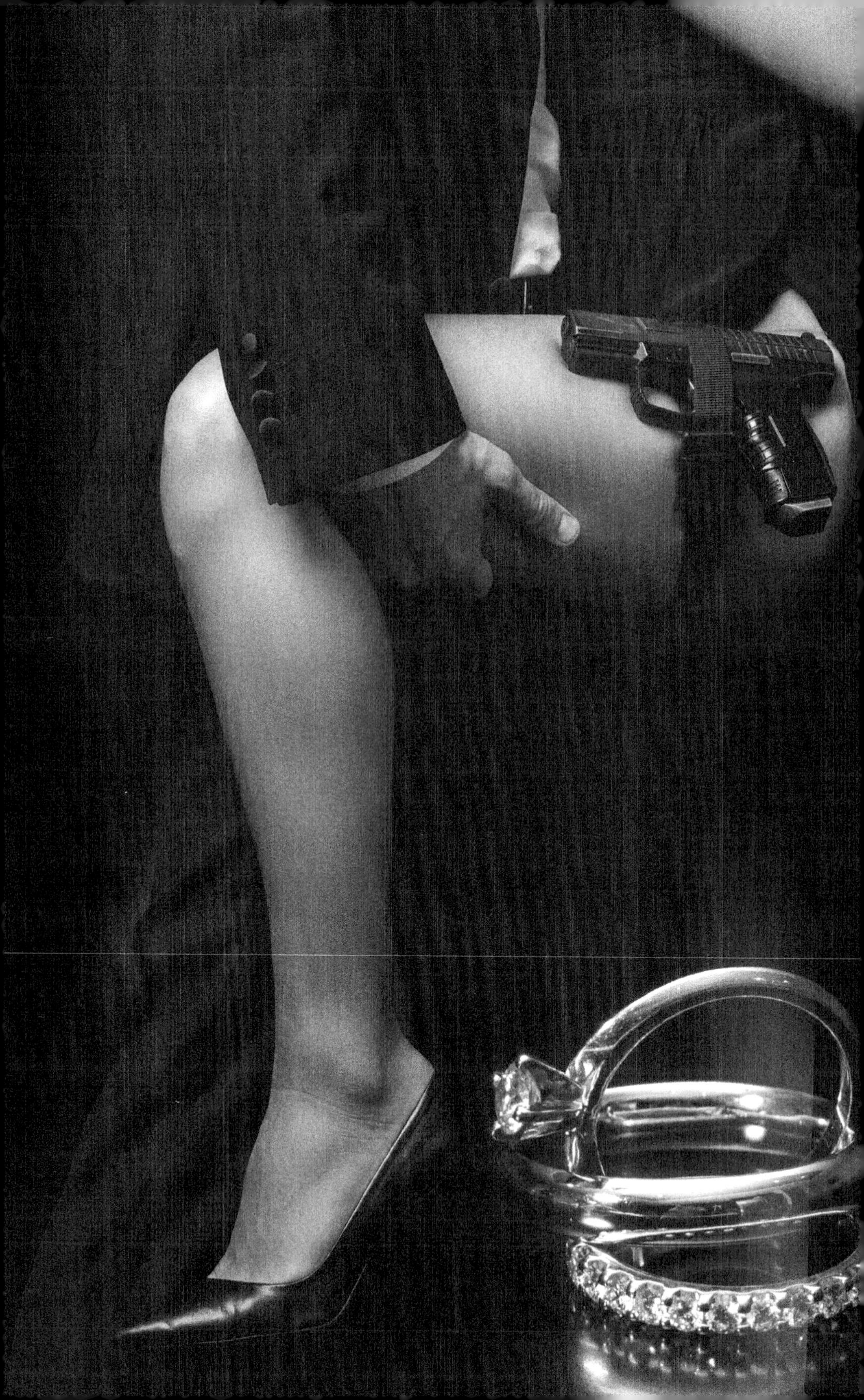

CHAPTER 15

Alaric

I lie on my side, running a finger up and down Layla's arm as she slumbers next to me. I swallow dryly as I stare at the perfect naked creature who is now my wife.

Wife.

I never thought that small word could hold such immense power over me, but it does. Just saying it out loud has my heart skipping a beat and my cock swelling painfully, needing to own her tight pussy once more and remind her she's mine.

But when Layla says it . . . then I'm fucking gone.

Unable to prevent it, I slide my other hand down my naked chest and wrap it around the base of my shaft, watching as her lips part in a sleepy smile. Groaning, I run my fist down the length, imagining plunging it into her hot little mouth. As if drawn by the sound, she purrs contentedly, slowly opening her eyelids to find me next to her already touching myself. I don't stop. I just keep leisurely stroking my cock as her lidded eyes drop to the sight and she gasps. I watch as she blinks twice, her tiny pink tongue darting out to wet her lips, and the sight makes my cock harden further in my grip. Having her gaze on me and seeing the arousal blooming across her face makes me speed up.

"Good morning, wife," I coo. I lean in to plant a tender kiss on her lips, tasting her sweetness. I squeeze the head of my cock to stop myself from coming from that one innocent touch.

"It is, isn't it?" She smiles shyly, reaching out to draw a tiny circle over my tattooed chest with her fingernail, right where the heart that beats her name lives.

I grunt at the light touch, needing her hands on me, needing more as I plow into her sweet, decadent cunt. It takes all the restraint I have and then some not to pick her up by her waist and plunge into that greedy little pussy with my weeping cock.

A part of me cringes for not having been gentle with her on our first night together. She came into our bedroom, wide-eyed and nervous, looking so fucking innocent and so unsure of what the night would hold. Yet her desire and curiosity drove her to give herself to me, willingly and passionately, and I made sure to take full advantage of all of it. I couldn't do anything but surrender. She's a siren, and I'm caught in her song—a trap I will willingly live in as long as I get to wake up with her in my arms forever and a day.

It only took one lick of her sweet cunt to know that no one had ever properly fucked her like she deserved. She was so starved for touch that even a chaste kiss along her soft skin had her undone beneath me. She was so responsive, so wet, and so willing to try everything to reach her pleasure, and when she clawed her nails into my back, I just lost it, rutting deep inside her until her womb was filled with my cum. The sight of it dripping from her raw, abused cunt is burned into my memory. I took her five more times after that, waking her throughout the night with my head between her silken thighs. I just couldn't get enough of her, and if she hadn't blacked out from her last orgasm, I probably would have fucked her five more times after that.

However, now in the light of day and faced with the marks I left on her frail body, I wonder if it was too much too soon. I skate my gaze over her lithe form and take stock of my lack of restraint. There are teeth marks around her succulent pink nipples and fresh bruises from my hands on her thighs. I can only imagine how her sweet pussy was stretched from the inside with my ten inches. The crown on my cock leaks at the vestiges of my claim on her, ready to do even worse and fuck her every which way until Sunday.

I'm a fucking sick man to get hard from the signs of my possessiveness, but I can't help it. I warned her that gentleness was not in my nature, yet I wonder if I can be for her. Maybe I can show her there is more to me than the rough man she has come to know.

"How sore are you, my love?" I ask, caressing her cheek, needing to know just how much damage I did to her inexperienced body last night.

She stretches on our bed, rolling like a kitten then inching closer to me, her teeth scraping on my jaw before planting a kiss on it.

"Deliciously sore," she purrs, her eyes heavy-lidded.

I weave my fingers in her hair and crane her neck back to look at me.

"Too sore to come on my tongue?"

She licks her lips, and pure lust burns in her emerald eyes as her body wiggles closer in invitation. "I don't think I'll ever be too sore for that," she whispers, her breath hitching.

"That's all I need to hear." I slap her ass, earning a little giggle from her. "Now be a good girl and jump on my face. I'm fucking ravenous, and you're my breakfast."

Even though she should be accustomed to my dirty mouth by

now, her cheeks blush a pretty shade of pink. One that has me wanting to corner her and share all the naughty things in my head at all times just to see her blush always stained there. Her hesitation to climb on me and give me what I want has me slapping her ass again, harder this time, with narrowed eyes.

"Argh," she whimpers, rubbing at her ass cheek as she pouts adorably.

"Don't make me wait, baby girl. If you do, sore or not, I'll fuck you raw until you can't walk. I'll spray every inch of you with my cum without letting you find release at all. Now, jump on my face and give me what's rightfully mine," I order, my voice sharp.

This time she doesn't falter, quickly sitting up on her knees. Her cheeks darken as she throws her leg over my neck and shimmies up until her pretty pink slit is poised above my greedy mouth. I take in her body, noticing her eyes are closed as she rests her head on the headboard and presses her hands to the wall to keep her steady. Smirking, I run my eyes over her dripping cunt, seeing the proof of her desire. She's already so drenched for me it practically trickles into my mouth. It was something she was embarrassed about last night, but me? I was overjoyed. The fact that she wants me just as badly as I want her?

Fucking heaven.

"Such a pretty little pussy," I praise, taking one long lick along the length of her slit.

The taste of her explodes on my tongue as I encircle my cock again and stroke it, unable to resist. I imagine my tight grip is her hot little cunt, but it's nowhere near close. I couldn't go back to just visualizing now, not after having her. My eyelids close of their own accord, her sweet nectar making me salivate like the feral animal she makes me.

Jesus.

I'll never get tired of this. Having her open for me, like the sweetest peach engulfing all my senses, is too much temptation for any man to say no to, let alone for a sinner like me.

"Hold onto something, baby. This may take a while," I warn, releasing my cock in favor of spreading her thighs wider for me.

Her hips roll on top of me, seeking more from my tongue. Unable to resist her body, I nibble on her throbbing clit, her breathing becoming shallower with every caress. She forgets all of her worries, just grinding down onto my mouth until I can barely breathe, but I'd die a happy man eating my wife like this. I scrape my teeth lightly over her sensitive nub, lapping up her juices as she starts slapping her hand on the wall, unable to keep the myriad of sensations wrecking her body contained. Her responsiveness to my touch is a heady feeling. Her little whimpers only heighten my arousal, and I eat her out with such fervor that all too soon her body begins to shake on top of me.

I slap her ass hard, the assault breaking her momentarily from her high, only for it to spark the sexual goddess I know lives inside her. She starts riding my face without any inhibition or embarrassment. Loving that Layla's timid barriers have crumbled, I let her fuck my face until she's close to stumbling over the precipice and shattering into a thousand little pieces. Her thighs begin to strangle me as the impending orgasm threatens to rip in her two, and like the twisted individual I am, I suck on my thumb before plunging into her small, puckered hole and then plow into her cunt with my tongue again.

"Alaric!" she wails, shaking above me as I fuck her good and proper with my tongue while my thumb defiles her ass.

The only thing that puts a damper on the whole erotic scene is that I can't see her face as she falls apart. My cock bobs in agony on my stomach, and precum coats my stomach as she falls into the wall, sated and trembling with aftershocks. Giving her pretty, tasty pussy one last lick, I pull my thumb free, making her whimper and fall back. I catch her and sit up, cradling her in my lap, feeling her round ass rubbing across my cock as she slumps into my form.

"That was . . . That was . . ." She's unable to find the words to describe what we just did.

"Perfect, wife. That's the word you're looking for." I smile, kissing the tip of her adorable nose.

"Yeah, perfect," she breathes, her gaze turning so soft that my heart literally breaks at its beauty.

I love her.

I've known it for a long time. It's a dangerous weakness for a man like me to have, but I could never resist Layla, and now that she is truly mine, I'll kill any motherfucker who tries to steal her away from me.

I did it once.

And I'd do it again in a heartbeat.

I lean in closer and press my lips to hers, loving how she parts them for me to truly claim every inch of her. I let her taste her release on my mouth to show her how fucking sweetly she came for me. When she deepens the kiss, her tongue ravishing mine, I pull away, knowing that if we continue on, then I'll end up fucking her shape into our mattress.

I try to ignore the hurt look she gives me for ending our kiss sooner than she would have liked.

"How about a quick shower before breakfast?" I smile, caressing her cheek with my knuckles.

Layla gives me a little conceding nod before nuzzling her face against my chest. I stand up from our bed, keeping a firm grip on the woman who has changed my life so completely. I stride to the bathroom and turn on the shower, holding her the entire time as it heats up. When steam fills the room and I'm happy with the temperature, I plant her feet on the tile floor of our shower. She lets out a relaxed sigh as the jets of water hit her tired limbs, but while Layla is good and content, my frown is stitched in place when I inspect the bruises decorating her creamy skin.

"What's wrong?" she questions, looking perplexed at the stern expression on my face.

"This doesn't bother you?" I ask, tweaking her nipples with my index finger and thumb before showing her my bite marks.

"No." She almost laughs, slicking back her hair as she tilts her head at me.

I grind my molars when I see the inside of her thighs also bear my mark.

"And this?" I snarl.

"No," she answers cheerfully.

I wrap my hand around her throat and drag her closer to me. Tilting her head back, I get in her face with a snarl on my lips and my eyes narrowed dangerously.

"If this marriage is going to work, Layla, you need to be honest with me. If there is anything I do that upsets or hurts you, I need to know."

She pushes up to the balls of her feet and places a tender kiss to my lips.

"You told me last night that you couldn't make love to me slow and gentle. I knew what I was getting into."

"Still—"

"Alaric, you're not listening to me. Last night was one of the best nights of my life. I don't say that lightly. Now shut up and take your shower. Zoey should be awake soon, and I need to make breakfast." She huffs in annoyance.

I pull my grip off her throat and let Layla do her thing. That dark side of me that whispers I shouldn't be left alone with nice pretty things continues to taunt me as she pours soap into her hands and runs it across her lithe body. When she repeats the action with shampoo to wash her hair, I'm still reprimanding myself for unleashing my most depraved urges on her. Layla stops rinsing the soapy suds off her creamy skin to gawk at me.

"You haven't even started," she begins, only to stop when she sees my hands curled into two tight fists at my sides.

Understanding washes over her, but instead of soothing my concerns, she pours a healthy amount of soap on her palms and begins to rub my chest with it. The lump in my throat refuses to go down as her gentle touch spreads all over my body. When her eyes fall to the hard, bobbing cock slapping against my stomach—I'm unable to resist her beauty, even in my anger and self-hatred—she throws me a mischievous grin.

"I know what you're thinking. You're thinking that you hurt me last night. That you're too much for me and that I can't handle a man like you. Let me show you just how wrong you are," she purrs, gliding her hand down to my stomach as she speaks.

Before I can get a word in, my jaw slackens as Layla falls to her knees before me, her tiny hands gripping my huge thighs. She digs her nails in slightly to hold me in place.

"What are you doing?" I croak, precum already coating the tip of my cock with how close her mouth is to it.

She throws me a little wink before wrapping her beautiful, luscious lips around my dick. Her movements are tentative and unsure, but so fucking perfect I slam my fist into the wall. Layla's eyes roll up to keep looking at me as she swallows me whole. The animal in me awakens as her gag reflex kicks in, so I weave my fingers through her hair and plunge down her throat. Tears fill her eyes and flow over her cheeks, and the sick part of me likes it.

"Why, Layla? Why tempt me like this? You already know what you're going to get," I snarl, fighting her hot little mouth as I fuck it hard and fast, giving her no choice but to hold onto my thighs.

A roar rips through me as I plunge my cock into her mouth over and over again. And just as I'm about to let her go, having proved my point, her hands skate around me and she digs her nails into my ass cheeks, preventing me from getting away. I hiss and stare in complete and utter awe as she keeps sucking me off like her life depends on it, her gaze never wavering from mine. Tears stream down her face, yet she never relents, never gives in—never surrenders.

This is what she's trying to tell me. She's not breakable, not fragile like fine china or some porcelain doll. She is made of flesh and bone and filled to the brim with hungry, dark desires that match my own. When she tips me over the edge with the way she starts humming around my steel length, her green eyes beam with triumph as she swallows every last drop of my release that I pump into her little mouth. She drinks it all, draining the strength and anger from me until my legs quiver. I have never come so hard or so fast. She leans back and pops her mouth from my softening cock, licking her lips clean of my release.

After I've returned from the nirvana she just gifted me, I pull her up and kiss her in a way that makes her knees weak once more, wanting her to experience an ounce of the pleasure she just gifted me.

"You've proven your point, wife," I confess, kissing her temple.

"Good," she whispers joyfully. "Now wash up. You've made me late for breakfast with your tantrum."

She sucks on my lower lip and gives it a bite before hopping out of the shower and going on her merry way. I can't help but laugh at the light she brings to my usual dark abyss. Not wanting to be away from her longer than I need to, I hurriedly wash and rinse my hair and jump out of the shower to get dressed. My mind is in a frenzied state, thinking of all the things we can do today, when my heart falls to the pit of my stomach with the sound of my phone ringing on my dresser. Still dripping with water, I pad naked over to it. My heart slows and coldness fills me, crushing my hope as I pick up the device and answer without a word. The familiar robotic voice on the other line steals any happiness I could have had today.

Goddamn it.

I hastily get dressed, my chest tightening when I enter our kitchen and see Layla cheerfully humming the same tune she had on my cock while stirring pancake mix in a bowl.

Shit.

I walk up behind her and wrap my arms around her waist, resting my chin on her shoulder.

"Unfortunately, I won't be able to stay for breakfast. A work thing came up that needs my attention. Shouldn't take too long though," I promise, and even I can hear the regret in my voice. I want to stay, I want to have breakfast with her, and never before have I ever been so torn.

"Hmm. Okay. I never did ask you what you do for a living." She sighs.

"Security," I reply instantly as she turns in my arms.

Her brows pinch together at my vague, one-word response.

I tip her chin up and deliver a kiss that has her forgetting all her doubts and questions.

"Here," I say, handing her my credit card. "Once Zoey wakes up and you both have breakfast, you two can go out and buy anything you need—clothes, shoes, toys, or just anything that will make this place feel like home."

Her nose crinkles at the black credit card, unsure if she should take it.

"Layla, take it," I order, my voice stern.

This time she relents and hides the plastic in her front pocket.

"Good girl," I praise before kissing the tip of her nose and rushing out the door.

"When will you be back?" she shouts behind me.

"As fast as I can, wife. As fast as I can," I yell back, closing our front door behind me.

The transformation comes over me as soon as I am out of her sight. Alaric her husband disappears, and cold ice flows through my veins, allowing me to do my job. I get into my car and drive like the wind to Brooklyn, praying that today's job will be quick and easy so I can come back home. The thought of turning down the job crossed my mind, but when I heard the password and the familiar digits and shuffled letters, I knew I couldn't. Although all my clients have their anonymity ensured, some like to use similar passwords so I can identify them as one of my most active clientele. This one in particular is responsible for half of my year's earnings, which means if I turned them down once, they wouldn't use my services again, branding me as unreliable.

And I can't have that.

My glowing reputation is my calling card.

If I piss off my biggest client, then the rest will also go in search of greener pastures.

Once I step into my brownstone, I rush to my office and go online to verify who my target is. The minute I read my client's portfolio on him, I groan in frustration. Apparently, I only have a small window to get the job done. My target is flying in from Zürich, making a pit stop at JFK, and then boarding the red-eye to California. If my calculations are right, then I have only a few hours to get the job done while he waits for his connecting flight. It's not going to be so cut and dry as I wish it were. JFK Airport sees an average of over five million passengers a day, and that's not to mention the other thirty-five thousand people it employs. The heavy security and police detail also throw kinks into making this an easy kill.

Fuck.

And on the first day of my honeymoon too.

Motherfuckers.

Whoever this guy is, he's going to pay for making me spend my day chasing his ass instead of my blushing bride's.

I list all the things I will need and book a midnight flight out of state as my way to get past security and into the boarding area. Guns and knives aren't going to cut it today, so I have to go with an old favorite that will ensure no one is the wiser to my true intentions. I run upstairs to my room and pile some old clothes into a duffel bag to add to the illusion I'm going for. Once I've triple checked that I have everything, I change into ripped jeans and a leather jacket to look the part of a traveling musician going to his next gig. I grab my duffel bag and the precious guitar case that holds my weapon of choice for today and head to JFK.

Unfortunately, when I get there, my target's flight from Zürich has been delayed three hours, which only decreases the time I have to get the fucker alone before he boards his next flight. I take a seat and wait it out, cracking my tense neck every so often. I'm not usually this antsy when doing a job. In fact, I can usually count on my nerves of steel to keep my heart rate down and my mind level-headed throughout.

But not today.

Today, I'm not the cold, calculating monster I should be.

Instead, my blood is boiling and I'm pissed at the world that I have to be here instead of where I really want to be—home with my wife.

I wonder if she took my advice to heart and went shopping with Zoey. A tug of a smile curves my lips as I recall how she took the credit card from me like it was going to bite her. I know she isn't used to people taking care of her, or even showering her with attention, but she'll get used to it. I vow I'm going to pamper the fuck out of her, and that one day, she'll wake up and forget she ever lived any other way. I also have to get some more meat on her bones. I love Layla exactly as she is, and I wouldn't change a goddamn thing, but she isn't skinny by choice or because of her metabolism. My girl is skin and bones because she's missed more meals than those poor homeless beggars that used to go into her diner in the hope she'd give them some soup.

The memory of how she would sneak them a bowl or sandwich when no one was looking is one that cuts deep inside me. Layla didn't bat an eye at stealing when it was to feed someone else, but when it came down to putting food in her own belly, she just couldn't do it, preferring to go hungry rather than taking something that didn't belong to her.

That shit is going to change.

My thoughts on Layla are brought to an unexpected halt when the display screen holding the flight information announces the arrival of the Zürich flight. A crack of a smile pulls at the corner of my lips when I realize that just thinking about my new bride made the hours fly by.

Hours that I could have spent with her.

My grin falls instantly off my face at the thought, and all the warm feelings I had disappear. In their place, resentful fury prevails.

I get up from my seat and pretend to aimlessly walk about until I find the man who brought me to this hellhole to begin with. He looks like your ordinary, run-of-the-mill banker, in his expensive suit and the ugliest Italian loafers I've ever set eyes on. I keep my distance from him, biding my time until I see my opening.

A little known fact I picked up about people who travel by plane is that not many are willing to use the bathroom forty thousand feet up in the air if they can prevent it. Even if it is a six-hour flight, most will do their best to hold it in like a good little virgin on prom night, while others give up the fight, drop their panties to their ankles, and get fucked. Since the idea of being bare-assed in a tiny cubicle in a flying death trap isn't everyone's cup of tea, it's very common that before passengers reach their gate, they make a quick pit stop at the bathroom to relieve themselves before takeoff. Judging by the way my target is guzzling down his Starbucks venti, I'd say he has about ten minutes before he's scouring the airport for the nearest can.

Just like clockwork, Mr. Ugly-Ass Loafers gets up from his seat and rushes to the nearest bathroom he can find. Taking this as my cue, I stroll after him, grab the out-of-service door tag from inside my jacket, and hang it on the knob before closing and locking the door behind me.

The sound of him whistling while he takes a piss irks me, yet I play my part and go to one of the urinals, pretending to take a leak. I zip back up and wash my hands just as he flushes the john and walks over to a nearby sink to do the same. Staring at my reflection in the mirror, I take a few paper towels to dry my hands before putting on my leather gloves. My heartbeat slows to an even rhythm as I grab my guitar wire from my pocket, waiting for the perfect moment to attack.

When he shuts off the tap and is about to pass me to get some paper towels, I wrap the metal garrote around his neck and pull. His eyes bulge from their sockets, and he tries to gasp for air as I pull him into a nearby stall. I close the toilet seat with my foot and use it for leverage. His loafers skate on the tile as he digs his fingers into his neck to pull the metal collar off him.

"Wife," he wheezes, spitting saliva every which way. "My wife."

"I wouldn't be talking about wives if I were you. I missed the whole day with mine because of your sorry ass," I growl, adding more pressure to the wire.

"Kids," he begs, his face turning purple from the lack of oxygen.

"Yeah, I've got one of those too, buddy. Sorry. Just isn't your day."

"Please," he wheezes, clawing at the wire.

Jesus H. Christ, I got a fucking talker on my hands.

Having had enough of his pitiful pleas for mercy, I twist the wire, pull it exactly at the precise spot where his spine joins the base of the neck, and break the fucker in one tight go.

Finally, some quiet.

I hold him under his shoulders and place the poor bastard on the toilet, taking a quick pic as proof to send to my employer, declaring another job well done. It's only as I'm buckling my seatbelt inside my car that his last words give me pause.

Wife. Kids.

A month ago, those words wouldn't have made a dent in my resolve. Today, however, I'm left here sitting in my car thinking about how his family will soon get the call that Mr. Ugly-Ass Loafers will never be coming home again. I rub at the light pang in my chest, imagining Layla and Zoey getting such a message.

Our little family has barely started, and my self-sabotaging mind is already going to a dark place where everything I hold dear is stolen away from me.

Fuck that.

I know what I am.

I'm a bad man who does even worse things, but like hell will I let any motherfucker steal my happiness away from me just by killing me.

Do I deserve my little family? Probably not.

I'm a killer without a shred of remorse, so to claim that I'm the best that Layla and Zoey could wish for in their lives is a fucking joke. I know they deserve better than me.

But will I fight tooth and nail to keep them? You're fucking right I will.

After returning to Brooklyn to clean up and change, I rush home, needing to wrap my arms around my wife and forget this horrid day ever happened. However, the minute my key turns in the lock, I know something is wrong. All the lights are turned off, except for the amber glow coming from the dining room. I stagger as I make my way there, finding Layla at the head of the dining table with untouched food on the plate in front of her.

Shit.

She made me a candlelit dinner.

Fuck.

With her head still bowed, she fidgets in her seat, gripping the hem of her dress.

"Where were you?" she asks softly, so softly I could hear a pin drop.

It breaks my fucking heart.

I'm a bastard.

"Work. I told you that before I left this morning," I whisper.

"It's after one in the morning, Alaric. Who works sixteen hours straight and doesn't have time to call or text his supposed wife that he won't make it home for dinner?" she snaps, her anger bubbling to the surface.

A hit man, baby. That's who.

"I'm sorry. It won't happen again," I respond evenly.

She raises her head and looks at me, her forlorn expression piercing a hole into my heart.

"I'm being silly, aren't I? I know I am. We don't know each other. Why should I expect anything from you? Especially something as stupid as a phone call," she replies, laughing nervously while shaking her head.

She stands and grabs the two plates of food before passing me and heading toward the kitchen. I follow her in and watch silently as she tosses the cold broiled salmon and vegetables into a trash can, kicking at it in frustration.

"You know, before I met you, I never would have done that—thrown perfectly good food away like that. But I can't bear to store it either. It only reminds me of how foolish I was to be excited to make dinner for you. Why should I care if you eat or not? Why should I care about anything related to you? I don't know you. I know nothing about you!" Her heated voice cracks at the end as I lunge over to her and grab her throat, pinning her to our kitchen island.

"Layla, listen to me," I growl, her penetrating gaze throwing daggers my way. "I'm not the type of man who apologizes for shit, so if I say I'm sorry, that's because I mean it."

Her fury starts to deflate, but only by a fraction. I take a long inhale, and her sweet scent gives me the courage I need to be honest with her.

"I want you. From the first time I laid eyes on you, I have wanted you. Now, to be able to call you my wife fills me with utter awe and pride. But you're not the only one who is new to this whole marriage thing. I've been on my own for a long time. I haven't had anyone worry over me or wonder where I am or if I've even eaten. I haven't had anyone care in a long fucking time, Layla."

"Well, now you do," she murmurs, her green eyes watering with hurt.

"I'll do better. I'll be better. I promise," I insist, releasing my grip from her throat. My heart aches at the thought of hurting her, at her waiting for me, at maybe losing her before I've even really had her.

Her shoulders slump as she worries her lip.

Even though it pains me to do so, I step away from her and give her some space. She fiddles with the hem of her dress once more, and this time I take stock of what she's wearing—a simple yet elegant sleeveless knitted dress that ends just below the knee.

"Is this new?"

She looks down at her cream dress and nods. "I only bought this one. Zoey and I spent most of the day buying school supplies for her to start school next Monday," she answers distractedly.

"Where is little Zoey?" I curl my hands to stop myself from reaching for her again, even though I'm silently begging her to look at me. To bridge this distance and touch me. To prove we are okay.

"Asleep, Alaric. Like I said, it's fucking one in the morning. How many twelve-year-olds do you know who stay up this late?"

Pissed, she turns her back on me, pressing her palms flat on the kitchen island to ensure she doesn't use those sharp nails on me—but fuck if the edge of fury in her tone doesn't make me want her to.

I lick my lips and lean closer, my swollen cock fitting perfectly in the crack of her ass. With my hands on her waist, I hide my head in the crook of her neck, inhaling her decadent scent.

"What's the real reason you're pissed at me, baby? Is it because

I didn't call, that I fucked up your dinner plans, or because deep down you missed me?" I question.

She brushes my hair back to look at my face.

"Honestly? Maybe . . . maybe the latter."

"Does that scare you?" I ask, wanting to know.

She nods.

"Yeah, that's what I thought, baby girl. It scares me too," I admit.

"Your hair's wet," she says matter-of-factly, and after a long pause, her brows pinch together as she runs her fingers through my freshly showered hair.

"Got caught in the rain," I lie, making a mental note to dry my fucking hair before I come home next time.

In retrospect, I didn't even need to shower tonight, but I could still feel my kill's stench of desperation in my pores and I didn't want to taint Layla's creamy skin with the filth.

"You're changing the subject," I interject, wanting to move past my mishap.

"Am I?"

"Hmm," I hum, nibbling on her neck. "You can say it, love. You're fucking pissed at me because you spent your day fantasizing about my fat cock fucking you raw, and I took my sweet ass time coming home to give you what you need."

"Did anyone ever tell you that you're full of yourself?" she rebukes, but the way her ass presses eagerly against my cock tells me she's just as needy as I am.

"The only thing that's going to be full is your tight cunt in about ten seconds. Now be a good girl and show me what's mine."

I palm her ass before hiking her dress up to her waist. Seeing the drenched splotch in the center of her panties makes me wild. Even when she's mad at me, she wants me. I rip them off her and throw them to the floor.

"Alaric," she whimpers in protest, but she knows as well as I do that this is happening.

"Bend over, wife. Let me see what I've been missing all day."

She leans onto the kitchen island, giving me a perfect view of her ass. I kick at her heels, making her spread her legs wide so her glistening pussy is also on display. Without a second to lose, I kneel and lick her from her clit to her crack. The little moan that escapes her is the cutest thing ever, but tonight I'm more inclined to hear her scream in ecstasy instead.

I'll beg for forgiveness with my head in her cunt and her taste on my tongue.

I dig my fingers into her thighs as my tongue plays with her clit and dives into her juices until my chin is coated in her cream. I eat her out like she's the greatest meal she could have ever prepared for me. Starved for her, I plunge my tongue into her hot wet core, becoming even more ravenous with how her pussy clenches around it.

Fuck!

I could eat her for days and still never be fully satisfied, needing more of her sweetness. More of her hunger. More of her.

"Alaric, please," she pleads, her knees threatening to buckle.

I stand up, grab each breast from behind, and pinch her taut nipples.

"Tell me what you want, wife. Use your words and it's yours. Just say it."

"I . . . I . . ." She hesitates, humping her wet slit on my crotch.

"Say it, baby. Remember, there is no shame in telling your husband what you want. It's only you and me, Layla. Say it."

"I need you inside me," she whispers.

"Not good enough, my love. Give me more," I order, placing wet kisses on her neck while I tease her breasts over her dress to the point of pain.

"God! Just fuck me, Alaric! Please!" she yells angrily.

I smile against her neck, giving it a bite while releasing my aching cock. She whimpers in my arms as my crown finds her soaked center.

"Is this what you want, wife? What's been missing from your day?"

"Yes," she mewls, biting into her lower lip so hard it pierces the flesh.

I grab her chin and capture her mouth with mine, sucking the droplets of blood onto my tongue as my cock inches inside of her. She's still so fucking tight. After the nightlong fuck session we had last night, her pussy still feels like it could strangle my cock in her hot, wet vise. Since I know she's still sore, I try my best to go slow, but my temptress has different plans. In one forceful push, she falls back onto my cock until it's at its hilt.

Fuck!

"Oh God!" she screams, her cunt swallowing me whole.

"So fucking impatient," I growl, pounding into her with my merciless thrusts. "You couldn't let me try to be at least a little gentle, could you?"

She shakes her head and then lets it fall to my shoulder, her heavy-lidded eyes burning with the same needy desire that pollutes my bloodstream.

"I don't want gentle. I want you."

This woman is going to kill me.

"You have me, baby. You fucking have me," I profess, wrapping her hair around my wrist and pushing her back down until her cheek is firmly pressed against the cold marble. "And I have you. Every inch of you," I add, trailing my gaze up her long legs, thighs, and ass, watching my girthy cock being swallowed by her pink cunt. "And one day," I say, dragging a finger down her slit and coating it with her arousal, "I'll fuck every inch of you. Your pretty mouth, this needy pussy, and your tight ass. All of you, mine for the taking."

She tries to arch her back when my digit penetrates her puckered hole, but my hand on her lower back prevents her from moving. Her legs begin to shake, the sensation of being full too much for her to handle. My ruthless thrusts speed up, and when I think she's prime enough to take it, I add another finger. On a loud cry, she yells out my name, her pussy strangling my cock in such a way that white spots cloud my vision. The earth-shattering orgasm blinds me as her cunt milks me dry, my cum dripping down her thighs from the sheer quantity of it all. I fall limply on top of her, my gaze catching her incandescent smile of pure happiness.

Perfection.

This woman was made for me in every way imaginable.

Her beautiful selfless heart.

Her sassy mouth that's quick to put me in my place.

And her gorgeous body that can take a beating of this magnitude and still be insatiable for more.

If there was ever any lingering doubt in my mind that this woman—my wife—owned my ass, then there isn't anymore.

I'm as much hers as she is mine.

CHAPTER 16

Layla

Being a housewife is . . . well, in one word, boring.

What do people do all day? I wake up in Alaric's arms, usually with him touching and kissing me, then he blows my mind and leaves me in bed as he showers and gets ready. When I can finally drag my jelly legs out of bed, I wash up, get dressed, and dry my hair before getting Zoey ready for school since she started back last week. So far, she's loving it, but I still worry since she's not fully recovered. I guess I'll always worry about her even when she's totally healed.

After I cook her a full breakfast, I walk her to school, ignoring her protests that she's old enough to walk alone. We might live in a better neighborhood than we did in Hell's Kitchen, but I'm not taking any chances.

But after that, I have nothing.

Alaric goes to work, doing whatever he does—which, don't even get me started on, since getting anything from that man that doesn't include a kiss or his cock is futile. I might sleep next to him every night, eat and play together as a family, and do all the things a husband and wife do, yet I hardly know anything about him. I thought time would help, but I'm slowly realizing he's a closed book that refuses to open. I just wish I knew how to get him to open up to me. He shouldered so many of my burdens, and yet he lets me help with none of his.

Drumming my fingers on the spotless worktop, I look at the clock again. I have five hours until Zoey is finished. What to do? I've already tidied and cleaned from floor to ceiling. I like to keep busy, and I'm used to working, but now I have nothing to do and the change is jarring.

When the front door suddenly opens, I jerk upright and rush through the foyer to see Alaric coming in. "Hi," I greet almost shyly.

He has no such reservations. He grins and yanks me closer, kissing me hard. Once Alaric pulls back, I'm breathless and blinking.

"Hey, baby girl, how's your day?"

"Good," I hedge.

He tilts his head and observes me carefully, his blue eyes locking me in place as if he's pulling back every layer of secrets I possess. "Layla," he warns.

Sighing, I wrap my arms around myself. "I don't want to seem ungrateful. I love the house and the life you've given us . . ."

"But?" he prompts nervously.

"But I'm bored," I blurt, wincing. "There's only so much cleaning I can do and TV I can watch. I'm used to working and being helpful. I just feel lost and a bit useless," I finally admit.

The slow grin that crawls across his lips has me huffing.

"What?" I snap.

"You could never be useless, baby girl. You want to do something? Then do it. Get a job if you want. You don't need to, but I understand that drive, the need to work, so do whatever you want."

"You mean it?" I perk up.

"Layla, you're not a prisoner here. You're my wife. I want to see you happy. Hell, go back to school if you want." He shrugs before wrapping me in his big arms. I melt like always. I may not know all of his secrets, but my body knows his.

"College?" I murmur. "But I didn't even finish high school."

"Precisely my point. Get your GED and then apply to college." He kisses my head and continues to hold me. "Why not? You're smart enough to get into NYU; I'm sure of it. You are smart enough to do anything you set your mind to, baby girl, and I will support you with whatever you want to do."

"What about tuition?" I ask softly.

"The day I married you, I told you I would take care of you and your sister's every need. Why would you going to college be any different from what I offered?" He frowns and pulls back to look at me, seemingly upset about my question.

"I know, I just . . . I don't want to feel like a burden to you," I murmur. "You've given us so much."

"And you've given me more."

"I've given you nothing." I scoff, turning and starting to walk away. He catches my hand and yanks me back to him. His chest presses against my back as he wraps his hand around my throat, squeezing. Alaric steals my air, and I wiggle as desire floods my veins at that dominant, confident move.

"You've given me a family," he murmurs, licking up my neck. "A home." He presses a gentle kiss to my pulse. "You've given me your body." I jerk and he chuckles, licking the shell of my ear until he's basically all that's holding me up as my pussy weeps. "You've given me a future, given me a life beyond my world.

You've given me everything, Layla, and you don't even realize it."

Kissing me one more time, he unwinds his arms and I stumble forward. Luckily, he catches me and sets me upright. "I forgot something for work. I won't be back too late though. Think about what you want to do, and remember, you can do anything in this world. I mean it, anything. You've got it all at your fingertips, baby girl, you just have to be brave enough to take it."

He leans in and kisses me once more before he disappears upstairs, leaving me staring after him. My hand drifts to the warmth on my lips as if to capture it forever, his words ringing inside my head.

Is he right?

Can I do anything?

Endless possibilities stretch before me.

It's both terrifying and exciting, and I turn and rush to the computer.

He's right, I'm still thinking like the old Layla. We've started fresh, and the new me can do anything, so what am I waiting for?

* * *

Alaric always keeps his promises. It's one thing I'm coming to love about him. He's not home late tonight so he cooks for us, laughing and joking with Zoey as she watches. I nurse a small glass of red wine, unable to stop the smile on my lips.

She's happy; she's laughing. There's no more worry or pain for her. She's adapted to this life like she was built for it, and it only assures me I did the right thing.

Alaric catches my eye and winks as he picks her up and spins her around before placing her on the counter to try the pasta he's making.

How did I get so lucky?

How could someone go from being a complete stranger to . . . this?

To everything?

After eating together like a proper family—something Zoey said—I take a bath. When I get out, I can't find either of them, so I wander to Zoey's room. I stop outside her door, and my mouth drops open in shock. I lean against the doorframe, silently watching.

He's perched on the edge of her bed which she's tucked into. "Please?" she begs, thrusting a book at him.

"Aren't you too old for bedtime stories, kid?"

"Nope." She pops the P on the end, pushing the book into his lap while wiggling excitedly under the covers.

She is too old for it, and we all know it.

But even though she's probably just messing with him, pushing the boundaries to see exactly how far he's willing to go, there is also an expectant twinkle in her eyes that says she hopes he'll submit to her every wish and be the father figure she has been deprived of all her life.

He hesitates, and he's obviously uncomfortable, but since it's obvious he can't seem to deny her anything, he takes the book out of her hands. Cracking it open, he clears his throat and starts to read, leaning his back against her bed frame. He gets so into it he switches voices and does hand gestures. It's adorable to watch, and Zoey's face just lights up. She giggles and urges him on, and it's the happiest I've ever seen her. She's a child again, not a solemn, worried, too old for her age, but an actual child.

And for that alone, I owe him everything.

He was wrong. I didn't give him a family or a future; he gave me one.

Eventually the story finishes and he closes the book. "Another?" she begs.

He grins and leans in. "Tomorrow?" he promises.

"I'll hold you to that," she retorts but settles down. "Goodnight, Ric."

He stills at the nickname, a bright, wide smile growing on his handsome face. "Goodnight, little Zoey." He stands and freezes when he spots me.

"Thank you," I mouth.

Winking, he turns off the light and wraps me in his arms. "Come on, baby girl, time for bed." There is no ulterior motive in that, yet my pussy clenches.

Stepping back, I smirk at him confidently. I need to show him that I crave him.

Need him.

"You'll have to catch me first," I dare and turn to race up the stairs. I hear his laugh as he gives me a head start.

"I'm coming, little Layla, and when I catch you, you're mine!" he yells, and then I hear his booted feet as he sprints after me. He's faster than I could have imagined, and I giggle as I slide down the hallway.

I should have known he would catch me. His arms wrap around my waist just as I reach the door to our room, lifting me easily off my feet. "Got you," he growls in my ear. "Now . . . what should I do with you?"

"Fuck me, I hope," I purr as he turns me. I wrap my legs and arms around him, grinning as he marches us into our bedroom and shuts the door without even looking.

"That's always the plan, love," he replies, and the next thing I know, I'm spun. I expect to land on the bed, but instead, my feet hit the carpet and my chest is pressed to the glass windows that line the front of our room. The contrast of the cool panes against my overheated skin makes me jolt and gasp as I push back into him. The desire I've been feeling since he handed me my future with a quick kiss and a promise, coupled with watching his caring nature with Zoey . . . Well, let's just say I've been a bundle of nerves all afternoon. My panties have been damp for hours as I've tried to ignore my need for this man.

This man who awoke a deep, carnal part of me—a part of me that makes me nothing more than a wet fucking woman around him who constantly craves his touch, his cock, his kiss.

And he knows it. He knows how badly I want him. He uses it like a weapon against me, teasing me until I almost combust and beg him to fuck me, but unlike other men, he isn't afraid to show me just how much he needs me too. He wants me just as badly.

Nothing with him is shameful. He owns every inch of his desire for me, and that is fucking addictive, even more than the mind-blowing orgasms he gives me every single time. Now, however, rather than slow, drawn-out fucking, I need a quick, satisfying, hard fuck to fill this void I've had all day without him.

Afterwards, we can do it slowly, but right now?

I need him inside of me more than I need my next breath.

"Alaric," I whisper, knowing what his name on my lips does to him. Staring out at the city lights, I groan when his huge hands press to the glass on either side of my head, pinning me in place. I should feel weak, trapped, but if anything, I feel safe. Excited. He offers me that when he's around—a space to relax and enjoy.

"Layla, you drive me crazy. Do you know what you do to me?"

Isn't that what I was just thinking?

He nudges my head, turning it to the side so he can run his nose along my neck to my ear where he bites. "I need you every minute of every day. You're all I think about in every waking moment. Even my dreams are filled with the taste and feel of you. I can't even concentrate at work," he finishes, kissing my neck again with a groan.

"I get wet whenever you even look at me," I admit, feeling brave since I'm not looking at him. He knows every inch of my body, including what makes me scream and what makes me laugh. He knows the stories behind any scars, like when I fell and sliced my foot at work. In this, we know each other better than anyone else. It gives me confidence and makes me own my desire for him. "Like now, I'm dripping." Reaching up, I grasp his hand and drag it down my body, sliding it under my dress to my panties.

He groans in my ear, pushing my hand aside and taking over. Alaric strokes those long, thick fingers across the wet material. "Fuck, I love how wet you get for me."

He must be feeling impatient too, because his fingers push aside my underwear and glide along my wetness. "Spread your legs for me, baby girl," he orders, and like the good, orgasm greedy girl I am, I do.

I use the glass to hold myself up while those talented fingers drag down my pussy, circle my hole, and then move back up to my clit. He flicks it, making me cry out. "That's it, let me hear you," he murmurs into my ear. He taps it over and over, alternating between that and slowly pushing a finger inside me.

But it's not enough.

I want faster, harder.

"Alaric, I need you to make me come," I demand, knowing he'll listen, and just like that I'm rewarded for asking for what I want, which makes me realize that's what he was waiting for.

He rips himself away with a snarl, one that has me clenching as

I remember all the ways this man has fucked me, claimed me, filled me, and stained my skin with his cum. Every time I look at him, I'm dripping wet, waiting for the next thing he will show me.

"Please," I beg, knowing he likes it when I'm vocal. I wiggle my ass and push it out. His deep, heavy breathing flows across my neck, and then suddenly his warmth is gone.

"Don't fucking move or I'll take that innocent little ass instead of your pussy and watch my cum drip from it," he calls, moving farther away into the room. The dirty words have me gasping as I imagine just that. The thought shouldn't turn me on, but as usual with Alaric, everything he says does.

He chuckles like he knows that, the cocky bastard.

Turning my head, I press my overheated cheek to the glass, letting it cool my skin as I wait. I grow cold and impatient as I hear him rummaging around for something.

"Aha," he murmurs, and then I hear his footsteps approach me and his warmth returns, pressed to my back along with something . . . cold. He trails it down my arm and across my side. "I got you a present today."

"You did?" I whisper, leaning into him.

"Yes, do you want to know what?" There's a challenge in his tone that has me considering it for a split second, but the truth is I want everything he has to offer.

"Yes," I purr as that coldness drags across my ass. When it touches my wet pussy, I shudder with a groan.

"It will feel so good, baby girl," he promises. "When I saw it, I knew I had to try it on you. I want to hear you scream because of it and watch you come apart again and again. I want to feel it around my cock as you drench it with that sweet release."

His words almost cause me to stiffen in anticipation, wondering what the gift is, but then suddenly, I know.

There's a low hum, and something wraps around my engorged clit. It feels like a gentle suction. The vibrations nearly have my eyes crossing, and my empty cunt clamps down as I fall farther forward. "Oh my God, what is that?" I murmur breathlessly.

The suction suddenly increases, like his mouth when he eats my cunt, but it's so much more. It's stronger, demanding pleasure from every corner of my being. My entire focus is drawn to my clit as I rock my hips, unable to stop myself from chasing the orgasm I can already feel building.

"It has different speeds. Let's see, shall we?"

And then it increases again.

The speed has my release slamming through me so sharply it's almost painful, shocking me at its intensity as my body jerks from the force.

The roaring inferno of my release surges through me so hard I swear I fall, but luckily Alaric is there to catch me. He holds me up, even as that pressure carries on. It's slower now, but it's enough that my orgasm doesn't truly abate. Instead, the rolling pressure simply builds back up again.

"Oh my fucking God," I whisper over and over, rolling my hips even as I try to stop. Each movement pushes me back into him. "Please, oh God, stop. No! Don't stop."

"I don't intend to, not until I see you come at least five more times. I want this little toy dripping with it before I suck it clean, wife."

The suction stays at that low hum, slowly building the pressure until I'm fucking myself against it. My abused clit almost aches, but it feels so fucking good. Except . . . I feel so empty. I need him inside me. I need to feel him stretching me and pounding into me at the same time.

"Alaric, fuck me now!" I cry out.

"Want to know another cool feature?" he murmurs instead as I whine in annoyance. He ignores that too. "It has a suction cup, so it can stick to walls, floors . . . windows." The pressure on my pussy spins, and when I push back, I look down to see a black and gold bullet as he sticks it to the window. His lithe hand releases it, and the device stays in place, tormenting my clit as his fingers fill my cunt once more. He thrusts them inside of me, twisting and turning and stretching me out. It sends me over the edge again. I come, screaming into the glass as I clamp around his fingers, and yet he doesn't turn it off. That infernal hum continues on, not letting me relax, and as soon as the wave of release is over, it's working on the next.

It's almost too much, but I couldn't stop it even if I tried.

Right now, I belong to Alaric, and he's acting like a possessive alpha who's taking what he wants.

"Good girl," he praises as his fingers pull from my fluttering channel. I hear him sucking them clean, and the thought makes me shiver. "Fuck, I'll never get enough of how you taste. I thought I knew heaven, but I was wrong. It's right here between these pretty thighs, and it's all mine."

"Please," I whine, dropping my head forward even as I push down into the suction. It's still not enough.

I need his cock.

He brushes his hand up my arm to my shoulder and then wraps his fingers around my neck as if to control me. He squeezes just enough to remind me that it's up to him when he takes me and when I come. Alaric controls me, and he's fucking torturing me and enjoying it.

I didn't even hear him get undressed, but I feel his hard cock pressing against my ass cheeks, his precum leaving a warm, wet trail across my skin. "I'll fuck you when I'm good and ready. Again."

"Again?" I repeat.

"Come again," he demands, tightening his grip around my throat as his other hand reaches down. I go to protest, already knowing what he's going to do, but I'm too late. He cranks up the speed, and just like that, I'm screaming into another release. I fall into the glass as my legs give out, black edging my vision from the strength of it.

Just as quickly as he sped it up, he lowers it again, and then his cock is pressing against my entrance and pushing inside, fighting my tight, fluttering channel. "So fucking wet. Goddamn, baby girl, I love the way you feel around my cock. So perfect, so fucking made for me."

He pushes in one hard inch at a time, stretching my cunt around him and forcing me firmer against the windows. That low hum still vibrates around my abused clit, and the pain and pleasure are too much. I'm nothing but a dripping, wordless mess as I take his cock.

I take it like the good girl he calls me. He bottoms out inside me, his balls slapping against my skin as he holds me in place with his body. He uses his grip on my neck to control me as he pulls out and slams back in, thrusting me into the windows from the force—yet not even that dislodges the toy. In fact, it hits a new angle that has me crying out and writhing from the pleasure.

Snarling in my ear, he bites down on my neck as he fucks me, filling me with his cock. His grip tightens as he releases his teeth and laves the bite with his tongue, taking away the sting.

"I fucking love your body and the way your cunt grips me like it never wants to let go. The little noises you make every time I push into you, the way this plump ass begs for my cock." He groans and speeds up, giving me everything I wanted, only on his terms.

"Alaric!" I scream as another orgasm rips through me, weaker than the rest but still there.

"Look out at the city, at what you can have. Any of it. All of it. All of me," he snarls, fighting my body. "It's all yours, Layla, and you?" His hand tightens on my throat. "You are all mine."

He pummels into me, hammering his massive cock into my raw, abused cunt. The pain melts into pleasure, and that low suction brings me to the edge again, but surely I can't, can I?

"Look at it, look at this world—the one I'm giving you," he demands, cutting off my air supply. I snap my eyes open, looking at the lights and the people walking below us, oblivious to the scene playing out above them. "If they look up, they will see you taking my cock like the dirty bitch you are, see you begging for me and loving it. They will see this tight little body plastered to my window."

Oh fuck.

His words fade into grunts, the sound of our bodies slapping together filling the room. My breasts are smashed against the glass so hard I can barely breathe, and my lungs scream for air as he continues to pound into me from behind. My pussy is so wet it squelches with every thrust, dripping down my thighs and his cock.

"I can't," I whimper. "I can't come again."

"You can and will," he snarls, grabbing my ass with his other hand and squeezing to the point of pain. "Now!" he yells, and just like that, I do.

I scream into the glass, almost blacking out from the force. I feel him thrust once, twice more before he stills, grunting into my ear as his warm cum fills me.

I remain in place, pinned on his cock and the vibrating toy, as tears slide down my mottled cheeks.

"Such a good girl," he murmurs as he pulls free of my body. He switches off the toy and pulls it from my abused clit, rubbing the bundle of nerves slowly as if to make it better. I fall backwards and he catches me, lifting me into his arms and turning us, but not before I see the prints all over the glass. For some reason, it makes me smile as I close my eyes and snuggle into his arms as he brings us to the bed.

I don't rest for long. I just lie here with my eyes closed as I float in the warmth and afterglow until I force my eyes open to see him watching me. He pulls me across his body so I'm sprawled over him, and then he strokes my cheek.

"You make me weak, Layla," he whispers.

"Is that a bad thing?" I murmur, watching him.

"Sometimes," he admits. "But I wouldn't trade it for the world."

I don't know what to say, so I don't talk. I just close my eyes and float again, even napping for a little bit.

Lying in his arms with our legs tangled, I feel free and happy. I was so scared of being his, but I've never regretted it at all. And in this moment, as I feel his heart race under my head while I stroke his strong, silky chest, tracing his tattoos, a truly happy smile blooms on my lips.

I've spent so long working, running, and living in the moment to provide for Zoey, I've never taken any time for myself, but then Alaric entered my life. He gave me everything I could ever want and need. But better than that, he gave me the ability to fall back in love with myself and finally dream of a future, and not just for Zoey, but for myself.

"I'd like you to meet someone," he murmurs, his chest rising beneath me. His hands tighten on my waist, stroking it like he needs the strength.

Lifting my head, I pop my chin on his pec and stare into his bright blue eyes.

"Who?" I ask curiously.

He swallows and searches my face before lifting his hand and stroking my cheek lovingly. I lean into the touch; I can't help it. "My father," he whispers.

His father?

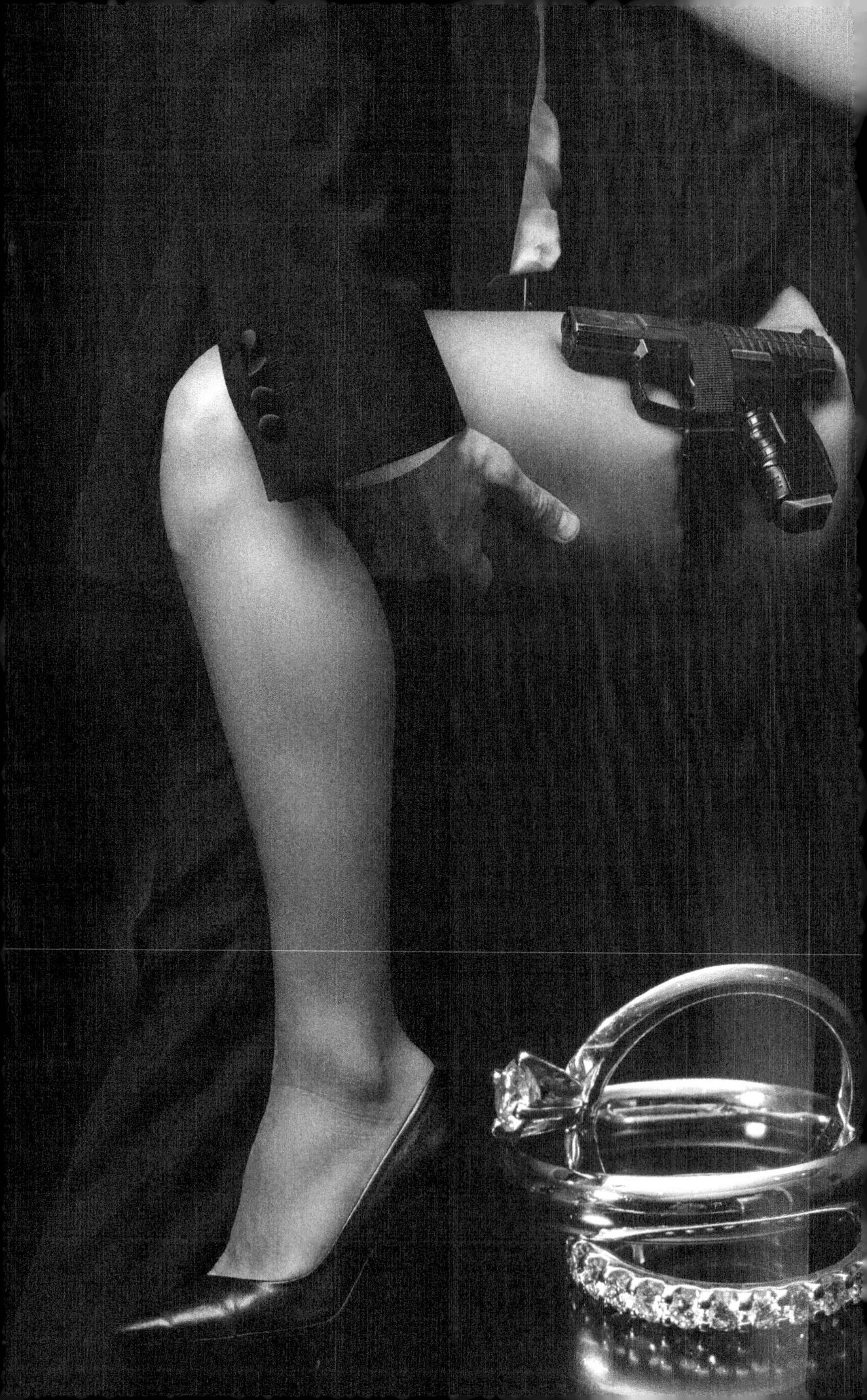

CHAPTER 17

Alaric

The next morning, I waste no time getting ready to take my girls to meet my father. The decision might have come to me unexpectedly, but once I made it, there was no point in hesitating or putting it off. I do find myself reaching for my little Layla as she gets ready though. When she's curling her hair back, I grab her hips and press my head to her back, needing her warmth.

I always feel weak when I'm with him.

He was once a great man, but now he's nothing but a shadow of himself. It hurts and haunts me, not only for what I've lost in a parent, but because of what I might become. Before her, that was my destiny, to sit alone, cold, and sick in a nursing home with no one to visit me but a monster like me. Now that I have her in my life, my future is suddenly hopeful, bright even. It's something I never would have considered possible for a man like me.

I have a family. I have happiness, whereas he only had me.

Where his darkness was thrust upon me, I will ensure my own

never touches the goodness that is Layla and Zoey. They will never know the demons like I was forced to.

I love my job, don't get me wrong, but my path was chosen for me and enforced by the man we are going to see. My whole childhood was molded around it, around training me and teaching me to be better than he could ever be. I learned to be cold, calculating, and uncaring for anyone and anything. Yet I loved him, and he loved me. I often saw the yearning in his eyes as he grew old and frail—yearning for something grander, more significant, like love. Something I struggled to express due to the very same things he taught me.

Now I'm peeling back those layers for her—my wife. I want him to meet her and see that I did what he never could, so that I will never die with the same regrets he will. I want my father to be proud and comforted knowing I'm finally happy. I know it's a concern of his, and no job or payout has ever felt as good as bragging to him about this.

I can't answer many of her questions, too nervous with the impending meeting, and Layla seems to notice. She offers me comfort instead, squeezing my hand as I lead her and Zoey to the car. When I go to shut the door behind her after she climbs in, she stops me, leans up, and kisses me, selflessly offering her support.

It sends a shot of warmth through my cold beating heart, restarting it once more. For her.

Only ever for her.

I smile for the first time this morning, like the sun breaking through the clouds, and when she sees it, hers grows. "Come on, Alaric. I want to meet the man who raised such an incredible man." She shuts her door, and I'm helpless but to comply with her order.

Helpless to give her anything less than everything she ever wants.

The drive to the home doesn't take long—he insisted on staying close, after all. Even in his state, he was the one to choose this senior home after making me list entrances and exits, security measures, and other people who lived there, including background checks. We can't park nearby, so I drop the girls off so they don't have to walk and find a spot before jogging to the entrance where they linger.

Zoey is clutching Layla's hand and looking around, and when she spots me, she grins widely, reaching out for my hand too. I don't know why, but that one gesture, that fucking smile, it's like a shot to my heart.

I actually stumble before taking her hand as I reach her side. "What's your dad like? I can't remember much of mine," she murmurs softly, innocently.

Layla's eyes close for a moment, and I quickly brush over her pain, not wanting to discuss it until she's ready to talk about that night. Kneeling, I brush Zoey's hair behind her ear and smile at her as tenderly as I know how to. "He's a wonderful man. He taught me everything I know. He's in . . . security too," I explain vaguely. "Or was. He was the best, the strongest man I ever knew. He taught me that strength, and although it didn't leave a lot of time for being a kid or just playing, I'm grateful all the same."

She nods, squeezing my hand and looking at Layla. "Layla was never a kid either, maybe that's why you work so well together." With that, Zoey turns on her heel and walks to the door, leaving us both staring after her.

Smart fucking kid.

"Maybe it is," I murmur, straightening. I take Layla's hand in mine as she stares after Zoey and raise it to my lips, kissing her knuckles. When she inhales and looks at me, satisfaction pours through me. "Come on, baby girl."

As we head inside the two-story brick building, I can't help but think of my words to Zoey. They were partly true, and even though I hate lying to her, it's for the best. How could I explain that on Saturday mornings I spent hours learning the best ways to kill a man when other kids were in the park playing baseball or football?

Or how on the weekdays when I missed school it was because he took me on a job and gave me my first kill?

Or when he showed me how to cut flesh from bones and how to dissolve bodies?

My father was the best hit man in the world . . . until me.

He taught me everything he knew, and like I was born to kill, I took his lessons and I made them better until I was untouchable, unkillable. By that point, he retired and lived vicariously through me. Even if I wanted to be someone different, someone better for Layla, I can't. Killing is all I know. My hands are so coated in blood that they will never be clean again. It never bothered me before . . . not until her.

Now, I'm aware that those same hands that have taken thousands of lives without remorse or a second thought are holding her so tightly, lovingly, and staining that perfect skin with the souls of the dead, and she doesn't even know it.

Maybe this was a bad idea, but as I lead them down the old, ugly carpeted hallway to his room at the end, I know there's no turning back. My father would have heard us coming, and if I didn't show? Well, I'm never too old to get my ass kicked, as he likes to remind me.

I crack my neck once we arrive outside the wooden door with the number thirteen hung in silver. I look at Layla once more, and her soft, encouraging smile has me knocking on the door and entering without waiting for a reply.

The TV is on in the corner, sitting on an outdated chest of

drawers as it plays some old war movie he loves so much. Two windows with a radiator between them line the wall next to it, looking out at the city—not that he can enjoy the view—and his huge Lay-Z-Boy is pointed right at it. It's where he's sitting now, with his slipper-clad feet propped up. He's dressed in some slacks and a white shirt, with a chunky gray cardigan over it. He's always been a sharp dresser, even now. The horrible carpet continues into here as well, with a tiny kitchen to the right and an open door to the left leading to his bedroom and bathroom.

It's nice, all things considered, and the furniture is placed in exact positions for him to know where to go, though I know he mostly sleeps in his chair anyway.

Clearing my throat, I tug Layla closer and shut the door behind us as Zoey hesitates near us. He makes no signs he's heard us, but I know he has. Nothing escapes my father. Not even the sound of a pin dropping.

"Dad," I call, leading the girls around to the sofa against the wall, which is only used for visitors like us. "I brought some friends."

"No shit, my boy," he replies, grabbing the remote and turning off the TV. Layla gasps when she sees him, and I wince.

"You look so much like him," she whispers, and that's when I comprehend she hasn't realized it yet. If the aviator sunglasses covering his eyes hasn't tipped her off, I don't know what will, but she's too busy looking at his styled gray hair, and yes, okay, facial features similar to mine, to notice that only a few people can get away with using shades indoors without looking like assholes.

My dad tilts his head like he can see her, something he works hard on. He says he finds it amusing to throw people off, to make them wonder if he really is blind. "And who's the beauty?" he asks.

"Dad, this is Layla. Layla, this is my father."

Layla steps forward, holding her hand out. "It's nice to meet you!" she gushes, but when he doesn't take her hand, she looks back at me nervously.

"You didn't do anything, baby. My father's blind," I explain slowly. Her eyes widen with recognition as she looks back at him, stuttering now.

"Ignore my grumpy son, it's fine. Happened ten years ago, stupid diabetes," Dad grumbles. "Come sit, sit."

Layla's mouth snaps shut, and she takes her seat, Zoey hopping up right next to her. She clearly feels awkward for not realizing he's unable to see, but she soon loosens up as I sit by her side, squeezing her knee consolingly. I wrap my arm around her shoulders to pull her closer, more for me than her, so I can feel her heat and curves against me.

"Layla is my wife, Dad. I got married," I tell him as I coil a strand of her hair around my finger, playing with it.

"Did ya? Fucking hell, you kidnap her or something?" He booms out a laugh. "Need me to kill him, girl?" he carries on jokingly.

Zoey giggles, and my dad stills.

"Alaric?" he growls, serious now.

"And this is Layla's baby sister Zoey," I offer softly. "Zoey, this is my father."

"You can call me Walter, little one," he tells her kindly, using a tone I've never heard before. "Now tell me everything."

I hesitate, but luckily Layla spins a story between truth and lie. She tells him about me courting her, visiting her at the diner, wooing her off her feet, helping her with Zoey and her health issues, and eventually asking her to marry me. She makes me seem like a hero when I am anything but.

"Why didn't you tell me you'd found someone, lad?" Walter finally asks when she's finished.

"I think he was nervous," Layla teases, answering for me, and it's a good thing, really, because I didn't have a clue what I would say. The truth is, I didn't want to explain how I stalked her and how I'm obsessed with her. But now that she's here at my side, smiling at him and looking at me like everything she just said is the gospel truth, my darker compulsions seem justified.

"Alaric nervous?" Walter laughs, leaning in. "I've only ever seen that once—"

"Dad, no." I groan, knowing where this is going.

"Tell us," Layla whispers like they are both in on the secret. Sighing, I lean back.

"He was about ten," my dad starts, telling them a truly embarrassing story about my childhood. Layla and Zoey both laugh, hanging on his every word, and despite my embarrassment, I can't help the huge smile forming on my lips. My dad likes them, that much is obvious, but more than that, he's welcoming them into the fold, into our small family of two. They fit right in here in my little family like they always belonged.

We stay for a few hours, and my dad gives them enough truth about my childhood to make it seem normal while keeping out the dark details. He never once stumbles over questions they ask and even turns it back on them. When he finds out how they spent some time living in foster care, I can sense his own anger and worry. He already cares for them, and since I've said they are my family, he's immediately accepted them as his own.

They are his, too, after all, and he might be blind and old, but he would kill anyone in this world to keep them safe.

"I better get the girls home, Pops," I say eventually, reluctant to leave. Usually, it's silent as we struggle to talk about anything other than work, but like with my life, Layla has filled it with joy and laughter once more.

After kissing his cheek, Layla says goodbye with a promise to come back soon, and then Zoey hugs him and runs after her sister.

I follow them, not wanting them out of my sight, and my hand is on the door when my father's voice stops me. "She's a keeper, lad. She obviously cares for you, and you her. I'm proud of you. Keep them safe and don't be strangers."

"I won't," I promise. "Thanks, Dad."

For some reason, his approval solidifies that I did the right thing by making Layla mine.

I hurry after my girls, feeling oddly choked up at the moment with my father. He doesn't often say he's proud of me. In fact, I can count the number of times I've heard it on one hand, but today he did, all because of the woman stealing my heart.

Who am I kidding? She stole it a long time ago.

I pull the car around and help them in. Once they are both inside, Zoey leans between the seats to look at us. "Layla, can I stay at a friend's house tonight?"

"What friend?" Layla asks, frowning back at her.

"Her name is Maddie. I met her at school. I told you about her. Well, she invited me for a sleepover!" Zoey is clearly excited with the idea of sleeping at a friend's house. Unlike Zoey's blatant glee of sleeping somewhere that isn't in her bed, it's obvious Layla isn't as keen. Her concern for her sister's well-being has been a constant in her life, and letting go of the reins is hard for her. Instead of giving Zoey the thumbs-up, Layla looks to me for advice. I lean into her, take her hand in mine, and plant a chaste kiss on it.

"It won't hurt Zoey to start being more social. She's a very smart girl and knows to call us if she doesn't feel comfortable."

"Right here." Zoey pouts, making me grin.

"She can take care of herself and knows not to do anything too strenuous. Let her go so she can have some fun. She deserves it after all she's been through," I murmur.

Layla debates it, I see it in her eyes, so I sweeten the pot. I grip her chin and pull her closer, dropping my voice so only she can hear. "If we have a night to ourselves, I can take you out to dinner and spoil you."

"Like a date?" she whispers, her gaze falling to my lips before flickering back up to mine.

"Why not? Isn't that what married couples do? Have date nights?"

She frowns, contemplating my proposal, so I kiss her, stealing her worries. "Where is your sense of adventure, Layla? We can have a nice meal, go out, hell, even see a movie. Whatever you want. Just us."

She nibbles on her lip as I wait for her answer, and I'm not sure why, but for some reason, this is important to me.

"Don't you think we are doing this backwards?" she finally responds. "We are already married. Do you think now is the time to date?" She laughs, the sound like sunshine breaking through the clouds.

"Better late than never, right?" I wink, kissing her before leaning back to look at Zoey who makes a gagging sound. "Whatcha say, Zoey bug? Want to go for a sleepover and I'll take Layla out?"

"Sounds perfect!" she replies, beaming.

Well then, it's decided.

Tonight, I'm going to wine and dine my girl until she falls madly in love with me.

Like the way I am with her.

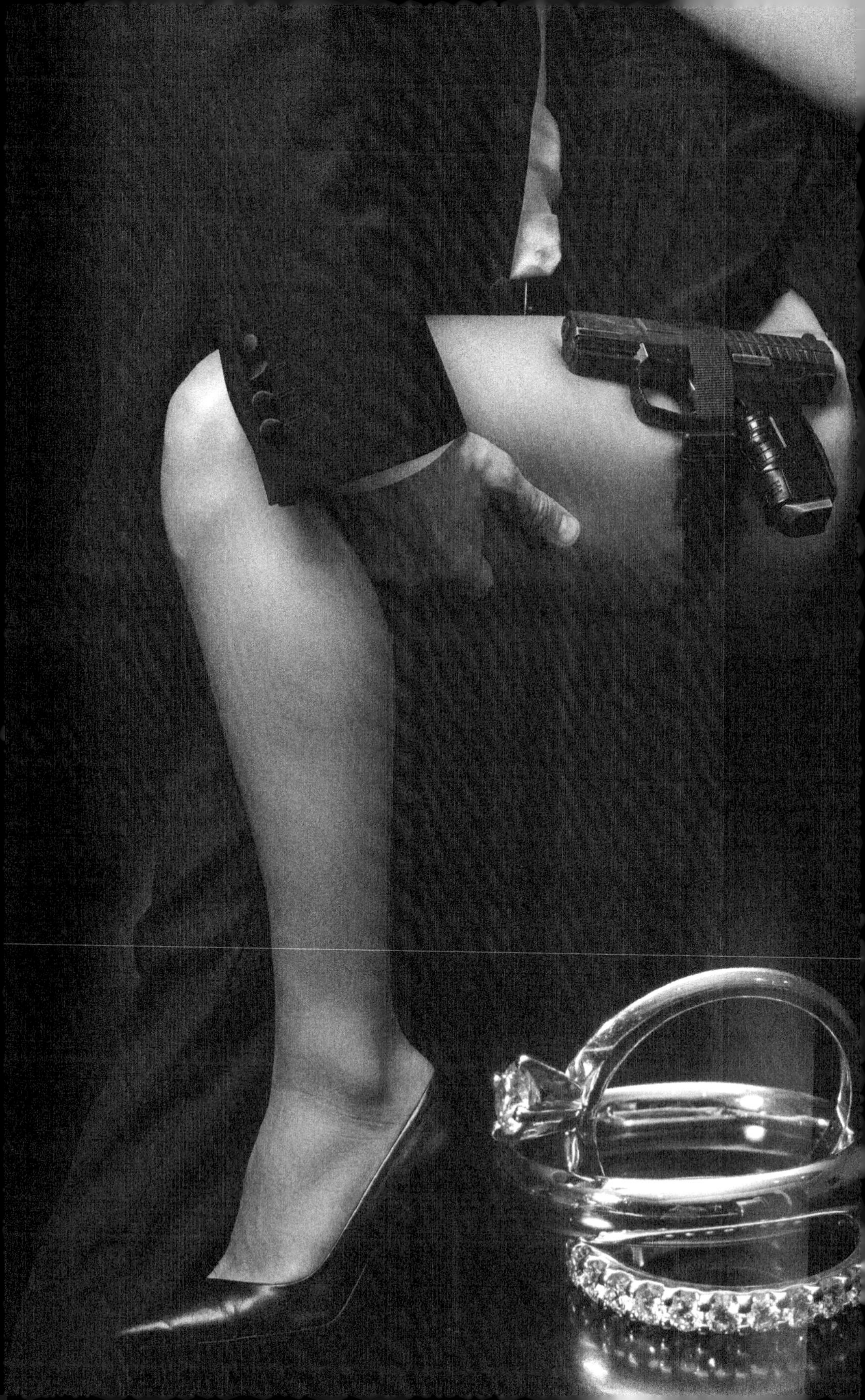

CHAPTER 18
Layla

"You're angry with me. Why?" Alaric asks, placing his wine glass on the table.

"Because I want to learn more about the man I'm sharing my life with and you're being evasive." I huff.

"Evasive?" He arches a brow.

"Yes!" I blurt out then seal my lips shut when I feel eyes from the other diners on me. I straighten my spine, plant a fake smile on my lips, and lower my voice. "Anytime I ask you something personal, Alaric, you evade the question."

"You asked me about my job. That isn't personal. It's boring," he retorts evenly.

"All I asked was how your day at work went."

"Like I said, boring."

"Fine," I concede. "Then tell me about your childhood."

"Tell me about yours."

"I asked you first, Alaric," I growl, starting to lose my patience with this infuriating man. "Or don't you care that I'm trying to make this marriage work?"

"I thought it was," he replies, sounding hurt, and the sudden pang in my chest has me losing steam.

"Not if I feel like I'm married to a stranger," I whisper, stretching my hand over the table to cover his.

Alaric's brows pull together in thought as he gives my hand a tight squeeze.

"What do you want to know?" he inquires, finally relenting.

"Everything. Anything. Just start from the beginning. Did you have a happy childhood?" I rush out, taking the opening.

"As happy as it could be. My father moved a lot for work, so I was always the new kid at school. We never stayed long enough in the same place for me to make friends." He shrugs, but there's a tinge of sadness in his voice I think he's unaware of.

"Sounds lonely."

"In the beginning, it was. I acted out because of it. I got myself into trouble just to get my father's attention, since he was basically the only one around. Mom passed away soon after I was born, so Pops was all I had, and I did anything to grab his attention."

"Did that work?" I ask, tilting my head.

"Eventually. When I turned eleven, I got busted for taking one of our neighbor's cars for a joy ride. Dad was pissed." He laughs.

"What did he do?"

"He told me if I had all this free time to act like an idiot, then I had enough of it for him to teach me to be a man. That's when he started teaching me the family business." His expression closes down, but I still ask.

"Security?" I arch a suspicious brow.

"Yes." He takes another swig of his drink.

"What could you do at eleven? Watch?" I tease.

Alaric cracks a smile.

"Definitely not. My father was more of a hands-on type of teacher. There were always small tasks I could do, even at a young age. Dad taught me all of them, and as I became good at whatever task he threw at me, we began to know each other. Before that, I don't think he really knew me or I him."

"Maybe you should take me to work with you," I joke.

"That's not happening," he states firmly.

"Why not? I might be good at it," I flirt, stroking his hand.

"Because I want better for you. I don't want you to have to do other people's bidding. I want you to finish school, get your degree, and then do something you really care about," he murmurs, lifting my hand to kiss it.

"I don't know what I want to do yet."

"That's okay. You have time to figure it out."

"Thank you. That means a lot to me. I never had that type of support before. People never really cared about what I wanted. It feels nice," I admit openly, sharing a part of me with him.

"What about you? Tell me about your childhood," he finally asks, his blue eyes locking me in place like always.

"I would rather not. It isn't the nicest of stories," I hedge, flinching at the reminder and pulling my hand away.

"Even so, I still want to know," he implores, his gaze patient and kind.

I worry my lower lip and take a sip of my red wine for courage, thankful Alaric requested a private booth in the Michelin-star restaurant to give us a semblance of privacy so we could talk freely like this.

"At first it was only my mother and me. I never knew who my father was, and I'm not sure my mother did either. She wasn't too mean to me when I was younger, just cold and unaffectionate. I think getting pregnant with me when she was so young made her resent me a little, but everything got worse as I started to grow up and become aware of things. Mom was a lot like your dad in that regard. She never stayed in one place for long, but that was more due to the fact that she couldn't keep a guy for more than a few months. We would live with them for a while, and when they got bored with her or couldn't handle a toddler messing with their things, they would kick us both out on the street."

My hands tremble as I remember those years and how she would always say it was my fault that we were kicked to the curb. Of course, the fact that she would steal or cheat on them was never the issue.

It was always me.

"What happened next?" Alaric croons, entwining our fingers to give me courage, and by some sort of miracle, his touch gives me the strength I need to muster through.

"Then Roy came along. He was the only one who stayed long enough to marry her. Mom was over the moon. She got pregnant with Gage and then Zoey, and even though she was still a shitty mom, at least she wasn't cruel or mean to them. She would even bake them birthday cakes sometimes. Maybe it was because she was older when she had them, or maybe it was just because she loved them when she couldn't love me."

I take another sip of wine, my throat drying with the memories that bombard me.

"I wish I could tell you that Roy was better than the others, but he wasn't. In fact, he was the worst of them all. He would find any excuse he could to beat up my mom. She would always have a fresh cut on her lip or a new bruise on her cheek, but she never once thought of leaving him." My voice hitches as the memories of her pain-filled screams echo in my head—of what came next.

"What about you? How did your stepfather treat you and your siblings?" Alaric asks, his voice bringing me back to the present.

"I wish I could tell you that his abusive ways were only directed at my mother, but they weren't. He never shied away from slapping us around. In all honesty, though, he wasn't very interested in us kids. For the most part, he left us alone and pretended we didn't even exist. We only got his attention when one of us did something he didn't like, and then he would discipline us. However, things changed once I got these." I point to my boobs. "His interest in me morphed from disinterest to curiosity. I couldn't pass him without his hands grabbing me in places he had no business touching. Sometimes I would act out just so he saw me less like the object he wanted to fuck and more like the petulant child he needed to discipline."

"Where was your mother during all this?" Alaric snarls, his eyes filling with anger as his hand tightens on mine. It feels nice for someone to be angry on my behalf, so I answer honestly.

"Drunk. High. Nursing a hangover or her own twenty rounds with him. She didn't care. As far as my mother was concerned, Roy could do whatever he wanted with me just as long as it kept the peace in the household." I snort bitterly.

"What changed?"

"Gage," I mutter, the sound of my kid brother's name pulling my heart into a viselike grip. "Roy was a gun nut. He had a whole collection of them stashed away in his garage. One day, he found Gage playing around with one of his rifles. Roy didn't like that. He didn't like that at all. Even though Gage was only eight, he punched and kicked him as if he were a grown man who could take such a beating. That's when my mother decided she'd had enough. We packed our stuff the very next day and left."

"What happened then?" he inquires, as if sensing this is where my story takes an even darker turn.

"Bad luck happened. Roy happened. He saw us making a run for it and followed us. My mom was always a shitty driver, but with Roy chasing us in his truck, she lost control of our car and slammed into a tree. Roy caught up with us on a deserted road and killed Mom and Gage. He shot me too," I mumble, touching the faint scar from the bullet wound on my shoulder. "I really thought he was going to kill us all, but then out of nowhere, an angel appeared and took the monster down. I never found out who shot Roy and saved Zoey and me from certain death, but whoever that person was, they were our saving grace, and I'll never be able to fully thank them for killing my stepfather."

I mean it. I wish I could remember who it was. The doctors said I had chosen to block out most of that day to protect myself, but a small part of me often wishes to find that person and thank them.

Alaric caresses the back of my hand with his thumb.

"No one will ever hurt you again, Layla. No one will lay a finger on your head, or Zoey's for that matter. I promise you that."

I feel a burning need to tell this man, this beautiful stranger who saved my sister, saved me, and irrefutably changed my life that I love him—that I've fallen madly in love with him. The only thing that keeps me from saying those words is my fear that he doesn't feel the same.

"Don't look at me like that, wife. Not if you're not prepared to deal with the consequences," he warns.

"And just how exactly am I looking at you, husband?" I murmur, licking my lips. The space between us heats, and the sadness changes, morphing into need that we are both clearly feeling.

"Like you're starving for my cock and not the steak on your plate," he answers unashamedly.

I choke on my wine, my cheeks blazing with heat. His piercing gaze has me shifting in my seat, and my clit throbs for his attention as I remember the way his huge cock feels inside me.

"You're still doing it," he growls under his breath.

"Am I?" I bat my eyelashes at him flirtatiously.

"You want to play, baby girl?" He cocks his brow.

"Depends on the game," I lick my lips.

"Get on your knees," he orders, those blue orbs narrowing dangerously.

"What?" I croak, thinking I must not have heard him right. "You mean here? Where everyone can see?"

"I don't care. You either get on your knees so I can feel that pretty mouth of yours on my fat cock, or I'll bend you over this table right now and fuck your sweet cunt. Your choice, Layla, but I won't ask you again."

My heart races at the threat in his eyes. I look around and see that everyone here is either distracted by the conversation they are having with their dates or too involved with the delicious food on their plates. I do as he says and slowly lower myself to the floor in front of him. The huge bulge in his pants tells me he's as eager and needy as I am.

"I'm waiting, Layla," he whispers, weaving his fingers through my hair. I run my tongue over my dried lips as I unzip his trousers and free the monster that was hiding underneath. I smile when I see he's commando, giving me easy access to him. With my gaze fixed on his, I swipe my tongue up the large vein on the side of his cock. The little hiss he lets out fuels my desire for him, and within seconds, my lips are wrapped around his huge shaft, sucking him for all I'm worth.

He curses under his breath and digs his fingers into my scalp, pushing my head down to take him deeper. I relax my jaw and throat to swallow him as far as I can, rubbing my thighs together with the salty taste of him on my tongue. Feeling them slick with my own desire, I want to push him to see if he really would fuck me here, but I also want to feel him explode down my throat.

"I love fucking your mouth almost as much as I love fucking that tight, dripping pussy of yours," he whispers lovingly as he slams down my throat.

Tears begin to form at the corners of my eyes, threatening to ruin my makeup, yet I can't find it in me to care. All I want is to make this man, this beautiful man before me, feel as good as he makes me feel every day. His cock swells in my mouth, and I grip his base with my hand as I jerk him off. My core feels so fucking empty without him, needing him and only him. Still, I persist, sucking him, licking him, and letting him thrust into the back of my throat until my tears fall down my face. I may be the one who's on my knees in a busy fancy restaurant where anyone could see, yet I feel so powerful it's intoxicating. Me, a girl who had a shitty start in life, is making this god of a man succumb to her every desire. When his grip on my hair tightens, I know he's close to coming undone. I speed up my tempo, giving him all of me, and soon his cum drips on my tongue. I milk him dry and swallow it all, feeling absolutely victorious as I lick his cock clean.

Alaric lifts me up and sits me on his knee, and my eyes widen in alarm when he shoves his hand between my thighs. I grab hold of his wrist, stopping his assault, and rip a deep growl of frustration from his throat.

"Everyone will see," I explain softly, releasing my hold on him.

"Let them. Let them all see that this pussy is mine and I can take it when I want, wherever I want," he retorts, inching closer to my soaked core.

When his fingers brush my slit, my eyes roll into the back of my head, and I stop objecting. He lets out a soft curse when he finds that I'm not wearing any underwear either.

"See? You want this just as much as I do. Why fight it? Why fight us?"

"I don't want to," I whisper.

"Then don't," he says, spreading my legs wider until I'm completely open for him, leaning back into the table to give him better access.

His deft fingers begin to toy with my clit as he nibbles on my neck. His touch feels so good, like a piece of heaven on earth, but as my greedy pussy begins to beg for his touch, my breathing becomes more erratic.

"That's my girl. Fuck my hand, baby. Show every last motherfucker in here who you belong to," he snarls.

With his order still hanging in the air between us, I do just that, fucking myself with his fingers. We can both hear the sound of my arousal as Alaric pushes two fingers inside me and starts thrusting into my pussy, my juices dripping all over his digits. I'm sure I'm going to leave a puddle on his pants, but judging by the heady stare Alaric is giving me, he couldn't care less. All he wants is for me to come. My orgasm is just as vital to him as his own, if not more so. When he adds another finger, I bite down on my bottom lip to keep from wailing. He always feels so good, be it his fingers, tongue, or cock. Everything this man does drives me wild with desire.

My vision starts to blur as the impending orgasm grows closer. I want to grab it, cradle it in my arms, and nurture it until it's big enough to shatter me into a thousand small, glorious pieces.

"I'm so close. So close," I whimper, needing him to push me over the edge.

And just like the dutiful lover I've come to rely on, Alaric latches his mouth onto my nipple through the fancy dress he bought me, biting down so exquisitely that I have no choice but to come. The only thing that muffles my loud cry is Alaric's other hand, which quickly covers my mouth. My soul slowly returns to my boneless, sated body, and my smile is so wide my cheeks hurt.

When someone clears their throat near our table, I finally look away from Alaric's smoldering gaze to find a man next to us. The waiter watches us hesitantly. I'm still on Alaric's lap, dazed with the orgasm he just gave me.

"Would you like dessert? The chef made an exquisite aux fraises et chocolat, this evening." He sounds slightly scared.

Alaric nods, and the waiter quickly rushes away.

"I think he knows what we just did. In fact, I think everyone knows." I eye a few curious glances from the restaurant's patrons.

"Fuck them. I want my dessert now," he growls, pulling me out of our seat.

"Where are we going?" I ask breathlessly, trying to keep up with his wide strides on these heels.

He parades me through the restaurant before urging me down a short hallway and into a dark alcove. Alaric pushes me into the tiny hideaway, the sound of dishes and chefs shouting announcing that the kitchen must be close by. But Alaric doesn't care. Instead, he swings me around and presses my cheek against the wall.

"Like I said, I want my dessert now," he states gruffly, lifting my dress to my waist so my ass is in full view of anyone who dares pass by. I moan when his fingers touch my sensitive slit, my legs parting instantly for him even though I just came. I'm a greedy fucking bitch, it seems, when it comes to him.

"You're fucking drenched, wife. This pussy is always so wet for me," he growls hungrily.

"It's your fault," I tease, looking over my shoulder and catching a glimpse of the ravenous man behind me. "You do this to me."

"Ah, love, and you fucking do this to me," he retorts, releasing my pussy to grasp his cock, rubbing it against the crack of my ass.

A little whimper leaves me as he continues to play with my clit.

"I can't get enough of you. Sometimes I think I'll go mad if I'm not deep inside you."

"Me too," I admit in a whisper.

His feral expression softens as he peppers my bare shoulder with kisses.

"You consume me, Layla. I'm nothing without you."

His loving words pull on my heartstrings, making me whimper with need.

"Make me yours. Please," I beg, my knees threatening to buckle if he doesn't fuck me.

With a nip at my shoulder, he stops his assault on my clit, and I feel his huge cock pressing against my hole, teasing me. As I'm about to act, he finally gives me what I want. A wail of relief escapes my lips as he thrusts his massive cock inside me, filling that emptiness with his love. He fists my hair and cranes my head back so he can devour my mouth as he pounds into me mercilessly.

Our lovemaking is just like our marriage—unexpected and all-consuming. Alaric plays my body like a fiddle, knowing exactly which buttons to push and which dirty words to use to tip me over the edge. And just as I expected, within seconds, I'm coming on his cock with his mouth on mine, swallowing the cry of ecstasy that leaves me. With three forceful thrusts, I feel his warm release fill me and begin to drip down my thighs. He grips my chin and delivers an earth-shattering kiss that leaves me breathless and at his mercy as my body becomes limp. When he breaks the kiss, I whimper in frustration, needing more of his love. No matter how much he lavishes me with it, I always want more. More. More. More. And I don't see that feeling ever changing. For the second time tonight, the words I love you burn my throat, needing to come out and tell this extraordinary man how much he means to me.

His blue eyes, the ones that always seem to see the very darkest corners of my soul, soften as he pulls down my dress and fixes my hair.

"Let's go home, baby."

"What about dinner? Dessert?" I murmur, still relearning how to breathe.

"We'll take it to go. I'd rather eat it off your body anyway." He smirks cockily.

The smile that crests my face is almost as big as the love I feel for him.

"I like that idea." I bite my bottom lip, tracing my thumb over his sharp jaw.

"I thought you would," he replies with a laugh, and the sound warms me from the inside more than any food or decadent wine ever could.

"So much for date night though." I pretend to pout.

"I promise I'll make it worth your while."

"You always do."

CHAPTER 19

Alaric

Wiping the bloody pliers with a rag, I return my gaze to the body fastened to the chair with bolts, which are impaled through his knees and hands. Poor bastard. He did something that pissed off my client, and my instructions were clear—he was to suffer before he died.

I don't usually take torture jobs, but once I did a background check, I couldn't not.

He's an escaped sex offender. He hurt kids. Countless numbers of them.

All I could think of when I read his profile was little Zoey. The money, the contract, none of it mattered as much as the anger inside me. I felt a burning need to kill this bastard, to make him hurt the way those kids did, to kill the monster. Even if it meant getting my hands dirty, it would be enough if it saved one child from his grasp. My own fury flowed out of me as I worked on him. I shocked him over and over, his screams the only sounds in this partially caved in warehouse I chose.

After the electricity, I pulled out every nail, broke each of his fingers and toes, and snapped his arms. I cut off his cock and balls, cauterizing the wound so he couldn't bleed out. No, that would have been too quick for him. I wanted him to feel the fear each of his victims felt. I dragged it out, making him scream and beg until his mouth bled with each mumbled plea. Eventually the wounds became too much and his heart gave out.

It still wasn't enough.

Grinding my teeth, I toss my tools back in the bag just as my phone rings—my personal one, not my work one, which means only one thing . . . Layla. I pull it out and accept the call. She never calls me at work, and a bad feeling starts to build in my stomach before her first words even reach my ears.

"Zoey's been hurt." She's panting, and there's panic in her voice.

"What? Where?" I demand, grabbing my bag and hoisting it up on my shoulder. I'll come back later to clean the rest of this mess up. It's risky, but Zoey and Layla are more important. I hear her running footsteps over the phone and her heavy breathing when she accidentally smacks into someone as they yell after her.

"Layla, talk to me," I demand as I rush through the warehouse and outside to my car. I place my phone on the stand as her voice switches over to the speaker.

"Her school called. All they could tell me is that she was climbing and playing on some stairs and fell. She was rushed to the hospital. I was in class. I'm too far. Oh God, Alaric," she rambles in complete and utter panic.

My heart stops before squeezing, and terror like I've never felt surges through me, but I breathe through it. I need to be there for her, for Zoey. They are both depending on me right now. Turning on the engine, I choose my words carefully. "I'm about ten minutes out. I'll go there now. If she's at the hospital, she's in the best place. Breathe deeply and take a moment before you get in an Uber and meet me there. Baby girl, she'll be okay. She's strong, remember that."

"She's so little," she cries, "and still so weak."

"Layla, listen to me," I order, my voice sharp. "This doesn't help her. She needs you now, okay? We can fall apart later together. I'll hold you while you cry, but right now, I need you to get to the hospital. I could swing by and pick you up, but then she would be alone."

"No, no, I'm okay. I'll meet you there," she replies hurriedly, but she seems calmer as I gun the engine, racing around the abandoned streets and back into the city toward the hospital. I stay on the phone the entire time with Layla, talking to her and trying to ease her panic, even as mine eats me alive.

Zoey.

Fuck, she better be okay.

She's Layla's entire world . . . mine too.

They both are.

I can't lose either of them.

There is no future, no me, without them now. Without Zoey's laugh, without her tiny hand in mine as she looks up at me so trustingly. Nights spent laughing and talking animatedly over dinner, or even just when we watch movies together with both of my girls tucked under blankets, eating popcorn. I never knew what love truly was until them, or what being alive actually meant.

It means being vulnerable. It means loving someone or more than one someone so deeply that you make yourself weak in the sense that anything could happen—they could leave; they could die—and you still fall because the highs are worth the lows.

I fell in love with Layla Johnson Holmes a long time ago, and somewhere along the way, Zoey became like my own child.

If she's not okay, not only will it break two hearts, but I know we wouldn't survive it.

"Alaric?" Layla whispers, fear still lacing her usual soft, laughing voice.

"It's going to be okay, baby girl. I'm almost there," I promise, slamming my foot on the pedal and running a red light. I don't give a fuck as I skid into a parking spot near the hospital. Leaping out, I take my keys and sprint toward the emergency room doors. "I'm here," I tell her as I run over to the reception desk.

"My wife's sister was rushed in from St. Augustine's. We don't know how badly she was hurt. Her name is Zoey Holmes. I legally adopted her when I married my wife," I rush out, realizing that I'm babbling, which is so unlike me.

I also realize I never told Layla or Zoey about me adopting her…a problem for another time.

The receptionist just nods and tells me to wait one second.

"She came in twenty minutes ago. She's been seen by a doctor and is currently in radiology. That's all I can tell you."

"Please," I snap before closing my eyes and breathing. It's not her fault, after all. Opening them again, I lean in closer, pleading with her. "Please, I just need to know if she's okay; she's our entire world. She's the only family we have."

The woman purses her lips but nods before typing quickly and looking around like she shouldn't be telling me this. "Her notes say they suspected a fractured arm, but they want to check her head because of her history. I'm sorry, that's all I can tell you. I'll let Zoey's doctor know you're here, and they'll call you back," she tells me reassuringly.

"Thank you." I sigh and step away, placing the phone to my

lips. "You hear that, baby girl? It's just a fractured arm. We can deal with that."

"Her head," she whispers worriedly, cars beeping in the background.

"She's hardheaded and stubborn like you, baby. I promise she'll be okay. Look after yourself. I'll be waiting for you when you get here, my love." When she says goodbye, I hang up. As I pocket my phone, my hands shaking, I finally let myself truly feel the utter terror, hope, worry, and anger.

There are so many emotions, unlike before when I was used to living without any. Not only did my two girls lighten my world and breathe life back into it, but they also breathed it back into me, and I'm struggling to contain all these new thoughts and worries. The protectiveness surging in me for my family overwhelms me.

I pace the waiting room, back and forth, focusing on the rhythmic motions to try and keep the fear at bay. About fifteen minutes later, Layla flies in like a storm, her eyes wild and hair everywhere. I catch her and pull her into my arms as she cries.

"Where is she? Is she okay?" she demands.

"They haven't—"

"Mr. and Mrs. Holmes?" comes a feminine voice. We break apart to see a middle-aged, friendly-looking female doctor waiting there. "I'm Zoey's doctor today, Dr. Cameron. Please follow me."

"Is she okay?" Layla questions, rushing after her and tugging me along with her.

"She'll be fine, I promise. Let me tell you and Zoey what's happening at the same time. Please, through here." She gestures, and we follow her into the emergency department and to the cubicle where Zoey is sitting up in the bed.

"Kid, you scared the shit out of me!" I exclaim, moving to her side and taking her arm that isn't raised.

"Zoey, oh my gosh, I was so worried!" Layla cries, holding her softly and kissing her.

She smiles, but her eyes are watery and her face is pale. "I'm okay. Sorry, I didn't mean to worry you."

"As you can see, Zoey has fractured her arm, but fortunately it's only in one place, and with the proper treatment, it should heal very well. Her head is fine; we had to check. She was lucky," the doctor explains. "So our next course of action is to cast her arm to heal the break. She will get some pain medication just in case, and we will want a CT on her head in seven days just to make sure everything is alright."

"Oh, thank God." Layla slumps, moving closer to my side.

"She's going to be okay," Dr. Cameron promises warmly, looking at Zoey. "She's one tough little girl. Let me prescribe some meds and cast her arm, and then you can take her home."

"Thank you, thank you so much," Layla gushes, reaching over to squeeze her hand. As the doctor leans in to check Zoey one last time, Layla rushes into my arms, sobs racking her body as all her worry finally dissipates. I wrap my arms around her, holding her as she presses closer to my chest, my own heart hurting.

"Shush, love," I murmur, hating her tears. I nod as the doctor leaves and rub Layla's back.

When she leans away, I wipe the tears from her beautiful face and stare into those glistening jewels that I fell in love with the first time I saw her. "Thank you, I . . ." Her words trail off as her eyes land on my wrist. "Alaric . . . whose blood is that?" she demands, her brows pinching together.

"What?" I follow her gaze, and ice floods my veins.

In my panic, I hadn't checked myself over. On the sleeve of my shirt is a bloodstain. It's red and clearly fresh, and there's enough that the person must be hurt.

"Are you hurt?" she asks as if following my line of thought.

"No, I'm okay," I promise when I see her worry for me. My poor wife has been through the wringer today, and I'm only adding to it. She reaches to check, as if she doesn't believe me. "Layla, I promise I'm okay," I assure her, seeing the concern in her eyes which quickly fades to confusion and then stark terror.

"Then whose is it?" she demands.

I freeze, unsure what to say.

"Alaric?" she prompts.

"What's happening?" Zoey asks, looking between us.

Sparing Zoey a reassuring look, I step closer to Layla. "Someone cut themselves at work, and I was helping them. I must have gotten it on my shirt," I lie blatantly, hating every word that spills from my lips. She frowns, but when Zoey calls for her, she nods and turns away.

I stand at her back, angry at myself and . . . worried for a whole new reason.

I don't think she believed me.

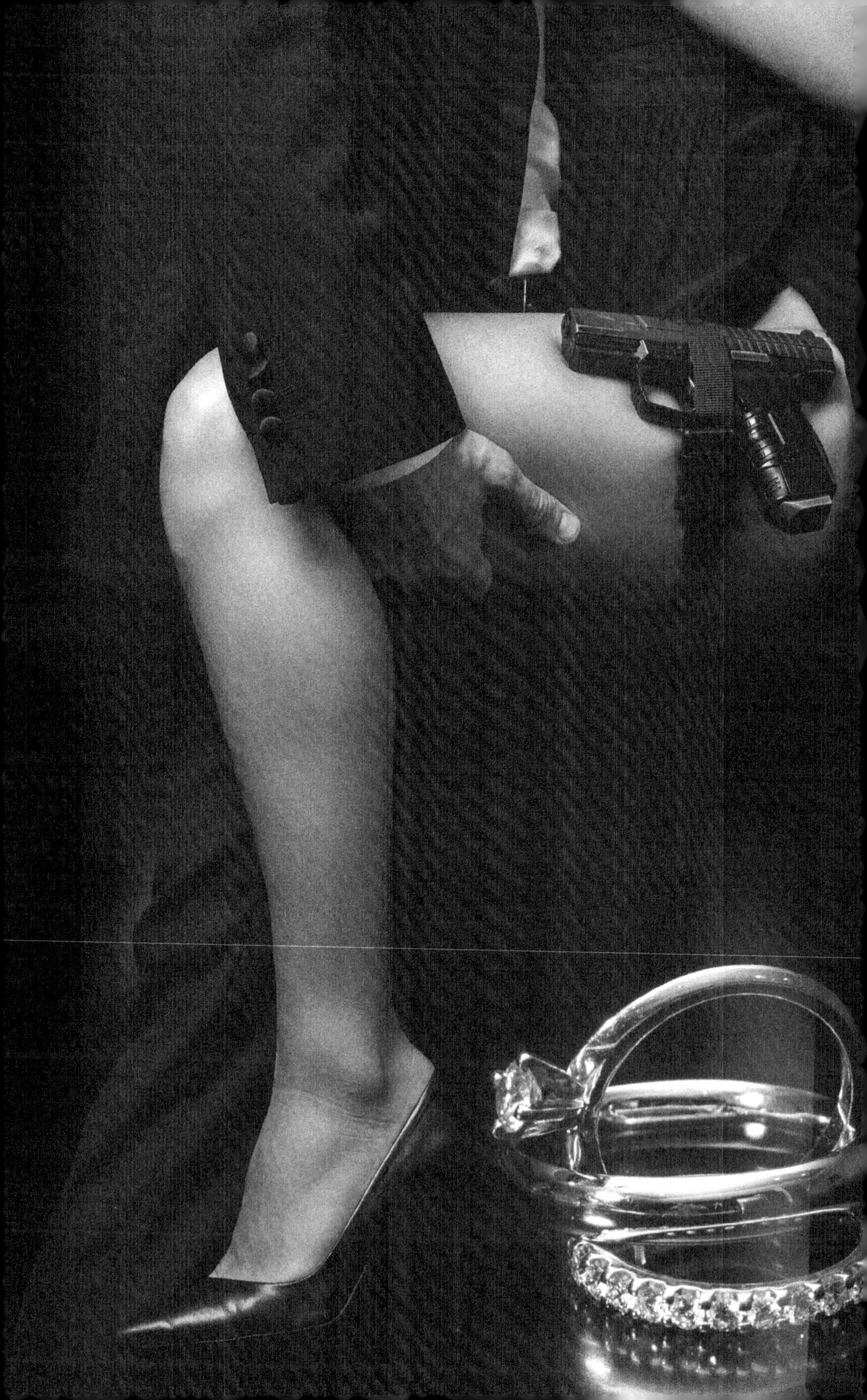

CHAPTER 20

Layla

I stand at the threshold of our bathroom door, watching Alaric shave his stubble clean. I itch to run my tongue up his jaw until my lips crash onto his. Knowing I'm blatantly gawking at him, he throws me a wink, beckoning for me to come closer. Without any hesitation, I hurry toward him, and his arm circles my waist before he perches me on the edge of the marble countertop.

"I wish your bosses didn't call you into work today," I complain, pouting like a needy infant who's frustrated she can't play with her toys.

"First of all, I'm my own boss. No one orders me to do shit." He smirks, wiping the rest of his shaving cream off his face with a towel, all while stroking my skin.

"No one?" I arch a mischievous brow, wrapping my legs around his waist and pulling him closer to me.

"No one but you," he whispers on a pained groan as I rub my needy pussy against the bulge that's currently growing in his pajama pants.

"So if I ordered you to stay home and make love to me all day, you'd obey?"

He begins to slide his hands up my thighs, widening them so I can rub against him better.

"As much as I'd like nothing more than to drop to my knees right now and eat that greedy pussy of yours, I do have some work that needs to be dealt with."

The frown on my lips is instant.

"Tell you what," he adds, seeing that my playful disposition is long gone. "It will be Christmas in a few weeks, and we haven't decorated the house yet. How about I do this one job I need to take care of, and then I come straight home before Zoey gets out of school and we three can go hunting for a Christmas tree."

"You're not playing fair," I mumble, wrapping my arms around him.

"Oh?" He grins widely.

"How can I be upset with you when you say and do all the right things? You make it very hard for me to hold a grudge."

"The only thing I ever want you to hold is my cock in your mouth, baby girl," he teases.

I bite my bottom lip, my mouth watering at the idea, when Alaric throws his head back with a deep laugh.

"I've created a monster," he teases, pulling me off the sink and palming my ass as he walks us into the bedroom.

"Are you saying you don't like knowing that your wife wants you every second of every day? That she misses you terribly when you leave?"

"No, wife. I fucking live to hear you say those words to me," he croons, laying me on our bed, his strong frame looming over mine. The heat that was in his eyes a second ago has now turned into something sweeter. My breath catches in my throat as he pierces me with those blue eyes of his, and all I see is love swimming in his gaze.

"I love to hear all your words," he whispers, the faint hint of vulnerability cracking my heart down the middle.

I love you, my heart screams out, but the words remain trapped inside me.

Why don't I just tell him how I feel? That this is no longer a marriage of convenience, but one I treasure above everything else. Why can't I tell my husband that I've fallen in love with him? Fallen so hard that I can't imagine a world without his beautiful face.

Why?

"Baby girl? Where did you go?" he asks when I grow silent.

"Umm . . . nowhere. I'm right here. But you, dear husband, need to get going if you want to keep your promise," I bluff, forcing excitement into my voice.

I read the uncertainty in his eyes, and just as he's fond of doing when my concerns arise, I pull him down to me and kiss him like it will be our last. He surrenders to my kiss, his tongue seeking refuge in my mouth. My heart flutters in my chest as he pulls my lower lip between his teeth, his cock now stabbing at my belly.

"Nope, none of that," I tease, slapping his shoulder and squirming away from him. "Go and take your shower before I really make you late for work."

When a genuine smile crests his lips, I know all his doubts and worries have vanished. He pulls himself off me, but not before throwing a suggestive wink over his shoulder.

"Go!" I laugh, tossing a pillow at him.

He chuckles all the way back to the bathroom, but as soon as I hear the shower running, my own smile slips off my face.

There is a reason why I haven't been able to open up to Alaric and tell him how I feel, and that falls down to the sick feeling in my gut that he's keeping secrets from me. Since I've known him, my husband hasn't been the most forthcoming with information about himself, but he's never once lied to me before last week.

When Zoey broke her arm and I confronted him about the blood on his sleeve, it was the first time he ever lied to my face. I need to know why. Nervous that I'm really doing this, I jump off the bed and walk to his bedside table where his work and home phone is. I have no way of knowing what his work phone's password is, but I know the one he uses to call Zoey and me by heart.

It's our wedding day.

I punch the numbers in, my nerves making me tremble as I download the Find My Friends app onto his phone. What I'm doing comes with a risk. Alaric might see it on his phone and question why I put it there. A private man like himself won't find it particularly funny that his wife of just a couple of months went through his things without permission, but it's a risk I have to take if I want answers. It's become painfully obvious that Alaric will not give them to me willingly, so if I have to succumb to stalking my husband to learn more about him, then so be it.

Once I've made sure that the phone is put back in its original place, I grab my robe and dash downstairs to make breakfast, acting like this is just a normal mundane Tuesday. On autopilot, I whip up some scrambled eggs, fried bacon, and chopped fruit while inwardly praying he doesn't pick up on my deceitful plan.

I'm probably blowing things out of proportion, and there is nothing for me to be worried about, but that sinking feeling in my gut refuses to let me back out now.

Both Zoey and Alaric arrive in the kitchen at the same time, animatedly talking about the movie we watched last night. I kiss my baby sister on the cheek then do the same to Alaric before telling them I'm going to dress so I can take Zoey to school.

I rush upstairs, my heart threatening to jump out of my chest as I close the door behind me. My eyes land on the bedside table, and I see that both phones are no longer there. I bang my head against the door, knowing there is no turning back now.

"Snap out of it, Layla. You need to know," I tell myself, but the pep talk does nothing to stop the ill feeling in my stomach.

Without a minute to lose, I get dressed in jeans and a simple sweater, brush my hair back into a ponytail, and add some mascara. Glancing at my reflection, I'm amazed at how put together I look while I'm a ball of nerves inside. I relax my shoulders and walk back downstairs. Alaric is already putting his and Zoey's plates into the dishwasher.

I'm a fool.

This thoughtful, caring man isn't hiding anything from me.

I'm just the paranoid idiot that can't accept a good thing when she gets it.

Oblivious of my self-deprecating thoughts, Alaric strolls toward me, puts his hand on my waist, and leans in to whisper in my ear.

"I'll be home around lunchtime. Make sure my favorite meal is ready for me. I want to see you naked on this counter with your legs spread wide so I can feast on your pretty pink pussy."

With that mental picture in my head, he cups my cheeks and kisses me until I have to lean against the counter just so my knees don't buckle. He grabs my ass and groans before passing me, kissing Zoey on the top of her head, and wishing us a good day.

I'm not sure if my pulse is beating madly due to the kiss or what I'm about to do next.

"Layla, is everything okay? You have a weird look on your face," Zoey observes, her curious gaze unsettling me further.

"Everything is fine, but it won't be if you're late for class. Come on. Chop-chop." I clap my hands to drive the point home.

Luckily for me, Zoey does as she's told, and within five minutes, we are both out the door. She goes on a tangent about school and her new friends, and I nod and hum every so often so she thinks I'm listening. I'm ashamed to say that I'm not, but I don't want to let on about what's truly going through my mind either. Once we reach St. Augustine's, I wave her off with a wide smile and wish her a good day. The minute she's gone, my smile falters, and I walk home, rethinking this whole plan.

I must be losing it.

What am I thinking?

Am I really going to stalk my own husband?

Jesus.

When I get home, I place my phone on the counter and just stare at it, debating my next step. A quick glance at the clock on the microwave tells me I just spent two precious hours talking to myself.

"Goddamn it!" I yell, picking up my phone. I grab my car keys and my coat and walk out of my house for the second time today. I slam my door shut and pull up my phone to click on the app. My forehead wrinkles when I discover that Alaric is currently in Hell's Kitchen, not too far from the diner I worked at.

What the hell is he doing there?

I guess there is only one way to find out. I start the car and make the twenty-minute drive over, glancing at my phone every once in a while to see if he is on the move. The dot on my phone does show some movement, but it stays in the nearby vicinity. The gods must also want me to get my answers, since there is vacant parking space waiting for me. I turn off the ignition and stare at my phone, my bottom lip now raw with my constant chewing. He's close. Real close. But where? Aside from a broken-down pawnshop and an out of business cleaners, there really isn't much of anything on this street.

Could he be in one of the deteriorating apartment buildings? And if so, what is he doing? This area doesn't indicate its inhabitants would have enough money to warrant private security. Hell, I lived just a few blocks from here, and I know that none of my neighbors had enough money to pay for their electric bill.

On shaky legs, I get out of the car, thinking that maybe I'll hear his voice and it will lead me to him. A cold chill runs down my spine, and I'm not sure if it's due to the December wind or my apprehension. I walk along the sidewalk, my eyes and ears peeled for anything regarding Alaric. My shoulders deflate when there is no sign of him, even though the app on my phone says I'm in the right spot.

I'm about to call it quits when a familiar grunt grabs my attention. My hackles rise when the sound of a body colliding against a wall reaches me. I swallow dryly and follow the sound into a hidden alleyway. With each step I take, the louder my heart beats in my chest. I don't know exactly what I'm seeing, but the large, broad form in the shadows is without a doubt my husband. It's only when he pulls himself into the light that I have a clear view of what's happening.

I stand frozen in place as I watch the man I love beat a total stranger to a bloody pulp. The only thing that slaps me awake from my stupor is when Alaric snaps the man's neck in one easy fluid move and then drops his corpse to the cold ground.

And that's when I scream.

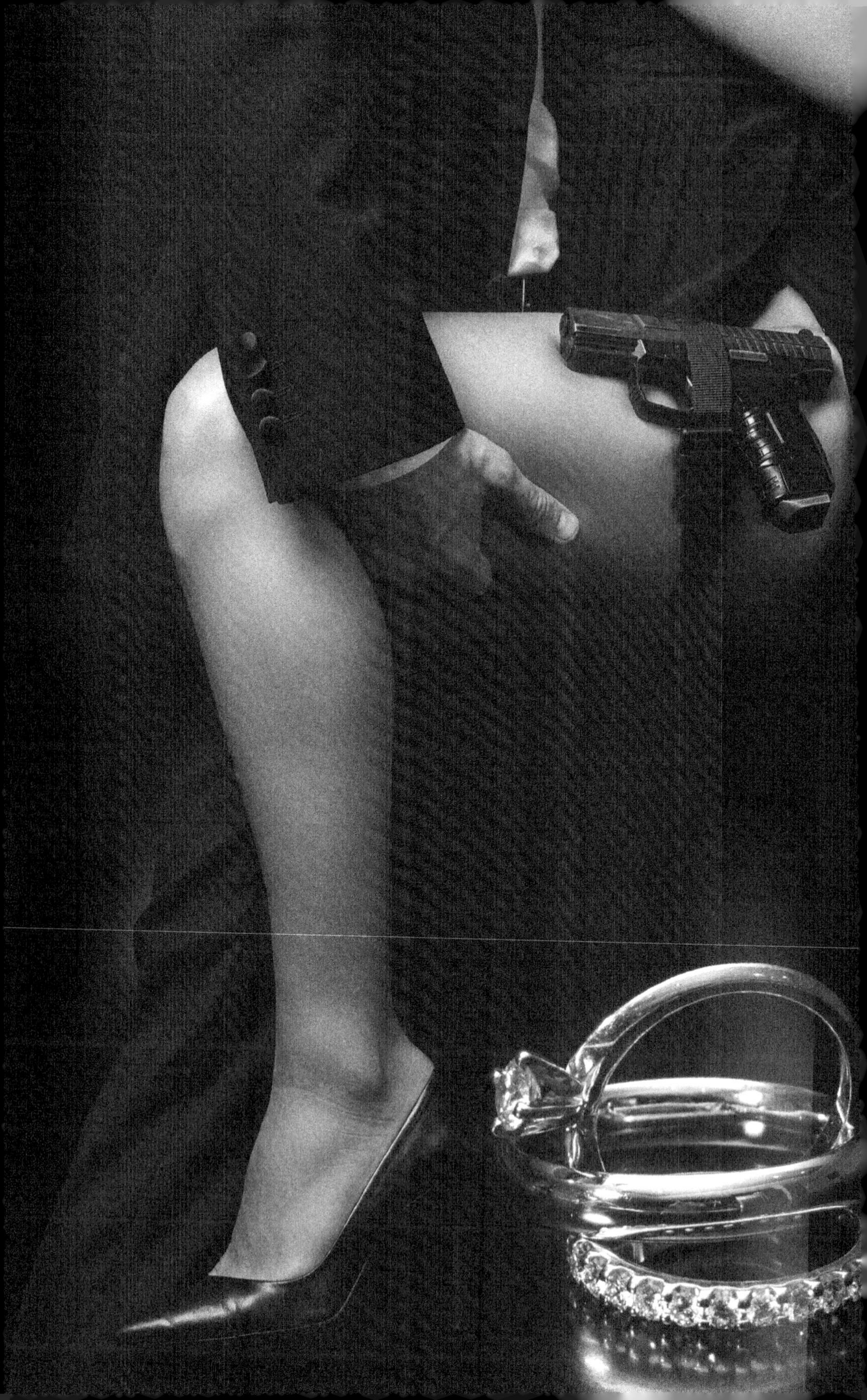

CHAPTER 21

Alaric

A scream splits the air.

High-pitched, horrified, and laced with fear, it makes me jerk around, wondering who has stumbled into the alley. I'm ready to bribe them when I suddenly see *her*.

My wife.

My Layla.

Her face is as white as a sheet, and her lips are parted as her scream tapers off. Her eyes are wide and filled with confusion and fear as she stares at me like I'm a stranger. She flicks her gaze to the bloody dead man on the ground then back to me. I quickly step in front of him to block her view, knowing it's already too late.

"Baby girl—" I reach for her, but she flinches.

Wincing, I drop my hands, realizing they are covered in my kill's blood. "Layla," I start, my voice gruff. My chest is heaving from the beating, and adrenaline still pumps through my veins, but another feeling courses through my body, one that is far more consuming—fear.

I love her. She's my wife, my whole world. I never wanted her to see me this way. Not like this. To everyone else, I'm a monster, a killer.

But to her? I'm just Alaric.

The man who loves her.

My heart twists in my chest as I see that changing before my very eyes. She stumbles back in shock, holding her hand up to ward me off as if I'm a stranger. Like I haven't held her while she cried, kissed her as she laughed, or felt her body pressed against mine. I actually see all those tender memories being replaced with this image.

Me, covered in blood, with a dead body at my feet.

"Who are you?" she whispers, her tone almost cold, numb.

She's in shock.

Fuck.

That realization spurs me into action. Even if she hates me, even if she doesn't want to touch me or be near me, I can't let her suffer alone right now. I grab my phone and send a quick confirmation that the hit is done, and then I check the scene to make sure I've left nothing behind. Satisfied, I slowly walk toward her, like she's a frightened animal ready to run from her prey.

Which she very well might.

My heart couldn't handle that. I would chase her.

I would follow her anywhere. She's my entire existence. She's the reason I laugh, smile, want to go home every night. She changed everything. She gave me a life. She gave me softness, excitement, and happiness.

Just by being mine.

All that teeters on the edge now, and I know if it crashes and falls . . . so will I.

"It's okay. I won't ever hurt you, you know that, love. Just come with me, okay? Let's get you warm and find you something to drink and we can both work through what you just saw. I'll answer anything you want. Just let me take you home," I implore, cooing at her as I step closer. She doesn't move or look at me as I gently touch her arms. No. She just stares at the dead body lying on the ground, shivering as if her bones are just as cold as his. Her gaze never wavers from the mangled corpse I fully intend to leave behind.

Fuck, she's almost catatonic.

I need to get her home and away from here, and quickly. Plus, anyone could have heard her scream, and I don't have time to deal with cops when my girl needs me. Wrapping my arm around her, I lead her away from the alley, hating how small and fragile she suddenly feels. She's so silent, like her soul no longer dwells in her body—as if I have already lost her.

Even more, I hate that I've left bloody handprints across her skin and clothes.

Fuck!

I know better. She should never have been touched by this side of my life. By the horrors I commit. By what I really am. I think there was always a part of me that knew she would eventually find out about this side of me, but I assumed I had more time. I'm not ready. I'm not ready to let her go. To lose her. Not like this.

I've faced many demons in my life, conquered many enemies and won every battle, yet the hardest fight of my life is still ahead of me—trying to keep my Layla.

I ignore the parked car across the street that I leased for her to use and guide her to my car around the block, carefully sitting her inside. She's so out of it that I even have to buckle her seatbelt to ensure she's safe. Once I'm certain she won't bolt, I shut the car door before rushing to the driver's seat and climbing in. Grabbing the wipes from my glove box, I quickly clean the blood off my hands, face, and arms before doing the same to her. All the while, she doesn't move or speak. It worries me, so I blast the heat and turn on the engine, wanting to get us home, to her safe space, as quickly as humanly possible.

Unfortunately, the drive feels like it takes forever. I clench the wheel so hard my knuckles turn white, making my hands ache, but it's still not enough. My anger at myself is starting to take over, even as I shoot her worried looks all the way home. She still hasn't spoken since we left Hell's Kitchen. Not a single word except that one burning question—*who are you?*

It rings in my head like an accusation. Who am I? Am I just a hired hit man? A killer? The monster people fear that hides in the shadows? Or am I the man she loves, her husband? Could I possibly be both? And if not, which one is an act?

I don't even know anymore.

What I do know is that I want to be the man I used to see in her eyes, the one she smiles at, laughs with, and trusts. I want to be the one who makes her happy, not this . . . monstrosity.

But maybe it's too late for all that now.

Or is it?

Layla is the most important thing in my life. More important than my job, my life, my business. She's everything. But have I realized it too late?

When we get home, I notice Zoey left a note saying she's sleeping over at her friend's house again, leaving just us. I rush my love upstairs and help her into a warm bath to clean off any traces of blood, knowing she probably feels dirty. After, I dress her. She remains silent all the while. Tucking her into bed, I kiss her head softly before grabbing some snacks and a cup of herbal tea for her.

She doesn't touch those either. Instead she turns onto her side, ignoring me.

"Baby—" I stroke her back, and when she doesn't move away from my gentle touch, I almost slump in relief. I quickly hurry to shower and then climb into bed with her. Pulling her close, I wrap her in my arms, needing to feel her. "I'm here. Whenever you are ready to talk, I'm here. You are safe; you are loved," I promise, kissing her cheek, but the shiver the gesture would usually elicit and her soft smile are gone.

Instead, we both just lie here until the hours pass. We watch the sunset through the window, and the silence hanging in the air between us is so loud, I almost choke on it. I wait for her to speak. I wait for anything.

But it never comes.

As I hold her throughout the night, I feel her slipping away. When I peek at her face, I see her eyes are clouded, distant, as she continues to stare at the city lights through our bedroom window with silent tears sliding down her face. She's stiff and unresponsive in my arms.

She might physically be right next to me, but her heart is already a million miles away.

I'm losing her.

* * *

Her silence terrifies me. Layla has never been one to hold back or fear anything. Even the day I met her, she was staring down death with a quiet strength that made me realize then and there this girl was special and worth saving.

Now? I stand hesitatingly before the bar in the kitchen where she sits, quietly nursing a mug of coffee. When I woke up this morning, she hadn't been in my arms. I got dressed in a panic before finding her here. I wonder how long she has been sitting here thinking.

"Please, say something," I beg.

And just like that, the spell is broken. She jerks her head up and meets my eyes. "What would you like me to say, *husband*?" She spits the word like an insult, making me flinch where no enemies ever could.

"Anything," I murmur.

"Okay, let's start with who the fuck you are. You obviously don't work in security, so what, you kill people?" When I hesitate to answer, she sneers and narrows her gaze on me. "I should have known. I'm so fucking dumb. All this money, the suit, and the cars. The strength I feel in your body, the blood on your clothes, and the scars on your chest, yet I never put it together. Never wanted to," she rambles before taking a sip of coffee as if to temper her anger.

"Please, don't blame yourself," I implore.

"I don't," she snarls, pushing to her feet and pressing her hand on the counter, glaring at me. "I blame you. I married you. I brought my sister into your house. I trusted our lives to you. I let you in my body. I . . . I fell in love with you." Her voice cracks as she finally says the words I've been dying to hear since I met her. Love has me stepping toward her, but with the coldness in her eyes, it's obvious I'm not welcome. "For months we have been living like husband and wife, and yet you are a complete stranger to me. So, Alaric, if that's even your name, who the fuck are you?"

"I'm still me, still Alaric," I start, but her eyes narrow into two tight slits.

"You are not. The Alaric I thought I knew wouldn't kill a man. Wouldn't snap a man's neck like it was nothing. I will only ask you once more before I walk out of that door and you will never see me or Zoey again."

Rubbing my head, I finally sit. "This isn't how I wanted to tell you."

"No? How did you imagine this going? Oh hi, baby girl, did you have a nice day? Does Zoey need help with her homework? Oh, and by the way, I kill people for a living. How about some pizza for dinner?" She snorts.

"Not like this!" I yell before wincing. "Fuck, I don't know. I don't even know if I would have ever told you. I liked that you didn't know, liked that you didn't look at me like everyone else, scared and knowing what I am—a killer." Shaking my head, I frown. "I guess it doesn't matter now. I'll tell you everything." I meet her eyes. "Which means I need to start at the beginning."

"Beginning?" she echoes, arching a suspicious brow.

Shit.

"Layla . . . Layla, I was the one who killed your stepfather."

The statement hangs heavily in the air as she gawks before sitting down heavily. "What?"

"You're right. I'm a killer, a monster. A professional hit man. I take jobs no one else could or would. I'm the best at it. I've taken hundreds, maybe even thousands of lives in my career. I never had a choice, or at least no one ever offered one to me. This is all I know. My father raised me to be like this. Before he retired, he was one himself." That makes her flinch, and her eyes widen when she realizes the man she so clearly liked and thought was going to be a good family member isn't who she thinks he is either. "I was taught young and worked hard to become the best at what I do. That day, the day you first came into my life, I was on a job. I think of it as destiny now. As if I were meant to be there, meant to be on that back road that day to see you, to save you." Licking my lips, I stare into her eyes. "To see you staring down the barrel of a shotgun."

"Don't," she whispers.

"You stood there so bravely, despite the fact he had just killed your brother and mother. You looked at me, and your eyes seared into my soul, and for the first time ever, I wanted to save a life, not take one. So I did. I shot and killed him. I saved you. And I've been watching you ever since." Reaching across for her hand, I implore her to understand, but she jerks her hand back like it's been burnt.

"I would check in every so often while you were at your aunt's, but more so when you moved here to the city where I lived, and I couldn't resist seeing you every day. At first, I told myself it was to ensure you were okay because I felt responsible for you. But the more I watched you, the more I fell in love with you, with the woman who silently, resiliently shouldered all the burdens. You did whatever it took to survive and did it with a smile. I couldn't stay away. I told myself it would never go further than me watching you and quietly pining over you, but when I saw you stripping" —I grin at the memory— "I knew, I just knew I had to save you one last time. But I promise you, Layla, everything I did was because I cared for you and Zoey. I never expected it to go so far, but you changed everything, and I was helpless as I was swept away in this new world—a world I wish I could truly live in just to be the man you lie next to every night."

She's quiet again, digesting all my rambled words.

"So everything . . . Everything was a fucking lie."

"No, not everything," I insist.

"No? What was the truth then?" she snarls. "You asking me to marry you? You telling me you worked in security? Letting me meet your father? Calling us a family? Making me believe that you cared for me? Maybe even loved me?" She inhales then, her eyes glassy. "How could I trust anything you ever say or do now?"

"Baby girl—" She flinches at the endearment, closing her eyes. "I'm sorry, I should have told you. I was just so fucking terrified of losing you. You were—*are* the only good thing in my life. I couldn't bear the thought of losing you. Even if you don't believe me now, I swear I do love you, Layla. You're my fucking heart. My whole world revolves around you. You are at the very center of it. My reason. My love."

My heart deflates as all my loving words fall on deaf ears. She's tuning me out, erecting walls around her heart, and refusing to let my love in.

"You know the worst part? I think maybe if you just had told me, I could understand, but the lies? That I can't handle." Taking a deep breath, she looks deep into my eyes. "I am thankful to you for saving us that day, and then again with the money for Zoey's surgery, but I can't do this. I can't be married to a stranger. To a murderer. To someone who could so easily kill someone one minute and make love to me the next. How could I possibly feel safe letting a man like you be around Zoey? No, I can't."

"Layla, please give me another—"

"No," she snaps. "I can't do this. I . . . I want a divorce!" she finally says, slumping as if every ounce of strength has left her body.

Me? I stagger in the chair. My heart stops and my soul turns cold as I stare at her. I was always so worried about losing her, and now I finally have. I was right: a monster like me would never deserve a woman like her.

It was better to have never had her than to feel this immense pain that blooms in my chest until I can barely breathe.

"I'll get my stuff and leave." I stand, the chair screeching with the force. Unable to stay, I hurry away, needing to get out of here before I break down. Before I finally crumble.

Never has someone landed a hit like this. I never let them close enough. But Layla?

She's my weakness.

And now I'm nothing.

I'm a broken man.

She doesn't call after me as I pack and leave. She watches me go, our eyes meeting one last time before I turn away and leave for good. I leave my keys behind, wanting her to feel safe. I can give her this one last thing, this home we made. The money, the safety, she can have it all.

None of it means anything without her anyway.

CHAPTER 22

Layla

H
e left.

Just like that, he left.

He didn't fight me on my request for a divorce. He didn't shout and yell at me to get out of his house. He didn't fall to his knees and beg for forgiveness.

He just . . . left.

I had been so angry and sure that ending this chapter in my life was what I wanted that my grief only surfaced with the loud bang of the front door. The sound's so final and so real that my knees buckle, making me slip to the floor as I sob my eyes out. Unable to stop the tears from falling, I let them do their worst as the river of misery pours out of me.

Even when I didn't know it, I always had Alaric in my life—my guardian, my angel, my protector—and now he's gone, and for the first time, I am truly alone.

I feel scared and lost, wishing we hadn't broken each other's hearts.

I wish we could be different and our lives could be perfect and happy, but that's a fantasy and not reality. This is real life. It's raw, fucked up, and filled with broken people just trying to survive and find happiness in those broken shards. Miraculously enough, for a while, I did.

With him.

Now that happiness is gone, and I can barely breathe with the thought of a life without him. Panic starts to take hold, and I rub my chest where it feels like a raw wound has ripped open inside it.

The tears eventually subside, and I fall asleep right there, curled up on the floor, holding my broken heart as I pray to the stars above that I haven't just made the worst mistake of my life.

The joyful life I always dreamed of having was just stolen from me, and to my shame, it wasn't some villain from my past who took it out of my hands. No, it was me who cruelly let go of the one chance I had for true love.

I'm my worst enemy.

I'm the villain in my story.

For that, my heartache will undoubtedly be my end, my ruin.

Without Alaric, what chance of happiness will I ever have?

* * *

It's been a week since I watched Alaric leave his house keys and walk through the front door without even a backward glance. I should be happy that he respected my wishes. I should be thrilled that he was the one who packed his things and left me and Zoey in this house. I should be fucking ecstatic that it was so easy to push a ruthless killer out the door and out of my life.

So why do I feel none of those things?

Why do I feel this terrible ache in my heart as if someone

punched a hole in my chest and is ripping me apart? I feel like I'm dying. Slowly. Ever so slowly with each second that he's gone. It hurts even more that I let my feelings slip and he didn't even seem to notice. I only realized the word "love" had slipped out when I was yelling after he left.

God, how did my life take such a turn?

A few months ago, I was living hand to mouth, trying to skate by while worrying that Zoey's health was deteriorating day by day and there was nothing I could do about it.

And then Alaric entered my life, with promises that he would remedy every wrong and save my beloved sister. All I had to do was marry him, and he would grant every wish I ever had.

Did he lie about that?

No.

He fulfilled my every demand and then some. Not only did he save my sister from certain death, but he gave us a home where she could flourish. Zoey has never been happier than she has been since Alaric came waltzing into our lives. Not only did he make sure she could attend the best private school in the district, but he gave her more than money could ever offer.

He gave her his time, attention, and love.

He went above and beyond all my stipulated demands when I agreed to be his wife. Zoey is a happy, healthy young girl because of him. But Alaric didn't only lavish my sweet sister with love; he spoiled me with it too. He showed me a world I never envisioned for myself. One where someone loved me with all his heart, body, and soul. He might be a killer and a liar, but no one can fake what we shared. Those long nights where he would coax my every nerve ending to sing for him. Those lazy Sunday mornings when he would open my thighs and feast on me like a starved man, ravenous to consume every inch of me.

No.

Alaric may have lied to me, but not about that.

Still, does it matter now?

It doesn't change who he is—a cold-blooded killer.

One that's paid very handsomely for his services and skills, proficient skills that he must have used on all his unsuspecting defenseless victims. If I let this farce of a marriage continue, would he use those same skills on Zoey and me? Make us disappear with a snap of his fingers as easily as I had watched him snap that man's neck back in the alley?

Oh God.

No. As much as I'm hurting, I could never put Zoey in that type of danger again. We survived one monster. I doubt we could endure another.

I was the one who killed your stepfather.

Alaric's last words to me felt like a truck slammed into my chest.

Even before I knew his name, he had already saved me.

Unable to contain it anymore, my tears start to fall on their own violent accord. I wrap myself around the baby-blue colored blanket I keep on the couch for those cold nights and pretend it's him holding me together as I fall apart.

Every night for the last seven days, I've wept for the future we could have had together, for the love I lost, and the family we were. I cry well into the early hours, knowing that when Zoey wakes up, I'll have to put on a brave face so she doesn't worry.

But as if she could hear my tormented thoughts, the sound of her bare feet drawing closer has me sitting up straight.

"Layla," my sister calls out from behind me.

I turn to find her wiping the sleep from her eyes as she walks over to sit on the couch beside me.

I shove my head into the blanket and quickly wipe my tears away, hoping she doesn't notice. Although my swollen eyes will be harder to explain.

"It's late, Zoey. What are you doing up?"

"Couldn't sleep. I could hear you crying from upstairs."

Shit.

"I'm sorry, sweet girl. It was just a sad movie that I was watching. I guess it moved me more than I realized."

"The TV isn't even on, Layla. Stop treating me like a child. I know the real reason why you've been crying every night. It's because Ric is gone."

I chew on my lower lip and offer her a nod. I won't lie to my sister. Not about this.

"When is he coming back?" she asks, hope shining in her eyes.

"He's not, sweetheart."

"Why not?" she demands.

"Because I asked him not to. He's not the man we thought he was, Zoey. It's best if he's no longer a part of our lives," I explain patiently, but every word feels like a lie on my tongue.

"I don't understand," she counters, her own eyes starting to water, and the sight only adds to my misery.

"I don't want to go into too much detail, but you just have to believe me that we are better off now that he's gone. Maybe when you're older, I'll be able to explain the things I found out about him. Maybe then you will see why I asked him to leave," I plead, hoping she will drop it so my already fragile heart won't break further.

She hugs her knees up to her chest and stares at me with understanding in her eyes.

"I know why. He told you what he did, didn't he?"

"What? What are you talking about, Zoey?" I murmur,

wondering if my sister knows more than I thought she did. Fear has me sitting up as I anxiously wait for her to elaborate.

"I remember," she starts, pretending to pick invisible lint from her pajamas. "I remember the day you told me to run into the field so Dad couldn't hurt me. I remember it like it was yesterday. You told me to run, but I didn't. I hid and watched you walk up to him, his mean grin plastered on his face. I saw how you confronted him, trying not to look at Gage's body on the street. I remember it all."

"Oh, Zoey." I clasp my hands over hers, pushing her to cuddle with me on the couch. "I'm so sorry, sweetheart. If I could, I'd take those memories away from you so you didn't ever have to think of them again."

"I'm glad I remember. Watching you confront my father so bravely made me want to be more like you. You made me want to be fearless, to look every monster in the eye and not be afraid."

"I was very afraid, Zoey. I was so afraid that he would catch you and do to you what he did to our brother and mother. That's where my bravery came from. It was all because of you," I tell her, hugging her close.

"That's not all I remember, Layla. I also remember what happened next. I saw everything. The black car driving toward you. The driver's window being rolled down and a gun being pointed at Dad. I saw the bullet that hit his skull. And then I saw his shotgun also fire a bullet into you. When you fell down onto the cement, it was the scariest thing I ever saw. But then the driver rushed out of his car and grabbed you, and I thought he was going to try and take you from me too. So I came out of my hiding place and ran to him, punching him in the leg to make him let you go. After he put you in the back seat, he dropped to his knee to look me in the eye. He told me that he was there to help us. He said he was going to take you to the hospital and that I should come with him. I remember, Layla. I remember all of it. I remember that man was our Ric."

"Why didn't you ever tell me this?" I question in utter shock.

"I don't know." She shrugs. "You seemed to want to forget it all, so I tried to do the same for you. At first I thought it was all in my head, that I must have imagined it all, but the more time I spent with Ric, the more I remembered. He saved us that day, and it's been Ric who keeps saving us. He will always be here to save us, don't you see?" she implores, her voice earnest.

"Even if that means he has blood on his hands?" I ask, wanting to know my sister's truest thoughts. She may be young, but she has survived more than most adults and has an intelligence that rivals even my own.

"No one's perfect." She shrugs, and then she gives me a genuine smile that fills my heart with hope. "But Ric is perfect for us."

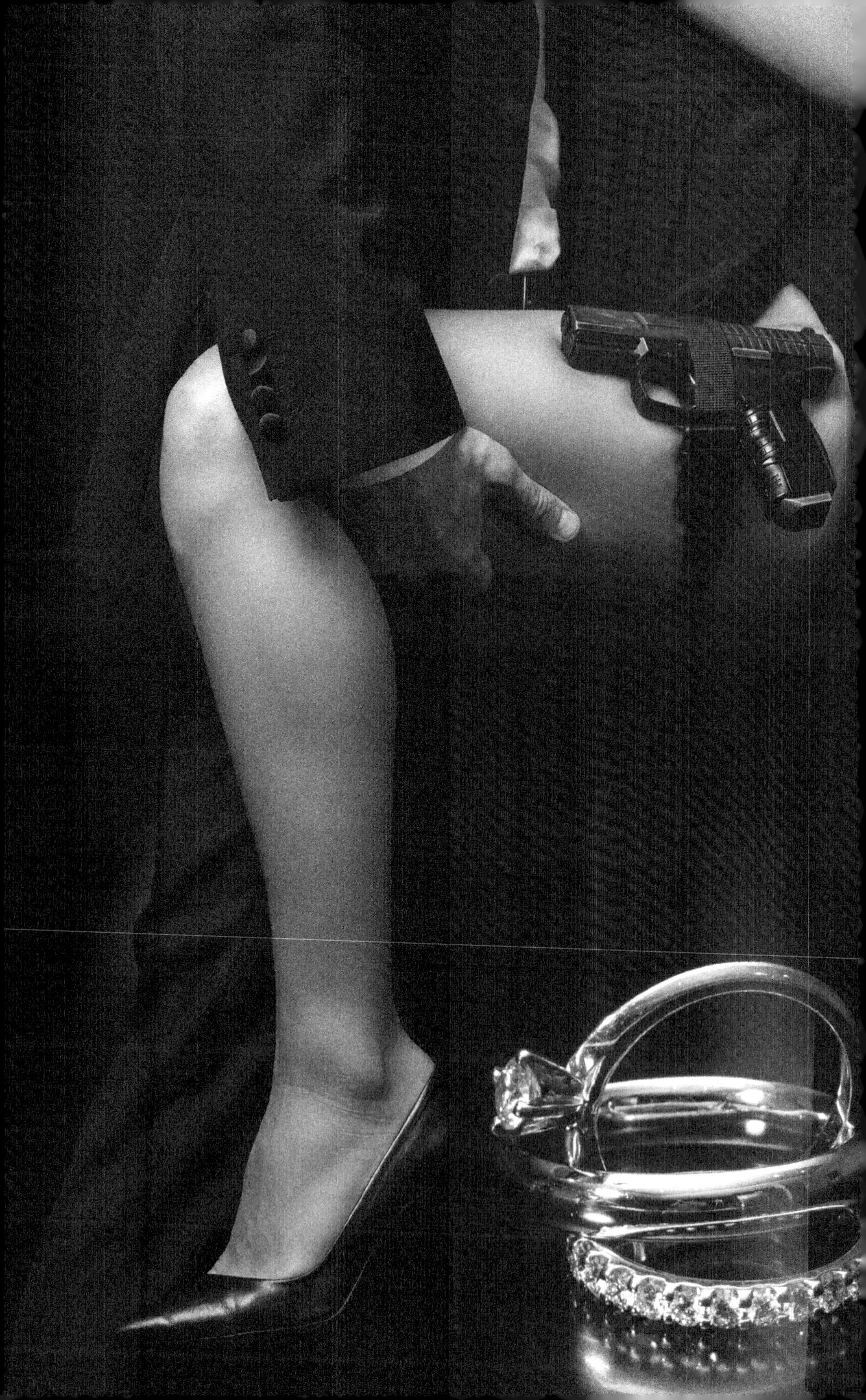

CHAPTER 23
Alaric

The folder feels heavy in my hands as I stand at the front door, ready to open it before I remember. Instead, I knock, wanting her to see I'm really trying. This is her house, not mine. In the divorce papers I'm holding, I made sure she would see that. I've made a savings account for Zoey, which I will add at least ten thousand dollars a month into, and a current account for Layla, so she will never have to worry about money. She gets the house. I have even bought her a new car, though she doesn't know that yet. That way she never has to rely on me or public transportation again.

I want her to be happy, to have everything she ever dreamed of or wanted.

I just wish it were with me, but I know that can't happen.

The door opens, framing Layla. She's wearing a beautiful flowing white dress with blue flowers dotted across it, and she steals my breath just like every time I lay eyes on her. The dress cascades like a waterfall down to her toned thighs, and it's cinched in at her curvy waist with her breasts pushed up. It's clearly new and expensive, and she looks fucking amazing in it. Yet I can't help but grin when I see her feet bare. Layla will always be a mix of the old her and the new.

"Hi," she greets shyly. "Come in." She turns away and wanders inside. I follow her into the kitchen where she grabs a mug. "Do you want coffee?"

"No, thank you."

For fuck's sake, Alaric, why did you say no?

Oh yes, because every moment in her presence is torture, knowing I can't touch her, kiss her, have her.

She's not mine anymore, and I have the papers to prove it. I wish I didn't, it hurts, but it's what she wants, and I would do anything to make her happy. Nodding silently, she faces me, her hands fidgeting with the dress as she looks me over. When her gaze lands on the folder in my hands, she stares.

"I have drawn everything up. If you have any changes, let me know. I've also marked the places to sign to make it easier for you," I begin, but when she continues to stare, I frown. "Bab—Layla, are you okay?"

Her shoulders lift almost absentmindedly as she turns away, but not before I see the tears in her eyes which she tries to cover. "Sorry, I'm fine."

"Layla," I murmur, "what's wrong?"

I step closer, drawn by her pain, needing to be there for her when she needs it the most. Even if, in the long run, it only hurts me more.

"Talk to me, what's wrong?" I beg.

Finally, she turns, her eyes red and glassy. "It's silly. I know I did this. I ended it and told you to leave. I want this . . . but . . ."

"But?" I prompt, hope blooming in my chest even though I

know it's stupid. I spent days trying to figure out how to fix this before realizing there was no fixing it. There was nothing I could do. She made her mind up, and she deserves to find and choose her own life and happiness.

Even if it's without me.

"Layla, isn't this what you wanted?" I ask when she doesn't respond.

"I thought it was," she whispers, meeting my eyes and swallowing. "But seeing the papers makes it all so real. I was so angry with you for lying to me, so mad at myself for believing all your excuses and not seeing the truth, but with this time apart, all I could do was think. I went back and forth about this. About us. You lied to me, and I hate that you did. You're not the man I thought you were . . . but then again, is anyone ever truly that person another makes them out to be in their head? Everything you did still stands. You still sacrificed everything for us and did everything for me even before I could remember you." Shaking her head, she reaches for the papers before stopping. "I asked myself if I could ever forgive you and give us another chance, a fresh start like you said. But there is so much history between us, I didn't know how. When it came down to it, all that really mattered was how I felt. Could I let you go? Could I end this before I really gave us a shot?"

"Layla," I whisper, begging her with my eyes to say what I think she's going to, even as that dark part of me calls me a fool.

"I . . . I don't know, Alaric. I want to. I know that, but what if nothing changes? What if we are just too wrong for each other? I don't like what you do for a job, but I understand why you do it. It doesn't make you a different man than the one who stood by my side the day Zoey went into surgery, or the man who reads her bedtime stories over and over just because she demands it. Nor does it make you any less of the man who would passionately kiss me and hold me so tight as he offered me the world . . ."

"Layla, what do you want?" I urge when she just trails off.

"I . . . I want you," she finally says after a lifetime. She holds my gaze as I stand frozen in disbelief, wondering if I heard her right. "Whatever that entails. I fell in love with you, Alaric. I love you. I do. I'm not accepting the lies you told me, but I think . . . I think maybe we could start again. I think we could be something truly amazing. That is, if you still want me? If you still want me to be your wife."

I just stare, unable to speak as she offers me everything I ever truly wanted but thought was lost.

"Alaric, I want to be married to you. I want to know everything, and I . . . I love you. Do you . . . Do you think . . ." I stop her, hating the worry in her eyes at my silence and the questions she should never have felt the need to ask. Covering the distance between us, I grip her throat and tilt her head back until she meets my eyes.

"I've wanted you since the day I met you. I will always want you, now and forever. There is nothing I want more in this world than to be your husband again."

"If that's true, I would like us to give it another go. But no lies this time, no matter how gruesome or uncomfortable they may make me. I can't live a life based on a lie," she begs, her eyes widening as she leans into me so sweetly. Her softness and warmth chase away the cold I've felt since she cast me aside, since she walked away from me.

"No lies," I promise. "You have me entirely, heart, body, and soul, Layla. I was ready to walk away, to give you up to make you happy, but I don't think I ever truly could. I'm drawn to you like a moth to a flame. I'm not a good man, baby girl, but you make me want to be."

"It's true that you're a killer, that you might be all sorts of bad . . . but you're my type of bad, and if this time apart has shown me anything, it's that I can't live without you," she murmurs, her voice so soft that it fixes my broken heart, and when she rises up on her toes and presses her lips to mine . . . ?

I am whole again.

"I love you," she whispers as she pulls away.

"I love you so fucking much," I snarl, dragging her closer and kissing her so hard that when I pull away, she's panting. I vow to myself to tell her how much I love her every moment of every day so she never doubts it. She groans, those beautiful breasts heaving with the desire—the same desire I see flooding those emerald orbs of hers when they blink open. "Now let me show you just how much, wife."

I don't have the patience to carry her upstairs. I need her right this second, need her to come across my tongue and then around my cock. I need to sink deep inside of her and stain every inch of her skin with my marks and cum until she is irrevocably mine.

Forever.

I hoist her up and drop her onto the counter, sweeping the folder off so its contents tumble to the floor, forgotten and unneeded.

I'm home.

She falls to her back, her legs hanging over the edge. Her green eyes glow with arousal and happiness as I lean down and blanket her body with mine. I slide my hands up her silken thighs to her hips, finding no panties.

"Fuck, is this for me, baby girl? You're goddamn naked under here."

"I hoped you'd have your wicked way with me." She grins.

I kiss her softly, tangling my tongue with hers before pulling back. "Wicked way? Love, when I'm done with you, you'll never forget who you belong to again. You'll be screaming my name for the neighbors to hear and begging me for more until you can't take it."

"Promise, promises," she purrs, arching her chest to draw my attention to her pebbled nipples pushing against the soft material of the dress.

Ignoring her taunt, I trail my lips down her chin and chest as she falls back with a moan. She wraps her legs around my waist and places her hands on my shoulders, pushing at the leather jacket I'm wearing. Nipping at her skin, I lean back slightly and help her strip it from me, tossing it aside before she grabs the bottom of my shirt. Winking at her, I grab it from the back and haul it over my head. Her eyes smolder as she licks her lips and runs her gaze across my chest.

Fuck.

I love the way she looks at me. Finally, all the hours spent training to make me the deadliest I could be has other benefits.

"Pants," she orders.

"Not yet," I growl, pressing my hand against her chest as she tries to rise to fight me. I push her onto her back before dragging her dress down, watching her rosy nipples tighten in the air as her breasts tumble free. Groaning, I stroke across her globes, tweaking and twisting one taut bud. Her moans fill the air as I watch it harden into a stiff, perfect peak, begging for my mouth like her little pussy as her hips roll desperately.

"So fucking responsive," I murmur, leaning down to suck her nipple into my mouth. Her chest arches, shoving it deeper into my mouth.

"Oh God, Alaric, please!"

I love the way she says my name, and I'll never get tired of it, so I make her call it again. I dig my teeth into her sensitive skin until she cries out, and then I soothe it with my tongue before pulling back and turning my head. I give her other breast the same treatment until both are flushed with my teeth marks circling her rosy, engorged nipples.

I glide my hands up her waist and under the dress, pulling it down farther until I have to step back and tug it, revealing her flushed, perfect body. But I'm too needy to just stare. I have to remind her how much I need and love her.

Forcing myself between her thighs, I grab her hips and lift, holding her aloft as I press her pink, wet pussy to my mouth. I lap at every inch of her core, her sweetness exploding across my tongue until I'm nothing but an animal eating her pussy. I dip my tongue inside of her to get more, and her noises get louder as she wiggles in my grip, riding my face like the good girl she is.

Her clit begs for my mouth, so I pull my tongue from her hole and lash there instead. She writhes, and I have to hold her still, her cries increasing as I suck and lick. When I bite down, she thrashes in my arms, her little hole clenching as she comes. She screams her release like I promised then sags in my grip after. I lick her through it, but I'm a greedy man and I want another.

Banding my arm across her peachy ass, I hold her against me as I stroke my fingers through her wetness and thrust them inside of her fluttering channel. She moans weakly as I curl them inside of her before pulling out and pushing them back in, watching her greedy cunt swallow them, glistening with her release.

"Good girl," I growl, licking around her hole to catch her cream as I fuck her with my fingers. I add a third, twisting and widening them until she's crying out again.

"Oh God, Alaric!" she yells. "I can't . . . I'm going to . . ."

Knowing she's right where I want her, I turn my hand and press my thumb to her little puckered hole, watching triumphantly as she seizes in my arms, milking my fingers as she comes again. She squirts her release, and I lap at her, desperate to catch it all, not wanting to waste a drop of my wife's delicious juices.

When she slumps again, I lower her to the counter, feeling her shiver. Her eyes are closed, her lips are parted, and her hair is wild.

She's so fucking beautiful. I kiss her stomach, ignoring my aching, rock-solid cock as she recovers. When she finally sits up, her legs shaking under my grip, I kiss her mouth, letting her taste her release as she eagerly slides her tongue across mine.

Stepping back, I watch her as she slips off the counter and moves toward me, her gaze intent and needy. She slides her hand up my chest and tweaks my nipple, sending a zing of pain through me and hardening my cock more.

"I need you."

Three words.

Three fucking words.

How could I resist?

Pushing her to her knees, I unzip my trousers, her eyes widening when I pull out my stiff cock and stroke it.

"Lean back," I order, and she does so quickly. "Good girl," I praise as she places her hands on the floor behind her to keep herself balanced. I step closer, still stroking my hard length, feeling my precum drip from my tip and splash onto her breasts. I can't help but grunt as I watch the bead roll down her skin. I did plan for that pretty mouth to suck my cock before I fucked her, but I have something better in mind.

Bending slightly, I release my cock for a moment. "Press your breasts together," I command.

She blinks, hesitating, and I narrow my eyes, so she quickly lifts her hands and pushes her breasts together like a fucking offering. Goddamn. I almost spill right there, but I hold myself back as I grab my cock once more. Slowly caressing the tip across her flushed globes, I paint them with my precum as she moans. I grab her hair with one hand, tilt her head back so I can look into those emerald eyes, and then do what I have been fantasizing about.

I push my cock between her breasts, thrusting like it's her tight little cunt. I fuck them, spilling more precum across them as I snap my hips forward.

"Oh God," she whimpers, spreading her legs wider so I can see her soaked cunt.

Fuck.

I release my cock from her tits and yank her up by the throat. She comes willingly, wide-eyed and needy as hell. My very own wife. "Bend that pretty ass over the counter," I order.

Turning, she does as I command and bends at the waist, pressing her chest to the marble counter. She sticks her plump ass out enticingly and stretches her hands out before her. I bite down on my fist as she parts her legs farther, seeing that raw, pink pussy I own. It drips with her need and release, her thighs glistening with it. Never has there been a more perfect sight.

Wrapping her hair around my hand, I yank her head back, meeting her eyes as I press against her back. "I'm going to fuck you hard and fast. I need you too much to do otherwise. I missed you too fucking much, missed this hot little body gripping my cock like the greedy cum-obsessed woman you are. But later . . ." I kiss her before biting her lip. "Later, I'm going to fuck you long and hard. I'm going to fill every hole with my cum. I'm going to fuck this sweet little worshipping mouth, that wet pussy, and your naughty, tight little ass until you pass out from exhaustion and pleasure."

"Alaric," she begs, pushing back.

She always wants me as much as I want her, and I can't hold back anymore.

I need her too badly; there's no more need for talking.

I need to fill my wife with my cock, to make her mine again.

For eternity.

"Don't you ever leave me again," she demands, turning her head and searching for my lips, so I kiss her deeply.

"Never," I vow. "Not even if you order me to. I'm yours and you are mine. I'll never leave your side, never hurt you, never abandon you. You are my entire reason for living, Layla Holmes, and I'll spend the rest of my days proving that to you and giving you the life you always deserved."

She stares at me with a sheen of tears in her eyes. "That was so fucking beautiful, but if you don't fuck me right now, I might die."

Reaching down, I circle my cock and drag it along her dripping cunt, making it good and wet with her release before notching it at her entrance. "Hold on, baby girl," I tell her, watching her fingers curl into the marble as I slam into her.

It's not gentle nor soft. I need her too much for that.

Pulling out of her clinging cunt with a snarl, I thrust back in, the slap of our skin loud as I hammer into her. Her cries grow louder and louder. I teased myself as much as her, and I can already feel my release building. Not having her in a while isn't helping, but I push back my orgasm, trying to make this last forever.

Even if it kills me so softly.

As she screams my name, she claws at the marble, pushing back to meet my brutal thrusts.

"Mine," I snarl, using my hand in her hair to pull her head up as I growl, clenching my teeth. "Say it, say you're mine."

"Yours, yours, yours," she chants, her pussy clenching around my cock.

I lose it.

I pummel into her, forcing her to take it over and over until I can't hold back anymore. My release explodes through me, forcing a yell from my throat as I jerk my hips. I fill her with my cum as she comes, groaning softly and clenching around me.

Dropping my head to her sweaty back, I just breathe as I feel her doing the same beneath me, our bodies still joined. Groaning, I step back, pulling my softening cock from her cunt, and I watch as my cum drips from it.

A claim.

"Alaric?" she mumbles, lifting her head tiredly as she reaches for me.

I grab her and wrap her in my arms. "I'm not going anywhere, my love. Not ever. I love you."

"I love you too," she breathes, closing her eyes as she snuggles into my chest. Leaning down, I kiss her forehead before carrying her up the stairs.

I'm ready to ravish her all day and all night long.

To start the rest of our lives together.

As husband and wife.

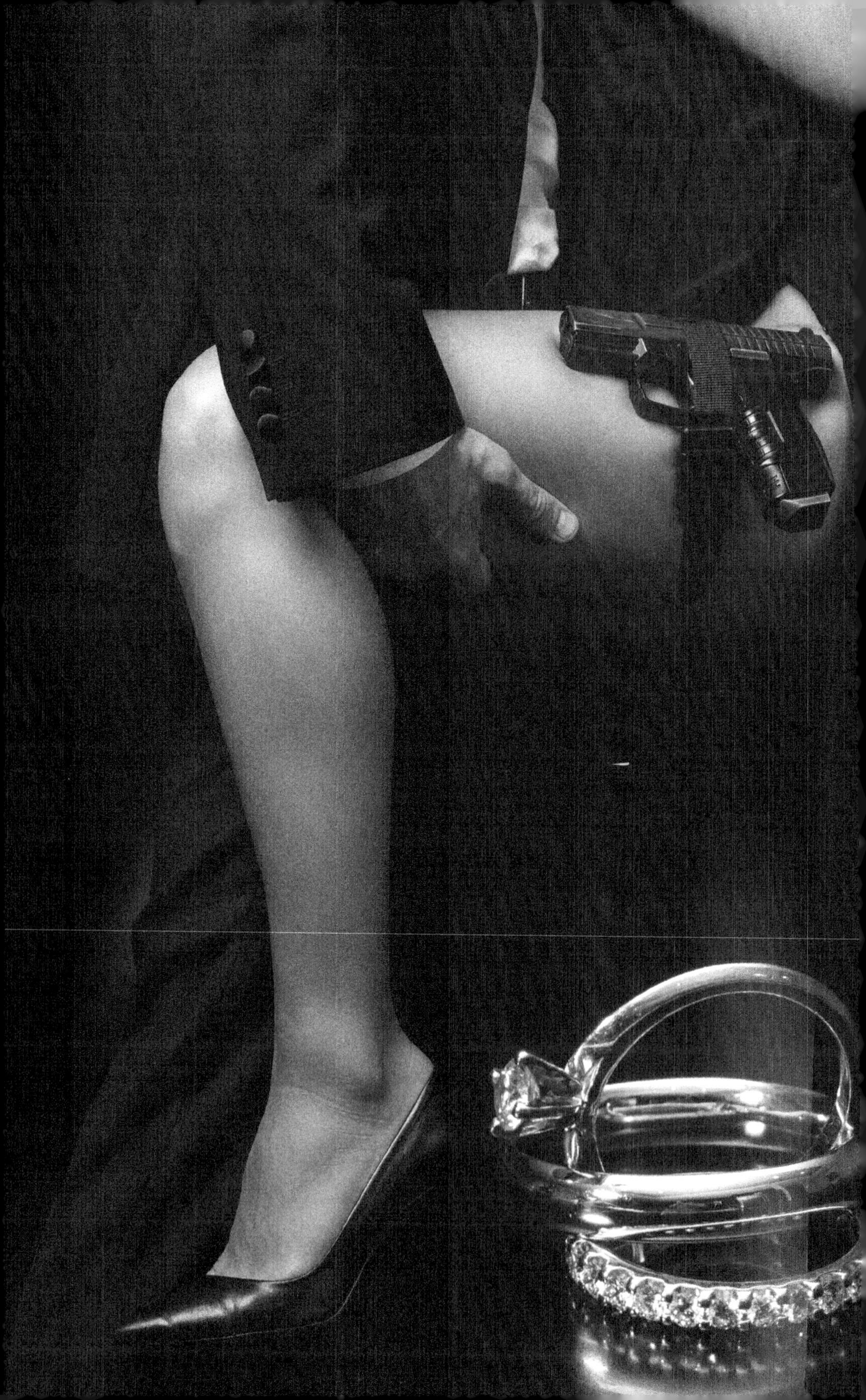

CHAPTER 24

Layla

I wake up curled in Alaric's arms. During the night, we made our way upstairs with a few pit stops, namely him deciding halfway up he couldn't wait before slamming me into the wall and taking me right there on the stairs, and then again on the hallway carpet before finally stumbling into bed and spending all night exploring each other, reconnecting until we were *us* once again. There was no longer anything between us but pleasure and love, like our destiny intended.

Now, I stroke his chest, tired and sore in the best possible way. His hands slide over my body, comforting me and him, as if to reassure himself I'm here. His mouth drops kisses on my head and hair, his leg twined with mine.

"I want to know more about your work," I finally say, making my husband suddenly stiffen under me. When I hear his heart skip a beat, I hold onto him tighter.

Is Alaric afraid I'll leave him again?

He is.

The way his breath hitches and his arms suddenly cocoon me is enough for me to know he fears I'll leave him if I find out more about his job.

Which is exactly why we need to do this.

Sitting up, I drop my chin on his chest and take his hands in mine. He stares into my eyes, searching for answers to questions he refuses to say out loud.

"We need to do this, my love. I need to see this. There can be nothing between us, no ounce of doubt or fear, or it's not fair. I love you, and you love me, but I can't only love half of you. I need to see that side of you too and embrace it. That's the only way this can work, the only way you'll be sure my love for you is unbreakable."

"And if you can't?" he asks, his voice cracking as he watches me sadly, like he's already lost me again.

"That's for me to decide," I tell him softly, kissing the skin over his racing heart. "But I need to do this. We need to do this. It's the only way we can survive."

CHAPTER 25
Alaric

I search Layla's gaze, seeing determination, hope, and reassurance reflected back at me. She thinks she can handle it, but I'm worried she can't. What if she sees that other side of me, the side that can kill and torture without even blinking, and it not only horrifies her again but is the reason she walks away from me for good this time?

She took my heart once and bled it dry, but now that I'm finally back in her arms where I belong, I don't want to do anything to jeopardize that.

At the end of the day, though, when it comes to my young bride, I'm a sucker and unable to deny her whatever she wants—even if it terrifies me.

I feel sick at the idea of her seeing *that* man, not this one who lies in bed with his wife, holding her so tenderly and protecting her always.

He would die before causing her an ounce of pain.

But the other Alaric? The one who takes pleasure in his work? I fear she'll never accept that man.

Her jade-green eyes stare into mine so lovingly that she actually gives me something I didn't think I had in me—hope.

Cupping her chin, I search her gaze once more before giving in. "Okay," I agree. "But when you see it, remember me like this, this man who loves you and would do anything and everything for you."

"I will," she promises, grinning as she sits up and straddles my waist. My hands go to her hips as I drag her close.

I need to feel and taste her since it might be the last time she allows me to.

I don't want what I do for a living to ruin the best thing to ever happen to me. It already came between us once, and I lost her for it, so I won't make that mistake again. There will be no secrets between us.

She will see every inch of me, and if she can handle it, then I am not only the luckiest man alive, but also the most possessive.

Because she will never escape me then.

Ever.

CHAPTER 26

Layla

I get ready, not really knowing what to wear. I don't even know where we are going, so I dress in some black jeans, a nude tank top, and leather jacket. Leaving my hair free since he loves it like that, I slip on my boots and give myself a once over, reminding myself to be open-minded.

Our future, as we know it, depends on it.

Once I'm ready, I find him downstairs, and I lean against the wall there, watching the change come over him. His shoulders stiffen when he slides on his jacket, his hands sure and hard as he checks his gun and puts it away. When he starts to check a duffel bag, I can actually see his face changing, morphing into something sinister.

No more smiles, no more soft eyes.

His eyes are bitter ice chips, cold and deadly, his lips are thin and mean, and his face seems sharper somehow, but I know that's not possible, and when he looks over at me, he runs his eyes over me critically before nodding.

"Let's go," he demands, holding out his hand to me, his voice as cold as the Arctic.

He's giving me one last out and trying to push me away. He's in work mode . . . killer mode.

I see the truth in his eyes. He thinks this will break us again, so he's trying to do it now before I see too much. I won't let him. I place my hand in his, and for a moment, those sapphire eyes flare with surprise and love before they cool once more.

"You will remain silent and behind me at all times, understood?" he demands as he leads me outside. I nod, wringing my hands as I watch him lock up our home. He takes my hand in his again and leads me to the car, slamming my door once I'm fully seated inside. He slides in behind the steering wheel, putting his bag in the back seat before peeling out of the parking spot.

I watch him out of the corner of my eye, sensing he's more on edge than he probably usually is in these situations. I should be afraid, and I am, but not of him. No, I'm afraid of what is going to happen because I don't know if I can handle it, but I need to know.

I can't give myself to him again without knowing.

Not just for my own aching heart, but for his. It wouldn't be fair.

Half an hour later, we pull up to an unmarked garage, and I get out. Without a word, he puts his bag in a plateless sedan, and when he sees me hesitating, he narrows his eyes.

"Get in," he orders.

I scramble to do as I'm told, and when I'm inside, I watch him add plates before sliding behind the wheel and pulling out. He can obviously feel my questioning gaze because he sighs.

"I can't have anyone tracking a hit back to me. We learn to change plates or steal cars. We learn how not to get caught, and I'm the best at never getting caught," he informs me.

He's not bragging; he's just speaking the truth.

I swallow my nerves and nod, looking out of the window. I feel his gaze tracing my face, but I need a minute to collect myself. I fear him for the same reasons I'm still alive right now. After all, he used those skills many years ago to save me.

To save Zoey.

That logic doesn't keep my heart from racing though.

We stop down a back street.

"Look at me."

I close my eyes, but his hand grips my chin and forces me to turn to him. "Look at me, baby girl. This is who I am. I can't change it. Not even for you. If you can't do this, we can go back, and I won't think less of you."

"No, I need to. I want to," I murmur.

He looks unconvinced, so I lean in and kiss him, needing the familiar reassurance of his strength and comfort. He's stiff and unresponsive at first, but just when I'm about to pull away, he groans against my lips. His hand slides into my hair and yanks me closer as he devours my lips.

When I whimper, he sweeps his tongue into my mouth, tangling it with mine until I lean into him, soft, pliant, and needy as hell, despite the fact he made me come more times than I could count last night.

I slide my hand up his thigh and find his stiff cock pressed against his pants. It seems I'm not the only one. I know this is out of fear for both of us.

Fear this will break us.

I can't seem to care, though, as I scramble over the console, settle on his lap, and grind against his huge member. He snarls and pulls back, tugging my hair until he can run his lips and teeth down my neck to nip my jumping pulse. "So fucking soft. Are you wet for me, wife?"

I groan, unable to form words, and he bites harder.

"I asked if you are wet for me."

Eyes hazy with lust, I lift my head, tugging at the strands of hair still wrapped in his fist. "Why don't you find out?" I dare brazenly.

He unbuttons my jeans and shoves his hand inside. Finding me wet as hell, he plunges his fingers inside my panties to stroke my soaked folds. "Always so fucking wet for me, baby girl. You can't get enough of my cock, can you?"

"No, fuck no." I moan, rolling my hips to try and get his fingers where I need them, but he ignores me, stroking along my lips and hole as I groan in frustration.

"Alaric!" I snap, and he chuckles as he pulls his fingers from my tight jeans and sucks them clean.

"Now when I'm killing this man, I'll do it with the taste of my wife coating my tongue," he murmurs. "Lean back," he orders without waiting for a reply.

I do as I'm told, resting my back against the steering wheel as he grabs my jeans, and we work together to get them down enough for him to rip away my panties. "Look how fucking pretty you are, baby girl, all glistening and swollen for me." He groans, his eyes locked on my cunt. I reach for him, but he pushes me away and unzips his own slacks, pulling out his huge, hard length.

"You're going to ride my cock fast and hard and come all over it, baby girl. I want to see you take your pleasure and make me yours."

Oh fuck.

Without waiting for a response, he lifts me and guides me to his cock. Holding my gaze, he leans back with his arms behind his head, making me take over. "Well, wife, if you want your pleasure, then get it," he demands.

Eyes flaring in anger, I sink onto his cock an inch at a time, having to work myself onto it despite how wet I am. Groaning, I lift up and try to take him all. He watches the entire time, hungry and unhelpful. I use his shoulders as leverage and slam myself down on him.

I take every inch of his incredible cock inside me, making us both cry out. Panting, I realize my eyes have closed, so I force them open and stare into his bright blue ones. His hands claw at the headrest as he watches me, his chest heaving.

"Good girl. Just like that. Take my big fat cock. It's just for you, baby girl, only ever for you."

Nodding, I use him as my anchor to ride him fast and hard. Between bouncing and rolling, I do as I am told and take my pleasure. "You feel so good." I whimper as I lift and drop faster, already reaching for that explosion I know will come.

"You feel better, wife. Fuck! I can feel how close you are. Practically milking my cock dry, aren't you?" His nostrils flare as my head drops back, and I lose myself in riding him.

I let him watch as I take every inch over and over until, finally, I come apart, falling off that edge with a scream. My pussy clamps around him, making him roar, and then his hands are on me, gripping my hips as he lifts me and impales me back on his length.

"So fucking tight, so fucking wet for me, wife. Fuck, I love watching you come, knowing it's for me. Only for me," he snarls, fighting my still clamping pussy as I scream louder. One release rolls into another as his fingers dance across my clit. When I slump, he doesn't stop. He slams me down on him harder and faster, until he stills and yells his own release, dragging me into another.

I actually black out for a moment, and when I come to, I'm

leaning against his rapidly rising and falling chest. He pets my back and hair. "Good girl, such a good girl," he praises. "Fuck, I love you so much." I snuggle closer with a sigh, and I'm sure he thinks I don't hear the next bit. "Can't fucking lose you, ever." His arms tighten before he releases me, and I sit back. He won't meet my eyes as he lifts me off him and tucks his cock away before helping me back into my jeans. Finally, he meets my eyes. His are sad, and I hate that.

"You own me mind, body, and soul," I tell him as I grip his face. "I need the same. I need to know and own all of you."

"Be careful what you wish for," he murmurs, but he kisses me anyway before helping me from the car and sliding out after me, transforming once more into a killer.

Not the man I love.

CHAPTER 27

Alaric

There was a job waiting for me that I had been considering agreeing to. This is that job. It's not an easy one, nor is it clean, but if she wants to see the man I am, then I'll show her. I'll throw her in at the deep end. This isn't a clear kill contract. In fact, the target is already inside the warehouse before us, waiting for me and the pain that will come.

The clients want him tortured before he's killed. They want me to record me ripping him to pieces until he dies of his wounds like an animal. They want him to suffer, and my wife has to watch as I do it.

If she can love me after this, then she can love me through anything.

Either way, when we step out of that warehouse, I'll know the truth and so will she.

"So, what can I expect?" she asks. "Gun fights, car chases..."

"Not this time, wife. This time it's something much worse." I refuse to sugarcoat it as we move over to the locked door, which I have the code to. "He was already captured by someone else and dumped here. They want me to extract information and make it hurt before he dies."

"They—they want you to—" She swallows as I look down at her paling face.

"Torture him." I arch my brow, giving her one last out before I turn the doorknob. "Still want to go ahead?"

Rolling her lips inwards, she tilts her chin up in defiance with a strength I both love and hate. "Yes," she says clearly. I had been hoping she would change her mind. Without waiting for anything else, I open the door and step inside, pulling her with me.

The door closes, and I lock it behind us. I don't lessen this for her. I refuse to. She wants to see me work, so she will get that. I won't change who I am, not even to keep her. I can't.

"Al—"

I cover her mouth. "No names," I hiss in the dark before leaving her there. I can almost hear her uncertainty as I make my way over to the back wall and hit the switch. Names aren't a big thing this time, since the man will die, but it's a good lesson to teach her about how I operate. The lights buzz on, and she shields her face, her gaze roving around, unsure and nervous, until they land on him.

Pure terror dilates her eyes as she stares behind me at the man tied to a chair. I drink it in, bathing in her fear, refusing to guide her over in case she rejects my touch. No, I need to be me—the killer.

I turn away from her and focus on him, trying to pretend she isn't here, which is hard when I hear her moving closer.

He's blindfolded and gagged, and his nails are broken from digging into the metal chair, trying to find a weakness. His ankles are tied to each cemented leg, and his hair sticks to his sweaty head.

"Who's there?" he mumbles around the gag, but I don't answer him.

He will talk when I want him to and not a moment before. I slowly strip off my jacket and roll up my sleeves before laying out my tools and checking each one. When I'm prepared, I glance over to find Layla there, her phone in her face. When I snatch it from her, I see she wasn't taking pictures or anything but googling the man behind me.

It must have taken her a while, but his face is recognizable enough even with the gag and blindfold. He's a cold rapist, one the police could never charge due to his money and the fact that he's a diplomat in this country. His list of crimes is longer than his bank account receipts, with victims as young as Zoey—which is why I wanted to take this job.

To get revenge for them, give them peace, and make their monster, their abuser, suffer.

I didn't want her to know though. I wanted Layla to think I was a bastard, a cruel evil man killing for the sake of it, but I guess there's no going back now. She will still have to watch me torture and kill a man, and no matter what kind of monster he is, that shit is never easy to swallow.

At all.

"I get an extra million for making you suffer," I tell him as I pocket her phone and stop before him.

Pulling off the blindfold, I smirk to see his eyes squeezed closed as if not seeing me will save him. I leave the gag in, not wanting to hear his blubbering just yet. Pulling out my phone, I set it up to record for the clients, purposely making sure Layla is out of it and they only see my back. After all, anonymity is key in this game.

After we are done here, I'll edit it so no faces or names are spoken and then send it over. For now, though, I look over at Layla as I run my hands over my tools, and when she winces, I stop on that one to see it's a hammer. Smirking, I turn back to the man, smacking it in my other palm. "This is going to hurt," I tell him conversationally before swinging the hammer down on his kneecap.

His eyes bulge, and his whole body arches in agony as he hollers behind his gag, spittle running down his chin. I watch it happen, and when he slumps, I finally reach forward and rip off the gag. "And this will as well," I remark, and without flourish, I smash the hammer down on his other kneecap.

His anguish-filled scream echoes around the warehouse, his body jerking in shock and pain as he begs.

"Mercy, please!"

"Did you show your victims mercy?" I demand. Gripping his limp, sweaty hair as I yank his head back until he meets my eyes. "Did you?"

"No," he whispers, his eyes glassy in shock.

"Then don't expect any from me. Now where were we?" I put the hammer down and pick up some barbed wire next, and then I slowly and meticulously wind it around both of his legs and pull until it cuts into his pants and skin. Blood runs down his knees and pools on the floor below the chair.

Layla makes a noise, and when I look back, she's pale, wide-eyed, and looking like she might vomit. "Leave," I demand, knowing she can't handle it, but seeing it firsthand fucking hurts, especially when her eyes flick to me and she looks at me like she doesn't know me.

I tried to warn her, but she didn't listen, and now I can see I've already lost her. Turning away before I beg her to stay, I get back to work, trying to tell myself I won't care if she leaves.

My heart splinters in my chest, making me wish for the days when it was cold and dead. Just like the man I'm torturing, I wish I could beg for mercy from her, but I know I wouldn't even if I could.

I would hand her my heart and soul all over again, even knowing she was going to shatter them.

I work for hours on the man, breaking each toe, finger, and rib before carving into his skin and electrocuting him. Crouched before him, I stare up at his blood-covered face and debate turning to look at Layla, but I know she's left.

She had to, right?

Then something unexpected happens.

Her hand lands on my shoulder.

Turning to gaze up at her with hope, I notice the determination in her eyes as they meet mine.

"Let me."

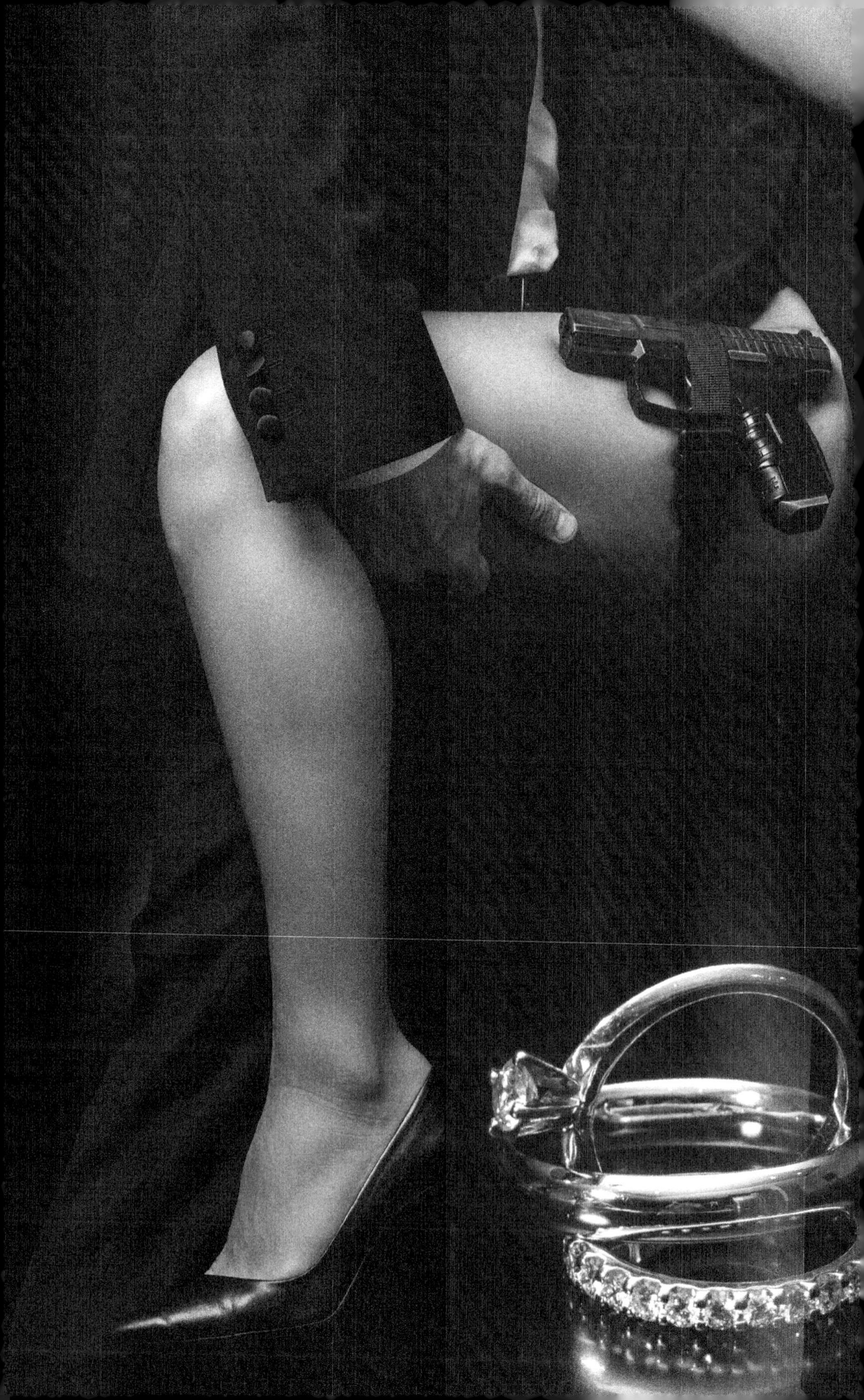

CHAPTER 28

Layla

My words echo around us he stares up at me, blood dotting his hands, arms, and cheeks. His eyes are cold, but he watches me carefully.

Let me.

It's all I could think to do. I was losing him. I saw it. He was testing me, and I failed. I was scared and horrified by what he was capable of, that's true, but the man he's doing it to? If what they say on the news is true, then he's more of a monster than Alaric will ever be.

Who is truly the devil here?

The man ridding the world of this evil by killing such a monster, or the man who the law cannot touch and remains free to cause even more suffering to his victims?

I don't know. Morals and ethics have long gone out of the window. Everything I should be feeling is wrapped up in my love for the man before me and my desperation not to lose him, no matter what.

For hours, I've watched him torture this man, and as those hours passed and my thoughts swung back and forth, I realized one thing —I'm not afraid of Alaric, not even now. I'm only afraid of losing him. He would never hurt Zoey or me, only the bad people in the world. It almost makes me happy to know there are men like my husband out here, men who rid the earth of scum like the pedophile coated in blood.

He talked during those hours, detailing all his crimes and victims, and it made me sick to my stomach. I don't know how Alaric is holding his composure, but every now and again, I see a flash of pure, electric hatred for the man, and I know he hates him and wants him to hurt.

It almost settles me in a way I never knew I needed.

All my life, I have been running and fighting to survive, but not anymore. I don't have to because he will fight for me and always protect me, and if one thing is clear, it's that the world needs men like Alaric, and so do I. Maybe if there were more men like him, men like Roy would think twice about killing their wives and kids.

He saved me when I was nothing but a stranger on the road, when no others would have. Without him, I would be dead. I have belonged to him fully ever since that day, and it's time I embraced this side of him. How could I hate him and be thankful for his ability to take lives and save us at the same time?

I can't.

I refuse to cower anymore. This is my husband, and I will love every dark jagged edge the same way he does me, because he's not alone anymore either, and it's time I showed him that.

I stepped forward and touched him with Gage's face flashing in my mind, almost feeling at peace when he looked up at me and those words escaped my lips. I know I need to prove to him I am worthy of him, just like he did for me.

I need to pass this test.

"Layla?" he asks in confusion, his brow furrowing as he watches me.

"I want to do it," I finally tell him. "You're getting ready to kill him, right?"

He inclines his head slightly as the man sobs. He stopped begging and fighting hours ago, just letting Alaric hurt him like he did those kids.

"You rid the world of one monster for me, so let me rid it of this one for you," I tell him, holding out my hand.

He gets to his feet, towering above me as he searches my gaze. I remain steady and strong, and then he slowly pulls out his gun and flicks off the safety before handing it over. He clearly doesn't think I'm going to do it, but I don't bother explaining myself. I just turn around, put the barrel of the gun to the man's head, and look into his eyes.

I need to see them, to remember them and what I am willing to do for the man I love—the very same thing he is willing to do for me.

And with that thought, I pull the trigger.

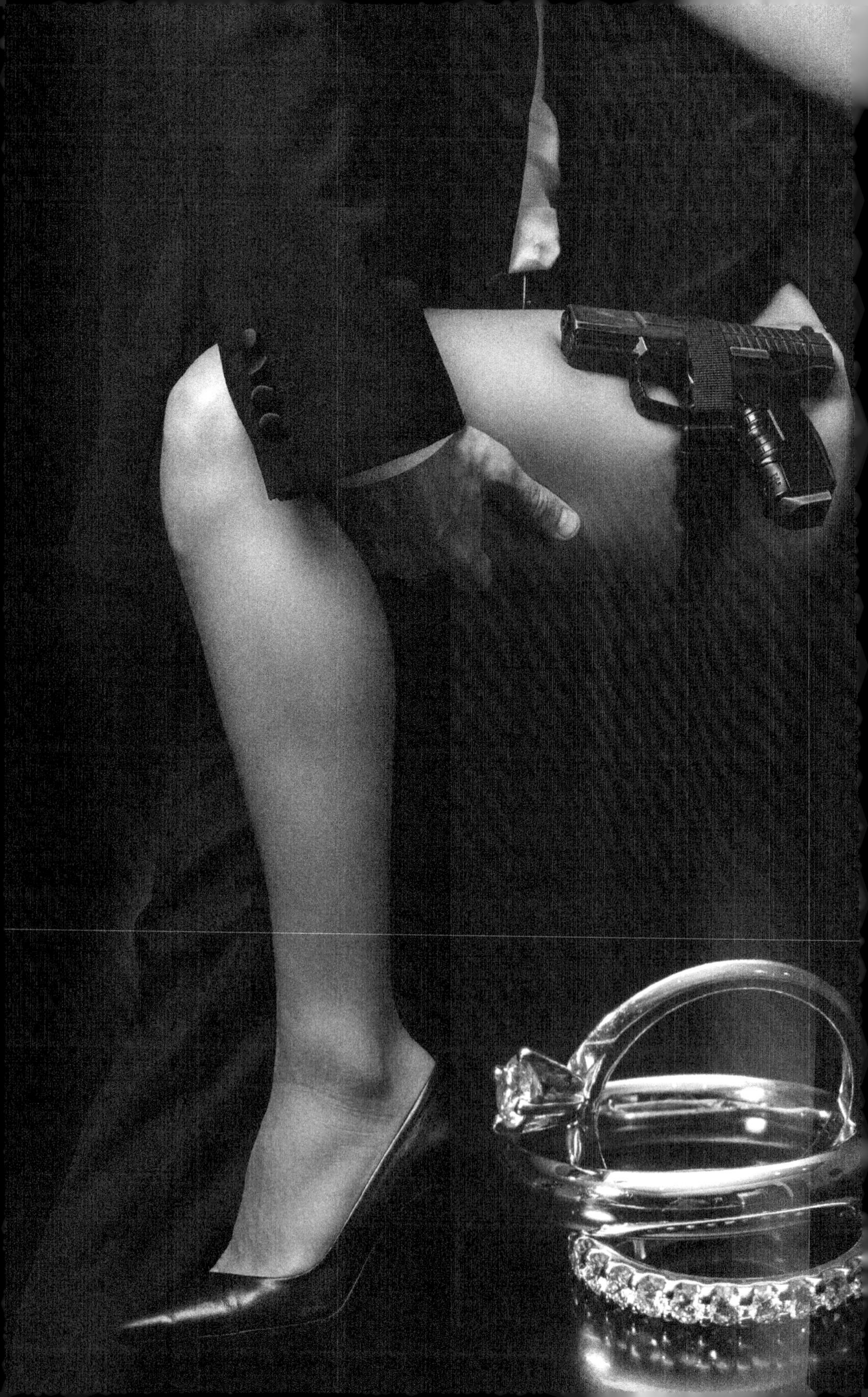

CHAPTER 29
Alaric

I stare at Layla in shock. She stumbles back and drops the gun, her face pale as she stares at his dead body. She looks at her hand like she can't believe she did it.

That makes two of us.

I gave it to her knowing she would run away, but she surprised me yet again.

She killed him.

"Baby girl," I coo softly, and she turns to me with wide, frightened eyes. I cautiously shuffle toward her with my arms out, and when I'm close enough, I wrap them around her. "You did so good. Everything is okay. You're okay. We're okay. I love you so much," I tell her, kissing her head and holding her as she begins to shake. I don't know how long we stand here before she pulls back, her eyes full of life again.

"I killed him," she whispers.

"You did. He was a bad man, Layla." I never should have let her take that gun and stain her soul like that. Guilt eats at me, but then she smiles, making me blink in shock.

"I killed him," she repeats in a stronger voice. "He hurt people, people like Zoey and Gage, and I killed him. I saved them." She looks up at me, her lips curled in a smile. "Fuck him, fuck them all. I can protect me. I can protect Zoey!"

That's when it hits me. This is what needed to happen to give her back her power—power Roy took away from her when he took her mother and brother.

She's alive in a way I've never seen before.

That's a lie. She's alive in the same way I am after a kill.

Adrenaline is pumping through her veins, and she feels satisfied for taking the life of an evil man in this fucked-up world. Our eyes meet, and something passes between us as her gaze darkens and fills with hunger that has my cock hardening.

"Layla," I say in warning, knowing what that look means.

She's not thinking clearly, but fuck! She slams her lips onto mine, and I'm helpless. I kiss her like a drowning man, desperate to feel her against me and know she's still mine. When she leaps up my body, I help her. My hands go to her ass and pull her close so not an inch of space is between us. When she moans, I swallow it down greedily.

I massage her perky, perfect ass as she rolls against me, the heat of her wet cunt dragging along my caged cock. Snarling, I turn and blindly slam her down onto the table, knocking my tools everywhere.

When I pull back and see them spread out on the floor in chaos, it makes me grin. It's the perfect fucking metaphor. My life was controlled and perfectly organized until she came along, and I wouldn't have it any other way.

"Layla." I try to breathe through the desire to slam into her wet cunt and prove she's still mine. "You probably need to rest—"

"Fuck resting, I want my husband," she snarls, her eyes alight with that fire that made me fall in love with her in the first place. "Now are you going to keep talking or fuck me?"

I stare at her rosy face, and my decision is made when I see that she's really here with me and needy. "Fuck you, always fuck you." I groan as I lean in to kiss her in a brutal, claiming kiss, reminding us both that we are together forever.

Nothing could break us now, and those last reservations and worries all float away, leaving me feeling lighter than I've felt in years as I drop to my knees. I run my mouth along her cheek and down her neck as she moans and tilts her head to give me access. Watching her eyes flutter closed in ecstasy, I nip her skin before kissing down her chest and then over her shirt to suck one of her tight little nipples into my mouth. She cries out, her legs clamping around me.

"Eyes on me, wife, as I make you come. You will give me everything as I watch you shatter for me. Only ever me," I demand as I release her nipple and give her other one the same treatment. She's as needy and restless as I am. Blood is smeared on her skin, so I quickly wipe my fingers off, not wanting that dirty bastard's blood anywhere near the perfection that is my wife's cunt. I don't bother pulling off her jeans. I grab a scalpel from the floor and cut a hole from the top of her mound to her ass. She gasps when cool air blows over her pink, glistening cunt, and I lick my lips.

"So fucking wet for me, wife, fuck, I love you." I groan, leaning in and inhaling deeply, locking the perfect musky scent of her arousal for me inside my brain forever. I ignore my throbbing cock, needing to make her come apart for me.

"I love you."

Chuckling, I seal my lips over her greedy cunt.

I give her everything she needs and wants. Her hands grip my hair, tugging me closer as I torture her in a different way than I was before. I lick and suck her pussy, avoiding her throbbing, swollen clit until she screams in frustration, and only then do I close my lips around her nub and suck.

I slam two fingers inside of her trembling hole, feeling her cunt tighten around them as she comes apart with a scream. I lick her through it, tasting her cum until she tugs me up. I resist at first, but she's a demanding little thing, so I crawl up her body. When she throws her legs around my waist and pulls me closer for a kiss, I grin.

When she pulls back, her cheeks red and eyes hazy in satisfaction, I fall in love again. "Fuck me, husband," she demands.

"Yes, wife," I murmur as I kiss her and pull out my hard cock, stroking myself before dragging my length across her dripping cunt. "Hold on, baby girl," I warn, nipping her lip, and when she goes to speak, I line up with her pussy and slam into her.

She screams and jerks against me as I drive every hard inch of my huge cock into her. I pull out and hammer back in with a hard, brutal thrust that has the table rocking.

"Alaric!" she yells, lifting her legs higher as her hips jerk. Gripping her tighter, I pull out and slam back in. Each thrust is harder and faster than before as I hammer into her, taking her the way I want.

I should have known my wife always gives as good as she gets as she lifts her hips to help me, her eyes ablaze with hunger. My hips stutter for a moment before I quicken my pace. The table rocks dangerously, the sound loud even over our breathing, but I don't care. I would never let her fall.

She leans back, dragging her hands up her body to twist her

nipples as I watch. The sight makes me harder, if that's even possible, and I know it won't be long before I'm coming in her tight, hot little body.

"I love you!" she cries out when I twist my hips to hit her oversensitive clit.

"Say it," I snarl, slamming into her. "Keep saying it while I make you come all over my cock."

"I love you, I love you, I love you," she chants, getting louder as we both reach for our peaks. Her nails dig into my shoulders, ripping at my clothes as she lifts her hips to meet my brutal thrusts, and when I reach down and flick her clit, she comes apart for me on a howl.

Snarling, I fight her tightening cunt, driving into her once, twice more before stilling with my own howl. I cry out my release as I fill her with it and make her mine forever.

Panting, I rest my head against her chest, feeling her racing heart as we both struggle to breathe. When her heart slows, and our breathing is more even, I lift my head and kiss her softly. "I love you so much, wife, so fucking much." I frame her cheeks with both hands then search her eyes. "Marry me," I blurt out.

She blinks before letting out a musical laugh that has my heart soaring. "We are already married, silly."

"No, for real this time. Marry me because you love me, because you want to." She sobers, staring at me in confusion, and I swallow my nerves. "Let's do it properly this time. The whole big day with traditions, friends, family, and vows. I want the whole world to know how fucking lucky I am to have you. I want the real deal. I want to look into your eyes and see love, not fear." She softens against me, her eyes gleaming with tears as I surge forward. "I want to do this for real. I want to be yours with nothing else between us. So, Layla, will you marry me for real this time?"

"Yes," she croaks before laughing and throwing her arms around me. "Yes, you brilliant, dangerous man, I will."

My heart bursts from my chest, or at least it feels like it as I kiss her, showing her everything I wish I could tell her, like how much she means to me and how I could never live without her . . .

How she saved me.

CHAPTER 30

Layla

It's my wedding day . . . *again*.

Alaric insisted we do this properly and that I get my dream wedding—not that I had ever dreamed of one before, but with him? Damn right I did. When he proposed yet again and suggested this, I was more than willing to take this man to be mine forever and to truly love him when I say I do.

He's right. If we are starting over and doing this properly, then we need to have this wedding. As I stare at the doors of the church, I can't help but grin. There isn't even an ounce of nervousness filling me like last time. In fact, I want to run down the aisle and offer myself to him forever. I know he feels the same. Last night we tried to spend the night apart to follow tradition, but halfway through the night, he woke me with his cock in my pussy claiming one night, never mind a few hours, was too much for him to be away from me ever again. *Swoon*. He was right, though, because I missed him something fierce and never wanted to wake up alone again.

And now I don't have to.

He's mine forever, and I am his.

The music starts, my cue, and I look over at Zoey and grin. She's beautiful. She didn't want a traditional princess dress. Oh no, she wanted to look like her hero Alaric and be here for both of us, since neither he nor I have any other real family—apart from his dad who is already in there with him.

The thought of our little family makes tears fill my eyes, and Zoey frowns at me as she adjusts her bow tie. "No crying, you'll ruin your makeup," she warns.

"You're right." I suck in a breath and blink the tears away so as not to ruin the hard work of the makeup artist who turned up this morning alongside a hairstylist. I planned to do my own, but when they showed up at my door, I wasn't surprised when they said they were a gift from Alaric. I did pick out my own dress and venue though. I just wanted us here, no one else, and he agreed, but I wanted a church wedding, and he was willing to give me whatever I wanted.

I hold a bouquet of beautiful lilies, sunflowers, and roses, and straighten my veil that trails behind me, making me feel like a princess.

Unlike my last wedding dress, this one makes me feel loved, beautiful, and like the wife I already am. The bodice of the stunning off-white dress—because fuck tradition—shows off my breasts before flaring out. The back is a crisscrossing strap, emphasizing the long train which blends with the veil. The bottom half is an off-white gauzy fabric that sparkles with diamonds arranged in a celestial pattern, and the capped sleeves cascade down in a beautiful cape. I feel like a goddess, and since I often thank the stars for Alaric, it seemed appropriate that I picked this dress.

I nod, and the wooden doors open. I start to walk down the aisle as the organ plays a soft love song, and then I see him. He stands with his back to me, and he's dressed in a black suit that fits him like a glove, showing off his amazing ass and muscles. He's so beautiful it hurts, and then he turns to me, and those blue eyes freeze me in place for a moment like they always do.

He gulps as his gaze runs down my body before flicking back up to meet mine. His eyes are glassy with tears as he mouths, "I love you."

I can't help but grin, and I speed up, almost running down the aisle to him.

Muttering, "Fuck it," he strides toward me. "I can't wait another moment to start our lives together," he tells me, taking both my hand and Zoey's before leading us to the front of the church. "You both look absolutely beautiful," he says, looking between us before winking at Zoe. She giggles and steps back, and then he focuses on me. "Baby girl . . ." He swallows, lost for words. "You are my everything."

"Let's not start with the vows yet." The pastor laughs, making both of us turn to him. Then, hand in hand, we get married. Zoey presents the rings, and he slides a new one onto my finger. It's more stunning than anything I could have ever imagined and so unique. It's a moss-colored diamond set in a rose gold band, with other diamonds surrounding it. It's beautiful and different, like us. When we can finally kiss, he dips me back, stealing my heart once more as he swallows my moan.

Zoey claps and cheers alongside Alaric's father, and when I straighten, I'm crying and laughing. She steps up to us and takes each of our hands. "I'm so happy."

"Me too," I reply, smiling at them. "So very, very happy."

She looks at Alaric, and he grins down at her. Nothing but love shines in his eyes.

"Thank you for being our angel all these years. Thank you for never giving up on us like everyone else did," Zoey tells him, and I watch as he falls to his knees before her, showing her vulnerability and respect.

"Never." He glances at me and then pulls me closer. "It's us three against the world, and it will never hurt you again, not as long as I'm around." A tear drips down his face as he kisses her cheek and then my hand. "You were the ones who saved me, and I will spend the rest of our lives earning that kind mercy. Now, how about we get out of here and start our lives together as a family?"

"I would love that," I whisper, and Zoey nods.

And so, hand in hand, we leave the church, ready to start our lives all over again.

For the first time since I was a child, I am ready and excited for the future.

* * *

Zoey was in on the plan to let us go on our honeymoon without her way before I knew that was the plan. It shouldn't have surprised me, but it did. We haven't ever been apart for this length of time, and although I'm worried about her, I try to enjoy our time in paradise like she begged me to.

It truly is paradise. He brought me to a private villa in the Bahamas, with our own butlers and beach and infinity pool. It's like a dream, and every day I get to see him sweaty, oiled, and half naked. Like now. I just sat up after napping on a lounger. He's relaxing with his eyes closed and a smile on his lips. His cut abs, chiseled arms, and chest glisten with the oil I insisted on covering him with, which turned into him fucking me until I screamed.

Without even cracking open an eye, his smile turns dirty. "Keep looking at me like that, wife, and I'll bend you over that lounger." He looks at me. "Again."

Shivering, I lick my lips as I run my eyes down his body. "Maybe later. I'm just enjoying the view at the moment, husband," I tease.

Shaking his head, he leans over and kisses me before sitting back. His phone goes off in a pile of clothes, and I narrow my eyes.

"That better not be work," I hiss and snag it quicker than he can.

He raises his eyebrow, his cheeks heating a little, and I open the notification—after all, the password is my name—but my jaw drops when I realize what it is. It isn't work . . .

It's a camera, and on it is Zoey.

"Alaric," I demand.

He grabs it and checks it before dropping it. "I was worried about her, and don't lie to me, I know you were too. If you thought I was going away for two weeks without a way to check on her, you were wrong, baby girl."

"You put cameras in her friend's house?" I ask.

"Yep." He grins proudly.

"Good." I relax back as he laughs.

"Really, wife?" He arches a suspicious brow, thinking this is some sort of trap I laid at his feet.

"Really. I was scared and missing her too, but I should have known you'd have a way to keep an eye on her, even from here." I watch him, and his eyes darken.

"Come here, wife," he demands, patting his thigh, and like the good, obedient wife I am, I slip off my lounger and drop onto his lap. I feel his hard length against me, making me moan. He tugs at the side of my white bikini bottoms, undoing the strings so they fall away, and then his hand slides up my back and holds me. "Lie back and let me taste my incredible wife. I'm fucking starving," he orders, and because it's what I want and I trust him to hold me up, I lean back as his incredible mouth seals over my pussy.

Right here, in paradise, under the bright blue sky with the ocean lapping against the shore mere feet away, I fall in love with my husband over and over and over again.

Who knew so much death could lead to so much life?

Epilogue
ALARIC

Five years later...

I bite into her shoulder, the jagged edge of my teeth piercing her skin and leaving my mark. She moans my name as I pound into her pussy from behind, her sweet cunt clenching around my cock to the point where white spots begin to blur my vision.

"Alaric," she whimpers loudly, uncaring of who might hear her wanton cries.

"Shh, wife. You don't want our guests to know what we're up to, do you?" I tease, slowing my thrusts purposely just to hear her needy, soft plea again.

"Alaric, if you don't make me come right this instant, you will have hell to pay. Fuck whoever hears me!" she growls, bending farther down across the hood of my car so I can have a perfect view of her ass.

I dig my fingers into her round, firm globes before I slap one ass cheek so hard that her juices begin to leave a puddle on the garage floor. Long gone is the skin and bones girl I tricked into marrying me. In her place is this goddess, this temptress, who plays with my body and heart with just a bat of her eyelashes.

"Who taught you to have such a dirty mouth that's begging to be fucked?"

"My husband," she purrs, licking her lips as she looks over her shoulder.

"You're fucking right I did," I growl, kissing her madly and increasing my tempo.

I swallow her little pants of pleasure as I ram into her over and over again, until her legs begin to shake, threatening to give out.

I'd never let my love fall like that though, and she knows it. Layla knows that despite whatever life throws at us, I will always be there to catch her, even if I'm the one doing all the hurting. I hurt her body so good that she goes to her knees and prays for an angel to save her, but it's no angel that arrives—no, it's the devil himself who answers her call. It's me, and I save her repeatedly by offering her my body, heart, and soul.

They are all hers to do with as she sees fit, after all.

Right now, all she wants is my cock to push her over the edge and give her the mind-blowing orgasm she craves. Like the dutiful husband I am, I'm more than happy to oblige her every whim and desire. I roll my hips behind her, with one hand on her waist while the other skates around her body to grab a handful of her breast.

"Alaric," she sings as she rises to the heavens and finds her glorious release.

I will never tire of this.

Watching my woman come in my arms is one of life's purest miracles, and Layla has made sure to spoil me with them since the day I put a ring on her finger. Just watching her come undone so beautifully has me following her over the edge, never willing to part from her for too long, even in this.

I drop my head onto her shoulder, hugging her tightly, our heaving chests slowing down simultaneously. I fix her skirt and pull her panties up from her ankles, smirking when I see my cum still dripping down her thigh. I run a finger through it before turning her around in my arms, her lips already parted for my treat.

"Such a good girl."

"I aim to please." She gives me a cocky wink.

"If I thought we could get away with it, I'd like to test that theory," I murmur, putting away my twitching cock that is more than ready to take her on again.

"Oh my God. The party!" Her eyes go wide as reality finally dawns on her. "The cake! I was only supposed to grab the birthday cake." She slaps my shoulder to push me away so she can dash over to the spare fridge we have in the garage. "I told everyone outside that I wouldn't be more than five minutes."

"Should have thought about that when you asked me to come help you, swaying those hips and that gorgeous ass in my face. You know damn well I can't fuck you in under five minutes. Even a quickie needs to be twenty minutes tops."

"Alaric, can you stop? Someone might hear you."

"Oh, I think our guests heard plenty, baby girl." I laugh, taking the ice cream cake off her hands.

She scrunches her nose at me and walks ahead, but the way she purposely jiggles her hips to catch my eye has me laughing my ass off.

This woman is perfection.

And all mine.

We climb the few stairs that lead us to the kitchen, only to find

Zoey stomping her foot with little Gage and Sophie tugging at her skirt as soon as we open the door.

"You two are an awful influence on me. You know that, right? Shameless. Absolutely shameless."

Layla's cheeks turn deep red at her sister's light teasing.

"Hand me the damn cake, Ric. My nephew and niece have been waiting to blow out their candles for over an hour." She tsks, shaking her head, but I see the little twinkle in her eye that says she's messing with us.

At seventeen, little Zoey has grown up to be a total smart-ass, and I couldn't be prouder. I love the kid as if she were my own. Fuck that. She is. She's my kid through and through. You only have to talk with her for five minutes to know how true those words are.

Layla crouches to pick up the other light of my life, my beautiful boy Gage, who instantly drops his head on her shoulder and begins to twirl a loose strand of his mom's hair. I follow my wife's lead and pick up his twin, Sophie, who squeals in excitement, pulling hard on my beard, reminding me yet again I have to shave the damn thing off.

"Come on, you two. Our friends are waiting," Zoey orders with a smile, leading us all to the backyard.

My heart swells ten times its size as I follow my girls through our home to celebrate the twins' second birthday. The halls are no longer empty but filled with family portraits and pictures of vacations and holidays, all announcing how our home is filled with so much love and joy. Sometimes it all feels surreal to me, and I have to pinch myself to remember that this is not a dream, but real life—the life Layla gave me.

Years before she brought light into my life, I used to think I would end up like my father in the end—alone, broken, filled with regret, and haunted by the blood on his hands.

But I have no such remorse, because each decision I've ever made has led me here.

To my family.

To my Layla.

To my home.

I follow them outside, grinning at the balloons, streamers, and the table of food to the left with a matching balloon tablecloth. All of our friends we've made over the years are gathered about, wearing smiles on their faces as they wait for us. The bouncy castle remains unoccupied at the back as we start to sing "Happy Birthday," and they join in.

When my son blows out the candles, I clap and kiss him on the cheek, making him giggle, and then I share a look with my wife. Her eyes shimmer with such happiness that my cold heart beats faster.

Only for her. For them.

Zoey takes my arm and kisses my cheek, making me grin down at her. I can't believe how grown up she is, but to me she will always be the little girl who stood face-to-face with a killer—me. I see that same girl in her eyes now. I know she's going to give me a run for my money when she turns eighteen and decides she no longer wants to follow all my strict rules, but moments like this, when there is love and happiness in her eyes, make all that future drama worthwhile.

I squeeze her briefly before I move to help Layla pass out the cake. When I hand out the next slice on a paper plate, a familiar scarred hand takes it. My eyes meet his unusual bright gray orbs. They are cold and dead, just like mine used to be. For a moment, the party fades as I stare into them. The jagged scar on the left side of his face, which he usually hides from everyone, is on clear display for a moment before he tugs his baseball cap down to conceal it and his identity.

He's taller than me, which he never lets me forget, and his muscular body is only growing by the day, which is necessary for the work he does.

The same work I used to do.

Gray, the man they are making me train to fill the hole I left when I handed in my resignation, doesn't have a family like I do.

The first day I met him, when he was a foul-mouthed teenager, he told me as much.

Gray doesn't have anyone to love or care about, and sometimes when I watch him in action, I wonder what I am unleashing on the world, because he enjoys it more than he should. He thrives on bloodshed and death and in the pain. For me, it was always just a job, but for him, it's his whole life—the sole reason for his existence.

His whole purpose is to take lives, and I'm the one who was chosen to mentor and teach him better ways in which he can go about it.

He inclines his head before fading into the background. I'm surprised he even came. I invited him in hopes it might help him integrate back into the world after the shitty hand he has been dealt, but now I regret having such an unbridled killer near my family.

Keeping my eye on him, I tug my family close, nodding and adding words into their conversations as I keep my eyes on him like a he's a bomb ready to go off.

Just like I predicted, it does, but not how I thought it would.

Zoey stands with her back to the outside wall, scrolling on her phone. She wears a grin curled on her lips when the neighbor's huge, teenage, football player son spots her and makes his way over. She's clearly annoyed and keeps edging away, and just when I'm about to haul his ass away, he grabs her ass and tries to drag her closer. I'm moving before she even slaps him. I know she can handle herself, I taught her how to deal with assholes like him, but she's still my daughter.

I'm halfway to them, but Gray is faster, moving like the ghost he is.

He materializes before the boy, whose face pales when he sees the death clearly written in Gray's eyes. Zoey's eyes widen, not just with fear, but also with interest—which I will need to deal with later. She watches Gray with something much deadlier than the horror and fear everyone else does. He's oblivious as he grips the young boy's neck and hauls him into the air, cutting off his air supply.

"Do. Not. Touch. Her. Again," he snarls, his dark voice filled with the wildness he tries to contain inside himself. He's about to lose it. I see it written on his face, especially when the boy spits out a reply like a fool.

"She liked it."

Sighing, I manage to move closer, blocking the view before Gray can snap the kid's neck, or worse. "Let him down," I order. Gray hesitates, his nostrils flaring. "Down now, Gray. If you kill him, I will have no choice but to deal with you after."

And by deal with him, I mean kill the fucker.

There is no way I can let him murder this kid in my home with so many fucking witnesses—my kids included—and let him off the hook.

Gray might be many things, but he's not stupid.

If he snaps this kid's neck, his head is next on my chopping block.

And he knows it.

So, despite the fact that he hates it, he slowly lowers the boy before standing over him, his fists balled at his sides. His body vibrates with barely contained violence—the strength of which even surprises me. "If I find out you touched her again, I'll come back for you. You won't even see me coming," he threatens, and the young boy actually pisses himself.

I don't blame him.

Even I'm wary when Gray turns his gaze from the kid and looks at me. "Never threaten me again."

"Leave," I snap, having had enough of this.

Gray steps into my space, meeting my eyes when no other would ever dare. "Never," he warns, and then he spins on his heel. He stills and meets Zoey's eyes, and something passes between them, something I really don't fucking like. I grab him by the scruff of his neck like the wild animal he is, drag him to the side gate, and throw him out.

"Stay away from my family, Gray, or you'll be dead quicker than you can react. I mean it. That's not a threat, but a promise." I slam the gate on his face, but some deep dark part of me knows that's not the end.

Layla is distracting everyone at the party, so I move in on Zoey, not happy with how her gaze is on the gate and hard for me to read. "Do not go near him, Zoey. I mean it. If he comes near you, hide and call me. He's dangerous."

Her eyes finally meet mine, bold and unafraid. "And you're not? Yet here I am, calling you my father." The minute I flinch, she softens, letting go of whatever other words she has in her arsenal that could cut me deeper than a blade. "I will, Ric. I'll stay away from your *friend*. Promise. Now let's get back to the party, okay?"

I nod and let her lead me back to my family. When Layla melts into my arms, I finally relax—it's the only time I ever can. Layla is the only person who can ever breach my solid exterior. She smiles up at me and pats my chest. "She's okay, husband. She can handle herself."

"That's what worries me, baby girl," I admit, leaning down to kiss her. As I taste her soft, sweet pink lips, I wish everyone else was gone so I could carry on, especially when she whimpers into my mouth. Pulling back, I meet those sparkling eyes I could spend the rest of my life losing myself in. "You're mine after this party."

"I'm yours forever," she teases, making me grin as she escapes the circle of my arms. "Now come on, husband, it's time to celebrate."

She giggles when I grab her hand and twirl her around as everyone dances to the music. I pick up Gage and spin him with us, making him laugh, and Zoey eventually joins in with Sophie until my whole family is around me. My life is so filled with love and laughter I almost can't believe it.

I don't deserve it, but fuck knows I will never give it, or them, up.

She's right: Layla is mine forever. They all are.

And this is just the beginning of our story.

The End

About the authors

Katie and Ivy have known each other since they began their author journey and have become fast friends over the years. Bonding over their love of books and crazy, maddening muses, they have always wanted to work together and finally did.

After deciding to take the plunge, the Deadly Love series was born… and matches like these are so deadly that they are bound to set your kindle on fire!

DEADLY LOVE SERIES
DEADLY AFFAIR
DEADLY MATCH
DEADLY ENCOUNTER

Want to read a snippet of the next story in the series, Deadly Match, which follows our broken bad boy Gray and a fiery Zoey who is all grown up? Turn the page now!

A Deadly Sneak Peek

OF DEADLY MATCH

ZOEY

I pull my knees tighter to my chest and press my face into them to muffle my sobs, not wanting to wake anyone. The cold, tiled bathroom floor chills the soles of my feet, and the nightdress Layla handed down to me, covered in holes, barely reaches my knees. The tile at my back has me shivering as I close my eyes against the sting of tears, my body shaking with the force of my pain.

Since Layla is heavily knocked out on her pain meds, and it's the only time I can get away from her and the other girls, I snuck out of our shared room. The eight other girls are sleeping in their cots, like I should be, but I can't. Instead, I'm huddled in the shared bathroom in the foster home we were dumped in when Layla was released from the hospital.

She almost died.

I almost lost her to…

Gage.

Mom.

I did lose them. I won't ever tell Layla that I remember it all—the sounds of the gunshots, the feel of their blood on my hands, and my own screams in my ears. I lost everyone I love apart from Layla. The only reason she is still here is because of the blue-eyed angel who stopped to save us.

Even thinking of him now has me crying harder, wishing he was here to protect us and save us from this life.

It's stupid to cry. I'm alive, and so is Layla. We are safe, even if this place gives me the creeps, but I miss them. I miss them so badly. I wish I hadn't gotten angry with Gage and yelled. I wish I could chase him around or sneak into his room to read with him at night.

Mom wasn't the best mother, but I loved her, and on those rare, good days she would bake for us. I miss the smell of her cookies and the sound of her laugh when I would steal one. Now, there is just a black hole where they were, and it hurts so much.

I miss home. I don't like it here.

I just want to go home.

Sometimes at night, I swear I hear screams, and none of them are mine.

I haven't told Layla this. She would run away with me and protect me at any cost, but she needs to heal so I won't lose her too. Instead, I try to ignore it and everything and everyone.

I hear footsteps, and I curl around myself—a habit I know Layla hates. It always made her eyes flash with anger before she stepped in front of me and took the blow. Maybe if I'm small enough, they will go away and leave me alone, but I still hear them next to me.

I feel their heat as they slide down the wall beside me. I don't look. I can't. I'm worried I will be punished for crying or being out of bed at this hour, but then a soft, slightly bigger than my own hand covers mine on my shaking knee.

Something about it makes me cry harder.

No words are spoken, and when the sun rises, he walks me back to my bed and tucks me in. At the door to my room, he looks back at me once. He's just a shadow in the dark, a boy, a face I can't make out, but it sticks with me.

That was the first night my protector came to me, promising he would never leave my side…

About K.A Knight

K.A Knight is an international bestselling indie author trying to get all of the stories and characters out of her head, writing the monsters that you love to hate. She loves reading and devours every book she can get her hands on, and she also has a worrying caffeine addiction.

She leads her double life in a sleepy English town, where she spends her days writing like a crazy person.

Read more at K.A Knight's website or join her Facebook Reader Group.
Sign up for exclusive content and my newsletter here
http://eepurl.com/drLLoj

About Ivy Fox

Ivy Fox is a USA Today bestselling author of angst-filled, contemporary romances, some of them with an unconventional #whychoose twist.

Ivy lives a blessed life, surrounded by her two most important men—her husband and son, but she also doesn't mind living with the fictional characters in her head that can't seem to shut up until she writes their story.

Books and romance are her passion.

A strong believer in happy endings and that love will always prevail in the end, both in life and in fiction.

Join her Facebook Reader Group - Ivy's Sassy Foxes or sign up for exclusive content and my newsletter here - https://www.ivyfoxauthor.com/

Also by K A Knight

THEIR CHAMPION SERIES

- The Wasteland
- The Summit
- The Cities
- The Nations
- Their Champion Coloring Book
- Their Champion Boxed Set

- The Forgotten
- The Lost
- The Damned
- Their Champion Companion Boxed Set

DAWNBREAKER SERIES

- Voyage to Ayama
- Dreaming of Ayama

THE LOST COVEN SERIES

- Aurora's Coven
- Aurora's Betrayal

HER MONSTERS SERIES

- Rage

- Hate

THE FALLEN GODS SERIES

- PrettyPainful
- Pretty Bloody
- PrettyStormy
- Pretty Wild
- Pretty Hot
- Pretty Faces
- Pretty Spelled
- Fallen Gods Boxed Set 1
- Fallen Gods Boxed Set 1

FORBIDDEN READS *(STANDALONES)*

- Daddy's Angel
- Stepbrothers' Darling

STANDALONES

- Scarlett Limerence
- Nadia's Salvation
- The Standby
- Den of Vipers
- Daddy's Angel
- Divers Heart
- Crown of Stars

AUDIOBOOKS

- The Wasteland
- The Summit
- Rage
- Hate
- Den of Vipers *(From Podium Audio)*
- Gangsters and Guns *(From Podium Audio)*
- Daddy's Angel *(From Podium Audio)*
- Stepbrother's Darling *(From Podium Audio)*
- Blade of Iris *(From Podium Audio)*
- Deadly Affair *(From Podium Audio)*

CO-AUTHOR PROJECTS - *Erin O'Kane*

HER FREAKS SERIES

- Circus Save Me
- Taming The Ringmaster
- Walking the Tightrope
- Boxed Set

STANDALONES

- The Hero Complex
- Dark Temptations (contains One Night Only and Circus Saves Christmas)

THE WILD BOYS SERIES

- The Wild Interview
- The Wild Tour
- The Wild Finale
- The Wild Boys Boxed Set

CO-AUTHOR PROJECTS - *Ivy Fox*

Deadly Love Series

- Deadly Affair
- Deadly Match
- Deadly Encounter

CO-AUTHOR PROJECTS - *Kendra Moreno*

STANDALONES

- Stolen Trophy

CO-AUTHOR PROJECTS - *Loxley Savage*

THE FORSAKEN SERIES

- Capturing Carmen
- Stealing Shiloh
- Harboring Harlow

STANDALONES

- Gangsters and Guns

OTHER CO-WRITES

- Shipwreck Souls *(with Kendra Moreno & Poppy Woods)*
- The Horror Emporium *(with Kendra Moreno & Poppy Woods)*

Also by Ivy Fox

The Society

- See No Evil
- Hear No Evil
- Fear No Evil
- Speak No Evil
- Do No Evil

After Hours Series

- The King

Reverse Harem Standalones & Series

Bad Influence Series

- Her Secret
- Archangels MC
- Room for Three

The Privileged of Pembroke High

- Heartless
- Soulless
- Faithless
- Ruthless
- Fearless
- Restless

Rotten Love Duet

- Rotten Girl
- Rotten Men

Mafia Wars

- Binding Rose

Co-Writes with K.A. Knight

Deadly Love Series

- Deadly Affair
- Deadly Match
- Deadly Encounter

Co-Writes with C.R. Jane

Breathe Me Duet

- Breathe Me
- Breathe You

Printed in Great Britain
by Amazon